PROLOGUE

The mining freighter MS Johannesburg slowed, remarkably smoothly given her immense bulk, size and age. As the two-kilometre long cargo vessel decelerated below light speed, she eased to port and slipped into a close proximity orbit around the vast "Snowflake" nebula; so called because when viewed from Earth, the Terran system, the deep space gas cloud exhibited a distinct, if a little skewed, hexagonal formation at its heart, which vaguely resembled a snowflake. Even though it was only from Earth this phenomenon was visible the name had been adopted through out the Alpha sector; such was the influence of the Terrans.

Captain Thomas Dalton, a mid-aged, greying, Welshman whose orange Titan Mining Fleet uniform was becoming a little too tight around his growing waist, ordered the ship's faster-than-light warp engines to power-down and for the induction engines to hold the ship on course at three quarters light speed.

"Aye Captain," responded the Johannesburg's helmsman, "Steady, three-quarters-Light. Holding course at 300 million Km".

300 million kilometres, "two clicks" is about twice the distance from the Earth to the Sun. It might seemed a great distance, but in Galactic terms the freighter was so close as to be almost inside the vast cloud, and the Johannesburg was a mere speck against the two-light-year circumference of the immense and highly volatile, hydrogen, sodium and sulphur dust cloud.

The Johannesburg was nearing the end of a year-long voyage, hauling an assortment of ore and minerals back and forth across the great expanse that was the Alpha sector. Her Captain had a choice of courses now. He could ease below light speed, as he had just done, and hug the perimeter of the great the nebula, or he could engage the faster than light warp engines and take a ten light-year detour route around the cloud. It wasn't possible to hug the shorter route and travel at warp speed. The cloud did not take well to warp plasma trails and had a nasty habit of burning out engine nacelles and blowing power conduits of any craft that attempted to make haste through or near it. The close proximity route required a more sedate velocity but it was still about a day faster.

As he eased the ship snugly to the edge of the cloud, Matt Sweeney, her young Australian, former "surfer jock" helmsman, deliberately and just for the fun of it, flipped Johannesburg's tail into the outer edge of the treacherous dust off their port-side. The 40 billion Kg mass of the ship, plus its cargo of diamond dust, caused the Johannesburg to fishtail, sparking a massive green, glowing scar across the face of the nebula as the ship's plasma trail ionised the gasses in the stellar smog.

"I said steady as she goes Mr. Sweeney," chided the Captain jokingly.

He was well aware that Sweeney was merely displaying a little high spiritedness that he and the rest of the crew felt at being almost home.

"Aye Captain. Steady," smiled Sweeney, as he deftly ran his fingers over the helm control and brought the ship smoothly back on course.

This final leg of their journey always made the Captain pause for thought. It was always the same cargo they hauled as they cruised homeward; the finest of diamond dust, used to line warp engine nacelles, streamlining the plasma flow through them, making them perform better, producing more speed; an essential in 24th century life. It was therefore ironic, thought Dalton, that three hundred years earlier, towards the end of the twenty first century, that diamonds had brought about the collapse of the World's economies and essentially created the world, no, the Universe in which they now lived.

The invention of the warp engine had been a long-time coming. Since the theory that proved it to be a possibility had been published in 2041, universities, engineers and science institute's greatest minds had strove to make faster than light space travel a reality. It was the Holy Grail, much like powered flight had been a hundred and fifty years before that. In 2089 warp speed finally became a reality and a ship, "The Odyssey" was built, powered by warp 2.5 engines and paid for by all of the governments of the World.

After its initial test; a sedate 14 hours voyage around the Terran solar-system, orbiting each of the eight planets plus Pluto, a four-month long expedition around the nearby stars in the Alpha sector was planned. The Odyssey returned triumphantly to Earth in 2094 having scanned and documented 9 stars, 25 planets and all of their moons. That's when the stock markets instantly flat-lined and then spectacularly crashed.

One of the smaller moons orbiting the fourth planet in the Alpha Centauri system was found to have a system of rings made almost entirely of super-dense carbon: diamonds. Suddenly it was realised that everything we humans had for centuries placed value on, because on Earth those things were scarce; valuable metals, minerals and suchlike, were available somewhere in the cosmos in ridiculous abundance and with the advent of warp speed, they were easily obtainable. Suddenly everything of value was worthless. The markets went through the floor. Chaos ensued.

On the brink of man's greatest adventure to the stars and beyond, economic meltdown brought the world terrifyingly to its knees. It was only the timely, if out of left field intervention by the President of the European Union, Charlotte Windsor, which had halted the blind global panic.

Former, Princess Charlotte Windsor, born into an elitist society and a family of immense wealth and privilege, on reaching her early twenties, had not just followed in the compassionate and crusading footsteps of her much love grandmother, Diana Princess of Wales, but had gone beyond. Growing up, Charlotte had taken her royal duties much more seriously than any of her siblings or cousins. Shaking the tree of the establishment, she had forgone merely attending functions and shaking hands with charity organisers and dignitaries to tirelessly and vigorously campaigning and fighting innumerable causes on behalf of the poor and disenfranchised. In her thirties, still single and fighting harder than ever, highlighting the plight of the impoverished, hungry and homeless around the globe, Charlotte relinquished her title and linage to the throne of the UK to become a thorn in the side of rulers and Presidents everywhere. Inevitably her all consuming passion for the fight, led the firebrand, erstwhile royal into politics and eventually, some would say predictably at the still sprightly age of 75 she had been elected President of the European Union.

As the financial markets plummeted, President Charlotte had steadied the populace. Her ambitious speech to the European people was simple yet galvanising. She rekindled hope, where despair and fear of a future without money, since it had lost all value, had numbed the masses with uncertainty and bewilderment. Life had been predictable and rationalised with the exchange of metal disks and printed-paper but was now unclear and torn. Her inspirational words quickly became a mantra across the continent, "If nothing has value, then everything is free, including our labour..... If we give that freely, then we can build more, faster, better than we could ever have imagined. Money has shackled humanity; let's grasp this opportunity. Let us be great."

A short, but chaotic period of widespread looting ensued, but that passed as people realised stealing for profit was history, since there was no longer money to make a profit from.

Charlotte promptly launched a monumental project, with the cooperation of North African states, to irrigate the barren deserts of Ethiopia.

"In the 1980's," She rallied, "the World fed Africa. Now let Africa feed the World."

She proposed laying a pipeline from wet northern Europe to the barren horn of Africa. There was no shortage of food in the world. Charlotte's aim was to demonstrate that fact and show that the world had more than we needed, and to assure the population that no one would starve, even though money would never change hands again.

Charlotte Windsor's speech was heard across the globe.

They came in their hundreds, their thousands...... they came in their millions and millions and millions, with picks, shovels and their bare hands. People, who had thought the world was at an end, had a renewed determination and a purpose to their lives again. It took three weeks.... THREE WEEKS, to dig the trench. Then pipes and pumping equipment were installed, given freely since money was now obsolete. In just over a month the world looked on in amazement at their achievement, as the waters flowed onto the parched earth, bringing it to life; from arid to arable. Crops were planted; an area the size of Texas and Oklahoma became lush, green and life giving.

"Until now we've been told that things could not be done, that they were impossible because they cost too much, that this or that wasn't economically viable," the President enthused, "well now we know different. Anything and everything is possible. Only lack of imagination can hold us back."

Within weeks, crops enough to feed all of Europe and Africa were sprouting. Similar projects were quickly implemented in Asia and North American. Money was gone but humanity found the greatest wealth in its self. The World and its people could do anything, and that's exactly what they did.

The stars awaited.

With nothing shackling the human race anymore we ventured forth into infinity with renewed vigour and belief, seeking out similar civilisations to ourselves. And we found them.

As warp technology improved and distances became less and less of an obstacle to exploration, most of the Alpha sector was soon easily within humanities reach.

We found life in abundance. Mostly simple bacterial life, which given a few million millennia would evolve, as we had done, but occasionally biologically advanced life. It was decided early on that unless a civilisation, our growing fleet happened-upon, had warp capabilities like our own, then we would avoid contact, for fear of contaminating that civilisation's unique evolution.

Our first contact with an advanced species similar to our own came in the mid-twenty second century; March 19th 2158 to be exact.

The SS Galileo, a long-range science and exploration vessel, was on route to a multiple star cluster, who's orbits were contracting so rapidly that scans had predicted an imminent and catastrophic collision between several of the systems planets, a rare event in the cosmos. So rare in fact that as the Galileo approached she detected several other ships already in position, also waiting to observe the impending cataclysmic impacts. None of them were Earth ships.

Captain David Robertson, an imposing figure at six-foot-three with a shaven head and a neatly manicured goatee beard, immediately ordered the Galileo's shields to be raised and to slow to manoeuvring thrusters. As the ship edged almost imperceptibly forward, like a child creeping down stairs to spy on his parent's party, Robertson instructed his security officer to scan the waiting vessels. As he did the security console flashed an alert, indicating that the Galileo was in-turn also being scanned, from multiple sources.

"They know we're here, Sir," announced the security officer.

The Galileo's crew as one held their breath, all thirty-seven of them to a man and woman through out the ship, froze as though merely blinking might provoke an adverse reaction. No one dared move. Second to Neil Armstrong's walk on the Moon, this was, in galactic terms, the most pivotal moment in human history; man's first real foray into the unknown.

The Captain instructed the helmsman to hold position for several minutes longer. They waited, and waited, expecting some kind of reaction to their unannounced presence. When eventually it was evident that none was forthcoming, and more importantly none of the waiting ships had charged their weapons, Robertson chose to carry-out Galileo's mission and ordered the ship into a position where the science team could better observe the approaching event.

"We're being hailed, Captain!" Exclaimed the ship's communications officer, from the rear of the bridge.

The Captain drew himself up to his full height; straightening the collar of his dark blue uniform, he stepped closer to the twelve foot-high view screen on the facing bulkhead of the bridge.

"On screen," He said with his usual authoritative boom, then quietly under his breath he added, "welcome to your first day at school, boys and girls," hoping his voice wasn't betraying the uncertainty his pounding heart was.

The screen shifted, and a pale, almost grey-skinned figure with very narrow, sharply angular features, white hair, blue lips and no visible ears, appeared. The alien was wearing a uniform, which was a simple loose fitting white robe. Beyond him, his bridge was clean metallic grey, giving the impression of an almost antiseptic environment. For a moment, because of lack of defining colour anywhere, Captain Robertson wondered if there was a screen malfunction, and the colour rendition was faulty.

"Back away," the alien demanded.

At first the Captain was stunned, not only that he was being spoken to in English, but also that the alien appeared more humanoid than he'd expected, he had no idea what he'd expected but he was sure it wasn't this. He quickly regained his composure and responded.

"We will not," he stated firmly. Stepping even closer to the screen he balled his fists, placing them defiantly on his hips to emphasise he intended to stand his ground, "We are here on a mission of exploration and we have as much right to be here as any." This wasn't how he'd hoped "First Contact" with another advanced civilisation would play out.

"I absolutely concur,...... Commander"

"Captain...... Captain Robertson," he corrected.

"My apologies..... Captain," continued the

stranger less abruptly, "but I do suggest that you back away, for your own safety. We have scanned your ship and have concluded that your defence shields are somewhat inadequate; they will not withstand the imminent detonations. Might I suggest, if you insist on being in such close proximity, that you manoeuvre to our Starboard-side and we shall extend our shields and there-by ensure your safety. Your scientific observations will not, I assure you, be impaired."

Hull shielding is an essential requirement to all faster than light vessels. Although "shields" do protect from weapons fire, a circumstance no Earth ship had yet encountered, that is not their primary function. They are designed to protect the speeding vessel from any errant dust, rocks and asteroids which may wander into its path, deflecting them safely out of harms way, since at velocities beyond light-speed it would be impossible and impractical to manoeuvre around such obstacles. A collision with a tiny speck of space dust may have merely scratched the paintwork of an older, lumbering rocket powered ship, at far greater velocities achievable in the twenty second century, that same tiny speck of dust would smash through the hull of a ship causing catastrophic damage and destruction. The Galileo's and all other Earth ships system of shielding was produced by positively charging its outer hull plating, polarising them, similar to emitting a massive magnetic field, thereby repelling all wandering space debris, keeping ship and crew safe within its intense bubble of protective energy. This simple yet effective system had, until now it seemed, proven more than satisfactory for our space faring needs. Captain Robertson's feelings were therefore a little hurt to find that one of his worlds greatest technological achievement was considered "inadequate".

"Ehhhh, that would be most eh, gracious," stammered Robertson swallowing his pride and attempting to continue the conversation in the same perfect grammatical phrasing the alien was employing. Turning his back to the screen to face his crew, Robertson found his bridge staff staring open-mouthed. "You heard the.......eh, man," he cajoled his helmsman, "Pull alongside to starboard, Mr. Suarez."

"Right, eh starboard, aye Sir....... Err, Captain alongside which ship?"

Besides the Galileo there were five other ships in orbit around the now tightly spiralling constellations, all of varying designs and obviously built on different worlds. Turning to face the screen again, Robertson was about to ask the alien for directions when his unasked question was answered.

"We are Vaurillian, Captain, from the planet Vaurilla. I am Commander Sorn. Our vessel is the elongated tubular construct with three engine nacelles. A word of caution though, the vessel between ours and yourselves, immediately to your port side, is Kraxian. They are a violent, warring species so I would suggest you give their vessel a very wide berth."

The Vaurillian Commander then cut the transmission short and the view screen retuned to displaying the rapidly circling stellar maelstrom that the gathered ships had come to witness.

"Like he says, nice and easy Lieutenant, lets not make any enemies on our first day in the playground with the big boys."

The total and complete obliteration of two solar systems took a little more than six hours. The violent and brutal rending of entire worlds from matter to mere atoms and dust was horrific and yet beautiful. The first explosion burst from the Galileo's view-screen flooding the bridge with an intense fury of blistering light, forcing the crew to avert their eyes. First one, then both stars smashed and savaged their orbiting planets and then each other. The shockwave that followed pounded their hull, ripping through the vacuum of space with a frightening ferocity that only nature at its rawest and most terrifying can muster. The crushing and concussive blast and those that followed, almost shook the Galileo apart, tossing her about like a child's toy on a string and were detected back home on Earth several days later. But the protection of the Vaurrilians shields held strong and both ships and the crews remained safe within the alien's protective envelope.

As the data from the catastrophic blast was being logged and studied by the Galileo's science teams the communications officer reported again that they were being hailed.

"On screen," the Captain instructed.

"Good day again Captain," the Vaurillian Commander nodded politely in greeting, "Our garnering of scientific data from the explosion is now complete. We shall now bid you farewell."

"Commander Sorn, if I may?" interrupted the Captain, "You speak English? How come?"

"No Captain." The alien Commander replied in an almost schoolmasterly tone. "I no more speak English than you speak Vaurillian. We are employing a technology, we call 'Universal Translator' to engage with each other. It is a simple computer program, which I believe you also have employed for some centuries on your home world to translate between your many and varied languages, but until now......, have had little use for in space travel."

"Ahh," was the only reply Captain Robertson could come up with, feeling a little stupid that the answer was so glaringly simple. "Our computer translation programs require a prior knowledge of the other language though, Commander."

"As do ours, Captain. We, and other races, have been observing your home world for some time. Earth, I believe it is called. Your species is not unknown to us Captain."

Galileo's security office once again interrupted his Captain, announcing that the Kraxian vessel and two of the others were breaking orbit and leaving, without incident.

"Should we be worried about the Kraxians?

And who were the other ships, Commander Robertson asked.

"The Kraxians of late, have become less worrisome, Captain, but I assure you they still pose a threat to peace in the sector. They have been empire builders until a few short years ago. Conquering for sport, and taking, simply because they can. In a vast Galaxy where much can be found in abundance; a rational which we have found to be most perplexing. The other ships," he continued, "the one resembling a bird-like design is Rassilian, close neighbours of Kraxa. They share a common border. I would be wary of both Captain. The third, the smaller of the three, is Tyreean. At present we are in dispute with the Tyreeans concerning a moon near our border with them. It surprises me that there was no attempt to further our conflict during the explosions. They are a tiresome and cantankerous species rather than dangerous. We find them to be most exasperating"

The Captain took mental notes; contact with these new spices in the future could prove problematic. "The other ship, the one that's still in orbit, who are they?" He asked.

"Ah, they are Macaitian, Captain...... Their world is distant; on the edge of the Alpha sector. They are largely unknown to us; though we have heard tails they invariably bring trouble. It is my personal opinion that they have designs on conquest; from what we understand, they deliberately create skirmishes and problems where none exist, as though testing the defences of worlds. Even the Kraxians are wary of them."

As they spoke the Commander was joined on-screen by another of his crew. The newcomer was smaller in stature but almost identical in grey colouring, white hair and long light coloured robes. When the newcomer spoke it was in a softer, higher tone; Captain Robertson deduced that she was female.

"My first officer, Captain."

"Pleased to meet you," Robertson smiled.

"Greetings," replied the female in the same flat emotionless tone her Commander had used.

It suddenly became apparent to Robertson, that during his conversation with the Commander, there had been a lack of tonal variation in the way the alien spoke. He hadn't really considered it until now, he'd thought it was just the Commander's monotonous, individual way of conversing, but he now realised this was a peculiarity of their spices. The Vaurillians appeared to be a rigid and emotionless people, and that they might not be Robertson's first choice of invite at a party.

Following genuine heartfelt farewells and enthusiastic invitations to formally visit each others home worlds the Vaurillian ship also departed the now ravaged star system, though not before strongly hinting at ways the Earth ship could improve its method of shielding. As Captain Robertson ordered the Galileo to do likewise and set a course for home, her security officer again was alerted to a deep and sustained scan emanating from the Macaitian ship. The scanning continued as the Galileo wheeled to port and vectored towards the Terran system only ceasing when she passed light speed. The Macaitians certainly seamed extremely interested in the capabilities and technology of others.

SS Galileo's and humanity's first encounter with advanced civilisations had passed fairly uneventfully but that would not always be the case. Over the next 200 years mankind learned more of their alpha sector neighbours, and there were many of them, and not all were benevolent or friendly.

Within a few months the first acknowledged visit by a Vaurillian ship to Earth was hailed as a major step forward into a bright new future. Trade agreements were set in place and ambassadors exchanged.

Since humans had evolved scientifically in isolation, we had devised unique systems and technologies aboard our ships. The Vaurillians were keen to understand and in some cases adopt our innovative designs, and so an exchange programme, sharing ideas and engineering was set in place. This further cultivated our blossoming relationship and encouraging humanity's favourable reputation within the Alpha sector.

Although humans endeavoured to work and explore peacefully in the galaxy, still reports of warring between different worlds reached Earth. A fortuitous discovery of a wrecked Tyreean fighter on an abandoned moon, from which several weapons and power systems were salvaged and improved upon, Earth ships were soon armed with laser weapons; the match of any in the sector. Although we knew our intentions to be peaceful we were aware that others were not so well disposed.

Some seven years on from first contact, a fully engaged fire-fight replaced sporadic scuffles in the ongoing quarrel between Vaurillia and Tyreea over their disputed moon. A sizeable fleet of Earth ships was dispatched to the region; not to aid our newfound Vaurillian friends, but to forcibly interject. Without firing a shot, nine Earth ships placed themselves in harms-way between the two warring fleets, refusing to budge until their respective governments agreed to a ceasefire and negotiations. Both factions were taken aback at the audacity of these newcomers to the galactic political games. Tyreea, although enraged at Earth's presumptuous intervention discovered a solid if grudging respect for the courage of Earthlings. That respect was soon reciprocated when Tyreea readily agreed to attempt diplomacy. Vaurillia, for all their reasoning and logic, was less willing to be drawn to the negotiating table. Earth being the "new kid on the block" held no preconceived attitudes or grudges towards other species in the sector, it was our intent to be friendly and cooperative to all. These older space faring worlds though had had centuries to feed and nurtured their fear, mistrust and dislike of each other, and found that letting go of their prejudices too much of a wrench. Earth's ambassador to Vaurillia was quick to point out to his hosts that the disputed moon was a useless, barren rock and that it merely marked an ancient boundary between territories, which no longer needed or required frontiers. That if mutual trust and cooperation were adopted then freedom of trade and movement throughout the sector would become not only inevitable but beneficial, and that old boundaries would be mere relics of a by-gone, less enlightened age.

Neither world had time to assemble a negotiation team before a fleet of thirty Kraxian "Battle Beasts"; their fastest and most powerful ships, amassed along the disputed border in a crude attempt to profit from the territorial unrest and expand their own imperial designs.

The unprecedented response to Kraxa's attempted invasion was something no one in the alpha sector had bargained for, or expected; Earth, Vaurillia and Tyreea, as one, turned on Kraxa. Without agreement, consultation or consensus; three separate worlds found themselves standing together, shoulder to shoulder against the warrior world with combined firepower beyond anything the Kraxian fleet could withstand. Whether it was the shock of being out-gunned, out-numbered or unexpected unity they found themselves up against, the Kraxian fleet retreated, bloodied and out manoeuvred back to Kraxa, their desert home world.

With a new found respect for each other Vaurillia and Tyreea's dispute was soon a thing of the past. Borders, not only between themselves but also between other worlds fast became relics of a fractious age; unnecessary barriers where there should have been bridges and collaboration.

    The Alpha sector was at last becoming less divided. Earth, over the next four decades hosted conciliatory negotiations between more than a hundred different worlds, which were at last seeing the folly of confrontation over consultation. By the early twenty fourth century an alliance of worlds had formed, brokered mainly by Earth and Tyreea. Vaurillians, for all their cerebral intellect were emotionless and could not see the logic in being excited and proactive towards achieving long lasting peace in the sector. There was still however, a slender trust between some worlds who seemed determined to nurse old grudges against neighbours, but as Macaitian attacks on distant, outlying worlds became more frequent, their unity solidified. The burgeoning informal coalition eventually became a recognised union, and the "Alpha Alliance" was born on the first of June 2350, formally uniting 73 planets and their star systems in a collaborative confederation. A further 19 planets were at that time recognised as being under the umbrella of the Alliance protection and in time they too would be formally integrated into the growing family of worlds.

    Soon even Kraxa would warm to the alliance when one of their out-posts was attacked by a

Macaitian raiding fleet, who by now had given-up any pretence that their intent was not conquest. An Alliance patrol was the first to respond to the SOS. Unable to repel the Macaitians they did manage to rescue almost the all of the outpost's personnel, bringing about an Alliance/Kraxian Empire accord, advancing stability, if not friendship between them.

This often-volatile treaty with Kraxa had one major stumble on its way to being ratified. There were some in the Alliance who could not stomach any kind of arrangement with the Empire, too many could not forget centuries of bloodshed, and a handful of Alliance renegades, humans and Vaurillians in association with Kraxian rebels, attempted to assassinate the Kraxian ambassador en-route to the peace accord. Some of his party died in the attack but he survived and the pact was sealed. The perpetrators of the attack were dealt with quickly and harshly by the Kraxa judicial system.

And so the Alliance grew, in numbers and strength. Fleets of ships, designed, constructed and manned in collaboration. The Alliance Fleet's strength in unity being greater than the sum of its many parts patrolled and protected the sector, maintaining peace and stability. The Fleet, their motto; "Without fear. Without Frontiers", became the only force able to withstand the onslaught of the ever-growing Macaitian incursions.

Which was why, now thirty years later and still so far from home, Captain Dalton was eager to get the MS Johannesburg quickly through this last leg of their journey.

"What was that?"

"What was that?" Dalton and his security officer, to the rear of the bridge demanded in unison.

As Sweeney, the helmsman, straightened the massive hull of the freighter quelling his errant, fishtailing joyride, a second slash of green scarring appeared across the face of the nebula above and behind the Johannesburg. A second ship, utilising matter-cloaking technology was tailing the freighter, so closely that it too had inadvertently ignited the gasses in the cloud.

"Hard to port. Warp nine, now!" bellowed Dalton as he slammed his fist on the large red button on the arm of his command chair.

Instantaneously a claxon resounded throughout the ship and the lights dimmed, diverting power from unnecessary auxiliary systems to life support, shields and weapons. An SOS was automatically transmitted to the Alliance Fleet. The MS Johannesburg was now in war mod.......

"It must be Macaitian," the security officer yelled as he attempted to scan and get a fix on the position of the tailing ship. "There's been rumours that they've perfected cloaking."

Several years ago unconfirmed reports of a badly damaged, but intact, Kraxian "battle beast" having been captured by the Macaitians, had filtered to Alliance Fleet. If such an event were true it was both unusual and troubling.... Unusual, because no Kraxian Commander had ever let his ship be captured by any enemy, ever; they invariably set their ships to self-destruct before they would face the humiliating indignity of capture. Troubling, because Kraxa had perfected a cloaking device, which concealed their ships, visibly and from sensors, about a hundred year earlier. It was a technology the Alliance had never found any response to and were powerless against.

It seemed the rumours were true......

As both the Johannesburg and invisible Macaitian vessel burst, at faster than light speed into the outer reaches of nebula cloud, they left a pair of flaming green tails in their wake as the cloud reacted angrily to their warp plasma trails. The Macaitian's trail veered sharply right and down as the invisible ship attempted to pull level with the Alliance freighter before the cloud around them became to dense and they would loose the freighter in the murk.

As Captain Dalton had hoped, the cloud around them suddenly fizzled with energy, sparking and spitting furiously, lighting up all around the racing ships.

"We're losing sensors Captain, the cloud's ionising because of our warp drive," the Science officer bellowed.

"That's good," Dalton smiled, "screen on."

As the cloud became denser they were becoming blind. They had no idea where the other ship was but then the Macaitian Captain would be having the same problem. Captain Dalton wanted the view screen on just in case they could make visual contact. It was unlikely but it was better than nothing. Suddenly a blast of bright orange laser cannon streaked across their bow.

"Woo, that was close," Sweeney laughed nervously, as the ship rocked, but he deftly and quickly steadied her back on course.

Any energy burst or energy field within the cloud pulsated and was magnified due to the composition of the unstable gasses in the nebula. The laser fire had caused a numbing shock wave that slammed into the Johannesburg's hull, like a tidal wave crashing to shore. But her shields held and Sweeney's surefooted balance and poise on a surfboard meant that he could feel and react to every ripple and vibration in the Johannesburg's deck plating beneath him making him more than a match for any disturbance in his course setting.

"No it wasn't," Dalton countered. "They're firing blind, hoping to catch us by chance."

Behind the Captain to his right, the communications officer abruptly interrupted, announcing, "Our SOS has been acknowledged, Captain. Endeavour is on an intercept course. She's only minutes from the nebula."

Alliance Fleet kept patrols in every region of the Alpha Sector for just such an eventuality. Clashes with the Macaitians were becoming a daily occurrence; a declaration of all out war was expected imminently.

The ship suddenly bucked, tossing the bridge crew from their seats, as she spun violently around her port bow.

"We've just lost warp drive and attitude control, Captain," Sweeney roared, scrambling back to his helm console and straightening the ship out of her spin.

The nebula had just dealt them a fateful blow, as it had done to many ships in the past, which had attempted to power through its volatile gasses. The Johannesburg was now a limping lumbering hulk. If the Macaitians got lucky and managed to find them, Dalton and her crew would have nowhere to run. They were now totally reliant on A.S. Endeavour.

"Hold us on course, maximum thrusters."

Another blistering blast of lasers strafed across the view screen.

"Dive, Matt. Take us out of their line of fire!"

Beyond the margins of the nebula the deep-space science vessel A.S. Endeavour closed on their target at warp 9.5; its maximum velocity. Her Captain, Nicolle Lockhart, sat tall and erect on the edge of her command chair gripping tightly to its arms. She was a tall and elegant beauty, with a milky complexion and high cheekbones. In her younger years at the Alliance Academy she had been the target for many an amorous males advances, and even now at 49, she was still very much a head-turner for all males, not only of her own species. Her once raven dark hair now had a single streak of grey in it, which she brushed back from her forehead giving her an added air of dark mystery. She was half French and half Scottish on her father's side; an exquisite blend of amour and aggression.

With a fait hint of a soft French accent, Captain Lockhart instructed her helmsman to slow to warp three and approach the edge of the cloud on a "zigzag" trajectory. Scanning the disturbances within the cloud, caused by warp engines and laser fire, from multiple angles, would give Endeavour's ship's sensors as much information on the estimated position of the Johannesburg and her attacker as possible. Swinging to starboard for the fourth time, having garnered as much data as the cloud would allow, the Endeavour's science team could just about pinpoint where both ships were. Captain Lockhart ordered her ship into an attack dive at warp five. Endeavour's elongated saucer silhouette with two engine nacelles below and one on top, mounted on a dorsal-fin, slammed through the clawing mist into the fray, trailing bright green in her wake; she had come to save the freighter and her crew, even if it meant sacrificing Endeavor's warp nacelles in the process.

Another barrage of dazzling orange laser arced across Captain Dalton's view screen but was suddenly answered by a welcome shaft of bright green lasers and then another; Alliance lasers cannons are green. The Endeavour had announced her timely arrival.

"Captain!" the Johannesburg's tactical officer, Commander Wicasa exclaimed. "There's some kind of an anomaly directly aft of us it wasn't there a second ago; it just suddenly appeared."

"He's right, Captain," the freighter's science officer, confirmed. "What ever it is, there's a massive gravitational force within it, and it's pulling us towards it."

"Maximum thrusters, Mr. Sweeney. What ever it is, get us away from it."

"Aye."

Both the Endeavour and the Macaitian ship continued their simultaneous barrage, firing rapidly and blindly into the grey swirl around them, more in hope than expectation of doing damage to their opponent. Each time they did the cloud lit up a dazzling, dancing and deadly light show. Unexpectedly the cloud began to clear a little. Indistinct shadowy shapes, trailing green vapor became visible as they moved through the murk. The Macaitian ship may have been utilizing cloaking technology but in the nebula, with an obvious green tail in its wake, it was as visible as either of the Alliance ships.

"Target the cloaked ship, fire all weapons!" ordered Captain Lockhart.

Onboard the Johannesburg Captain Dalton issued the same command. Both ships simultaneously unleashed a fury of concentrated energy on one set of co-ordinates.

Whump!!!!!

A concussive blast wave punched through the cloud, radiating from the Macaitian ship as its cloaking failed under intense fire. The shockwave pitched all three vessels, bouncing them around like insects in a hurricane, as the Macaitian ship suddenly became as visible as the other two. Defending herself, she loosed a volley of lasers on both Alliance ships. The Endeavour's shields held, only weakening by a fraction, but the Johannesburg took a direct hit to her port thrusters. Without attitude control the Johannesburg swung wildly through a shallow ark only slowing as she swung within range of the gravitational pull of the widening anomaly to her rear.

The anomaly's gravitational pull was increasing. The reason the three ships could see each other more and more clearly was because the nebula's toxic cloud was thinning as the dust particles within it were sucked through the anomalies widening aperture.

"Captain!" the Endeavour's tactical officer, ensign Walter Cheung exclaimed, There's some kind of gravitational anomaly directly aft of the Johannesburg. She's being pulled towards it!"

The young Chinese Ensign Cheung was only just out of the Alliance Academy, it had been his twenty first birthday just two days before The Endeavour had set off on this current mission patrolling far edges of the nebula. He had only returned to the Alliance Fleet Academy in Dallas from his parent's home in Kowloon to be told of this; his first posting. This was his first tour of duty, his first encounter with opposing forces and his first time under fire, but he had a cool head on his shoulders and Captain Lockhart had personally requested him for her crew.

Lockhart had a brief and rare moment of pause as she weighed-up her options. The freighter had no warp drive and now had only reduced thrusters; it was being pulled towards the anomaly and no longer had the power to pull away. She had to get the Johannesburg away from the gravitational anomaly, while holding the Macaitian at bay. Endeavour's tractor beam was useless; to engage it she'd have to drop her own shields leaving Endeavour defenseless.

"Place us behind the freighter," she instructed her helmsman, "Use our shields to push the Johannesburg away from the anomaly!"

As the helmsman swung the Endeavour aft of the stricken freighter and engaged her warp drive, attempting to push her dead weight to safety, the anomaly widened further still.

"Captain!" Lockhart's Vaurillian science officer, Lt Constarectacek Jevak, called, as he made himself heard over the groaning of the ship's hull as it strained to push the mass of the freighter in front of her whilst being pulled by increasing gravitational attraction of the anomaly to her rear. "The anomaly is widening! It appears to be increasing in dimension in relation to the magnitude of thrust emanating from Endeavour's and the Macaitian warp drives."

The Lieutenant's first name being unpronounceable to any but another Vaurillian, he was normally referred to as simply, Mr. Jevak or just Jevak. As with almost all Alliance ships the science officer post was always given to a Vaurillian since their cold logic and deductive reasoning was unfaltering.

"Have you any idea what the anomaly is?" Lockhart asked, the urgency in her voice palpable.

"I can not explain it Captain, but it would appear to be a rip in space. The composition of the nebula coupled with the concentrated warp energy and weapon fire, seems to have destabilized the fabric of space in the immediate vicinity. Our efforts to rescue the freighter and hold the Macaitian at bay are only serving to increase the dimensions of the fracture."

The Macaitian again targeted both Alliance ships.

The Johannesburg's shields faltered and she took a direct hit to the bridge. The bulkhead above Captain Dalton's command chair buckled and split showering him with a ton of molten hull. At the same time the view screen exploded. Commander Wicasa leapt from his station at tactical, shielding his eyes from slashing fragments of the screen, he hauled the burning debris away from his commanding officer, but he knew instantly Dalton was dead, he'd been dead before anyone on the bridge had time to react.

"Extend our shields to protect the Johannesburg!" Lockhart called to Cheung.

FOR THE WANT OF A NAIL

Extending Endeavour's shield over such a vast distance, to encompass the massive bulk of the freighter, weakened them considerably. They were designed to accommodate a starship possibly two, but certainly not the immense bulk of a vast freighter, its lumbering cargo and a starship. With both ships now inside the Endeavour's diluted bubble though, Captain Lockhart was able to deploy her ship's tractor beam and began pulling the stricken freighter away from the anomaly's gravity well.

"Full warp power!" Lockhart instructed her helmsman.

Both the Endeavor and Johannesburg began inching away from the gravitational pull of the anomaly, but only for a brief moment. The nebula's loathing of warp nacelles became evident again. Endeavour's starboard engine instantly flamed and died.

The powerful thrust of warp power from Endeavour had widened the anomaly further. The gravitational pull from whatever was on the other side of the hole in space was immense and it was again dragging the Johannesburg towards it.

With the Endeavour's shields now over extended and her engines faltering, the Macaitian took the offering of the now vulnerable opponents to unleash a full volley of laser fire across both ships. A vast hole in the side of the freighter exploded, venting its engine room. Bodies and burning debris erupted from its hull, pluming across space. Since both the Johannesburg and Endeavour were enclosed within the same defensive bubble, much of the debris smashed into the Alliance Defense vessel slashing ruptures in its outer hull.

Jevak worked furiously across his science console, his full attention focused on the danger now posed by the growing mouth of the gravity well to their rear. Besides the mounting pull of immense gravity, there was also a colossal radiation source; heat and growing intense light, emanating from the anomaly, none of which he found encouraging or fascinating.

Lockhart knew that tethering her ship to the dead weight of the freighter was crippling her own ship and restricting her ability to defend either, she felt "hogtied". It was obvious she had to take more positive, aggressive approach to the enemy.

"Full port-side spread of ion torpedoes. Target their weapons."

Cheung did as instructed. A three second burst of light pulses exploded from Endeavour's port-side launchers, angling towards the Macaitian's laser cannons. The enemy's Captain, as Lockhart hoped he would, angling his defence shields towards the incoming assault. Lockhart was about to instruct her helmsman to dive and accelerate to the Macaitian's starboard side, when the hull plating below the bridge exploded upwards hurling everyone including the Captain from their posts. Lockhart smashed her head breaking her nose and dislocating her left shoulder as she landed. Dazed, she looked around. Her young helmsman lay at her feet, his head askew with a deep gouge across his temple and half a meter of deck plating protruding from his chest. Nicolle knew he was dead. Scrambling across her fallen crewman- she could grieve later, she pulled the debris aside, clearing his console, and with her good arm took control of the helm. She swung the ship to starboard and rushed the Macaitian on his now unprotected side.

"Fire all lasers." She roared.

The space between the two opposing ships crackled with brilliant, burning lances of laser fire as they twisted around each other. The barrage continued unabated for a full minute, each ship's defense shields weakened by degree, but still both Captains raged against the other, refusing to give, hurling everything they had at their enemy. To both Captains, the Johannesburg had become secondary to the battle they were now engaged in.

The Macaitian's shields weakened first, a single laser burst to its engine room crippled its warp reactor leaving it with only maneuvering thrusters, which meant it could still battle, but it was going nowhere.

"Captain," Jevak called, but refrained from shouting.

Shouting is a physical manifestation of emotions such as fear or anxiety, and Vaurillians are an emotionless species.

In their adolescence, which occurs in their early thirties because they are long-lived by human standards, they, both male and female, go through a ceremony; a right of passage called "Purgat". The "Purgats" meditate for weeks, sometimes months at a time locked away in rooms of confinement. Chemicals are burned and inhaled; to take them to a heightened state of awareness and in a drug induced stupor they achieve a startling mental clarity and enlightenment. Their minds become more focused, leaving them brilliant but cold; the emotional side of their brains having been purged; physically burned away by the chemicals. It is ironic that as a species, even before they undertake the ritual, Vaurillians are the most empathic race in the known Galaxy, almost to the point of being telepathic. They are intensely attuned with emotions of others, becoming even more so after undergoing "Purgat", but at the cost of their own emotions.

"Captain, the Johannesburg is slipping through the fissure."

"What's on the other side, Jevak?"

"I still can not be certain, the cloud particles rushing through are blunting our sensors, but I would hazard that there could be a star, possibly a red giant of immense magnitude in very close proximity to the fissure's aperture. By my calculations, if there is a star, the aperture may even open into its corona."

"Captain, we lost our tractor beam in that last barrage," Cheung advised. "Even if we could deploy it, we can't pull the freighter back through."

Lockhart knew the Johannesburg, without protective shields, would burn-up in a star in a few seconds, killing all of her crew, if she deserted them to carry on the fight.

"We're going after them!"

She ran her good hand across the helm console, nimbly fingering the gloss black surface, spun the Endeavour on a sixpence, then punched the ship to her maximum warp speed, given that she was down to one engine nacelle. In half a second they were through the fissure, once again alongside the freighter. As they did, the Macaitian kept up its relentless barrage through the aperture, raining laser fire on both Alliance ships.

The Johannesburg's outer hull was already beginning to glow red as she spiraled towards the surface of the waiting star.

"Teleport Room!" Nicolle roared.

The ship's computer system picked-up the Captain's voice command and immediately opened a communication link, "comm-link" to the Teleportation operator.

"Teleport here Captain," came the reply from seven decks bellow.

"Lock on to all life signs on the freighter and beam them out of there."

The teleport operator, utilizing the ship's computer systems for data analysis, scanned the freighter for signs of biological life, quickly determined which were alive and activated the teleportation beam.

Teleportation technology, where-by an object can be disassembled, down to its molecules, converted into energy, and that energy transported, at light speed to a distant location, then reassembled back to its original form, has been in existence since the early twenty-first century. A rudimentary "Teleport" was first achieved at the Delft University in Holland, when quantum data was sent from one electron to another ten feet away. Since then only the inability of computers and their lack of processing power, to successfully evaluate the mass, composition, movement and size of an atom quickly enough to enable it to be disassembled and rebuilt before the object disintegrated or worse, died was soon over come with the advent of warp technology; warp technology changed everything.

The Macaitian ship continued its onslaught from the other side of the fissure, firing only at the Endeavour now, since the Johannesburg was already doomed. Nicolle ordered Cheung to target the Macaitian's damaged engine room.

The two explosions occurred simultaneously; the Alliance freighter broke-up and ruptured her warp reactor as she tumbled helplessly to the star's crushing gravity, at the same time as the Macaitian's warp reactor breached under the Endeavour's relentless fire. The seismic, crushing, detonation of two warp reactors ripped through the vacuum of space with a raging fury, pummeling the Endeavour, smashing against the ship's outer hull. The blinding, numbing light of the detonations, swallowed the starship, engulfing it in a raging tsunami of debris. The incandescent explosions dwarfed the light from the star, searing the blackness around them. Hull plating buckled and ripped from the Endeavour, only her protective bubble of shielding held the starship together, preventing her destruction. The explosions tossed the tiny, by comparison, starship, tumbling aft over nose for half a light-year across the firmament until she finally came to rest, listing crazily, broken but intact.

When the explosions and light finally subsided the fissure was gone. Only Endeavour and the red giant star she was now orbiting wildly, remained. The identical, simultaneous explosions on both sides of the rift had collapsed it, closing the doorway they had entered through.

The stars around the forlorn Alliance ship looked strange and unfamiliar. Wherever Endeavour was, she was far from home, broken and alone.

CHAPTER 1

Extended periods of inactivity frustrated Nicolle. The more prolonged the lull, the deeper her irritation. She was ever industrious and craved the heat of the moment. There were goals to be realized and unexplored new horizons beckoning her constantly. The reason: quite simply, her family history had set her personal bar very high.

Her maternal great, great, great, great grandfather, Claude Mathieu had been the revered physicist; the head of the science team, which had developed the faster than light warp engine nearly three hundred years before she was born. It was a immense honor and an undoubted door opener that she was descended from such a respected scientific icon, who's work had opened the cosmos to human exploration and eventually given rise to the Alliance, but it was also a millstone around her neck. Much more was expected of Nicolle, especially from herself, and for that reason she pushed herself more than she expected of others.

Since Endeavour's unplanned arrival in the Gamma Sector a little over six years ago, Nicolle's beckoning horizons were a far cry from what she had imagined when she had first enlisted at the Alliance Fleet Academy. Those horizons tended now to couch danger at almost every turn, rather than the wonder and excitement of discovery she had sought when she had sign-up. That was after all why she had been so eager to enlist at the Academy: the thrill of exploration. She was without doubt an alpha personality: bold, decisive and quick to action, though never impulsive. She thrived on pushing her personal envelope to its limits, challenging the boundaries of her potential. Actively seeking out her uncertainties, facing them down and vigorously testing and prodding at her limitations. Patience, Nicolle had realised long ago, may be a virtue, but it was never one of hers. Unless she was in the thick of it she was decidedly frustrated. It was therefore uncharacteristic that she should now be in a leisurely mood, her thirst for action and the next alien horizon temporarily quenched.

Captain Nicolle Lockhart could scarcely remember a time when she had happily accepted a prolonged period of what she would have normally considered tedium.

It was late evening. She was relaxing in the mess-hall, sipping coffee and swapping old stories and tales of daring with three members of her senior staff and, as she was proud to say, three of her dearest friends. For that is what they were, more than comrades, much more than colleagues, friends.

It was now six long years since A.S. Endeavour and her crew had followed the doomed freighter Johannesburg through the fissure and found themselves far removed from home. They'd realised immediately they were no longer in the Alpha Sector. The stars were unfamiliar. But by scanning the position of galaxies beyond our own they were able to ascertain their new position relative to Earth. The initial surprise and disbelief soon gave way to dread at the sheer scale and enormity of the situation and their predicament; they were more than seventy thousand light-years on the far side of the galaxy. So impossibly far from Alliance space, that even at the ship's maximum warp, it would take much, much longer than their lifetimes to reach home again. She and her crew were very much alone.

Endeavour's enforced isolation from the rest of Alliance Fleet had brought all of the crew closer together, like a surrogate family in this unfamiliar corner of the galaxy. They were the only family any of them now had. Her crew. Her friends.

Nicolle shifted in her chair, stretching her back like a contented cat, as she eased herself into a more comfortable position. Behind her, through the curved view ports, the vast nebula they were currently orbiting, mirrored her peaceful demeanour as its colossal cumulous clouds billowed and puffed, drifting lazily by.

It was hard to imagine, given how untroubled the crew appeared, that they were so far from home. Further than any human had ever travelled. Farther than it was possible to communicate, even using 'hyperspace transmissions '. And one hundred years from now, even at their average warp speed of 6.3, Endeavour would still be little more than half way home; still well beyond communication range with the Alliance's farthest outpost.

Endeavour was lost and so far from home that light which had left Earth seventy thousand years ago was only now reaching her, in a place so distant and alien as to be nightmarish to the creatures whose images those photons of light carried. Were it possible to isolate and extract the images of that distant blue speck, life on Earth would be the stuff, not of history, but archaeology. Our ancient ancestors, not yet human, no longer ape, taking those first tentative steps upon the ladder of evolution. The first primates to exhibit evidence of self-awareness and conceptual, abstract thought as opposed to instinct born reaction, had only recently set the spark to the flame of that evolution. Fuelling a brain that would lift mans gaze to the heavens, his imagination to the stars and Endeavour to this lonely and remote edge of the galaxy.

The relentless journey home, though never far from her thoughts, was firmly to the back of Nicolle's mind for the moment. She was off-duty and planned to enjoy her downtime. And if current trends were anything to go by there was very little chance of this evening's get together being interrupted.

Until two days ago they had been traversing a sparsely populated sector of Gar-jevan space; an oasis in the constant danger the Gamma Sector had come to represent. The locals were friendly, happily allowing them to pass through, even offering assistance if it were needed. Apart from that their last encounter with any other vessel had been three weeks ago; a friendly Morrmarian trader who had exchanged much needed supplies for some expertise in anti-matter flow from Endeavour's Chief Engineer.

Zerttral and Vadeusan ships which had harassed them since their arrival in this sector, were so conspicuous by their absence in this region, they had almost become bad memories. Long-range scans had detected nothing but empty space for a distance of at least sixty light-years in all directions. No warp trails, nothing untoward or remotely threatening. Things were most definitely quiet. And as far as Nicolle was concerned, she was more than happy for them to remain that way. Her coffee was hot, the company was good and there were countless tales to wile away the hours.

Flash!!

Her attention was suddenly caught by a blinding burst of incandescent white light, exploding through the view-ports behind her. The shafts of shocking white radiance split the room, casting stark haunting shadows of the groups around her, to the far walls.

Momentarily, she glanced from her companions. The clamour and noise of the busy mess-hall briefly hushed as many eyes in the room turned towards the view-ports, and the breathtaking, sporadic light show taking place beyond them. Unfazed by the bedazzling interruption, Nicolle returned to the conversation at the table.

For the past 48 hours Endeavour had been in close orbit around a class-eight nebula, the source of the dazzling, intermittent light display. Some of those off duty in the mess-hall who still found the display beguiling, gasped in awe as the lights in the vast swirl of gas and dust sparked furiously again and again in ever changing colours and hues. Those who had seen more class-eight nebulas than they could count on the fingers and toes of an adult Drisart, merely carried on chatting.

As Matt Sweeney, one of the many of the Johannesburg's crew who had been rescued at the last minute before its destruction, had nonchalantly commented shortly after their arrival around the phenomenon: "It makes for nice wall-paper, for those of us with quarters on the port side."

He, like the captain had encountered more than his fair share of gas nebulas, many of which he had even successfully navigated.

Several days ago, at lieutenant Jevak's request, a slight detour had been arranged from their general heading, to investigate the gas cloud now venting its fury one hundred thousand meters to port. The captain had readily agreed, welcoming the opportunity to resume Endeavours primary function as a ship of discovery and exploration. Besides, it would give the crew some much-needed relief from the usual dodging and running from the Gamma Sector's unfriendly natives.

Cradling her coffee cup in both hands, she stared dreamily into its golden brown depths, lost in the memory of the story she was recounting. Her ice blue eyes betrayed a mischievous sparkle, as she cast a playful glance around the table at her three friends.

"…..and since port and starboard are relative to whether you're upside down or not," Nicolle explained, a sly grin teasing wickedly at the corner of her lips. "They didn't have clue where we were," bursting into fits of laughter and almost spilling her coffee at the memory, she added. "……but then, neither did we."

Around the table Lieutenant Matt Sweeney, Commander Wicasa and Ensign Walter, or as he'd become known amongst the crew, "Wattie", Cheung echoed her raucous laughter.

Wattie spluttered, almost chocking on his coffee. "That's not in the manual." he coughed, shocked at his Captains revelation of dishonesty.

Endeavour had been Wattie's first tour of duty after graduating from Alliance Fleet Academy and he was still a little naive where commanding officers were concerned. Although his bubble had been burst long ago, part of him still wanted to cling to the illusion that captains could walk on water.

"Well it should be," insisted Matt, still laughing as the room split with light again. "Not everything should to be done by the book."

Nicolle's penetrating gaze locked on Matt as the laughter subsided. The book, she thought: Matt could write a book about the book, and the pages he had ripped from it. That had once been her hotheaded young helmsman's undoing. He had been a brilliant young student at Alliance Fleet some years earlier, but his insubordination and reluctance to accept authority had been his downfall. Alliance Fleet had seen fit to part company with young Mr Sweeney casting him into the wilderness, denying him his thrill for speed at the helm of a starship. He found his solace instead at the bottom of a bottle. Fortunately he'd later found his way again, working his ticket, piloting freighters for The Titan mining company. Like all of Johannesburg's surviving crew, he'd been conscripted. After all, he was the best pilot in the Sector, and Nicolle liked his maverick spirit. He reminded her of her younger self..... sometimes.

"A little unorthodox," Wicasa commented, "but it showed initiative. No one's ever beaten the Academy's simulators."

Commander Wicasa, like Mr Sweeney had been a conscript to Endeavour's crew. Captain Nicolle had lost several of her key crewmembers during the firefight with the Macaitian. Her "Number One" Commander Muller had perished when Endeavour's starboard nacelle had flamed, exploding power conduits in Engineering Section. She'd lost many of her brave crew as they fought to quell the flames that threatened to incinerate the warp reactor's cooling system, putting the whole ship at risk.

In the six years Captain Lockhart had gotten to know her new second-in-command, Wicasa, she'd come to trust his judgement implicitly. Though they didn't always agree, it was his job to second guess her and propose alternative strategies to hers. The tall, barrel-chested Inuit Indian who's long dark hair was always swept back in a pony-tail was an excellent sounding board for Nicolle, they worked comfortably, collaboratively together like two sides of the same coin, his name from the Dakota tribe means "Sage", wise one, he was younger than the Captain but to her that's what he'd become; her wise constant rock.

Born in Greenland, he'd joined the Titan Freight Company fifteen years earlier, in his mid-twenties. He'd reasoned that since space was desolate, empty and cold, just like home, he'd fit right-in there.

Wattie shook his head incredulously. "I can't believe you re-aligned the gyroscopic relays. That's cheating!" he exclaimed.

Stretching back in her seat, Nicolle slowly wagged a finger at him in that 'wise old school teacher' fashion she often adopted when imparting her experience to junior members of the crew.

"No, no, not cheating," she said pensively, furrowing her brow while she slowly shook her head.

The Captain, pausing briefly for effect, purposefully leant forward to rest her elbows firmly on the table. Doing a very passable impression of stern, she locked her steely gaze on the young ensign giving him her most withering, intense stare: more for Matt and Wicasa's benefit and amusement than anything else.

"I don't like to get beat," she explained.

"And that, ensign, is why she sits in the captains chair," Wicasa said with a sidelong wink at the Ensign.

"Yes Salix," the Captain said, turning her attention to Endeavours chef as he approached the table.

Since the four bridge officers had arrived in the mess hall over an hour ago, Salix had been furiously juggling pots and pans in the galley, creating another of his gastronomic surprises. Now his latest 'masterpiece' was evidently complete, as he triumphantly placed a dish before the Captain.

"What's this?" she asked.

Looking a little apprehensive, as he always did at moments like this; namely when his credibility as a chef was about to be called into question. Salix suspiciously eyed the others at the table before replying.

"Just a little something I've been preparing," he replied sheepishly, before adding. "It's a bit special. I'd like you to be the first to try it, Captain."

"Oh oh," Matt said. "Then by implication, you'd like the rest of us to try it too." Adding, with a heavy dollop of sarcasm, "Maybe we'd better alert the doctor."

Lockhart shot Sweeney a withering look. He held his tongue, quickly getting the message that the Captain wouldn't approve of Matt's use of Salix for jocular target practice, at least not this time. Encouragingly she smiled at the little flame haired Tallurian.

"I'd love to Salix," she said. "What is it?"

The only member of the crew indigenous to the Gamma Sector, Salix had felt out of place aboard the starship. His knowledge of his native sector, and its unfamiliar species, had proven invaluable on countless occasions. But six years into their journey they had left behind his field of expertise, and his home world long ago, leaving him feeling a little surplus to requirements.

The captain therefore felt it necessary to nurture and encourage him, and since energy restrictions often curtailed the use of food replicators, she appointed him Endeavour's chef. A position the little Tallurian had taken to enthusiastically, throwing himself into the role with passion, if not talent.

"Just try it," he urged, hoping for a positive response. "I think you'll like it."

Uncertain, she picked up a spoon, and prodded the strange contents of the shallow metal dish, breaking through the crust to the filling below. A strange greenish goo, with a distinctly purple tinge oozed slowly out.

Food shouldn't be that colour, Nicolle

thought, eyeing the offering suspiciously, at least not edible food.

Given some of Salix's previous attempts at gastronomic conjuring, Nicolle was a little reluctant to rush into a stomach-upset. As ship's captain she fully accepted the responsibilities of leadership and the risks it involved. Bravery in the face of the enemy was part-and-parcel of the job, but bravery in the face of her own chef must be above and beyond the call of duty.

Looking up, she half hoped Salix was as surprised as she was at the strange colour of the ooze slowly covering the bottom of her plate. Instead he just carried on smiling and nodding whilst his bushy red eyebrows almost danced with enthusiasm.

She turned to the others at the table, hoping for some glimmer of support, though was not surprised when none was forthcoming. They were all wearing the same fixed smiles, like startled rabbits, and that 'thank God I'm not the Captain' expression, that so many starship Captains had come to 'cherish'.

No help there then, she thought, sighing, as she prodded a little further. Well, he's never actually killed anyone with his cooking, and I suppose he must have tried it himself.

As she lifted a small, very.... very small piece tentatively to her mouth, the nebula suddenly sparked again.

Flash! Right on cue, filling the room with stark, black, haunting shadows.

Matt seized the moment and gasped, hiding his eyes in mock terror. Every one saw the humour, laughing a little nervously: all except Salix that is. Not to be diverted the Tallurian carried on smiling his encouragement at the Captain.

Ah well, here goes nothing, she thought. With resigned uncertainly she lifted the spoon to her lips and tasted the dubious offering.

Slowly her face brightened.

'"Salix...mmm... Oh Salix, this I delicious!" she exclaimed, surprising even herself at her enthusiasm. "Mmm..., it really is, absolutely delicious." Scooping another, larger spoonful, she pressed him again. "Okay, so tell me, what is it?"

"It's just a simple pie, captain," he shrugged coyly.

"Come on Salix," coaxed Wicasa. "We know you're dying to tell us."

Salix could hardly contain himself. He was so proud of this new culinary creation; he felt he would boil over if he weren't allowed to explain how he had worked his magic, conjuring this piece de resistance.

"The filling, ah... the filling is a cornucopia of delicately spiced Morrmarian apples, blended with the fine, aromatic juices of the Gar-Jeff mountain grape, left to marinade and ferment for exactly the right amount of time to bring-out their pungent heady sweetness." He caught his breath, almost gushing with child-like enthusiasm, before re-launching at his description. "Then rolled lovingly in the most delicate, creamy pastry." Then added triumphantly. "And served, for your delectation," he finished, half bowing to the captain.

Nicolle returned his bow with a slight nod and an appreciative smile. "This really is absolutely delicious Salix. You've surpassed yourself."

Pushing the dish into the centre of the table, she motioned for the others to sample it too. "Here try some, go on tuck-in."

The dish was passed around the table, gingerly at first, then with mounting enthusiasm. The sound of the mess-hall door swishing open then closed again, as Lieutenant Jevak entered, was almost drowned-out by the growing clamour of praise suddenly being heaped on a delighted Salix.

As Jevak approached the table he was intrigued by the commotion. Matt had turned his attention from the fast disappearing fare to the delighted, ever-grinning chef.

"So these must be the apples we got from that Morrmairian freighter a couple of weeks back?" he asked.

"That's right," replied Salix, fussing around the table.

"Then I suppose you could call this... Morrm's apple pie."

Everyone within earshot groaned their reluctant appreciation at another of Matt's perfectly orchestrated puns; all except Salix and Jevak that is. The normally jovial Tallurian did not appreciate the joke being directed at his creation, and Jevak of course, now standing to the Captain's side, like all Vaurillians, just did not appreciate humour.

"Sorry," offered Matt. "Just a little joke."

"Yeh," agreed Wicasa, dismissively. "Only just."

Wicasa's jibe earning another appreciative ripple of laughter.

"Mmm. Humour," observed Jevak, in that emotionless, almost disdainful manner by which Vaurillians view the superfluous recreational activities of all other species. "I have never understood the human need to interject it at every conceivable opportunity," He cocked his head to one side, grimacing slightly, to emphasise his observation. Then poured salt into the wound by adding, "Even when inappropriate."

"Harmless fun, Jevak, just harmless fun. It lightens the heavy load and helps lift the weary foot one more step down the long road," interrupted the Captain, jumping to the defence of every humanoid in the Universe not blessed with the good fortune to be born on Vaurillia. Though she needn't have bothered, since the word "fun" was as alien to the ship's science and security officer as "fair-play" was to a Macaitian.

Jevak, as with all Vaurillians could no more appreciate the emotional humanoid condition, as a blind man could appreciate the colour green. Explaining joy, anger, frustration, and the deepest of all, love, to a Vaurillian was futile. Their race had abandoned their emotions for the higher attainment of pure logic centuries ago. Cold and emotionless, no Vaurillian could ever appreciate the complexities of just simply.... feeling. Their lives were ruled, not by the their hearts, since their emotions had been chemically purged, but by their brilliantly incisive heads. For that reason, almost every Alliance starship in the galaxy since the Alliance was formed has had a Vaurillian science officer. Their affinity for cold, clinical deduction having proven invaluable to every Captain.

Wearing an obviously fake, pained expression, Matt looked up at Jevak, his eyes heavy with exaggerated sadness. "Oh Jevak," he sighed, shaking his blond curly head. "It pains me to see you so sad." Adding sarcastically. "Here try some of Salix' apple pie, it might restore your usual bubbly demeanour." Winking at Salix, Matt suddenly gushed excitedly, "I've just had flash of genius. We could market your apple pie. Just imagine; 'So delicious, it can even bring a smile to a Vaurillian's lips'." Sweeney spread his arms wide, his hands mapping-out the words printed high on an imaginary billboard. "It can't fail. We'll be rich."

Salix felt obliged to join-in the assault on Jevak. "Go on Mr Vaurillian, try it," he said elbowing him gently in the ribs. "I'd go so far as to say, it might even take the starch out of your neck."

"Thank you, but no. I have no need of sustenance at this moment," he replied, stoically, ignoring their attempts to goad him. "Perhaps later." Quickly changing the subject he glanced out of the view-port behind the Captain, at the nebula, then added. "Captain, may I speak with you?"

Nicolle noticed the glance and instantly rose to her feet. "Certainly," she said. "I was about to make my way to the bridge anyway. Walk with me." Placing her spoon on the table she looked across to Salix. "Save some of that for me, would you? I'll have it later."

"Oh absolutely, Captain," gushed the delighted little chef. "I'll have it sent to your quarters."

"It really is delicious," said Nicolle, as she and Jevak made their way to the door. "You should've tried some."

"I take it, Mr Salix has been giving vent to his culinary genius again?" enquired Jevak.

Nicolle looked at him a little quizzically. Were it not for the fact that Jevak was Vaurillian, she would have sworn that he was being sarcastic, but she knew any implication by her to that effect, would bring the standard Vaurillian response; that he 'could see no reason for insults'. Sometimes she was sure that his species did have a sense of humour. Theirs was the only planet in on the joke, and they were having a laugh at the rest of the galaxies expense.

Stepping into the corridor, the door swished immediately closed behind them. Nicolle again leapt to the defence of her chef.

"Salix puts in a lot of effort," she pointed-out. "He tries hard to please the crew, and it usually goes unappreciated."

Turning right, into the main access corridor, which ran the length of the entire deck, they fell into step, making for the nearest turbo-lift.

The dimly lit corridor curved gently to the right, following the external contour of the vast hull. It was well past eighteen hundred hours and so, as has always been the case in vessels deprived of sunlight, the lighting levels in all public, none working areas of the ship had been dimmed. Mimicking the hours of darkness, afforded some semblance of rhythm to the crews body clocks.

"Anyway," she continued, as they strolled, "Salix isn't the reason you wanted to speak with me. I take it you've found something?"

"Nothing conclusive."

Nicolle eyed him wickedly; she was off-duty and still felt in a playful mood. "Then why all the excitement?" she asked.

It was Jevak's turn to look quizzical. "Captain?"

"Well," she explained. "You rush all the way from your duty station to the mess, when you could have used the comm. Secret nods and winks. You drag me away from my leisure time. Come-on Jevak, you can hardly contain yourself." Fixing him with a grin she added sarcastically. "In fact, if I didn't know you better, I'd say you were positively buzzing with excitement."

Nicolle could see him visibly stiffen before making his stoic, measured reply. She was having a little fun at his expense; teasing him wickedly, and she knew it. But they were friends and she knew that he trusted his human colleagues, who, though often a little childish, would never be deliberately malicious or hurtful.

He cocked his head slightly, furrowing his brow in that inimitable Vaurillian manner as he maintained his unperturbed even flat, tone. "I am merely keeping my commanding officer appraised of an ongoing situation, Captain… I see no reason for insults."

Nicolle smiled as she got the obligatory, 'No need for insults', Vaurillian response; satisfied that she'd successfully hit his species fabled raw nerve, she assured him; "Only pulling your leg, Jevak."

Her mischievous wink, as they fell into step, only served to compound Jevak's "insulted" demeanour.

"Come-on," she relented. Feeling a little guilty, she adopting a more business-like manner. "Okay, what have you got?"

Jevak re-composed himself.

"As I have said captain, the readings are inconclusive. As expected, the nebula is reflecting most of our sensor scans."

Although Nicolle had been having a bit of fun at his expense, she knew her science office well enough to know that he would never have ignored the comm system in order to find her in person, if he had not thought it necessary. Jevak must have found something of significance, so she pressed him further.

"What's your best guess then?"

"I am familiar with the human concept of 'guessing'; a rather haphazard method of reaching a largely unsubstantiated conclusion. I would never presume to be so inaccurate."

Nicolle sighed. Jevak wasn't being intentionally obstructive with his reply, only thorough. But the Vaurillian habit of constantly justifying their logic could grate sometimes. She found herself wondered again, as she'd often done, as had many a starship Captain, that maybe Vaurillians did have a sense of humour. Their persistent habit of appearing mortally offended when their cold logic was questioned was maybe their way of deliberately annoying every other species in the Galaxy, just to see the irritation on their non-Vaurillian faces. It was their little secret joke, which only they were in on.

She held her breath, counted to four then tried again. "Okay then, what's your best hypotheses?" she persevered.

"The cloud would appear to be a stellar nursery," he said, adopting his usual meticulous manner. "I would speculate that probably twin stars are in very close orbit, at its heart; that would account for the cyclic nature of the energy bursts we have been witnessing."

"Mmm. Twin stars," she pondered for a moment. "Sounds interesting. But we're hardly the first ship to encounter such a phenomenon; twin or otherwise." She clasped her hands behind her back as they walked, then added. "There's something else, isn't there. Come-on Jevak, out with it."

He hesitated for a moment, considering his reply. As they turned a corner he stopped. Nicolle took a few more steps, and then turned to face him.

"There is Captain, but I….. I am reluctant to, as you humans say, 'put my head on the block'. Again he paused, seeming reluctant to offer his findings. Nicolle knew he was being cautious. "I have also detected very faint Neutrino emissions, emanating from the cloud."

The captain's face lit-up.

"A worm hole," she said, suddenly very attentive, her voice betraying both anticipation and scepticism. Nicolle's eyes turned from Jevak to the bulkhead behind him, focusing not on the curved, life preserving metal of the ship's skin, but on a point in space somewhere distant off the port bough. "A worm hole," she repeated quietly, to no one close enough to hear.

News like this was what they hoped for every day.

Seventy thousand light-years, even for a ship capable of Warp 9.5, was almost an inconceivable distance. It was farther than could possibly be covered in two, possibly three lifetimes, but that daunting journey was what lay between Endeavour and home: an impossible, unimaginable distance.

Six long years ago, in the blink of an eye, the fissure had spirited them across the vast swirling spiral of the entire Milkyway galaxy. Leaving them stranded, lost and alone so impossibly far from home. They were further from home than any Alliance ship had ever travelled; beyond imagination, beyond the expanse of any known star-chart, far beyond hope of contact.... But never beyond hope.

Every minute since that fateful day, Nicolle and her crew had strove to close that colossal distance again, inching ever nearer to home, mile-by-mile, click by click, light-year by endless light-year. Although the vast, unimaginable distance was daunting she knew, believed whole-heartedly with every fibre of her being, that some how, they would find a way to recross that vast expanse. But she also knew, as well as their own resourcefulness and enterprise they needed good fortune on their side too.

In fact they had already, by mere good fortune on several occasions successfully trimmed sizeable distances from their journey, although not by much. On each of these instances closing the distance back towards the Alpha Sector by several dozen light-years... a small amount in Galactic terms but never the less always a step closer. On each of these occasions they had detected neutrinos: the telltale signature of a wormhole.

Wormholes are naturally occurring spatial anomalies. They are like doorways in space, instantly connecting two remote and completely unrelated points. Allowing a ship to travel from point 'A' to 'D' without having to pass 'B' and 'C' to get there. It was like stepping through a door, and instead of finding yourself on the street outside; you were suddenly transported to, for example, the Sahara dessert. But looking back you could still see the door and beyond it the room you had just left.

These chance encounters had provided Endeavour with shortcuts that had so far slashed their journey by almost twenty five years; almost a quarter of the way to the centre of the galaxy: an eighth of their total journey, but that still left them a long, long way from home.

A few months ago, though, another encounter with a wormhole had been less fortuitous. This particular anomaly had carried them completely in the wrong direction. It had delivered them back, almost to where they had started their journey six years earlier, cancelling all of the progress they had made in the intervening years. On realising their error, Nicolle had ordered an immediate 180 degree about turn, retracing their steps, back into the anomaly and back to where they had come from.

A cruel twist of fate; had they encountered that particular wormhole when they had first arrived in the Gamma Sector, twenty five light years could have been slashed from their journey instantly, and the subsequent six years spent taking them even closer to home.

Although they had encountered other smaller setbacks, their journey had, on the whole, been Alliance-bound, and Nicolle was sure that somewhere out there, there was a wormhole that would take them even closer to familiar space, and she was even more certain she would find it.

"Captain," said Jevak, his voice dragging her back from her musings. "I feel I must advise restraint."

Although spared emotional entanglement himself, he was fully aware how excitable his crewmates could be. The mere hint of a possibility could have rumour and speculation of certainties and unquestionable specifics sweeping the ship. He did not want that. Humans could be unbearable when disappointed.

"Whilst neutrinos are characteristically an indication that a wormhole is present," he continued. "The levels I have detected are far below expected parameters. We cannot be certain that a fully formed wormhole is present... And also, should there be a wormhole within the cloud, who is to say where it might lead."

Nicolle paused a moment before replying. Jevak was right of course; wishful thinking rarely brought anything but disappointment but there was nothing wrong with a little guarded optimism and hoping for a 'yellow brick road'. Besides, without hope what was the point of going on? Hope had gotten them this far and it would get them all the way home.

The Captain resumed walking slowly and Jevak fell into step beside her.

"Care to speculate?" she eventually asked.

"It is almost certain that the dust cloud is masking the true level of the emissions," he explained. "The true levels could in actual fact be far in excess of those we have so far detected. In which case there would undoubtedly be a wormhole present. Alternatively, and this is a possibility, the emissions may simply be a unique property of this particular nebula. That……." he added reluctantly, "would not be unusual."

Nicolle nodded, a resigned acknowledgement of Jevak's caution, that this might be another unfortunate blind ally.

The science officer continued. "As you are aware, nebulas, by their very natures are different in all cases. Each may, depending on the elements condensing within their clouds……"

"Yes Jevak," she interrupted, in an effort to hurry the conversation along. "I am well aware of basic astro-physics, and that this might be another false alarm. I'd like to be certain of what we're looking at here. And even if there's only a micro-wormhole in there, that'll trim little more than an afternoon off of our journey, something's are better than nothing. Besides," she said, shrugging to show her indifference at the possibility of another disappointment, "It costs nothing to dream."

They halted as they arrived at the lift. The door swished open, but neither made to enter.

"I had anticipated this might be your reaction," he said. "Might I therefore suggest that we, if nothing else, confirm the existence of a wormhole? In order to facilitate that, we would be required to take the ship into the nebula."

Nicolle frowned. There weren't a lot of options to consider here, she thought, but going blindly into another nebula was never a good one; they had proved that six years ago. She paced beside the lift door, reluctant to enter. She was never indecisive, but this was an occasion where some degree of caution would be prudent. Warp engines could fail, almost eaten away by lethal concoctions inside certain clouds... even with the protection of shields.

Jevak eventually added, prompting her to the inevitable decision: "Our sensors are of little use out here, Captain."

"Yes, and when we go in we'll lose them completely."

She stopped pacing. Nicolle had been through nebulas before, occasionally for exploration, but more often to hide from danger: it was a standard evasion tactic. Inside a nebula, if your sensors were inoperable, then so at least were the enemies. That was the beauty of dense matter clouds. But then it was also the problem with them too. Inside them you were totally blind, and susceptible to whatever elements the cloud contained.

"I suspect this cloud may not be of uniform density," Jevak stated flatly. Raising what little eyebrow his grey skin exhibited. "We may be able to confirm visually and therefore not require sensors."

Pausing again to consider her decision, she knew he was probably right. They both knew their basic astro-physics. If there was a stellar nursery at the centre of this nebula, then the gravimetric shear of the two orbiting stars should have created a sphere of clear space at the heart of the cloud.

She nodded her agreement. "Make preparations."

Stepping into the lift she lightly touched her communications bracelet on her left wrist. It chirped in response. Adopting her authoritative command voice she issued her orders. "Captain to senior staff. Report to the bridge."

Jevak followed her into the lift and the door swished swiftly shut behind him. "Bridge." He demanded of the mechanism.

CHAPTER 2

The bridge was bustling; a hum of super efficient activity ebbed and flowed about her. Nicolle stood alone, leaning on the metal rail that bordered the raised walkway behind her command chair, whilst all around her the crew readied the ship for action. As always she was unnecessarily tense at moments like this, being Captain, there was little for her to do and as a result she found it difficult to settle.

She slowly surveying the bridge: her command. Her rigid, unyielding stance made her shoulders stand proud. Captain Lockhart resembled a stalking cat intent on her prey. But that is exactly what she was; her mind was again set on a purpose and she was focused. There was a new horizon beckoning.

Throughout her distinguished Alliance Fleet career Nicolle had been renowned as a woman of action. The young Ensign Lockhart was inevitably always first to volunteer for any away mission: the more dangerous the better. She was hungry for action, desperate to prove her worth to her superiors and especially to herself. That was why she had been earmarked so early in her career for fast track promotion. Now as commander of her own vessel she found it alien to take a backseat and let others do the work. As with all command posts, it was her job to observe, theorise, strategize and utilise. The hands-on-stuff was for her subordinates. She accepted that, she had to, but inside she felt knotted, as though she were being restrained on a tight leash.

That in her opinion, she had the finest crew in the fleet, and a ship that was second to none, did not make this part of the job any easier. She still longed to get her sleeves rolled-up and her hands dirty. The feeling of redundancy, no matter how temporary, which this part of the job brought with it, never sat easily with her.

Earlier she had called the ship's senior staff together, in the conference room, and set out her objective: to enter the nebula. She had also explained why. The news had been met enthusiastically, as she expected it would be. The rest of the crew were as anxious to end their isolation, as she was, and the prospect of trimming a few light-years from their journey was always relished. It was now with her senior staff and their subordinates to make that decision and her objective, reality.

Around her, all of the bridge stations were manned. For' ad and slightly to her left, Matt Sweeney was at helm control. Behind her, against the rear bulkhead, Jevak and Cheung busied themselves at Science and Tactical. And at her feet, next to her own chair, Wicasa, co-ordinated and monitored ship-wide systems. The remaining stations against the port and starboard bulkheads: weapons, communications, and engineering were also manned.

Everyone's attention was firmly on their consoles; their fingers flitted and darted across the gloss black surfaces. Every crewmember throughout the ship was at this moment, playing their essential part in this symphony of bleeps, chirps and flashing lights, which brought Endeavour, this colossus of twenty-fourth century engineering, to life. Except Nicolle, she continued surveying her command and feeling restrained.

Suddenly the bridge was engulfed by a shock of light so intense it blurred the edges of every person and object around her. The overwhelming radiance swamped the bridge like the flood from a bursting dam; a light so intense, so shocking it physically hurt.

Nicolle averted her eyes, burying her face in the crook of her arm. Around her the crew did likewise, shielding their eyes from certain blindness. The nebula was again venting its anger; its light display magnified a thousand times on their main view screen. Although the intervention of the screen's built-in safety filters had protected the crew, the shields could still barely contain the searing luminescence as it penetrated the nerve centre of their ship.

Since arriving in orbit, Jevak's observations of the nebula had determined that the energy eruptions within the cloud, varied significantly in magnitude. The energy being discharged was immense, but its source and cause, and its full intensity, still could not be determined because of their sensors inability to penetrate the phenomenon.

As the light's magnitude subsided, and her vision returned, Nicolle quickly scanned the bridge to ensure her crew were unharmed: they were, though they were still a little blinded and numb from the shock. They quickly resumed their duties as their training dictated. They were Alliance Fleet and they had a job to do.

She turned her attention again to the screen, which flickered erratically as it returned to normal. The image of the dust cloud, which now was the focus of all their attention, was docile again, only a few fingers of energy rippling here and there through its insubstantial mass, belying the fury this inanimate giant could apparently unleash.

Until Jevak had made known his theory, that the cloud might contain a wormhole, Nicolle like many others on board had given the nebula little thought; it was after all just another cloud of choking dust and lethal gas, of which she had encountered many. She had always thought of them as visually impressive, and largely obstructive. But now, this particular stellar phenomenon filled her mind. She was anxious to satisfy her curiosity, or have her hopes dashed.

She found herself staring intently, without realising, at the immense billowing clouds of stellar dust and gases, so vast the Terran solar system could easily be swallowed many time over within its vast expanses. What would they find in its interior?

That was their job, to find out.

There was a movement near her foot. Wicasa glanced up at her; preparations must be nearing completion.

Captain Lockhart straightened, stepping away from the rail.

Wicasa again glanced her way. This time she caught the slightest of nods; the ship was ready. It was time to go to work.

Nicolle stepped briskly down to the command level of the bridge. Without a rearward glance, she asked, "What's the outer diameter of the nebula?"

"Along the axis we are currently facing, approximately 3700 billion kilometres Captain," Jevak quickly replied, without having to consult the readout on his console; he knew this nebula so intimately now.

Taking her seat the Captain immediately scanned her own miniature console, located in the armrest of her command chair.

"I'd like some room to manoeuvre as we go in," she announced loudly, so that everyone on the bridge could hear. "If there is a stellar nursery in there, I don't want us getting so close that we become a permanent feature of its matter stream." Again, without a rearward glance, she instructed, "Mr Chueng, count us in to 50 billion kilometres," pausing, as she looked around her, "Then we'll assess the situation."

"Aye, Captain," Wattie acknowledged.

Wicasa leaned towards her. "If I might suggest, Captain?" he said, "We'll be flying blind after we enter the cloud, it might be a good idea to deploy a navigation beacon."

"The cloud density is sixty three parts per hundred, commander," Jevak interjected. "The beacon's pulse would only be detectable for a few million kilometres beyond the nebula's perimeter. It would be of little use."

"Better than nothing at all, Jevak," Lockhart assured her science officer. Turning to Wattie, she said simply; "Mr Cheung."

"Beacon deployed, Captain," came the instantaneous response from the eager Ensign, almost before the Captain had finished speaking.

Her crew were outstanding, they responded to her, sometimes she thought, almost telepathically. Cheung had anticipated her order, readying the beacon without being told. This was the finest crew in the fleet, she thought, smiling with satisfaction to herself.

"Mr. Sweeney, take us in. Nice and slowly, one quarter light speed."

"One quarter light speed, ma'am," he acknowledged.

"Shields to maximum."

"Shields up," confirmed Jevak.

A focused hush fell across the bridge. All eyes were on the main view screen, as the cloud began to swell, expanding gradually until it filled the entire screen.

The ship edged forward, a mere trifling speck against the vast cosmic majesty of the billowing nebula. The constantly shifting reds and blues of the progressively swelling cloud reflected and shimmered varying degrees of violet on the gleaming hull of the tiny vessel as it crossed the void between them. Slowly, eventually, Endeavour entered the cloud. It seemed to envelope and consume the insignificant little craft, like a feeding amoeba devouring some microscopic piece of organic matter.

"Sensors have just gone off line," announced Jevak.

"Straight and true, Mr Sweeney," said the Captain in her best reassuring tone, though it was completely unnecessary; a crew of their experience needed little reassurance simply because it had become a trifle misty outside.

As the dense cloud closed in around the ship, Mr Cheung maintained his close monitoring of their measured progress. "Three hundred billion kilometres, Captain," he announced. "Beacon is still transmitting, directly aft."

"Hold this line, Mr Sweeney," Lockhart reaffirmed.

Without warning the screen again exploded. Another blast of energy detonated in a blinding shock of white light, adjacent to the ship. Endeavour pitched and shook. Both Lockhart and Wicasa were almost thrown from their chairs by the violent upheaval. The others around them held tight to their consoles for stability.

"Shields are holding. No depreciation," assured Jevak. "That was the most intense discharge thus far, Captain," he added.

"Thanks for that reassuring, 'Thus far', " said Sweeney, setting himself upright again as the quaking subsided. "Hopefully that's as bad as it'll get."

Lockhart looked back towards Jevak and asked, "Can we expect worse?"

"Uncertain, Captain. Sensors could provide no data as to the source of the pulses prior to entering the nebula, and their magnitude and direction would appear to be completely random," he replied.

She twisted in her chair to look over at Wattie.

The young Ensign understood the look. Without prompting he confirmed, "Beacon still transmitting directly aft, Captain." Then added. "Becoming very faint though."

Turning to face the screen again she glanced over to helm control. "Maintain course and speed, Mr Sweeney."

"Aye Captain."

Everything again fell silent. Nicolle shifted in her chair as an expectant hush descended around her. She stared attentively at the main screen waiting for Wattie's next call, which she knew was inevitable. She did not have long to wait; and was not disappointed.

Wattie looked up from his console. "We just

lost the beacon," he said, with barely concealed resignation.

Lockhart sighed, though not despondently. "It would seem we're in your capable hands now Mr. Sweeney. She's all yours," she said, nodding her consent.

Wicasa glanced at the Captain, giving her a sly wink and a smile as he aimed a playful dig at their helmsman. "And try not to dent her, Matt," he said, provoking a chuckle from Wattie.

Not to be outdone, Cheung then added his own little dig. "Remember fly-boy, any scratches come out of your pay," he said, getting a laugh from everyone on the bridge; except Jevak, of course.

Sweeney feigned embarrassment. "Oh please, please people," he said, never taking his eyes, or hands off the console in front of him, maintaining full control of Endeavour at all time. "This overwhelming display of trust is making me blush. Please, try to restrain yourselves." Then he added cheekily, "I have done this before, you know."

From the rear of the bridge Wattie sniggered. Nodding towards the main screen, he joked, "Hay didn't we just pass that patch of cloud a few minutes back. It looks familiar. I think we're going in circles."

"Oh yeh, very funny!" exclaimed Sweeney. "Why don't you try this? I just make it look easy."

Nicolle immediately jumped to Matt's defence.

"Okay, okay everyone settle down," she

said, restraining a smile at the friendly teasing. "We've nothing but the utmost faith in you Matt, and you know that." Then added, feigning sympathy, because Matt's attempts at hurt feelings had been so feeble. "Take no notice of them. Okay, okay everyone," she said, getting everyone's minds back to the job in hand. "Just get us safely to the centre of the cloud, and find us a quick way back out, if we need to."

Lockhart enjoyed the playful banter that was common on her bridge, and often indulged in it herself. They were all friends here, and although their duty was paramount, the odd bit of verbal jousting never went amiss. And besides she was Captain, so no one ever got the last word with her, (command has its privileges). This is where she felt comfortable. In this chair, with these fine Alliance Fleet officers around her. This is where she felt at one with the universe. It had been a long road getting to this chair, but it was where she belonged. Even if it did mean she had to curtail her desire to get into the thick of things.

No sooner had she eased herself back into her comfortable mind-set, than she was shaken violently from it. Endeavour again shuddered as another explosion detonated above them and close to port. The cloud around the ship lit-up, brilliant white, dousing the red and blue tones of the nebula.

"Shields still holding," reported Jevak.

"Keep her steady Mr. Sweeney," urged Lockhart.

"Compensating."

Sweeney's fingers ran deftly over the smooth, gloss, black surface of his console. Returning the ship to a bearing which he was blind to, and his instruments were ignorant of, but which his gut told him was the way ahead. As a pilot he had no peers. His body seemed to sense every twist and turn of the ship, though it obviously could not; the damping systems made that impossible. For every degree they shifted from their course Sweeney could find them a way back again. Though no one on the bridge ever voiced it, they all firmly believed he could thread Endeavours warp trail through the eye of a needle, and probably tie it in a neat bow as well.

Their progress felt slow, though at one quarter light speed, which could take a ship from the Earth to it's Moon and back in a few moments, they were hardly standing still; it was their blindness which seemed to make time drag. It was like swimming through treacle. Though the tones and colours of the cloud shifted and changed depending on its chemical composition at any given point, there was nothing to differentiate one patch of obscurity from another. All they could do was press forward.

"One hundred and fifty billion kilometres," announced Cheung.

Lockhart glanced back towards Jevak. "Anything?" she asked.

"Sensors are still ineffective," he replied.

That was what they had expected.

The bridge fell silent again, every one anticipating further explosions, the only punctuation to the constricting bleakness.

As they eased forward as slowly as they dared through the dense cloud, there seemed to be no discernable forward movement, Lockhart was reminded of the tails she'd been told as a young girl, of the fog as it rolled in on Edinburgh's Forth estuary, engulfing the whole city, leaving only the upright sections of the old railway bridge visible. That of course was before Alliance Fleet technology had given them control of Earths weather. Coupled with the pollution of the era, those misty days could become killers as the fog turned to toxic smog. Though that was hardly in the same league as the lethal mix of gases and dust which at present enveloped Endeavour. How strange she thought, that on the other side of the Galaxy something so extreme and alien and unrelated, could still bring unexpected thoughts of home rushing to you.

If inactivity made Lockhart cranky, flying blind, literally flying blind, with no sensors for back-up, was making her more so; though she could never let the crew see. She usually made a point of coming onto the bridge as preparations to get underway were nearing completion, thus sparing herself the irritation of feeling surplus. But now they were underway she still felt like a third leg. Looking towards Matt's helm station, she inwardly longed to be piloting the ship, as she would have been doing less than ten years ago, when she was still a Lieutenant. She had to remind herself that the ship was in Matt's very capable hands, there was no reason to be anxious, but it still rankled that her sole contribution to their mission, at the moment seemed to be to stare intently at a fog filled screen.

She found herself tapping her foot, and not to any particular tune. Glancing to her left she discovered Wicasa smiling at her. Returning the smile she instantly ceased the toe tapping. Nicolle wondered if he knew what was going through her mind. He usually did. He had a knack of second guessing her; but as usual, those bright dark eyes of his just put her at ease again, as they always did.

Before she could indulge in anymore-introspective analysis another observation came from Wattie. "Passing one hundred billion kilometres," he called.

"Slow to manoeuvring thrusters," Lockhart ordered.

"Aye Captain, slowing," acknowledged Sweeney.

Endeavour shuddered as another explosion detonated somewhere distant and behind them.

"Steady as she goes," the captain added.

Sweeney did not reply. He understood the order was rhetorical, and so continued to maintained course and speed, as she expected of him.

"Approaching fifty billion kilometres, Captain," announced Cheung.

"So far, so good," said Wicasa, encouragingly.

As though on cue, just to prove Wicasa's optimism wrong, the ship lurched and pitched, more violently than before. Wattie was thrown hard against his console, knocking the wind out of him. Lockhart steadied herself. "You were saying?" she replied.

"We have partial sensors, Captain," announced Jevak, loudly. "The cloud is thinning, Density down to thirty parts per hundred, and continuing to fall."

Rising to her feet she was about to enquire if the Neutrino levels had increased, when Wattie's voice, tinged with a little more urgency than made her comfortable, suddenly fixed her attention.

"Captain. Coming up on something, dead ahead!" he exclaimed.

She turned to face the screen.

Although the clouds density was ebbing, the image on the screen was still obscure and shadowy, like a heavy mist of condensation on a cold window, movement could be detected, but shape and form were still indistinguishable. They were approaching something... Something that was moving very fast.

Two hazy, luminous, red orbs slowly pulsated at either side of the screen. Between them a brighter, blue, intermittent glow, darted and snapped.

Nicolle strolled calmly to the rear of Sweeney's chair. Resting her arms along the back of it she lent forward and said quietly in his ear. "I know I'm teaching grandma to suck eggs here, but let's not do anything impulsive. Slow and steady," she said giving him a friendly pat on the shoulder, then headed back to her command chair.

"Exactly what I was thinking," Sweeney replied, squinting at the view screen, trying to discern the shapes.

Turning to Jevak, Lockhart asked. "Well?"

The Vaurillian stared intently at his monitor. "I am detecting massive, fluctuating electromagnetic pulses. As the cloud thins the readings are increasing exponentially.

"Shields?" she asked.

"Still no depreciation," he confirmed, to her relief.

"Matt," Lockhart said, "Be ready to put some distance between us and what ever that is, if we need to."

"On the starting blocks, Captain," he assured her.

The cloud continued to thin, like veils being lifted before them. The more they closed the distance the clearer the image became.

"Cloud density down to eighteen parts per hundred," Jevak announced, whilst furiously processing information though the computer.

The cloud suddenly dissolved before them, opening up to reveal an empty, almost spherical chamber, as Jevak had predicted. Its vaulted sides stretching into the distance like a vast cathedral, large enough to shelter an entire star system.

The walls of the immense chamber puffed

and billowed, continually shifting. Occasionally a rogue wisp encroached into the cavern, but the sides, in the main held together, never losing their curved geometric contour.

"All stop," ordered the Captain.

Endeavour smoothed to a halt, coming to rest on the interior of the immense sphere, like a speck of wind blown dust in a football stadium.

Lockhart strode to the centre of the bridge. Her hands balled into fists, resting on her hips. "Well," she said, her eyes wide with astonishment at the majestic sight they were beholding. "You were certainly right about the stellar-nursery, but that doesn't nearly describe this."

Jevak glanced up from his console. The sight that greeted him would have been considered awe-inspiring, had he the unfettered emotions to appreciate it. He merely raised an eyebrow.

On any tour of duty with Alliance Fleet, it quickly becomes apparent to any new recruit just how insignificant they, their planet and their species really are beside the colossal majesty of creation. The universe is a diverse, beautiful, strange and profoundly humbling place. And few on board A.S. Endeavour had encountered anything so visually breathtaking as that which they were presently sitting abeam of.

The void at the heart of the nebula enclosed a pair of embryo stars in close, rapid orbit around each other. Jevak's initial sensor scans revealed that they were both of identical composition to the nebula, which enveloped them.

Approximately seventeen and a half million years earlier, a very short period of time in cosmic terms, a single large planet; a gas giant much like our own Jupiter, had occupied this space. Also like Jupiter, this gas giant was in actual fact a star, which in its infancy had failed to ignite and had, again like Jupiter, remained dormant.

But in this star's case, that dormancy had terminated in a single, shocking, catastrophic event: a meteorite, an immense mountain of rock, had collided with it.

The meteorite had been colossal, almost twice as large as Earth's moon, composed mainly of iron and magnesium. The mass of the two bodies, and the gravitational pull of the gas planet had accelerated the collision to beyond 2500 kilometres per second, at the point of impact.

The meteor had cut through the giants' thick outer layer of hydrogen in a millisecond. In that brief time the friction created, had been enough to cause its temperature to soar to more than 30,000 degrees Kelvin, instantly igniting the hydrogen around it.

As luck or misfortune would have it, just below the hydrogen level had been a thin layer of oxygen, and as any fourteen year-old high school student will tell you; one of the by-products of burning hydrogen in oxygen is water. The magnesium in the meteor instantly reacted with the resultant water in the way magnesium always does and instantly flashed to a million degrees Kelvin, igniting the dead planet and transforming it, briefly, into a star.

The explosion was of such cataclysmic magnitude that the radiation pulse was detected, millions of years later, on the far side of the Galaxy, on Earth.

In the early 1970's, observatories across the World, innocently scanning the heavens for anomalous radio waves and signs of alien life, detected the radiation pulse. Their relatively primitive technology though, had been unable to determine its origin; in those days a radiation pulse was just a pulse. Unfortunately, as a result of the paranoia of the times, it was wrongly perceived as a nuclear detonation some where on the planet's surface. Armed forces across the globe were scrambled; missiles fuelled and readied and failsafe points attained. The World readied for war.

Although it was never made known to the general population at the time, NATO's war threat was elevated, for months, to DEFCON 1; the closest the world had ever come to the horror of all out nuclear war.

And now, far removed, in an other time, another place, an Earth ship, of discovery rather than war was now sitting broadside to the perpetrator of that, almost catastrophic, galactic nuclear hoax.

The meteor's momentum had not halted with the collision with the gas planet. The explosion had smashed through the new star, splitting it in two, sending both halves spinning in wild arcs around each other, spilling molten debris millions of kilometres out into the cold void.

In the passing millennia the debris had cooled, eventually shrouding the twin stars in the dust cloud that now hid them.

These stellar twins had pacified, and reconciled their untamed rotations around each other, into a single orbit, spinning about a shared central pivot, like two dead weights on either end of a rope. Slowly their gravitational pull magnified as their orbits decreased, spiralling them ever closer, towards each other. Their relentless convergence accelerating their orbits: ever tighter ever faster, ever closer they spun.

And now as Endeavour's bridge crew marvelled at the awesome, humbling spectacle on their view screen, the stellar twins were orbiting each other at a wild, ferocious pace; completing a single rotation about their central, pivotal point every thirteen hours.

One of the stars, being about half as large again as its twin, at their current pace of rotation, was causing an imbalance, pulling unevenly, generating an oscillating effect in their orbit. Compelling the two colossal bodies to twist and tear at the other. Each ripping at its sibling: leaching matter and energy, one from the other, in a continual molten stream between them, like an umbilical cord, binding them forever together.

Their metal cores, a gift from the meteorite

that had created them, rotating about each other at such a terrifying velocity, were generating an immense electro-magnetic field. This was the force responsible for repelling the dust cloud and keeping it at bay. But it was also the force responsible for creating a more immediate danger. The electromagnetic field was inducing static, far beyond Jevak's ability to quantify it. It was also the source of the sporadic explosions; the erratic discharge of energy through the surrounding clouds. And it was that which now held Endeavours crew in awe. Massive discharges of energy were snaking back and forth, like vicious tendrils of lightning, whipping, and leaping between the stars, spitting terrifying giga watts of energy at each other and across the inner surface of the dust cloud.

Now and then a ribbon of energy leapt from the breach, escaped into the nebula, exploding in an incandescent flash within the cloud, briefly flooding the hollow sphere with brilliant white light.

Hidden, and almost unseen, within this malevolent dance of light and menace, near the hub of the star's orbit, just off centre of their pivotal point, was a patch of motionless darkness. Amongst this brightness and perpetual motion, this dark shimmering void seamed out of place. But there it was, radiating a faint blue glow; Captain Lockhart's reason for placing them in danger. The gateway to somewhere else. The wormhole they had come in search of.

Sweeney had been holding his breath since

the cloud had cleared. Finally he released it letting out a low, continuous whistle. "Are there anymore at home like you?" he said, astonished.

"I'd suspect not," replied Wicasa, equally overwhelmed.

Lockhart was the first to jolt herself from their awe-struck surprise. "Analysis, Jevak," she said, bringing everyone to their senses. "What're the neutrino readings?"

"As I suspected, Captain, the cloud was indeed masking the emissions. The neutrino levels are within expected parameters for the presence of a fully formed wormhole."

"Is it stable?"

"At the moment it would appear to be relatively stable," he replied, "It would seem to have existed within these conditions for some considerable time, but the gravimetric shear of the stars, on each other and on the wormhole its self, could collapse the phenomenon at any moment. I would suggest that there is a very delicate balance in operation here."

"What about those energy ribbons?" enquired Wicasa, just as a bright fork of luminescence leapt furiously from one of the stars, scraping and scratching at its twin. Tendrils of raw energy, thousands of kilometres long, whipped back and forth between the colossal orbs, then lunged into the void towards the ship, like a immense claw slashing and scraping its fury at the tiny craft which had dared to enter its' domain.

"A more immediate danger, Commander," confirmed Jevak, visibly recoiling, as the ribbons fell short of connecting with the ship, and exploded across the screen. "Far in excess of 4 Million giga watts in every discharge; more than the combined laser power of eight starships."

"And sitting neatly in our path," said Wicasa.

Lockhart almost leapt to the top level of the bridge. Standing beside Jevak she looked over his console. "Would there be any way into the wormhole, avoiding the energy ribbons?" she asked him.

"Impossible. Even approaching from above or below the stars' orbits would take us well within their sphere of attraction," he assured her.

She turned her attention to the screen again.

Like a pair of gargantuan sphinx, the plasma spitting stars sat either side of their charge, daring Endeavour to approach: defying them to come within reach of their deadly claws.

Wicasa drew a heavy sigh. "We're going to have to run the gauntlet," he said. " And I doubt our shields would ever withstand a direct hit from even one of those blasts."

Lockhart thought for a moment, considering their options. "Let's not get ahead of ourselves," she said. "Let's at least establish where this doorway exits first, then I'll decide whether it's worth putting our heads in the lions mouth. Wattie, class four probe, if you please."

"Probe away Captain," he reported momentarily, confirming her order.

The sleek, black, meter and a half long probe issued silently from beneath Endeavour's elliptical hull, immediately angling into its pre-determined flight path, accelerating directly towards the wormhole.

Nicolle watched intently, as the slender blue thread of the probe's tail dwindled into the distance, becoming little more than a receding speck of light. Finally it dimmed, becoming invisible against the overwhelming brightness of the twin stars. She continued watching attentively, edging slowly towards the rail behind her chair, whilst playing alternative scenarios through her mind.

Nicolle spent the few short moments of the probe's flight, running numerous unwelcome scenarios and possibilities through her keen tactical awareness: playing Devil's advocate. She found herself pondering the possibility that if the probe did not make it, destroyed by the energy ribbons, or torn apart by the gravitational shear of the stars, could she dare risk putting the ship in the same danger? Suppose it did make it through unharmed, but failed to send back telemetry, due to damage; again could she risk the ship? Command was like a chess game: it was her job to consider the unthinkable and to strategise several moves in advance, to be prepared for adverse circumstances and to deal with them.

As the probe approached the stars' sphere of exertion it wavered slightly, tugged by their combined gravitational shear, then corrected, realigning along its original trajectory. Jevak continued to monitor its telemetry data, during its few short minutes of flight, via its onboard sensors. As it passed through the energy field the bridge fell silent. All eyes watched the screen; waiting for the bright flash that would herald the little projectile's failure. They continued to wait, and wait. The flash never came.

"The probe has successfully entered the worm hole," Jevak eventually reported, relieving the mounting tension. "It has sustained no damage."

Again they waited, with escalating anticipation.

Jevak looked over his console, quickly computing calculations. "It has safely exited on the far side," he said. "Carrying out stellar scan of the region." Slowly he looked up from his console. "Captain," he said calmly. "The probe is home… It is in the Alpha Sector."

CHAPTER 3

Nicolle gazed pensively out of her conference room view port.

Her thoughts were light-years away; her mind troubled. She had been staring out of the viewport for only a few moments, but already she was all but oblivious to the stellar maelstrom beyond the nine-foot high, curved diamond rectangle.

Diamond was in common usage in Alliance ships; being the hardest, transparent element in the known Universe, it was used, as now, to facilitate large transparent sections of ship's hulls, while maintaining the strength and rigidity of a vessel able to travel at more than the speed of light.

Outside the deep amber radiance, of the circling twins, reflected off the inner surface of the cloud, bathing the ship from stem to stern in a soft copper glow and casting long, stark shadows to the wall behind her.

The smouldering, auburn was reminiscent of vast, burning, sunsets she had enjoyed on long summer evenings back home in Bordeaux. She never tired of hearing her father tell her mother that the sunset was a merely poor imitation of the lights in her fiery hair. She smiled briefly at the thought of her parents. The possibility of enjoying those tranquil times again, soon, should have quieted her agitated mind, but that was not the case, for the source of this red sky was the cause of her dilemma.

As with any command structure, problems always filter down the ranks; they never travel in the opposite direction. It therefore followed that since Nicolle had a problem the rest of the crew also had a problem. That was the reason why she had called her senior staff together in the conference room.

Behind her, around the table, sat Sweeney, Wicasa, Cheung, Jevak, and the ship's half Human, half Kraxian, chief engineer Cosique Tarr'gn. The five of them were noisily debating options, as to whether it was advisable to enter the wormhole, and if so, how to make it safely across the energy barrier the infant stars were generating. The discussion had been bouncing around the table for the last twenty minutes or so, like a grenade with its pin out. Sweeney's position was unshakable; he was adamant that there was only one option.

"Well I don't see that there's a choice. If we want to get home, we go in," he said resolutely.

Not for the first time did Lockhart recognize much of her younger self in Matt. He was head strong and impetuous. He seldom saw danger as a life threatening possibility.

Nicolle remained at the view-port, grinning to herself, as an old joke suddenly came involuntarily to mind. Bawdy as it was, it was a joke she had often retold in some of her more inebriated moments, in the bars of the academy campus. She had even told it in mixed company in the officer's mess: well that was Kraxian ale for you. The joke had concerned an old bull and a younger one, watching cows grazing at the top of a hill. The younger of the two bulls suggested running up the hill and having sex with one of the cows. The older bull offered an alternative; they should walk up the hill and have sex with all of them.

She stifled a snigger. Matt, she thought, would have them all running up the hill.

Flash! Nicolle froze.

The warm soft glow of the fiery orbs was suddenly swamped by an intense blinding arc of blue, as a massive fork of electrons, slashed across the cloud base and seared through it to explode deep inside the nebula.

She breathed again.

A timely reminder, that the barrier was capable of repelling, and destroying, any foolish attempt at incursion.

Lockhart returned to the table, casting her gaze around the room, at each of her assembled officers. As she took her seat Wattie was rebuffing Matt's argument, to rush the wormhole, and damn the consequences.

"That's just crazy," he said. "If there's no way past the barrier, it'd be suicide to even attempt the wormhole."

Nicolle knew how limited their options were. The data from the probe, as it passed through the stars' gravitational field, had been meticulously analysed by Jevak, and his finding had been far from encouraging. The supercharged barrier was generating a static field so intense it had scorched the probes hull and almost liquefied its circuitry. It had barely survived the transit.

"Well the probe made it through, what makes you think we can't?" Matt replied.

Wicasa leaned forward intently. "Is that possible? Could anything larger than the probe make it through?" he asked Jevak.

"Negative," the Vaurillian assured them, "The probe's size was a contributing factor to its' safe passage, but the primary reason for its survival was its propulsion. Endeavours size and more importantly, its warp field would act as a magnet to the charged barrier."

Sweeney sighed, shaking his head in frustration. "I don't believe we're having to discuss this," he said, "We have an open door here. The best chance we'll probably ever get to go home. Home, people!" he repeated, exasperated. "Yes there's a risk, but that's the territory that goes with this uniform," he argued, tugging at the Alliance Fleet badge on the chest of his black and red tunic for emphasis. "You all understood that when you signed-up, even us who've joined since the fissure. That is what they meant when they said, 'Without fear. Without Frontiers'."

Lockhart intervened. "I can appreciate your urgency, Matt," she said quietly, calmly. "We all want to get home, no one more than me."

"Well I say we take a chance," Matt persisted.

"I agree, Captain," offered Cosique, who had been quietly listening to the discussion until now. "Between here and the alpha Sector, there may be no other short cuts. This maybe our only opportunity to get home."

Lockhart held up both hands, palms outward, to silence the clamour. "Okay, okay, people," she said, "This is not a debating chamber. It's also, unfortunately, not a democracy."

She rose to her feet again and paced slowly round the table.

"I've already come to a decision. We're going in. So let's stop the arguing now. What I need from you all, are options. If we can't eliminate the risk from those energy discharges, I want to at least minimise them."

Reaching the opposite end of the table, she rounded on the company. Leaning forward enthusiastically she rested both hands firmly on the conference table's glossed ebony surface. Nicolle scanned their faces, looking each of them in the eye. "So... Let's have some ideas." she encouraged.

Jevak was the first to offer. "Captain, I have been monitoring the energy levels in the electromagnetic discharges. They are not constant. But they are," he added, sounding as hopeful as a Vaurillian can. "Predictably cyclic in configuration. There is a slight, decline in energy output when both stars' are at 180 degrees to the mouth of the wormhole." He glanced at the Captain, his eyes showing little encouragement. "It might possibly offer a window."

"When's the next low point?" she asked, pacing back towards her own chair at the far end of the table, but not taking a seat.

"One hour, twenty seven minutes and forty three seconds."

Wicasa didn't like Jevak's emphasis on 'slight'. "Will the drop be enough for us to pass through, safely?" he pressed.

"Unfortunately there is no guarantee of complete safety, Commander. But, if we are to enter, it would appear to be our best option," replied Jevak.

Lockhart bit her lip. When she was weighing options she liked to have something to occupy her. Usually it was a mug of strong coffee playing around in her hands. But needs must, and a bottom lip was just as good.

"The field is cyclic," she said rhetorically, her voice dropping almost to a whisper, "cyclic"....

An idea was slowly taking form.

She stopped her pacing, and eased herself gently back into her chair while thoughtfully running a hand through the grey streak in her hair. "In the old days, before first contact," she said. "Earth ships experimented with rotating shield frequency as a crude method of repelling space debris."

"Affirmative," Jevak replied, ponderously, wondering where this was leading.

"Could rotating the shield's frequency in that same manner, and offering a constantly changing opposite charge, repel the barriers electro-magnetic charge?"

"It is feasible that we could present the barrier with an opposing charge. But the mechanics of varying the shields, to the exact cycle of the barrier, as rapidly as would be required, may prove difficult."

"Make it possible." She said, not so much by way of an order, rather as positive encouragement.

Cosique quickly considered Jevak's suggestion, then offered her own. "Captain, before The Alliance developed proper shielding," she said. "starships protected them selves by polarising their hull plating. It was never fully effective against laser fire, but it may help to repel electro-static charge."

"Would that affect the shields harmonics?" Nicolle asked Jevak.

"Not if both, shields and hull polarity are rotated in unison," he replied.

"Okay," she said, eyeing both of them. "Co-ordinate your efforts."

Nicolle was becoming more enthusiastic. The possibility of getting home was suddenly becoming within their grasp.

She got to her feet. "Okay, people, we have One hour and twenty seven minutes, ..."

"One hour and twenty four minutes, now, Captain," Jevak corrected her.

"One hour and twenty four minutes," she

smiled. Though the expression did not last long, it was quickly replaced by her more serious, Captain's face. It was time to go to work.

"I want every spare watt of power diverted to the shields," she explained, now issuing direct orders. "Every joule that's not being used. Every food replicator and hologram-suite shut down to re-route their power." Pacing around the table again, she continued barking orders. "Since every one'll be at their stations, shut down life support to every corridor, cargo bay, crews quarters, and the galley. If there's a light bulb not being used, I want its power diverted. Okay?"

She liked to leave briefings on a positive, upbeat note and added. "I know a little restaurant just off St. Peter's Square, where I'd like you all to join me for breakfast tomorrow morning, so let's make this work... Stations every one."

As they rose to leave, Wattie shook his head in disbelief. "Why here, why of all places would the only wormhole we need to get into, be so damn hard to get near?" he asked to no one in particular.

Walking to the door, Jevak explained. "Where else? The fabric of space has been so weakened in this region, by the gravitational shear of the twins; the conditions are more than ideal."

Wicasa, who had been noticeably silent during most of the briefing, dallied as the rest of the senior staff left, apparently seeking a private audience with the Captain. As the door swished closed behind the last of them, Lockhart made for the replicator and requested her usual cup of strong coffee. "I got the impression you weren't in favour of this," she said.

He nodded towards the furious riot of lightning beyond the view port, as they made for the table to take their seats again. "Fools rush in where angels fear to tread, and all that," he explained.

"Is that what you think, that this is a fool's errand?" she asked, surprised by his response.

"That's not what I said," rushing to his own defence. "For what it's worth, I think you've make the right decision," he assured her. "It's just that I wouldn't want anyone to get the impression this was going to be an easy ride. I'm just playing Devil's advocate. We're sitting within touching distance of the doorway home. But we may not even make it that far, we may not even make it through the door."

"I don't think anyone's under any illusion," she said, shaking her head, "We're all fully aware of the dangers." Then added, gravely, lowering her voice almost to a whisper, though there was no one near to hear. "I don't think well make it through with-out casualties, if we make it at all."

"I know... We all do... But you still made the right decision," he said, reassuring her, managing to sound optimistic about a dire decision.

Looking out of the window at where her fears became nightmares, Nicolle reflected. "Do you know what frightens me most?" she asked, cradling her hot coffee. "It's not knowing how many of my crew I'll have to sacrifice, getting the rest of us home?"

"That's the fundamental nature of command, Nicolle," he said softly, not in any attempt to ease the burden she shouldered because he could not. She was their Captain and the burden was hers alone to carry. All he could do was try to reassure her of the crew's belief in her. "Command isn't about the easy choices, but then you know that," he explained. "What sets a leader apart is their crew's willingness to follow, because they believe in that leader." Gesturing towards the door, he added, "and they, believe in you. They believe that you'll make the difficult choices honestly and without prejudice. And that when the time comes, and any of us is required to lay-down our lives, that you'll make that choice, only when there is absolute necessity, and with the understanding..." He paused briefly; he had never been this open and honest with any Commanding Officer. He had an unending respect and admiration for Nicolle, as a person and as a Commanding Officer. He knew that command weighed heavy on her, though she never let it show, and she bore it resolutely and bravely. And he knew that this decision had been made with painful regret for the inevitable loss of life that would undoubtedly result. But that she had made it honestly. He also knew that in her darker moments, she felt the loneliness of her burden.

Locking on her forlorn gaze he continued. "... That you would willingly trade places with any of us, and that you would gladly lay-down you own life to spare your crew."

Lockhart stared into the distance. "I promised I'd get this crew home, and I meant all of them."

"That's just not possible, Nicolle. Like Matt said, it's the risk that goes with the uniform. We all accept that not all of us are going to see home again. Whether we get home this way, or if it takes years to find another route, we won't all make it." He rose and made his way to the door. As it swished open, he turned to face her again. "But when the time comes, all we ask is that you have the courage to lead us." He smiled wanly and made to leave. She had her demons to wrestle and that was something she had to do in solitude.

"You know," she said, attempting again to lift the gloom from their mood. "They say that where ever you are in life, or what ever life has thrown at you, there is an old Beatle's song appropriate to your situation?"

"I've heard that said," he smiled, this time warmly. "Why, which one were you thinking of...? 'Across The Universe?'... 'The Long And Winding Road?' ...Or maybe", He said playful, "'Get Back'?"

Lockhart returned the smile. "You know you're Lennon and McCartney."

"Doesn't every one?" he shrugged.

"I was thinking more along the lines of, 'With A Little Help From My Friends'."

As he turned to leave, Wicasa nodded his appreciation. "Remember, we have a breakfast date in Rome," he reminded her.

Cradling her coffee cup a little closer, she turned again to face the warm shafts of orange light, which cut through the darkness of the now empty room.

They were much more than her crew: her friends, her family.

* * * * *

Adjacent to the helm console on the port-side bulkhead, the door to the conference room swished open, and Captain Lockhart breezed onto the bridge. Though she still viewed their venture with more than a little trepidation, there was a buoyant air of optimism about her that had been absent an hour and twenty minutes before. The feeling of optimism had also percolated down through the crew, and the whole ship now felt a little brighter. A decision had been made, and however perilous, their fate was now in their own hands. That act of self-determination had been enough to raise their spirits. The nettle was about to be grasped.

They were going home.

As she slid onto her chair, Wicasa glanced up from his console on which he had been reviewing the ship's state of readiness.

"It's funny to think we could be home in a few hours," he said brightly.

Lockhart lifted her eyes to the main viewer. "We still have the small matter of an E.M. field to navigate," she replied quietly, not wishing to dampen the crew's mood, then asked, "Status?"

Endeavour was as near perfect as it was possible to be, given its six years absence from Alliance Fleet's care and the damage it had sustained coming through the fissure. It was not quite space dock pristine any more, but in many ways, as a result of pilfered technology and other acquired replacement systems that had been found in the Gamma Sector, it was better. The absence of unsolicited interfering from Zerttral and Vadeusan patrols over the previous three weeks or more, had freed-up the crew, to dissect the ship with fine toothcombs, evaluating, stripping and overhauling everything from Warp drive to replicators. She was as ready as she could be. So, when the order had been given, there had been little to do apart from diverting power to where they knew it was going to be needed, and building-in auxiliary back up's to handle the anticipated power overloads.

"All decks report ready, Captain," Wicasa responded.

"Jevak, how long to the optimum window?" she called, to the rear of the bridge.

"Four minutes, thirty five seconds, Captain."

"Matt, at full warp, how long to the E.M. field, and then the wormhole?" She enquired.

"Forty eight seconds to the E.M. field, then another twelve to the mouth of the wormhole," replied Sweeney.

"On my mark I want full warp, everything she's got."

"Aye-aye, Ma'am," he replied enthusiastically. Confidently brushing his fingers over the coloured indicators on his console to set course heading, and co-ordinates then awaited the final order.

Lockhart inclined her head slightly. "Bridge to engineering," she said, slightly louder than conversation level.

"Engineering here, Captain," replied Cosique, via the ship's comm system, from twelve decks below.

"Give me full power to the warp-drive. Everything else you can muster, everything, divert to the shields."

"Yes ma'am, you have full power," she replied, bringing the warp engines to pulsating readiness.

Through out the ship, the crew were responding with a vigour and enthusiasm she had not encountered for a long time. The prospect of getting home was inspiring them. She dearly hoped this was not going to be tragic case of, "Hello, Goodbye."

"Okay, people. There's no time like the present," Captain Nicolle Lockhart announced as she slowly cast her eye around the bridge, smiling optimistically at each of her crew. "Let's do this and let's do it right... Time to go home. Mister Sweeney, three quarters light-speed."

"With pleasure, Captain," he replied punching his console's touch sensitive surface to bring the sub-light induction engines online, then added sarcastically. "So long Gamma Sector, it's been a whole lotta fun."

"E.M. field approaching minimum," Jevak announced from the rear of the bridge.

"Shields up!" ordered Nicolle.

"Shields to maximum.... Rotating polarity," responded Cheung.

"Warp nine, Matt... now!"

Endeavour responded instantly, bursting forward. For an instant the ship appeared to be in two places at once. Her image stretched from where she had been, to where she was heading. Hurtling towards the massive burning orbs, she closed the fifty billion-kilometre distances to the stars electromagnetic barrier in a few heartbeats.

"Fifteen seconds to the barrier," Jevak announced, as they approached the threshold.

The shielding envelope around Endeavour, began to glow as it closed on the barrier, crackling and hissing with a mounting fury of static. With out warning a fork of blue whipped free of the E.M. sphere, directly at the hurtling ship, spitting and tearing at the protective shroud around it. The ship heaved to port.

"Hold her steady," Lockhart called.

"Compensating," grunted Sweeney as he fought to hold Endeavour on her heading.

"Shields down to 68 per cent," Jevak reported.

The energy ribbons retracted again. Retreating to the edge of the barrier, like a boxer jabbing and punching, then falling back before commencing another assault. Which it duly did. Again the barrier crackled, sending a bright fork of energy at the approaching starship. This time exploding against the shields, pitching Endeavour viciously.

Lockhart held tight to her chair, as all about her the crew were thrown around like rag dolls. "Wattie," she called. "Is the shield rotation having any effect?"

"Almost none!" exclaimed Cheung, steadying himself across his console. "The EM field's polarity is alternating so rapidly, the computer is barely keeping up."

"Do what you can," she grimaced, knowing that Wattie was already doing everything humanly possible.

Another barrage exploded against their diminishing shields, throwing everyone off balance. The ship heaved violently upwards and to port. Lockhart was thrown clear of her chair, catching the armrest as she fell, cracking two of her ribs, and splitting her head as she landed with a sickening thump. As she tried to get up her head swam and a warm trickle of blood momentarily blinded her as she smeared it with the back of her hand, across her eyes.

Wicasa jumped to her aid. Helping her to her seat, she stifled a moan. "Divert everything to the forward shields," she groaned.

"Shields down to 49 per cent." Jevak responded, then added with more immediacy. "Passing through the barrier... Shields down again to 40 per cent, but still holding."

"We're going to make it," cried Cheung.

"We're not out of harms way yet," bellowed Wicasa, steadying Lockhart into her command chair. She made to move, but he restrained her.

As he looked at her, a question and answer passed between them wordlessly. Wicasa nodded his understanding, knowing what her next order would be. "Re-direct all power to the aft shields," he called to Jevak.

The barrier's immediate response was awesome and terrifying. It unleashed a savage bolt of dazzling blue, which smashed through what remained of Endeavour's now flimsy shields, hurling the helpless craft off its heading, away from the mouth of the wormhole, towards its rim.

Like dozens of enormous rasping whips; ribbons of energy, thousands of kilometres long, lashed Endeavours outer hull, snaking over her like a neon net, tearing at the unprotected hull plating. Explosions peppered the aft section adjacent to the dorsal fin engine nacelle, ripping gouges through it.

"I can't hold her, she's drifting!" yelled Sweeney, as he strained to pull the ship back on course.

The bulkhead behind Wattie suddenly exploded, engulfing him and his console in flames and throwing him clear across the bridge. He landed with a sickening crunch, smashing his shoulder. He lay still, his uniform and skin smouldering. Before anyone could get to him, the ship convulsed again. The deck plates beneath their feet seemed to heave upwards, twisting and buckling the ship like a flimsy toy. Above their heads more explosions brought down hull plating and bulkheads. Within a few seconds choking smoke and grinding metal filled the bridge. Flames spewed from Wattie's console, up the bulkhead and across the ceiling.

"She's responding!" shouted Sweeney, coughing on the acrid smoke.

"Pull her round, Matt!" groaned Lockhart.

Wicasa hurried to Wattie's aid. He didn't make it. Before he got as far as helm control another bulkhead collapsed pinning both him and Wattie to the floor.

Slowly the ship responded. Inching round to its original course.

"Entering wormhole," shouted Jevak above the noise of Endeavour's death throws. "Captain, two ribbons approaching, magnitude... beyond sensor capabilities."

"Brace for impact," she coughed, struggling to hold herself upright.

As the tiny ship disappeared down the gaping throat of the wormhole, two dazzling tongues of raw energy gave chase, attracted by her warp trail, plunging into the phenomenon in their wake.

The first impacted along the starboard nacelle. Ribbons of blue crackled, lashed, split and danced across the engine, tearing at it, ripping hull plating free; scorching and burning with abandon. Then a single ribbon arced from one nacelle to the other, leaping the distance between the two. In a burst of terrifying power, both nacelles exploded in a shock of crimson light.

The second ribbon stabbed directly at the ship's heart, impacting directly above the bridge. Outer and inner hull plates melted and exploded as the ribbon whipped and slashed, gouging a deep swathe through Endeavours protective skin, tearing a gapping wound above the heads of Lockhart and her officers.

For a brief second the vacuum of space intruded into their protected cocoon. Gravity was lost and air vented outwards. Instantly the ship's safety systems responded to the incursion, establishing a containment force field over the breach.

To Lockhart's right there was piercing scream. A bolt of blue suddenly burst from the control panels at the auxiliary engineering station, buzzing and crackling as it burned through every system.

Ensign Rossi took the full force as the blast erupted from the wall adjacent to the station, showered the entire bridge with burning fragments.

The vicious tendril of blue energy licked at the air, whipping and snapping a foot or so distance from her. Rossi felt as though her skin was being scoured by thousands of tiny, burning white-hot, needles, stabbing repeatedly at her. Her skin felt like it was on fire. Then it leapt directly at her. Rossi screamed as she was thrown backwards twenty feet across the bridge. But her screams died, as did she, long before what was left of her, crashed lifelessly to the deck.

Lockhart clutched at her broken side. Gulping down a lung-full of air, she threw herself to Rossi's aid. As more explosions rained debris around them, she turned the Ensign's still smouldering, limp form onto her back. What she found was horrific. From her left temple to her right hip, Rossi's uniform and flesh had been seared away, exposing a gouge, burned through her ribcage to her spinal column. Her chest cavity was a blackened void, all of her vital organs: heart, lungs, everything had been incinerated.

Helpless to save the fine, young officer, Lockhart turned her face to the heavens. Her eyes found the gaping four-metre wound in Endeavours hull, above their heads, through which the inside of the wormhole was visible; muted shades of greys, blues and browns rushed by. She fought to hold down her anger, stifling a scream, borne of rage.

Suddenly she was blinded.

The second energy ribbon, which had slashed the wound in the bridge, glanced off the main hull as it made to stab again. Leaping above Endeavour it split, forking into hundreds of stabbing fingers of ferocious energy. Then it burst in a plume of blinding intensity, as its fatal touch stroked the inner wall of the wormhole.

Flash!

From end to end the wormhole flooded with searing white light.

Lockhart groaned as the un-filtered light assaulted her eyes. She rolled away from the hole above her head, shielding her eyes from the painful light, burying her face in the crook of Rossi's lifeless neck. The light was so intense it hurt; so bright every nerve fibre in her body tingled at its touch.

Endeavour seemed lost, shrouded in an incandescent nothing. Beyond her Tri-tungsten hull only light existed.

Then, just as suddenly, the light dissolved, and was gone.

The walls of the wormhole resumed their race, hurtling past them again.

Suddenly they were out. Like a bullet from the muzzle of a gun, they exploded from the mouth of the wormhole, back into normal space: into the Alpha Sector...Home.

Free of the electro-magnetic onslaught, Sweeney quickly regained control of the ship by firing all manoeuvring thrusters; with warp and induction engines ripped apart they were his only option. Endeavour shuddered and rolled to a very untidy halt; anything that was not fixed to a deck was thrown at the for' ad bulkheads. Inertial dampers were evidently off-line too.

Endeavour spun slowly to a halt eventually hanging dead in space, askew, like a wasted autumn leaf, waiting to fall. Smoke plumes and explosions peppering her once beautiful hull.

But they had made it. They were home.

Jevak was the first to react. Hugging his console, unable to support his weight on his shattered right leg, he grunted painfully. "Shall I issue a distress call, Captain?"

Lockhart blinked, readjusting her eyes, after the shock of the light. She could make-out shapes, which were slowly becoming tangible. She looked again at the body of Ensign Rossi, still clasped in her arms, and the devastation around her. Her vision was restoring, and her alarm intensifying.

"Yes," she grunted eventually.

Matt left his post and struggled over the twisted debris to help the Captain. "Are you okay?" he gasped, choking on the clawing smoke.

Above them the bulkhead exploded again showering the bridge with sparks, flames and deadly fragments. Gently Matt took Rossi's smouldering body in his arms, taking her from the Captain.

"I'll look after her," he said. It was his way of letting her know, 'You have more pressing things to attend to, and we need you to be Captain again'".

Grasping her injured ribs Nicolle struggled to her feet. Squinting, to refocus her dimmed eyes and smearing more blood across them, she looked around the bridge, this time really seeing the devastation. She was their Captain and it was time to put her ship in order.

Raising her voice to the comm-system she grimaced, "Damage crews, report!"

"Captain," Jevak groaned, "I have been attempting to hail Alliance Fleet." Even through the pain he was enduring, he looked perplexed. "I have attempted to raise them on all Alliance Fleet channels, but as yet... have received no reply. In fact all Alliance Fleet channels are empty, not even white noise."

Having laid Rossi's body aside, Matt began pulling Wicasa and Cheung free of the fallen bulkhead. Lockhart struggled to assist him. "Have Communications been damaged?" she asked, grimacing as she pulled Wicasa clear.

"Negative, I have been intercepting Kraxian, Vaurillian, Tyreean and even Macaitian transmissions. It is only Alliance channels which seem affected."

There was nothing she could say that would assist Jevak just now. She had to secure her ship, assist her fallen crew. All she could do was advise him to keep trying.

CHAPTER 4

The past eight days since their undignified return, battered and bloodied, to the Alpha Sector had been exhausting and the situation they now found themselves in was becoming increasingly alarming.

The crew had been almost overwhelmed by the extent of damage the ship had sustained. Widespread repairs had occupied all of their waking hours, but they still found time to worry about the lack of communication from Alliance Fleet. Tension and irritability throughout the ship was mounting. A situation, which had initially been merely perplexing, had quickly descended to distressing, fuelling rumours of a cataclysmic, Alpha-sector war.

In eight days none of their faster than light hyper-transmissions, or, more worrying, their distress calls had been acknowledged, and that was just impossible. There were dozens of reasons why they might be unable to contact Alliance Fleet Command for a few hours, even a day or so, but not for eight days. And there were absolutely no reasons why they should be unable to contact the entire fleet.

Every known line of communication employed by The Alliance was vacant of all traffic. Static filled every single channel. Even the antiquated network of navigation beacons, which though now obsolete, having been set in place more than two hundred years ago, but which should still have been transmitting, were silent. As a result Lockhart had deemed it imperative that Standing Order No. 157 be invoked. That requires that any ship unable to contact Alliance Fleet Command for more than forty-eight hours must make their best possible speed to the Terran system, and that the ship should assume 'silent-running'. Which was exactly what they were now doing. Until they ascertain the reason for the Alliance's silence, it was prudent not to advertise their position or circumstances to any hyperspace transmissions eavesdroppers.

Unfortunately, unbeknown to them, the damage had already been done.

Jevak, while maintaining communication silence, continued to monitor all other hyperspace transmissions. Scanning for anything that might shed some light on a situation that every one on the ship already considered to be inconceivable and were becoming fearful of. What possible reason could there be, that might prevent Alliance Fleet from contacting them? After eight days though, the disquiet amongst the crew was escalating. Speculation as to why their distress calls had gone unanswered was understandably rife. The general consensus was that the unthinkable had happened: In their six-year absence the war against the Macaitians had gone badly and that the Alliance had been defeated; or worse, that.... Earth had been totally annihilated. Although the idea was appalling, no matter how Nicolle stacked the variables, it was none the less a possibility the Earth had been destroyed, and that had to be considered.

Intercepted transmissions from Vaurillia, Tyreea, Kraxa and even Rassila and many other worlds across the sector, were still referring to the ongoing war, and that on many fronts the situation sounded desperately critical. During Endeavour's absence the war had, it seemed escalated beyond imagination.

But it was still difficult to accept that Earth alone could have fallen to Macaitia, even if it was the heart of The Alliance and therefore a prime target. It had always been widely believed that the Rassilian Empire would eventually, if reluctantly stand with The Alliance and Kraxa and that with combined superior numbers and ships, the uneasy union would ultimately defeat the invasion.

The deliberations and theories were rife amongst the crew and only added to the growing worry and uncertainties about home and families: Had our so-called allies turned tail at the first sign of trouble, and sacrificed Earth to save them selves? Possibly, but that didn't explain why it appeared that Earth was the only Alliance world absent from the continuing war. Speculation could go on forever; nothing would quell the crew's growing fears, out here in the inter-stellar void, too far from home. The explanation was waiting for them nineteen hours away on Earth.

Though still badly crippled they were making their best possible speed. Endeavour had become a lumbering wreck following her transit through the wormhole. Almost every system on the ship had had been damaged or destroyed. Three crewmembers were dead, and another eighty-seven badly injured. Their prompt return to the Alpha Sector had cost them dearly.

In the immediate aftermath of their exit from the wormhole the warp reactor had gone critical, threatening to destroy the ship. The final assault by the energy ribbon which had fried the engine nacelles had overloaded and ruptured virtually every conduit in the warp manifold, emptying the coolant system and flooding the engineering section with super-heated plasma, allowing the warp reactor to go into meltdown. Ensign Petrov had been the last to evacuate the area as it flooded. Her lungs had been scalded as she raced for the descending blast doors, and had barely made it under the narrowing gap, before the whole section was swamped with lethal, boiling gasses; she was now in sick-bay, still critical.

For a time the situation had become grave. It had been touch-and-go as to whether they would need to dump the warp reactor in order to save the ship from being vaporised. Their drastic situation had called for drastic action; and original thinking.

With so many of the external hull plates already damaged or missing; thereby opening numerous decks to the freezing vacuum of space, Lockhart concluded that the only way to prevent the warp reactor from going into melt-down, and at the same time vent the leaked plasma that was threatening to liquefy her ship from the inside, was to deliberately remove a few more bulk-heads and hull plates. The vacuum of space being a constant minus 270 degrees centigrade was easily cold enough to prevent the warp reactor from going critical, buying them enough time to rebuild the cooling system and save the warp reactor.

It had taken most of the first two days back in the Alpha Sector, with every member of the crew working in rotating shifts, just to vent main engineering and make it possible to work in safety without the need for bio-suits. The most gruelling part of the operation had required Chief engineer Cosique Tarr'gn to lead a three-man repair team on an arduous, three hour, zero gravity hike across the entire length of the external aft section of the ship, to remove three of the outer hull plates. The exhausting trek to reach the target plates had been unavoidable, since the nearest, still operational airlock was situated at the wrong end of the ship.

As her team had emerged from the airlock, Cosique stumbled attempting unsuccessfully to plant her magnetic boots firmly on Endeavour's savaged outer hull. The deep gouges at her feet made stability almost impossible. The dreadful scars, slashed into the ship's once pristine outer skin, were painfully deep even by the faint, cold light of the distant stars. Some of the scars were so deep they looked like ploughed furrows. The energy ribbons had slashed and burned into the almost impenetrable tri-nanocrystalline plating, melting the dense metal, and dissolving it as though it were little more than ice in the Sun. Then in the icy vacuum that surrounded them, the metal had re-solidified: freezing instantly to produce these deep, un-even painful ruts.

It had then taken the team a further four hours, and several replenishments of their oxygen supplies to complete the gruelling task of manually removing each of the required plates. The emergency explosive bolts which secure each three-metre square plate, which should have allowed the plates to be jettisoned easily at the touch of a button, having failed, along with almost every other system on the ship. With engineering now purged of the lethal mix of plasma and gasses, repairs to all of the other dependant systems could now begin.

The task before them though, was immense, and under normal circumstances should have required a complete refit in a space dock, lasting months or years. But that was a luxury they did not have. They were still far from home, on their own, with nothing but the damaged resources at hand.

Although both warp and induction engines had been comprehensively damaged, the make shift repairs to the slower, induction engines by cannibalising all three of the Endeavour's shuttlecrafts, had at least gotten them underway. The warp drive had taken the worst of the energy ribbon's punishment and required more manpower than Nicolle was prepared to spare; it would have to wait. Their induction engines would suffice for the time being; at least they were now homeward bound. Permanent repairs could be undertaken en route.

Before finally departing the wormhole though, Nicolle had one final, painful duty to attend to. Besides Ensign Rossi, Lieutenants Harris and Levakk had also given their lives in the line of duty; they had both been in the armoury, when one of the ribbons struck.

The track of spitting, blue energy had sliced through the hull tearing a swath along three decks and eleven sections to the rear of the main hull, breaching directly above the heads of the crewmen. A containment field had secured the breach initially, but failed when the lower starboard nacelle exploded during the final assault. Debris from the nacelle had sliced through the containment field venting the armoury to the vacuum of space, sucking them both out to freezing death.

A final sensor sweep, before their departure, was initiated to search for and recover the bodies of their fallen colleagues. Lockhart was determined that she would keep her promise to get everyone home; her brave officers would at least receive a fitting burial on Earth. But their bodies were never found. Although sensors were barely operational, there was still enough resolution power to differentiate organic matter against a background of the cosmic vacuum, but there was just no trace of either officer.

The sensor sweep also failed, it was discovered later, to locate their probe, sent through to determine the wormhole's exit. It had apparently also gone missing. In fact it was not just missing, there was no evidence that it had ever been there: no residual ion trail, no debris, nothing at all.

Nicolle therefore determined that, until they could establish otherwise, sensors were unreliable and that the whole system would require to be purged, re-established, then calibrated. But that was well down the repair priority list. There was much more to do before restoration of sensors became operationally imperative.

For the first five days on the journey home, Endeavour had struggled, like a wounded leviathan. She was on a direct heading, at half light-speed. Faster would have been preferable, but pushing the engines in their current fragile condition would have been reckless; they may have been working, but as Cosique had said, 'string and sealing wax came readily to mind'.

By the sixth day out from the wormhole, they had closed half the distance home. Replicators, which using teleporter technology could reduce matter to its molecules then reconstruct the energy in any form required, had been brought back on line, and spares for the impulse engines were now being replicated rather than robbed from their now disabled shuttles. The induction engines were now operating at their maximum, and so within two more days had gotten them quickly to the edge of Alliance space. The warp engines, though, were still very much under repair. Cosique had established repair teams which had worked constantly round the clock, and she had promised that they would be in a position to re-energise the warp field in about another 72 hours, but that was still a conservative estimate.

    Lockhart's frustration was mounting by the day, their slow of progress in repairing damaged systems was unavoidable, the crew were working as fast as they could with the limited resources they had, but now after eight days Endeavour was still barely functional. Lasers were still inoperative, shields were down, as were the teleporters, but they could all wait. No one would be teleporting anywhere for at least the next day or so. As for shields, they would just have to hope that concealing their position would negate the need for protection. Ion torpedo launch systems were severely fused, though they could, if required, still be deployed manually, so they at least had defence systems. On a more positive note, though, the ship's structural integrity had at last been re-established. Once again the shuttles had been called upon to sacrifice some of their hull plating to shore up the worst of the gaping wounds in Endeavours sides. All of the essential systems were now at least, repairable, even if their being restored was not quite imminent. On the surface the ship looked almost as good as new. But they were closing in on Earth and with still no contact from Alliance Fleet, Nicolle did not yet know what her damaged ship was going to have to deal with when they arrived. She looked almost fit for the hero's welcome she richly deserved, but with still no contact from Earth, a hero's welcome from whom?

Wolf 359, the universally recognised frontier of the Alliance's heart, was now behind them. They had passed it late yesterday at about twenty two hundred hours, and to their initial relief they had found no sign of any battle, no burning hulls, no crushed wreckage; the remains of their brave, defeated fleet. Then the bewilderment set-in again, if there was no evidence of any devastating battle then why not?

As Endeavour slowly approached the outer margins of familiar worlds, they had dreaded the prospect of realising their fears. Their escalating uncertainty had primed them to expect the worst, to find the region littered with the wreckage of battle, a graveyard of Alliance and Macaitian ships, stretching as far as the eye could see. The smashed and smoking remains of a horrific battle. But there was nothing. No debris, no shattered hulls to indicate that any kind of conflict had take place. Nothing.

If Earth had fallen to an invading fleet, this is where the trail of destruction and death would have started. Wolf 359 was the fleet's rallying point, beyond which no invading force had ever penetrated. This is where their comrades would have made their final stand.

Though the absence of debris had been a relief, it had only served to deepen their concern and multiply their confusion. Wreckage would have at least confirmed their fears, but its absence only added to the mystery. Why was their no answer from home?

Captain Lockhart was now more anxious than ever to get home, and the closer they got without contact, the more anxious she was becoming. The tension that was permeating the ship was almost tangible; the fear that the loved ones they had longed to see again, might be dead, and that there was no home to return to, had been gnawing at all of them. Only one thing eats at morale more effectively than disinformation, and that is no information at all; the mind then has all the fuel it needs to conjure its own destructive scenarios.

Rumours were sweeping the ship like a virus. The latest was that the Macaitians must have some new and terrifying, planet-killing weapon, which they had unleashed on Earth. A weapon, which only targeted organic matter, vaporising it leaving inorganic matter unscathed. Rumours like this were unsettling, especially since there was no evidence to the contrary and no warm friendly voice from Alliance Fleet, telling them "well done, come-on home."

FOR THE WANT OF A NAIL

It was late in the evening and Wolf 359 was now more than 24 hours behind them. For the first time in three days Nicolle joined her friends in the mess hall for some relaxing company; it was crowded. She had just completed another gruelling nineteen-hour shift as part of "gamma" repair team, in main engineering. Along with the rest of the bridge crew, The Captain had abandoned her normal duties in order to speed the repair of the ship. Everyone's shoulders were to the grindstone, and it was proving exhausting. If she had been frustrated that command offered little opportunity for hands-on work that was quickly being worked out of her system.

This evening had been only the second time, since their catastrophic passage through the wormhole that she had managed to snatch some "down time"; and it was much appreciated. Along with everyone else who had gathered in the mess, she needed this time to help her wind down. The gruelling manual labour helped to keep everyone's minds focused on the task in hand, but thoughts of home were never far away.

Around the table with her were Jevak, Wicasa, Cosique and Sweeney. Salix was in the galley doing his best to keep up with the demand for coffee.

"So you don't go along with the new weapon theory?" Cosique inquired of Jevak.

"Most definitely not," he replied, dismissing the idea.

123

"Care to share the reason with us," asked Lockhart, nestling her coffee in both hands.

"Any weapon, Captain, no matter how devastating," he explained. "Would require to be deployed on, or at its target. In doing so the enemy would still require to evade the fleet. The fleet would in-turn, inevitably attempt to engage that enemy. The absence of wreckage would suggest that no enemy was engaged, and that therefore none of this has occurred."

"Besides," added Sweeney, in support of Jevak's explanation. "There's been no mention of any weapons of mass destruction or any thing else, in any Kraxian or Vaurillian communications we've intercepted. It's hardly something they'd keep under their hats."

Their conversation was not private, nor was it intended to be. The mess hall was for the crew to mix and socialise. Others near the table began taking notice of what was being discussed.

"Captain?" interjected a young ensign, standing just behind Jevak. "We've been away from the alpha Sector for a long time, perhaps, if there is such a weapon, it was used a while back." The girl was obviously troubled and looking to her commander for encouragement. "It maybe that it's just not be the first topic of conversation anymore."

Lockhart scanned the assembled crew; everyone's eyes were on her. From the door to the galley their table had become the focus of attention. She put her coffee cup down and rose to her feet. She had to put their minds at ease, or at least ease their fears.

"I know you're all worried," she said softly, as she stood on her chair to get a better view of the assembled crew.

Standing head and shoulders above them, she could see every worried face, every anxious pair of eyes. She could tell instantly, it was etched on all of them, how deeply troubled they all were. They were scared, worried and uncertain. They were looking to her for some kind of reassurance. Nicolle was not sure how she was going accomplish this, because she was not even certain she believed her own reasoning. But she had to somehow waylay their fears, but looking into their eyes she knew she could never lie to them.

"I am too," Nicolle continued, as the room fell silent. "And I wish there were some way that I could lay your fears to rest, but being honest, I can't. I know as much as you, about the situation back home. All I can say is that I cannot believe that some... some super weapon has wiped out our entire species. There's no evidence beyond lack of communication from Alliance Fleet to indicate anything is different at home, or that anything in the sector is different."

"But sir," interrupted the young ensign again. "It's been almost nine days, and Alliance Fleet still haven't acknowledged us. That just doesn't make sense."

Lockhart had to agree. "I know, Morag," she said, maintaining a calm air. "None of what we've found since returning has made sense. But I still don't believe we're all that's left of the human race. I mean, let's be honest, even in the event of an all-out Galactic war, an entire civilisation could not be wiped-out," she concluded doggedly.

Wicasa rose to his feet, to lend support to the Captain. "Exactly," he said calmly. "Even if there were such a weapon, and all life on Earth had been exterminated, that still doesn't explain why we've not heard from the rest of the fleet, or the Martian colonies. Not all of the human race is resident on Earth, there would always be some one left, somewhere, to answer us."

Lockhart nodded her agreement and continued. "There would still be pockets of survivors scattered all through the Sector, and no matter how wide spread they were, we would still be able to contact them; they should at least have picked up Endeavour's distress calls." Extending her hands, palms down to indicate calmness she added. "I think, at best the Macaitians may have found a way of jamming Alliance hyperspace transmissions. That, I genuinely believe, is the most rational explanation for what's happened. And anything else is just unsubstantiated guesswork. We're all scientists and engineers," she said scanning the room, picking out individuals and making deliberate eye contact. "We work in exacting environments where only provable hypotheses are accepted, and we should all know better than to indulge in such fanciful conjecture. ....Anyway," she smiled warmly. "Tomorrow we'll know for definite what's been going on in our absence. We'll be entering the Terran system at about..." She looked at Jevak for confirmation.

He straightened, eyeing the gathered crew. "At precisely 13 hundred hours, 17 minuets and...."

"About lunch time," Nicolle interrupted, drawing a snigger from the assembled throng. The speech was having the desired effect; their mood was lightening. "Salix, let's make sure lunch is served early," she added, raising her voice to the back of the room ensuring the Talluriann could hear.

"So let's not lose our heads. There is a plausible explanation for what's been happening, and what ever it is it'll all be made clear tomorrow. So let's sleep well, all of us. And be ready for the biggest home-coming welcome, Alliance Fleet has ever mustered."

Getting down from her chair, the room buzzed with optimistic anticipation. Wicasa held out a hand to assist her.

"Do you really believe that?" he asked in a whisper as she brushed passed him.

"Of course I do. And even if I didn't I wouldn't admit it to the crew, besides there is no evidence to the contrary. And until I see anything that proves me wrong, with my own eyes, I wont believe anything else. Anyway, only tomorrow knows what tomorrow'll bring. It's been a long eight days, and tomorrow could be even longer," she said finishing the last of her coffee. Turning to Jevak she said. "Let's recommence hailing Alliance Fleet. This close to home it shouldn't matter if anyone else intercepts it."

He nodded in compliance. "Aye Captain."

Nicolle bid every one at the table a good night and made her way to her quarters. Though she was exhausted, she slept fitfully that night, snatching only a few hours in short bursts. Her impromptu speech had calmed the crew's fears, but not dispelled them entirely. There were too many unanswered questions. Questions that kept running through her mind, chasing away much needed sleep.

* * * * *

Captain Lockhart emerged from the lift onto the bridge. She had not been part of the repair team, which had put this area of the ship back together again. Her expertise in warp-flow had confined her mainly to engineering consequently this was her first day back at her post in nine days.

She paused for a moment to look around her. The assigned repair teams had done a fine job; it was hard to tell that this technological nerve centre, of pristine gleaming metal, had looked like a melted gumboot, several days earlier. Slowly she stepped up to the rail, behind her command chair, gently leaning on it, she surveyed her domain appraising the meticulous workmanship; it looked fine, and it felt fine.

She was back where she belonged.

Wicasa, Sweeney, Jevak, Cheung and Ensign Lawrence were already on the bridge, manning their stations.

Elizabeth Lawrence was a pretty, petite girl of twenty-two, who had studied tirelessly to get into Alliance Fleet, whilst working on her parent's small farm in Wyoming. Like Cheung she'd had been fresh out of the academy when Endeavour had departed Earth. In life she and Ensign Rossi had been inseparable friends; like sisters. Now she was her dead friend's replacement at the bridge auxiliary engineering station.

Lockhart's eyes went immediately to where the tiny, now battle hardened veteran, was running test programmes through the engineering consoles. She knew exactly, the pain Lawrence was suffering. Her heart went out to her.

"There was nothing you could have done," Wicasa said sympathetically, seeing the pain mirrored in his Captain's eyes, as he mounted the stairs to stand beside her.

Lockhart sighed heavily. "I know," she said mournfully. "I just wanted to get us all home." They locked eyes. "Was it too much to ask?"

"Given what we went through, it was little short of a miracle any of us made it. You did all you could; you got your crew home, Nicolle."

As a mark of respect for the woman and for the rank, Wicasa never used her Christian name on the bridge, but sometimes friends had to be friends.

She glanced to the main view screen. "Not quite yet," she said setting her mind to business.

The bridge view-screen displayed the for'a'd

view along their course heading; the spangled black expanse of infinity around them. There were only a few points of starlight dotted in the darkness, one of which, at the centre of the screen, was growing larger as Endeavour closed the distance.

Stepping down to the lower deck of the bridge, Nicolle glanced back at Jevak. "Report," she demanded briskly, getting down to the immediate task in hand.

"We have entered the Terran system Captain." He replied. "Neptune's orbit was negotiated a few moments ago. We will shortly be with in range of the Mars perimeter."

"Are we still hailing?"

"Affirmative," he replied shaking his head. "There has still been no acknowledgment."

"Slow to one quarter-light, Mr Sweeney."

"Slowing to one quarter, Captain," the helmsman confirmed.

The Mars perimeter was an automatic defence system, designed to detect and verify the identity of any approaching ship. Every Alliance starship was fitted with a transponder, which emitted a unique signature. On approach the system automatically detected, identified and hailed friendly vessels with a recorded message, and registered their arrival with Alliance Fleet Command. Unfriendly vessels were more harshly dealt with.

Incorporated within the system were sensors, sensitive enough to detect even the displacement of space dust around a cloaked vessel. The detection of any such vessel was met with a more forceful response. Once exposed, an encroaching ship was immediately targeted, then hailed. If no recognised response was forthcoming, the system's built-in firepower was calculated to disable or destroy any known technology. Since the whole installation was fully automatic, and was never manned, so even if the unimaginable had occurred on Earth, the perimeter should still be active and hail their arrival.

The minutes dragged by. Lockhart took her seat and waited for the computer-activated chirp that would signal their automatic recognition. A hush descended on the bridge and throughout the ship. Lockhart could feel the silence it was almost tangible. On all decks, in every section, the hush was mirrored. 286 crewmembers held their collective breath, and waited for the automated welcome.

And waited.

"Crossing the perimeter's boundaries," reported Jevak. He waited another few seconds before looking-up and adding, "No response."

"Anything on sensors?" Wicasa asked hopefully.

"Sensors are still operating at barely minimum resolution, commander. It is almost impossible to get precise readings. I can be certain, though, that there are no life readings on the surface, and the atmosphere is thin, predominantly carbon dioxide with traces of nitrogen and argon."

"What about the biospheres?"

"Nothing. There is no evidence of habitation. No debris on the surface, or in orbit." Jevak continued. "To all intents and purposes, Mars would appear to be just as it was prior to colonisation."

"Should we divert?" Wicasa asked the Captain.

"No. Take us in, Mr Sweeney; Earth, standard orbit," Lockhart directed.

"Aye Ma'am," Matt responded briskly, setting vectors and co-ordinates. He spun in his chair to face the Captain, and then asked a general question of everyone present. "Could we have travelled in time somehow? Could that be why there's no sign of the Alliance?"

Nicolle had also considered that as a possibility, but as yet had no evidence to confirm it as fact.

Cheung intervened. "No Captain. I'd have to say we haven't. All hyperspace transmissions we've intercepted; Kraxian, Tyreean, Vaurillian, they all make reference to the Macaitian invasion, and how badly they're faring. All of which puts us in our own time. This is the twenty forth century."

Lockhart frowned. "I'm getting tired of puzzles," she sighed, with enduring frustration. "Engineering! How long till we have warp power restored?"

"Another two or three hours at best, Captain," replied Cosique via the 'com'. "We do have partial weapons, though. Lasers are still off line but ion torpedoes and launchers are now fully operational again."

"Well that's something at least," Nicolle said, betraying the relief in her voice. "Keep working on the warp drive, Cosique. If we need to get out of here, I want to make it as quickly as possible."

"Yes ma'am."

"Earth is now within sensor range," Jevak announced.

"Well?" Asked Wicasa, still harbouring hope.

"I can detect no orbiting satellites," Jevak said, rapidly scanning the information being presented by his console. "No weather stations, no space dock, no evidence of the lunar colonies... and still no orbiting debris." He added finally.

Lockhart leapt to her feet. "Magnify!" she demanded.

The screen shifted, altering its focus.

The lower half of the rectangular screen was now filled with the familiar arc of the of Earths northern hemisphere. Icy white at its apex, darkening to deep blue towards the equator, against a black, spangled shroud. Wisps of cloud drifted gently across the azure North Atlantic Ocean, which turned slowly, twenty-five thousand kilometres below them.

For six long years, they had grown used to the idea that they might never see this sight again, and yet here it was; home. For a brief second they forgot their situation; their worries fell away. Six pairs of eyes just stared, like rabbits caught in headlights, even Jevak.

Nicolle stood transfixed. It was almost dream

like. She had seen this, all of this, happening over and over again in dreams; only in dreams, so this could only be a dream. It felt like her mind were moving through treacle. Time seamed to have slowed, almost to a stand still as she stared spellbound at the azure arc. It seemed so unreal, so unbelievable yet here she was, here they all were. They had made it. Home.

Suddenly Nicolle was shocked from her stunned silence, as her mind abruptly registered what her eyes were seeing. The hemisphere below them was in complete darkness; the Sun was over the Indian Ocean, on the far side of the planet and yet she could see no lights, no sign of habitation. She had seen the Earth from this elevation on countless occasions. Street lighting, bathing towns and cities, should all be visible. Freeways, like fine gossamer threads meandering in the darkness between the bright pools of habitation should be illuminating the whole of the North American continent directly below them. New York, Washington, as far south as Florida should all be burning brightly. On the extreme right of the screen Paris, London, and Barcelona should also have been bristling, sparkling like fairgrounds. But everywhere was in complete darkness. Not one light shone anywhere on the planet.

Lockhart caught her breath. Spinning sharply on her heals she called. "Jevak, Life signs?"

He ran his fingers deftly across his console. "With sensor impairment, I can not guarantee accuracy....Unlike Mars, the surface is barely accessible through the Earth's denser atmosphere...." Slowly he looked up from the display, His eyes betrayed his disbelief. "Captain...The population is less than one billion. I can detect no cities; at most there are possibly several large towns, none of which are geographically where they should be. The densest centres population are mostly around the equatorial regions.... There are no detectable power sources, in fact.... no indication of any technology what so ever."

CHAPTER 5

Of course she had considered the possibility. From the moment Alliance Fleet had failed to respond to their hails and she had given the order, setting a course directly for Earth, Lockhart had played every feasible scenario, and even some infeasible, through her brilliantly analytical mind. But in every conceivable case, no matter how plausible or implausible, the conclusion she had invariably arrived at had always come out the same; that the situation they now found themselves in was quite simply impossible.

Even the old Sherlock Holmes' deduction, that: 'When you have eliminated the impossible, what ever remains, however improbable, must be the truth,' did little to temper her mounting disquiet.

Throughout the previous nine days, Nicolle had vigorously challenged all of the negative, morale sapping, rumours sweeping the ship. Countering them with, what she believed to be, reason and common sense. She had constantly reassured the crew that there was nothing to worry about. After all how could there be? There had to be some rational explanation for Alliance Fleet's silence. The idea that in their six year absence, one of The Alliances many enemies had developed a weapon capable of destroying an entire planet, and then systematically dismantled and obliterated all evidence of that culture from every corner of the Sector beggared belief. Other than Alliance Fleet's non-response, there was nothing to indicate that anything was amiss back home. Until now.

Now there was no denying it. She was faced with the awful truth; there was no home to return to. Earth had faced some cataclysmic attack. All that they had known had been wiped from the face of the planet. The population had been decimated. Almost seven billion people gone, annihilated. Their home, their world was destroyed.

As though in a nightmare, for that was exactly what this was; a nightmare come true, she stood rooted to the spot, seemingly unable to move. Her eyes grew wider in disbelief, staring incredulously at the screen, unable to breath, as the shocking gravity of desolation assaulted her. The bridge fell deathly silent; a burden of fear and loss choked the air around them. The walls of the bridge seemed to close in, constricting Nicolle's awareness to all but the image on the screen.

Dragging her attention from the screen, she spun on the science station. "What else? Why's there no debris?" She demanded, painfully.

"There is no evidence to indicate that there should be, Captain." Jevak replied at a loss for a rational explanation.

"How reliable are the sensor readings?"

"Excepting the fact that they are operating at a reduced power output," The Vaurillian replied. "All sensor readings are within expected parameters."

"Damn this, I'm getting tired of riddles and questions," She said turning to Wicasa. "I want answers." Raising her voice a little to the comm-system she hailed engineering.

"Do we have teleporters?" Lockhart asked, hurriedly.

"Teleporter room two is back on line Captain." Cosique replied, sensing the Captain's urgency, as she slid from under a plasma flow conduit. "It's been reconfigured to accommodate our current power deficit. The buffers and foot pads were salvaged from one of the shuttle's emergency teleport system"

"That's good news." Lockhart smiled; encouraged that she was no longer impotent.

"The shuttle's buffering matrix wasn't entirely compatible with the ship's systems," continued Cosique. "But they've been modified to interface."

"Thanks, good work Cosique," Lockhart concluded eagerly. Stepping purposefully to the centre of the bridge she scrutinised the screen again, as though daring the image of their barren home to further deny her answers. Without turning she gave the order. "Wicasa, assemble a landing party."

Almost before the Captain had finished speaking, her second in command was moving towards the lift at the rear of the bridge. "Matt, Wattie, you're with me," he said as the automatic doors opened before him.

All three entered the lift together. Wicasa tapped his 'comm' bracelet, it chirped in response. "Security," he said. "Have someone join the landing party in teleport room two, and issue hand lasers for four."

"Aye, sir," a male voice replied.

"Deck five." ordered Cheung, as the lift began its decent in response.

"So we finally made it home," Sweeney said, without much cheer.

"Hardly the way we'd expected it," Wicasa replied, similarly bleakly. Staring straight ahead, the Commander was now too concerned with their mission on the surface, to indulge in the niceties of their usual banter... They all were.

On the bridge the Captain paced irately, occasionally glancing up at the screen. Her mind raced with possible theories, scenarios and strategies to explain their plight. Like multiple chess games, all being played-out in unison on a galactic scale. Nothing made sense to her, but she was desperately trying to make their unfathomable predicament fit some rational model of reality she could accommodate.

Again she felt restrained; she hungered to be on the surface, seeing first-hand what had occurred during Endeavours absence, but according to Alliance Fleet protocols it was the first officers' place to lead the landing party. Not for the first time did she long for the old days when Captains, especially the maverick ones, regularly lead landing parties. But for the time being, resolving this enigma was out of her hands, all she could do was wait for Wicasa to report-in.

Command was so damned frustrating.

As Lockhart tuned to retrace her steps across the deck, for the fourth or fifth time Jevak's fingers deftly flitting across his console caught her attention. Even with his head bowed she could still see his eyebrow lift in that manner Vaurillian's have when the have been surprised.

Mounting the stairs to the science station she asked. "What've you found?"

"Captain," he said, sounding a little bewildered. "I have reconfigured the sensors to a narrower field cycle, which has produced a similar effect to increasing their power output."

"And?"

He furrowed his brow a little more. "I am now detecting a single, relatively large, metallic object on the surface, which would appear to be made of steel. Given the apparent absence of any other technology, it would appear to be unique."

Lockhart joined him at the science station. "Let me see. Can you make out what it is?"

"Inconclusive, even after reconfiguring the sensors, the object was still barely detectable."

"Well it's all we have to go on. Patch the co-ordinates through to the teleporter room." She lightly touched her 'comm' bracelet. "Wicasa."

Five decks below in teleporter room two, the landing party was now complete. They had been joined by Lieutenant Ar-Cann, a young Tyreean officer who had also been a member of Wicasa's crew on the Johannesburg, and was now second in command of Endeavours security team.

"Yes Captain?" Wicasa responded, as he and the other gathered lasers, hand held scanners, known as palm-corders and flashlights.

"We've found something; a large metallic object of some kind, on the North American eastern seaboard, it would appear to be in the Philadelphia area. Jevak is passing the co-ordinates now."

"Aye Captain. Are there any sizable populations close by?" he asked as he joined the others on the teleporter pads.

"A fairly small settlement, about 6000 metres west of the teleport co-ordinates." She paused momentarily, to consider their situation then continued; her tone was cautious. "Wicasa... Let's assume, for the time being, that Earth's no longer ours, treat it as hostile territory, okay?...Be careful."

"Understood, Captain..... Initiate," He said, nodding to the teleport Chief.

Wicasa was in a hurry to get to the surface, he was as eager for answers as the Captain.

A myriad of vertical, translucent blue light shafts simultaneously descended from above, shrouding the four figures on the pads. Each of the figures glowed and flickered within a display of bright stars as a harmonic whine pulsated the air around the dazzling light columns. The glowing pillars of blue shifted and moved as the figures within became progressively less distinct. Their outlines blurred as the landing party dissolved molecule by molecule. Reaching a zenith, the buzz climbed an octave as the lights dissipated, revealing an empty teleporter.

*********** ***************** **********

It was dark. The waning three-quarter moon offered little illumination as it eased behind another of the gathering storm clouds. A chill breeze blew briefly, ruffling the stunted, meagre vegetation on the eastward facing, exposed slope. The four pillars of blue light, which descended from thin air to the damp earth eight feet below, momentarily banished the darkness from the deserted hillside. The shimmering particles within the light columns gradually coalesced and arranged forming hazy indistinct figures: slowly amassing to assume the forms of the landing party.

The four figures, still bathed in blue light, were all but complete, when the teleport sequence suddenly reversed, and all four began to dematerialise again.

"Teleport room!" Lockhart roared at the

'comm' system. "What's happening?

The reforming pillars of light were accompanied by a sudden, ear-splitting whine, which vibrated through the deck plates, bulkheads and the teleport console.

"The pattern buffers are unstable, Captain. I can't maintain a lock on them!" the teleport chief roared trying to make himself heard above the metallic scream.

The noise reached a crescendo where its screech was almost inaudible, but still stung like a drill-bit being pushed through his eardrums, when it suddenly stopped. The teleport chief flinched, shielding his face, as his console exploded, showering him with shards of burning fragments and slamming him backwards against the bulkhead. He cradled his face in his hands, stifling an agonising groan as his legs gave way under him and he crashed to his knees. Flames leaped from the twisted control panels above him, flashing across the ceiling.

The Chief struggled to his feet; his hands and face soaked with blood. A four-inch shard of the console's laminate surface had taken his right eye out, tearing his face open to his jaw. His head swam from the searing pain and loss of blood, as he struggled to stay conscious.

Trying desperately to focus with his remaining eye, he could barely make-out the figures glowing within the light columns a few feet away. Growing weak from shock, he knew he had to do something before he inevitably lost consciousness.

His colleagues would die, their atoms scattered in oblivion, if he did not re-establish the teleport sequence; and he was the only one who could. Ignoring the searing pain he struggled to his feet. Plunging his hands in to the flames, he fought down panic and fear.

The four figures began to glow on the teleport pads then one by one began dematerialising again.

"Captain... I'm...I'm losing them!" the chief exclaimed via the 'comm'.

On the bridge Jevak rapidly stabbed his fingers across his console. "The teleports are haemorrhaging power through a damaged conduit in the main power grid," he urgently explained to the Captain, who was still at his side.

"Can you do anything?" she asked hurriedly.

Springing from his own station to the auxiliary engineering station to his right, where Ensign Lawrence stepped aside giving him access, Jevak shouted. "Chief Cunningham... Maintain a lock. I will reroute power through the transponder couplings to the two remaining, vacant pads. Reconfigure the buffers to those pads, and bring them back two at a time."

"Belay that order, Chief!" intervened the Captain. Rounding on Jevak she explained. "I want them on the surface, we've no other way of getting them down there."

It was less dangerous to the away-team, for the teleport procedure to be reversed and return them to the ship. Jevak's first concern had been for lives of his colleagues: an automatic reaction. The Captain's first concern would normally have been the same, but she needed answers and she needed them now. There was more at stake than the lives of four Alliance officers, and failure was too a high a price to pay for a teleport malfunction.

Jevak nodded his acknowledgment. "Chief Cunningham, continue with the teleport procedure; reconfigure the matter shells to the two remaining pads. I will reroute power as I have suggested."

"Aye sir!" Grunted the teleport Chief, as he stumbled towards the flames, now ferociously consuming most of the console. "I.... I'm holding two of them in the buffers now Lieutenant!" Beating back the flames with his bare hands he once again set the teleport sequence.

On the surface two of the figures began to sparkle, and slowly materialise. Matt and Wattie became manifest as the sparkling diminished.

"Teleport room, what's happening?" shouted Sweeney, as he slapped his comm-bracelet.

"We are attempting to complete the teleport Mr Sweeney, please stand by," Jevak said, seemingly unruffled. "Chief Cunningham...."

Again the teleport Chief bravely thrust his hands back into the flames. He screamed as his arms and hands blistered and boiled, the stench of his own burning flesh almost choking him. His compulsion to save his fellow officers and friends was greater than his agony. He had to do his duty.

Suddenly one by one, the teleport pads began to explode.

"We're losing them. We've only two serviceable pads left!"

"Activate now!" urged Jevak, flinching at the teleport Chief's agonising screams.

"Medical emergency! Doctor report to teleport room two, immediately!" Lockhart shouted at the comm-system.

On the surface two figures began sparkling in the same spot where Matt and Wattie had appeared a moment earlier, then faded again.

The figures once again resumed sparkling on the teleport pads. One of the two remaining pads exploded under the feet of one of the materialising figures. Chief Cunningham's hands and arms up to his neck were by now ablaze, screaming blindly as the flesh pealed from his arms he pushed on, thrusting his wasted hands once again into the blaze. His tunic ignited, flames licked up and around his head. Flailing helplessly as inferno devoured him the two figures flickered as they began to dematerialise again. Flash! A shower of burning debris and smoke filled the teleport cove. The last pad exploded. Both human outlines instantly vanished.

Sweeney and Cheung stepped to the side as only one single figure resumed sparkling a few metres in front of them. Slowly the figure took shape, molecule by molecule until finally Wicasa stood with them.

"Teleport room!" Wicasa shouted, almost

punching his comm-bracelet. "Lieutenant Ar-Cann isn't with me, what's happening up there?....What's happening?!"

From the teleport room the Doctor's alarmed voice replied, "Chief Cunningham's been badly burned, Wicasa, stand by."

It had taken the Doctor mere seconds to get from his sickbay, to teleport room two. In Alliance ships all teleport facilities are on the same deck and sickbay is adjacent to all of them. It was considered prudent to have a medical facility close to the teleports since returning landing parties frequently required medical assistance, such was the nature of missions to the surfaces of strange worlds with strange bacteria and viruses.

"Bridge!" The Doctor bellowed at the comm-system as he rushed to the aid of the Chief.

"Doctor!...Quickly! Complete the teleport sequence, now!" Jevak urged.

Momentarily disregarding the needs of Chief Cunningham, the Doctor plunged his impervious arms deep into the blazing inferno now engulfing the length of the teleport console and burning a column from deck to ceiling. As the flames leapt at him, consuming his face, he recoiled for an instant: an automatic, though completely unnecessary response from some redundant subdivision of his cybernetic programming.

The ship's physician, as with all Alliance vessels, was a standard issue Mk3 medical cyber-unit; a machine built to look and act human. All other posts on the ship – science, engineering etc were related disciplines and as such were, to an extent interchangeable, since the personnel had similar understandings of how and why different aspects of the ship worked. The ship's Doctor though required a unique understanding of all non-mechanical living matter on the ship, be it human, Vaurillian or any other, and so was indispensable. His program was embedded within the ship's computer core and could be downloaded, in an emergency into any mechanical module. So even if the Doctor was physically destroyed the ship could still have the skill of a surgeon.

The Mk3 unit was constructed to be of average height, average build and looks with a slightly darker than caucasian complexion, black swept back hair and a moustache. The moustache, it was felt gave the unit an air of maturity and an embodiment of trust, an emotion that humans seemed to require in their Doctor.

Steadying himself and adjusting his response to the nonexistent danger the flames represented to him, the Doctor again lunged into the blaze.

The remaining figure began sparkling faintly again, as the teleport beam's hum filled the cove in which the matter pads were situated. Since none of the pads were now operational the shapeless figure shimmered briefly before dispersing.

"Doctor, have you got him?" Shouted Wicasa. "....Doctor....Doctor!"?

After a moments pause, which seemed endless, the Doctor finally replied, his voice was quiet, measured.

"Lieutenant Ar-Cann didn't make it....." He drew a deep breath. "Thankfully what we got back didn't survive."

"Damn!" Wicasa raged, angrily stabbing the heel of his boot into the damp earth. As he turned to face Matt and Wattie, though, the empty, lost look in his eyes told them anger was the least of his emotions; Wicasa had lost a friend.

For a few heartbeats there was silence. On the bridge, in the teleport room and on the surface, no one spoke. Over the years their perilous journey had robbed them of many of their friends. No matter how often it was encountered, losing someone close never got any easier.... and they prayed it never would.

Eventually Lockhart broke the silence. "Doctor,... how's Chief Cunningham?" She asked anxiously.

"He has sever head trauma and suffered first-degree burns to most of his upper torso, head... and lungs, but," he reassured, confident of Twenty-forth century medicine, "he'll survive."

"Get him to the infirmary, immediately. ... Landing party."

"Yes Captain?" answered Wicasa.

"I'm sorry Wicasa," Offered Lockhart, sympathetically.

She knew all to well how he felt. Ar-Cann had served under Wicasa for four years on several Titan

149

mining ships, before both joined Endeavour. Almost ten years together… you get very close to people you serve with for that long.

"There's nothing you could have done…… You have your mission."

"Understood Captain," He said, visibly shaken. Pushing past Sweeney and Cheung he muttered. "Let's go."

Matt and Wattie fell-in step behind him.

As they made their way amongst the spars bracken bushes, Wicasa remained subdued. Since entering the "Snowflake" nebula, six years ago, this protracted mission had cost them dearly; too many lives had already been lost finding a way home. Turning into the chill breeze they each silently reflected on how many more of them would yet be sacrificed before this mission was over.

Activating their arm-mounted flashlights and flipping open their palm-corders, their hand held scanners, they quickly scrutinize they area around them. As they moved slowly but carefully over the coarse terrain they found the going slow. The grass, such as there was, was damp under foot. The twilight dew had descended heavily that evening, and even the ground between the meagre tufts of greenery was wet and slippery.

"This way," said Cheung, his breathe hanging as a fine mist in the chill night air. "About an other hundred metres," he said, indicating a north-easterly direction.

They continued for several more minutes

until eventually Wicasa slowed his pace. Levelling his palm-corder to scan the rise to their left, he again became perplexed. His findings were definitely not what they had been expecting, not if there had been a war.

"I'm not reading evidence of an kind of battle," he said, not knowing whether to be relieved or not.

Cheung agreed. "There's no scorched earth, no radiation above what could occur naturally, no atmospheric ionisation. Apart from an unusually high level of oxygen in the atmosphere, there's nothing we wouldn't expect."

"Why the raised oxygen levels?" asked Matt.

Wattie returned Sweeney's blank look; he was as much in the dark as the others.

Wicasa stopped. Turning slowly through 360 degrees he scanned the area around them to a distance of three miles in all directions to confirm Cheung's findings.

Inhaling deeply he said. "Air's fresh too. No pollution or disease from mass corpse decay." Shrugging he turned his flashlight and palm-corder on the ground at their feet. "Vegetation, insect life, all normal. There isn't even any indication there's ever been any kind of construction around here". An owl hooted high to their left, startling them, as it circled, searching for its prey, Wicasa followed the sound with his scanner. "Everything's normal, exactly as we'd expect to find it. There's nothing showing-up that's out of the ordinary. Definitely nothing that could account for the loss of almost seven billion people," he said at a loss.

Although the ship's sensors had sustained extensive damage during the passage through the wormhole, and therefore could easily be deceived by any number of atmospheric variables, the landing party's palm-corders had been unaffected by the massive energy assault. Their hand-held devices should therefore have been providing them with reliable, credible data. But they could still shed no light on what had occurred here: which was, as far as they could tell, apparently nothing. From what they could gather, It was as though nearly seven billion people had just simply packed-up and left, taking every evidence of their existence and culture with them.

Resuming their hike over the rough, undulating terrain, skidding a few times where the ground was particularly wet, they continued northeasterly. Meticulously scanning as they went, they became more troubled. Their scans continued to prove unhelpful, confirming that everything was normal, except that their whole civilisation was gone.

The moon slipping from its hiding place behind the gathering clouds, low in the eastern sky, reflected its cold light off the thread of a wide stream, snaking past them about half a mile to their right. In this half-light they could just make out a bend about two miles upstream, where it turned north.

Despairing at the lack of consistent information being offered by their instruments, Matt lowered his scanner and swung his flashlight towards the distant stream, to determine their situation with his own eyes.

The ground fell away steeply for about twenty feet or so, and then levelled out again to a plateau, which disappeared in the darkness about thirty feet away. His flashlight punched through the heavy, damp air like a solid cone of light. Squinting, he strained to peer through the faint mist that hung close to the ground where it fell away.

"You know," he said. "I've been to Philly a few times… and I kind of remember it being busier than this." Adding, even more sarcastically. "Few taller buildings, big cracked bell. That kind of thing." Sweeney's indomitable, dry sense of humour could always be relied upon to surface especially when it was at its most inappropriate. It never helped situations but it sometimes relieved tensions. "Just where exactly are we supposed to be?" He asked.

Adjusting his palm-corder to determine global positioning, Wicasa replied. "By these readings we're supposed to be somewhere… Somewhere in the 'Aqua Park'."

Philadelphia's aqua park had evolved from the ashes of the old Naval Dockyards, which had occupied a vast area to the south of the city during the 20th and early 21st centuries.

"I don't see it… I don't mean I can't actually see it…obviously. I mean I don't see the Aqua Park slotting into this landscape."

Sweeney looked around. "We can't be. That would make that the Delaware," he exclaimed, indicating towards the narrow tributary. "It's far too narrow; it should be more than eight hundred metres wide here. They used to build naval ships in the 'Aqua Park' before it became a leisure facility. You couldn't launch a ship into that," he said, pointing his flashlight arm in the direction of the stream. "George Washington could have jumped across that without getting his feet wet, never mind having to sail across."

"That's what the co-ordinates say," replied Wicasa, sounding more and more exasperated.

"Commander, maybe we are," shouted Cheung from the top of the next rise.

Wicasa and Sweeney hurried to join him. Cresting the low hill they found the object they had teleported down to locate. Though none of them expected it to be what they saw.

Scuffing down the steep gradient the three of them circled the huge object, running their torch beams over its surface, whilst thoroughly scanning it with all of their instruments. Wicasa stepped closer and ran his hand over its dull, flat surface, which curved outwards above his head as it towered over him.

"This has been here for centuries," he said doubting his own findings. "But how could it have been?"

Running his palm-corder over it, Cheung started to say. "Approximately......"

"Approximately four hundred and twenty years, give or take," cut in Sweeney.

"How can you be so sure?" asked Wicasa.

"It's Second World War design. A diesel powered, steel hull, battle cruiser. It's been here a long time."

"How'd it get so far inland?" Cheung asked, becoming more bemused.

"That's a good question." Wicasa said, kneeling to grab a handful of earth and scan it. "This area hasn't been under water in a lot longer than four hundred years. And that excuse for a river, isn't tidal. This shouldn't be here."

Sweeney edged along the, grey painted keel towards the front of the vessel, looking it over. Its surface was mottled and broken. Its dried, cracked paintwork, had flaked and crumbled long ago, exposing the metal underneath, which had long since turned to rust, staining the ancient paintwork with streaks of brown.

The crushing weight of the vessel had, over time, compressed the soil beneath it, sinking the hull up to a metre or more into the soft earth. The whole ship was resting at an angle, listing towards the slope of the hill they had descended; propped-up and prevented from falling further by an outcrop of rock.

As nature always does, the local eco-system had not been long in staking its claim to the twentieth century wreckage. Weeds, grass and bushes had penetrated its steel plating, through stress fractures and rust holes near ground level. And, with the passage of time, where wind-blown soil had accumulated in crevices and angles in the main structure, bushes and clinging ivy had found a lifeline, clinging precariously to the bridge superstructure and conning towers. Built to withstand the fury of battle, this twentieth century war machine could not withstand the relentless march of Mother Nature.

"No one's been near this in a long, long time," said Sweeney, stating the obvious. "Probably not since it was grounded."

Gravity had played its part in the disfigurement inflicted on the vast leviathan. Near his feet, Sweeney found the remains of the radar mast, and both of its twin funnels. They had long since dislodged from their positions high above and to the rear of the superstructure, and were now little more than fragments of desiccated rust, crumbling in the wet earth, midway along the keel. Matt stopped to examine what remained, even the larger fragments were like dry parchment, crumbling to dust at his touch.

About five metres from the leading edge of the keel, Sweeney discovered what was left of the ship's registration markings, they were difficult to distinguish, the paintwork having deteriorated so much over the centuries. Wattie came over to join him; both ran the beams of their flashlights over the two metre high letters.

"D. E...." Sweeney read. "The rest of it looks like 1, 7, maybe 8 or 3. it's hard to tell. The rust's really eaten into it here. It was an escort ship, part of a destroyer battle group."

Wicasa joined them. "How do you know that?" he asked.

"D. stands for destroyer, E for escort," he replied with just the right amount of smugness not to offend. "She was probably part of the Atlantic convoys."

Matt's hobby, before being lost on the far side of the galaxy, had been all things twentieth century, preferably mechanical and especially 'boys toys'. On the Johannesburg he'd kept and maintained two old Triumph motorcycles and a beautiful old E-Type Jaguar he had lovingly, and meticulously restored himself and also converted to run on non-polluting, hydrogen gas. The old freighter had been so large he could drive them up and down the mile and half long cargo holds for fun, or sometimes to get to trouble spots in the thrusters system. There were hover shuttles for that job, but his 'toys' made the long journeys along the freighter's two kilometre power conduit much more fun.

Wicasa shone his torch across the ground to their right. There were a dozen or more brass shell casings scattered around a gapping wound in the ship's hull. Brass tarnishes in air but does not oxidise as quickly as steel, so unlike the hull these casings were still pretty much intact. The hole the casings were scattered around was about a metre in diameter bellow the waterline, just aft of the bow. Wicasa crouched warily, shining his torch through the opening, into the bowels of the wreck. The edges of the hole were jagged with rust, and bent outwards. As he lightly touched the rusted lip, to steady himself, a chunk of the oxidised metal dislodged, crumbled and disintegrated to dust at the Commander's feet.

"So you're an expert in old battle ships, as well as old movies and automobiles, then?" Cheung teased.

"Guess I was just born out of time."

"Guess you were," confirmed Wicasa, his voice echoing flatly in the lower decks of the ship. "Let's have a look inside."

Scrambling through the damp opening, almost on all fours, Wicasa found himself in a dark ancient world: a different time. A time when so much of Man's endeavour and ingenuity had been directed towards hostility and destruction; in-fact back then it was almost government policy. He took a few steps into the darkness, his footsteps echoing dully off the rusted steel walls. The stale air was heavy with the acrid stench of decaying metal and stagnant water. As he directed his flashlight high up into the blackness, he accidentally kicked something that made the devil of a noise, clanging and echoing round the hold.

Wattie and Sweeney scrambled through behind him. "What was that?" Wattie asked, surprised by the din.

All three scanned the floor with their beams. There was a virtual carpet of discarded brass shell casings, hundreds of them, strewn around them. Matt crouched, picking one up to examine it. He turned it over in his hand looking closely at its base and then did the same with several more.

"These have all been deliberately dismantled. The shell's been removed and the propellant extracted," he said, with certainty.

"How can you tell?" Wicasa enquired.

"On their base, they have this circular area." He demonstrated, turning one upside down. "In the centre of it, just here, there would be a punched indentation, where the firing pin struck the detonation cap, if the shell had been fired. None of these have any indentations. They've all been taken apart to remove the explosive filling." Looking back at the hole they had entered through he added. "And it looks as though one went off, accidentally. That hole's been made by something exploding outwards, not by an attack.

"That's a hell of a lot of explosives," Wicasa judged, looking around at the discarded shells littering the hold.

"It would certainly make one hell of a big bang," Matt confirmed, kicking some of them out of his way.

"Come on, let's get going," Wicasa said urging them on again.

This decaying, dinosaur of destruction was another conundrum; out of its time and out of place on a world, which its self was out of place; and the Commander was becoming weary of conundrums.

The inclined keel was slick with four hundred years of congealed moisture. Droplets of water still dripped from the once white, but now filthy, brown, rust streaked roof. The piles of shells, coupled with the slippery hull plates made for dangerously unsure footing.

"Careful," warned Wicasa aiming his palmcorder around the vast hold. "There isn't a lot of solid metal left in these plates, so let's not spend any more time in here than we have to. The whole structure is pretty unstable, it could collapse around us without much persuasion."

The still air was heavy with dampness and mould, as they set off tentatively, in single file, along the ridge of the inner keel. The angle at the base of the hull plates was packed with moist earth, which had found its way into the hold through rust cracks and openings, to accumulate where gravity deposited it. Wattie was in the middle of the line, Wicasa leading the way, with Matt bringing up the rear.

As they shuffled into the darkness Sweeney' attention strayed to the shells for a moment. He failed to notice when, a few feet in front, Wattie lost his footing on a loose weld joint, and stumbled. Matt made to grab at him, but missed. Bouncing across shell cases as he landed, the noise of Wattie's fall echoed of the steel walls and reverberated through the lower decks. As Matt and Wicasa helped him to his feet they caught the echo of a deep, throaty growl from somewhere up ahead.

"We're not alone," whispered Matt.

Turning and crouching in the same movement, Wicasa and Matt swung their torches towards the half open, watertight hatch in the bulkhead, about fifteen feet directly in front of them. Scrambling to his feet Wattie aimed his flashlight in the same direction. None of them had time to consult their palm-corders to determine what danger lay in wait, or to draw their weapons. A second growl, from just beyond the hatch was suddenly followed by a shadowy blur which rushed at them. A few feet before reaching Wicasa the shape veered at the slope of the hull, scrambling on the wet surface, snarling as it desperately tried to evade their bright beams. Its footing was unsteady. It slipped, crashing into Matt, tumbling on top of him, as they both hit the deck. Sweeney raised an arm; an instinctive, defensive reaction, just in time, to deflect the creature. It snapped at him. Its gaping jaws missing his hand by millimetres. Then it was gone; out of the hole behind them.

"A wolf!" Wattie exclaimed, shining his flashlight in the wake fleeing beast. "A pretty small one at that. The poor thing was more frightened of us," he said laughing with relief.

"Easy for you to laugh. It wasn't you on the wrong end of mister Big Bad, there," said Sweeney, brushing himself off as he got back to his feet.

"A little far from home," Wicasa noted. "They're not known for venturing this far-east, or south. Are you okay?"

"Yeh," Matt nodded.

"Come on. It was alone." Wicasa reassured them, checking his palm-corder to be certain that the wolves mate was not also lying in wait.

The hatch in the bulkhead at the far end of the hold was open barely enough for them to squeeze through. Which was just as well, since its hinges had long since rusted beyond movement. Beyond it was a long, narrow access corridor just wide enough for a man to pass along with barely inches to spare either side. From what Wicasa could tell, it ran the full length of the ship; his torch beam certainly could not find its far end.

Assuming the same formation, Wicasa leading the way with Matt again bringing-up the rear, they pushed their way further into the wreck, the confined space now stifling the sound of their footsteps.

"Cramped conditions to work in," Wattie said, his voice muffled by the dead walls of oxidised steel enclosing them.

"This was just an access corridor," Sweeney said, putting his colleague right, as he tapped the welded bulkheads on either side of him with his fist. "Looks like these were the fuel storage tanks. They're double skinned, and they're empty."

Their progress along the confined passageway was difficult and demanding. The intrusion of mud through the keel, and the years of moisture and slime oozing down the inclined walls made it difficult to get a steady footing or a handhold. The listing angle that the ship had come to rest at was making things even more awkward; it was like one of the assault courses they had been made to tackle at The Academy. The bulkhead to their left fell away, while the right inclined up over their heads. The simplest way of negotiating the complication, they found, was to edge their way along, hand over hand, with their backs to the overhanging wall.

Their progress was slow, but determined.

"What's up ahead?" asked Wicasa.

"Should be the engine room," Sweeney grunted as he fought to keep his footing.

A few claustrophobic minutes later the corridor finally opened up as they reached its end. A second corridor cut across it, forming a 'T' shape at the intersection, giving them room to move around. Directly in front of them was a battened, sealed hatch, beyond which, as Matt predicted, was the engine room. To their left and right, at the ends of the shorter, intersecting corridor they found steps leading up to the next deck.

This far into the bowels of the ship there was less mud intrusion, and what remained of the deck plates were relatively sturdy and clean, though still slick. Wicasa edged up the slope of the moist deck, shining his torch beam up the stairwell to their right. There was little to see but more damp darkness and rusted bulkheads. Meanwhile Sweeney and Cheung turned their attention to the engine room hatch. They found it was rusted shut and not likely to move without considerable force, which given the flimsy condition of the vessel was not advisable.

"Where would the Captain's cabin be?" Wicasa asked without turning.

"Below, and aft of the bridge," Sweeney replied, coming over to join him. "Two decks up," he added, his gaze following Wicasa's beam up, into the darkness overhead.

Droplets of water dripped continually from the decks above. Their four centuries of dripping, marked by thin stalactites of brown slime dangling around the stairwell and down the fragile corroded stairs, like lank locks of muddy hair.

"What do you think?" Wicasa asked.

"Not much solid metal left in them," Sweeney replied, casting a worried eye over the dilapidated steps. "What about them?" he asked, nodding at the stairs on the reclining wall.

Wattie eased down the slope to the opposite end of the corridor, running his palm-corder over the lower stairs. "Same here," he said. "Pretty far gone."

Sweeney grasped the handrail nearest to him and gave it a solid tug; it stayed in place. "Only one way to find out, and since I'm the lightest."

"By that same reasoning, since I'm the heaviest," insisted Wicasa. "If it'll hold my weight, then it should hold you two."

Without waiting for further argument he secured his palm-corder on his belt and firmly grabbed both handrails. Carefully placing his right foot on the bottom rung, the Commander tentatively eased more of his weight on to it until his left foot was fully off the deck. Then he repeated the procedure, sliding his left foot gently on to the next step, until gradually his full weight was on the steps. Both steps held.

"So far so good," he said, more in hope.

The stairs were steep, rising more than three metres to the next deck, but spanning only a metre. Space on board these old tubs was a premium. Every thing had to fit into small spaces, even the crew. There were fourteen stairs up to the next deck. By the fifth the stairwell was creaking under Wicasa's weight and it seamed to be taking forever for him to reach the top.

Crack!

The sixth step splintered with hardly any pressure at all. Collapsing, it sent a shower of desiccated rust and powder crashing to the deck around Matt and Wattie's feet.

Wicasa grabbed at the handrails to stead himself. To his left, the weld holding the stairs to the inner hull, split. The ancient wreck groaned as the stairs shifted violently to his right. Quickly he shifted his feet up to the next step, spreading his weight as evenly as possible. But the quick movement only served to hasten the metal husk's disintegration. The hull shuddered as the stairs separated from it, splitting the joining welds from top to bottom. As the stairs gave way beneath him Wicasa launched himself at the hatch to the next deck, now just above his head, just in time for the buckled steps to collapse around Matt and Wattie's feet.

Dangling from the opening above, by his fingertips, he heaved himself up, cautiously spreading his weight as much as he could, while Matt and Wattie grabbed an ankle each and pushed. Hauling himself through the hatch, Wicasa rolled on to his back and lay still for a brief second, to be certain the weakened deck was not also about to collapse around him, dropping him once again to the deck below. Pulling in a lung-full of air he steadied himself,

Below him Cheung scanned the decking plates on the upper level. "It's okay," he called. "The upper decks haven't corroded as much. They've still got a fairly high metal content. They should hold."

Shuffling back towards the hatch, Wicasa rolled onto his stomach. "It's pointless trying them," he said, nodding towards the stairs on the reclining hull. "Here," he said, stretching a hand towards Matt.

Grasping the offered hand firmly Sweeney hauled himself up, while below Wattie again pushed. Both Matt and Wicasa then reached down to the waiting Cheung and hauled him up as well.

Getting to their feet, all three instinctively reverted to Alliance Fleet training. Back to back, facing into possible danger, they directed their torch beams into the darkness on all sides. They were not expecting trouble so weapons were not drawn, but they were always at the ready.

Similar to the deck configuration below, they

found themselves at an intersection of two passageways: one running the entire length of the ship, for'ad to aft, and a shorter one running port to starboard, cutting across it. At the centre of the intersection a single stairway, this time, rose steeply to the third deck. Behind them, off the main passageway Wicasa could make-out doors spaced at regular intervals, to where he imagined, were the officer's quarters. Ratings, as far as he remembered, slept at their stations, in hammocks slung between bulkheads, or on top of the munitions, down it the bowels of the ship.

Sweeney tapped the handrail of the stairs with his flashlight. Instead of a dull thunk, it reverberated with a thin, but definite clang.

"Sounds like there is a bit more metal in these," he said optimistically.

Wicasa again took the lead to the next deck, taking each of the fragile steps slowly. Under his weight, the antiquated metal groaned its displeasure at being disturbed from its protracted slumber. Paint from the rails and steps along with several millimetres of rust, crumbled and fell in a shower to the deck every time he moved, but this time the stairs held. There was no give in any of the aging weld joints either: the centre of the ship had apparently faired better with the passage of time. The metal content of the steel plates around them was still surprisingly high.

Matt emerged from the stairwell, on to deck number 3 last, Wicasa and Wattie were already searching the immediate area, probing the darkness with their lights and palm-corders.

"Which way?" Wicasa asked as Matt joined the search.

Sweeney looked around to get his bearings. "We're amidships, must be this way," he said leading off along the main passageway, which again ran the length of the ship.

The air was still damp, even here where there had been less corrosion. The smell of ages hung heavily in the stale atmosphere. Playing their lights around them, they searched the corridor as they moved slowly and carefully along it. Debris lay in every corner; pieces of the collapsed vessel: discarded clothing, dampness and slime. Passing several doors, left and right, they made cursory searches in each of the cabins behind them. They all looked the same; filthy and abandoned.

About half way along the passageway they found what they were looking for. Fixed to the narrow, wooden door was a small sign, which read 'Captain'.

CHAPTER 6

    The door was unlocked, slightly ajar, but it declined to open further. The hinges had seized solid long ago and would no longer function as designed. A little persuasion though, from Matt and Wattie's shoulders, and a considerable amount of brute force from Wicasa's right boot finally made the obstinate hinges see reason. They eventually gave: splitting away from the door, leaving the cracked wood to fall, twisted against the bulkhead.
    The cabin was in much the same condition as the others they had passed-by on the passageway behind them, except that it was marginally larger: about eight feet by six. By their own vessels standards that was almost prison cell like, but by what they had seen, was obviously spacious to the crew of this ship. Wicasa moved ahead of the other two, probing his flashlight into the corners. He noticed instantly how the cabin was misshapen. The far wall, the inside of the hull, was bevelled inwards and a crack ran down its elevation from top to bottom. The rocky outcrop that was holding the ship upright, was slowly crushing its way through the rotten hull. It was clear that gravity and time were taking their toll and that the ship would inev-

itably, someday in the not too distant future, crumble finally to the rocks below.

The wooden bunk, over against the right hand wall, had been stripped bare; any sign of sheets or mattress were long gone, though the frame was still intact, if a little rotten. At the foot of the bunk, smashed picture frames littered one of the corners, but there was no sign of any of the pictures. The walls, they noticed, were bare of any of the 'pin-up' type photographs, which they had come across in almost all of the other cabins they had looked into; but then they had not expected the Captain to indulge in anything like that.

On the left hand wall, above where they had set the door to rest, there hung a small ornate metal plaque. The inscription was barely legible under four hundred years of dust and dampness. Wicasa removed it and wiped it down with his sleeve.

"U.S.S. Eldridge," he shrugged, looking at Matt.

"Doesn't mean anything to me," Sweeney replied, blankly.

Laying the plaque on the desk, adjacent to the bunk, Wicasa began searching through the desk drawers. Meanwhile Wattie and Matt continued rifling the rest of the cabin.

"Look at this," Wattie said, wiping cobwebs from a discoloured brass sextant, abandoned on the top of one of the shelves, above the bunk. "I've only ever seen these in museums. It's hard to believe they could really navigate with them."

"Simple, but ingenious," Wicasa said with an admiring respect. "You really have to marvel at their bravery. Not that the Captain of this ship would ever have needed to use one of these. But can you imagine the earliest sailors, setting off across that first frontier, with nothing but a star to guide them. That must've taken real guts"

Matt opened the cupboard behind where the cabin door had been. "Looks like they left in a hurry, but they've been choosy about what they took," he said, removing the Captains dress white uniform. Which was no longer white or dress.

"Do you think it was abandoned at sea, then drifted here?" Asked Wattie.

"No," Matt replied, indicating to the stripped bunk. "You wouldn't take a mattress with you on a life boat. And none of the other cabins had mattresses either."

As the other two fanned-out to quickly cover as much of the cabin as possible, searching through the remainder of the cupboards, Wicasa concentrated on the desk. He pulled out all of the drawers, finding one or two difficult to dislodge: the wood having expanded in the permanently damp air, and so had to smash his way into them. He found them all to be empty except one. At the very back of one of the bottom drawers he found a dusty bundle tightly wedged into the confined space. Unwrapping the discoloured grey oilskin, which was wrapped tightly around it, he called the others over.

"Here," he said laying a large book on the desk.

"The ship's log. Maybe this'll tell us something."

They hastily joined him, holding their torches up to flood the desktop with as much light as possible. They were all eager to know the history of the wreck.

"Don't think it's got much to tell, doesn't look all that thick," remarked Matt jokingly.

As Wicasa opened it, the metallic damp stench around them, which they had almost become accustomed to, was joined by a trace of dry and musty. The book may have been protected from the oxidising damp air, but fungus could not be deterred by mere oilskin. Most of its pages were missing, which was why the book was so thin. Running his flashlight down the inner spine Matt pointed out where a knife or something similar had cut almost all of the pages from the log. "They've been removed deliberately," he said.

Wicasa flicked to the first page, which confirmed the vessel's designation. Printed proudly, in thick black ink, the words:

United States Navy
D.E. 173
U.S.S. Eldridge.

Turning over a few pages he found the Captain's first entry. Pre-printed at the top of the page was the date; unfortunately though that was almost the only thing that could read, with any degree of certainty. Mould on every page had all but obliterated the Captain's had written notes. Who ever had hidden this log away, and taken such trouble to preserve it, had obviously not counted on it being four hundred years until it was discovered.

"Not much use," Matt noted, as he brought his torch in closer to lend a hand.

"I don't know," Wicasa said, a little more optimistically, flicking back and forwards a few pages. "She was a brand new ship by the looks of things. This was her launch date; 25 July 1943. Here," He said scanning further down the page. "This looks like... 'Sea trial'."

Turning to the next page, then the next then another, he was unable to distinguish anything else that was legible. Shaking his head he flicked over another six or seven pages, then stopped. "15 August 1943," he read. "This could be 'weapons work-up'."

"Could be," confirmed Wattie, eagerly looking over Matt's shoulder.

Scanning down the rest of the page, none of them could make out anything else except a letter here and there.

Skipping to the last page Wicasa said. "I wonder why the pages were cut here? 28 October 1943." Running his torch down the page he stopped halfway down. "Look, here, there's some thing written a little heavier than the rest." He attempted to wipe some of the mould off; to little effect. "Project Ranb...." He said shrugging.

"I think it's Rainbow." Wattie said squinting a little and tilting his head to see better. "Yeh, yeh Rainbow. It looks like it's repeated further down. It definitely ends, b.o.w. Must be Rainbow."

"Some sort of mission?" Matt said, looking around them at the mess. "And it looks like it was her last, maybe her only"

Wicasa closed the log and carefully wrapped it again. "There's nothing more this can tell us. Take another look around Wattie, see if there's any thing else. Matt, find us a way up to the bridge."

Matt headed into the passageway leaving Wattie and Wicasa to conclude their search.

After searching everywhere else, Wicasa finally ran his flashlight under the desk, then the bunk. All he found were discarded bits of cloth, which he assumed were the remains of old clothes, bits of crockery; a piece with the ship's crest on it, but nothing of any consequence.

Wiping the filth off of a small shelf, fixed to the bulkhead, at the top end of the bunk, Wattie discovered the Captains compass. It was a large, circular, brass construction with a glass face, embedded in the centre of the shelf, and fitted flush with the wood. He had seen these antiques working before, but he was always struck by their crude dependability. Having searched every other corner, crevice and cupboard with Wicasa, Wattie was now just casually killing time; there was nowhere left to search, and by the looks of things nothing to find.

For nothing more than amusement he reconfigured his palm-corder to emit a magnetic pulse. Moving the scanner in an ark around the instrument, he watched as the floating dial moved to follow the pulse, and then follow his magnetic lure back as he moved his hand in the opposite direction, like the arched neck of a cobra following the hypnotic melody of the charmers pipe. Releasing it from his magnetic grip, the dial then swung back to its resting position. By his palm-corders readings though it came to rest a few degrees shy of north. Slapping the flat of his hand on the shelf he attempted to free the snagged dial. It jumped a little with the impact but did little else, remaining a few degrees shy of north. Shrugging he turned to Wicasa.

"Looks like they just abandoned it," he said, exhaling in frustration.

Wicasa got to his feet. Tapping his comm-bracelet, he hailed the ship.

"Yes Commander?" Replied Captain Lockhart.

"Captain, we've found the metallic object we picked up on sensors. It's a little strange. It's the remains of a World War Two battle ship; the U.S.S. Eldridge."

"Any indication of what it's doing there?"

"None. It looks as though no one's been near it in the four hundred years since it was abandoned here. It looks like the crew just walked away."

"Another Marie Celeste?"

"A good comparison, Captain," Wicasa agreed. "Except there's no hot meal still waiting in the galley, just years of dust and filth."

"The computer's back on line. We'll check historical data to see if we can come up with anything on her." Lockhart primed herself for her next question; she was expecting her worst nightmares to be confirmed. "How are things looking on the surface?"

"It's just as the ship's sensors found, Captain. There's no evidence of any conflict. No excessive radiation. No scorched Earth. But there's also no ruined city. Nothing at all, just open countryside and this wreck...which shouldn't be here."

Lockhart's frustrations had not been abated. It was beginning to look like getting a landing party to the surface was only throwing up more questions, instead of providing answers. Nicolle was becoming increasingly irritated. She frowned. "Keep me informed. Lockhart out."

Wattie, still scanning the cabin with his torch said. "There's nothing of any help here Commander, only discarded personal effects."

"Let's have a look top side... Matt!" Wicasa called as they emerged from the cabin into the dank passageway again.

His call was answered with a muffled, "Here!" From a stairwell adjacent to the Captains cabin.

The stairs lead through a circular hatch in the deck plates above, to a landing where a door exited to the main deck and another set of stairs lead further up to the superstructure, and the bridge. This was the Captains direct route to both.

"Have you found anything?" Wicasa called up to Sweeney.

"The stairs leading up to the bridge are rusted so badly they're crumbling under my weight," he replied. "But we can get out on to the main deck from here. Maybe there's another way up to the bridge from outside. It's okay, those stairs are solid enough, come on up," Sweeney reassured them.

Wicasa lead the way. Sweeney was right, the stairs were still solid, but the creaking and shifting was a little unsettling.

As all three emerged onto the main deck, a chill breeze blew across the exposed hull from the river, which was on their port side.

"This is a pretty cold night, considering it's still early autumn," Cheung said rubbing his arms to fend off the chill.

Wicasa shivered as he directed his torch beam across the imposing, grey superstructure. It rose high above them, stark and impenetrable like a castle wall atop a sheer cliff. Rising about fifteen metres above the deck it almost doubled the height of the ship. All of the windows and portholes around the bridge were smashed, thick bushes growing in wind-blown soil where several of the glass panes should have been.

"Lets split-up. Wattie you take aft, I'll try for' ad. Matt you see if there's another way up to the bridge."

Wicasa edged his way gingerly around the base of the superstructure. The deck was slick, and sloped to starboard at about twenty-five degrees. He slipped as the sky suddenly lit-up with all the fury at nature's disposal. Whilst they had been below decks the storm front had rolled-in overhead. Lightning split the heavens, starkly illuminating the old wreck.

Seeing the Eldridge, in its entirety, stranded on this bleak hillside, for the first time, Wicasa realised just how incongruous, and out of place, she looked, so far from her natural environment she may as well have been on the Moon.

As the lightening abated the darkness again closed in, save for the faint glow offered by the now clouded Moon, and the harsh, probing beam of his flashlight.

Rounding the base of the superstructure, the for'ad deck opened up before him. He swept the beam across the inclined deck, picking out a few distinct shapes, some of which he recognised, but a few that were unfamiliar.

Forty feet in front of him he found the muscles of the old tub; two massive 4.5-inch guns mounted on turntable assemblies, sitting about twelve feet back from the bow. The turntables allowed each of the guns to pivot through nearly 180 degrees, giving coverage to the entire front of the ship and most of port and starboard.

Directly behind the guns, though several yards back, at the base of the superstructure, was what appeared to be a large, black painted ball. It was approximately six feet high, with a section cut away at its base so it sat flush with the deck. He found the structure curious, not just because it was painted black, making it standout from the rest of the ship, blighting the vessel's smooth camouflage lines, but also because it seemed so out of place here. He had a rough, rudimentary knowledge of twentieth century war machines, but he had no idea what this was.

Pulling out his palm-corder, he scanned it as he carefully circled the sphere. Its surface was smooth; there were no visible weld ridges to betray its construction. Unlike the rest of the ship this oddity was non-reflective; the dull moonlight, which glinted off the deck and guns, seemed to be swallowed by the black painted globe.

Moving to its far side he found a sealed hatch, which exactly matched the rest of the sphere. The hatch was oval, and about two feet high, just large enough for a man to enter, and curved to facilitate a precise fitting to its housing. Six batons, equally spaced around the hatch, held it secure and watertight.

Wicasa released each of them in turn; to his surprise they moved easily. So far these were the only metal fittings they had found anywhere on the vessel, that were not rusted solid. The hatch its self also moved without being forced; it sucked in air as he separated it from its housing.

Scanning the breach with his tri-corder, his expression quickly changed from surprise to disbelief.

"Right about now, Jevak would be saying, 'Curious'," he thought, involuntarily raising an eyebrow to mimic his Vaurillian colleague.

The sphere's skin was composed of very high quality stainless steel, which was why there was absolutely no corrosion in or around the massive globe. And four hundred years on it was the only part of the U.S.S. Eldridge that was still completely intact.

Although he knew very little about twentieth century maritime construction, he did know that stainless steel was something that ships of this era were not built of. This was very out of place.

Swinging the hatch open he squeezed inside.

The interior, wall of the globe was covered in severely decomposed, copper coils, hundreds of them. Slotting and fitting together like honeycombs. The copper wire tightly wound in to each of the coils had oxidised long ago rendering the metal an insubstantial, powdery green. Even the watertight seal of the hatch could not prevent the eventual corrosion of the copper, since it oxidises even in air. Whatever this was, he thought shaking his head, it was...Slowly it came to him... generator, it was a generator, for producing electricity. He was standing inside a massive electrical generator.

Sweeney called to him from beyond the hatch. "Wicasa?"

"In here."

Matt eased through the narrow hatch. There was just enough space for the two of them to stand side by side.

"What do you make of this?" Asked Wicasa.

"I've just found two more aft of the bridge, and it looks like there are another two beyond where the smoke stacks were. They're quantum field generators," said Matt in amazement.

"And that's standard fittings for a twenty century battle ship," Wicasa replied sarcastically. "Care to speculate?"

Sweeney looked around them, bewildered. "Beats me. They're not connected to any of the ship's systems; they'd produce way too much power for that anyway." He delayed further speculation while he adjusted his palm-corder, and then commenced scanning again. "The way they're configured, all they'd produce is a massive electro magnetic field around the ship."

"Wicasa, Matt!" Wattie shouted, almost hysterically from somewhere aft.

The ensign's dread shouts cut short their deliberating. Hurriedly squeezing from the sphere, they bolted towards the rear of the ship. Cheung's yells had sounded alarmed. Once again both of them instinctively reverted to Alliance Fleet training, assuming a threat posture: weapons drawn, torches quickly scanning all corners and ambush zones.

About forty metres passed the bridge, beyond the rear most black spheres, which Matt had found earlier, they discovered Cheung kneeling on the lower slope of the deck. His back was to them, so neither could see what, if anything, had happened to him.

"Wattie?" Wicasa shouted.

Cheung got to his feet, edging slowly away from something lying on the deck. At first neither

Wicasa nor Sweeney could not understand Wattie's shock at the find. At his feet were what appeared to be pieces of a human skeleton; a piece of skull, a section of ribcage and an arm, still attached at the shoulder. All long since stripped bear of flesh. It was hardly the first human remains Wattie had encountered, so neither could understand his alarm.

Matt bent over the remains to scan them more closely. "My god!" he exclaimed, filching in horror. "They're imbedded in the deck." His eyes grew wider as he played his palm-corder over the rusted metal at his feet. "The bones are embedded in the metal plates at a molecular level. This body was... fused to the deck."

What Wattie had discovered were not pieces of bones, but a complete skeleton; its bones merged with the metal of the ship. Only part of the skeleton was visible above the deck, the rest was possibly still dangling in a cabin somewhere below their feet.

The three crewmates stared at the find, caught by the same dreadful thought: that this was a terrifying way to die. They had all heard the stories about how, in the early days of teleport technology, horrifying errors had occurred, which had killed dozens in this same way. Co-ordinate miscalculations, confinement beam inaccuracies, had all resulted in crewmen re-materialising partly or even completely inside solid rock, or within walls. Their bodies fused at the molecular level with the object they had materialised within.

Sweeney swallowed hard. He'd heard that death was usually instantaneous in cases like this. He hoped, for this poor souls sake that that was true. Recomposing himself he scanned the bones further. "This is impossible. These are as old as the ship."

"There's another two back there, and three more fused in the bulkheads near the rear guns," Wattie added, still shocked.

"Dear God, what happened here?" Wicasa exclaimed.

As he made to tap his comm-bracelet, to report their latest findings to the captain, it chirped of its own accord.

"Lockhart to landing party."

"Wicasa here, Captain," he acknowledged.

"We've found some historical data on your mysterious U.S.S Eldridge, Commander," she said "But there seems to be some conflicting information."

"I'll bet there is," Matt cut-in, sarcastically.

Ignoring Sweeney's comment, Lockhart continued. "According to unconfirmed sources, and by that I mean urbane myths, the U.S.S. Eldridge was supposedly involved in some top secret military experiment to make the ship invisible to enemy radar, during the autumn of 1943."

"Project Rainbow," Wicasa said confidently.

"That's right." The Captain confirmed, her tone betraying the furrowed brow Wicasa knew she undoubtedly had at this moment.

"We found the ship's log," he said, answering her unasked question. "The last entry appears to have been made on the day of the experiment."

"Apparently, according to the same unofficial reports, the experiment went tragically wrong," the Captain continued. "As its specially constructed generators powered-up, seemingly the ship was engulfed in a thick green fog," she said in a tone that betrayed the fact that she did not believe a word of what she was reading. "When the fog dispersed the Eldridge had completely vanished, having been, supposedly, teleported 600 Kilometres to the naval shipyards at Norfolk, Virginia. Then some ten minutes later it re-appeared back in Philadelphia, some of the crew spontaneously combusting, while others were imbedded in decks and bulkheads whilst the ship was re-materialising."

Wicasa said nothing, but glanced down at the half embedded skeleton.

Lockhart restrained a dismissive laugh as she continued. "But that was impossible for twentieth century technology."

"Right now I'd have to disagree with that assumption, Captain," Sweeney interrupted. "We've found five massive generators capable of producing a quantum field powerful enough to teleport this ship over vast distances, through time, or even across dimensions, maybe"

"Commander," interrupted Jevak, who was at the Captain's shoulder, at the science station. "These reports are by, as they were referred to at the time, hysterical U.F.O. spotters and conspiracy theorists. The project became known in later years as 'The Philadelphia Experiment'," he said unemotionally, but still asserting that the reports had to be nonsense. "The official reports by the United States Government of the time, rejected the entire scenario. They maintained that not only was the Eldridge not involved in any such experiment, it was not even launched until approximately two months after the alleged event."

"Well Jevak," Wicasa sighed, "I'm looking at a skeleton fused through a bulkhead, that says that official report was a cover-up."

Lockhart looked at Jevak in disbelief.

The Vaurillian hesitated before continuing. Wicasa's reply had taken him completely by surprise.

"Commander," he paused again, a little uncertain of his own findings now. "I am confused. Given that either of these reports, the official one or the conspiracy theorists, are in fact complete fabrications, they both later go on to confirm exactly the same outcome for the Eldridge. The ship was decommissioned several years later and sold to the Greek government, who eventually scrapped her towards the end of the twentieth centaury. So...?"

Lockhart finished his question for him. "So how come you've found her in exactly the condition she would have been in if she had been abandoned 400 years ago, on the day of the experiment. That doesn't make sense. That ship wasn't abandoned. Both the official report and the conspiracy theory both confirmed that she went into service, and had a forty year career."

"Not much of what we've found so far does make much sense, Captain," Wicasa agreed.

He stepped over to the ship's railings to look across the dark open moorland, towards the faint glow of the near-by settlement. Lightening burst through the gathering clouds overhead, illuminating the rough undulating heath around the ship. "I don't think there's any more this old wreck can tell us. I suggest we make our way inland to the settlement. Maybe we'll find an answer there."

"Captain, I agree with the Commander," Jevak interrupted. "But might I suggest caution."

"Exactly what I was thinking," Lockhart agreed. "Okay Wicasa, but let's treat this as a hostile environment. This maybe home, but none of it is what we expected. Until we're sure of what's happened, let's continue assume there's a threat."

"Understood," Wicasa replied.

"Report in when you reach the settlement, Commander. Lockhart out."

CHAPTER 7

'Standard orbit' is Alliance Fleet terminology for a geo-synchronis orbit: that is to say, maintaining a position above a single point on the planet surface below, by matching the velocity of the ship, to the rotation of the planet, there-by remaining above that single point. Endeavour was now in standard orbit, one thousand five hundred kilometres above where the city of Washington ought to have been…but was not.

When they had entered orbit, a little over four hours ago, the Sun had been beyond their horizon, over India. It was now directly over Western Africa, and Endeavour, as a result of their synchronised orbit, was now being bathed in Sunlight, casting her small shadow towards the Moon, far off to their rear.

On the planet surface, that pre-dawn period of twilight can appear to last some considerable time. From the initial greying of the sky, to the first shaft of the morning Sun breaking over the horizon, would give the impression that the division line between day and night is indistinct and blurred. But from space the division is a very definite, distinct line, to one side day, to the other night. That line was now slowly, almost imperceptibly, creeping across the Atlantic, far beneath them. And the first rays of the new dawn would be breaking over the landing party in a little more than two hours.

Their last contact with the landing party, prior to them setting out for the settlement, had been forty-five minuets ago, so they should soon, thought Lockhart, be approaching the settlement.

Backing silently away from the science station, deep in thought, where she and Jevak had been processing data, Nicolle eased herself into a sitting position on the rail behind her Command chair.

"We're missing something here," She said exasperated. "Something so obvious it's staring us in the face. We must be"

She and Jevak had gone over and over all the data their impaired sensors had been able to gather since exiting the wormhole, and every piece historical data available to them. But still could not come up with any reasonable hypotheses for the situation they and the landing party now found them selves in. It was like trying to piece together a jigsaw puzzle with no picture as a guide, and whilst being blindfolded.

She sighed heavily then raised her voice to the comm-system, "Bridge to engineering."

"Yes, Captain?" responded Cosique.

"How are the repairs coming along?" Lockhart asked. Feeling uneasy about being vulnerable in the dark.

"We'll have laser cannons in about an hour, maybe a little more," Cosique replied enthusiastically, but sounding exhausted. "Warp capability and teleports, maybe about an hour or two longer. We've had to cannibalise the last emergency teleport circuits out of the second shuttle. They're only intended for short-range teleport, so we'll have to get pretty low in the atmosphere to retrieve the landing party."

"That's okay, we're prepared for that."

Nicolle hated having to push the repair teams any more than she already was. Some of them had not slept for more than forty-eight hours. But for ship safety and immediate operational capability it was unavoidable and necessary.

"I know you're already stretched, Cosique," she said sympathetically. "But is there anything you can do about the sensors?"

Cosique thought for a moment. It was difficult keeping her tired mind on what she already had in hand without taking on more. "Well... well since we're not going anywhere at the moment Captain, we could temporarily patch power from the impulse engines through the main sensor array, that could give..." She sighed wearily, trying to do the maths in her tired mind. "Maybe...maybe a nine per cent increase."

"That might be enough. Do it," Lockhart said eagerly. Then added, appreciatively. "Thanks Cosique."

* * * * *

Low, over the distant hills to the southwest, the waning moon slid between clouds again, plunging the broken landscape into darkness. In less than an hour it would set beyond the western horizon, giving them cover as they entered the settlement. What was left of the night was becoming colder. The chill in the pre-dawn air was more intense now, and even through their temperature regulating uniforms they could still feel the chill.

Flash.

Their rutted surroundings became starkly visible again, with dazzling clarity. A delay of ten or twelve seconds and the inevitable crack of thunder followed, pounding the air like a drum. The storm still hung in the air and seemed to be following them; thankfully though, it had not yet deteriorated into rain.

From the deck of the Eldridge, the terrain between the river and the distant settlement had appeared relatively undemanding: a comparatively flat plain that swept gently up from the meagre river. There were few hills to speak of, only low mounds, exactly as Wicasa had remembered Philadelphia to be. As he surveyed the darkened plane before them, the Commander found himself recalling his last visit to the old city's Aqua Park, almost eight years ago. He could see the city in his minds eye, slotting buildings and streets into the empty landscape around them. To the north east where the Delaware turned inland, heading towards Lambertville, the hills banked moderately, sweeping south across the flat plain where the settlement now lay, nearly four miles away. He estimated that the settlement must be a little more than half way between the river and where West Chester should have been. From there the grassy plain continued south, extending round to their left, to where the aerodrome should have been; the old airport at New Castle. The land still looked as it should do, everything was there, just waiting for the old city to be superimposed.

Within half a mile or so after their descent from the old wreck, by rope; retracing their steps back through the unstable hull had not been advisable, they had found their way virtually barred by a deep gully. The trench was about fifty feet wide and about the same deep, and stretching as far as the eye could see in both directions north and south. Its sides were steep and treacherous; loose rock and shale, which gave way too easily underfoot. Their descent into it had been awkward, both Wicasa and Wattie had slipped, tumbling to the base of the gorge. Fortunately, only sustaining a few cuts and bruises.

The floor of the trench, they found, was a thick, deep tangle of bramble bushes. From above the growth it had not appeared to pose much of an obstacle, since the depth of the bush could not be gauged, but trying to get through it had proved painful and time consuming. The bushes were old; they had been there a long time and had entwined themselves quite effectively, each clasping their neighbours' branches with claw like thorns. Negotiating the dense briars had eventually required the use of lasers to cut a path. Ascending the far side of the gully had proven equally awkward, but cut and bruised they pressed on.

Unfortunately they found that a direct route to the settlement was impossible. The way ahead was again barred within another half mile, this time by marshland, which they had ploughed into before realising. The marsh was not deep, but its thick glooping consistency was sufficient an obstacle to make their passage through almost impossible. It was dark and their footing was unsure. Each step sucked them to their knees in stagnant, freezing, mud. Pulling a foot out, before taking another difficult step became exhausting.

As the moon reappeared from behind another cloud the extent of the problem became obvious. As far as they could see the watery quagmire extended another quarter, probably nearer half a mile before them. A new route had therefore to be decided upon.

They retraced their steps back to the edge of the marsh then wheeled to the south. Within half an hour the saturated, wet earth became firmer, enabling them to turn west again, skirting the southern edges of the marshland. Here the ground was solid, and allowed them to make better time, but they were now quite some way behind schedule.

As they quickly covered the distance around the marsh, attempting to make-up time, it occurred to Wicasa how perfect a defence construction the combination of the gorge and the marsh would have been, had there been anything beyond them to protect. They were a perfect deterrent to any would be trespasser. He could not know, none of the landing party could, that that was exactly what they were; defences built long ago.

The flat terrain almost immediately changed, the landscape soon became rocky. Boulders, some as large as a man littered the ground. Picking their way carefully between them, playing their lights back and forth, they rounded a grassy rise, which sloped gently to their left. As the ground levelled out again the rocks became fewer, affording them manuverability to pick-up the pace again.

It had taken them more than an hour and a half, following their descent from the Eldridge, to cover two miles as the crow flies. They were now well behind schedule and the Captain would have expected them to have reported-in long before now.

Eventually they intersected a rutted dirt track, which cut across their path, running north to south. Turning north they were now heading at last, directly for the settlement. They would finally be able to make up for lost time. About four hundred meters south of the settlement Wicasa signalled to the others to halt. Keeping low and shielding their torch beams as much as possible, they crouched low into the tall grass at the side of the track.

"Cut the lights," he whispered.

As they extinguished their torch beams, their shadows merged with the intense blackness that surrounded them, consuming them. Up ahead, the darkness highlighted the outline of the settlement against the warm orange corona of its streetlights. As their eyes slowly adjusted to the blackness they could pick-out a few bright lights; single lights, which shone from random un-shuttered windows, like holes cut into the night. They also began to distinguish streets, or alleyways cut between the houses, running into the light, to the heart of the small hamlet.

It looked peaceful.

Wicasa indicated a dimly lit alleyway half a dozen houses to the left of the road. "Keep low," he whispered.

Searching the road for movement, he darted off at a crouch. Sweeney and Cheung followed in single file. All the way to the edge of the village they each maintained a ten-yard spacing between them. Though they were scientists, first and foremost, they were also Alliance Fleet, and their military training came instinctively to them, especially in situations like this. It was easier to pick-off three figures moving together as a group, than it was to take-out three individuals.

As they approached the alleyway they diverged, seeking cover. Sweeney moved quickly to the right of the opening, while Cheung took the left. Wicasa fell back, remaining in the shadows beyond the village perimeter. Shifting from side to side, like a crouching tiger, he assessed the opening. When he was certain there was nothing moving he nodded silently to the others and all three slid silently, surreptitiously into the village.

Keeping to the shadows against the walls of the houses on either side, they paused, to catch their breath, and to assess the situation. The alleyway was narrow, seven, maybe eight feet separated one house from its neighbour, and at ground level there was little light, almost dark, providing excellent cover.

On both sides of them the houses were of similar construction; low single story, wooden structures with over hanging, thatched roofs. Their walls were of rough wooden trunks, not milled or treated wood, but whole tree trunks, trimmed to size, laid on top of each other then cut and jointed at the corners to fit tightly together. The ill-fitting gaps between each trunk had then been shored-up with clay and horsehair making the building weather tight. They were exactly like the log cabins they had seen illustrated in history books.

Where these differed from those old illustrations though, was in the gap below each house. These buildings had been raised off the ground on short wooden stilts. This provided an air gap, of about eighteen inches between the underside of the floor and the ground beneath, to prevent dampness intrusion.

Wicasa led the way to the far end of the alley. It opened out on to a wide cobbled street, dimly lit by oil lamps, which hung under the porches at the front of each house.

None of them had any pre-conceived notion of what they would find when they reached the village, but a living museum was most certainly pretty far down the list of expectations.

Keeping close to the shadows of the over hanging roofs they darted to the opposite side of the cobbled street and into the next alleyway.

*   *   *   *   *

"Sensors are coming back on line, Captain," Jevak announced, looking up from his consol.

"Any improvement?" Lockhart inquired.

"Cosique has achieved a twelve percent increase in their resolution," he said as he raised an eyebrow in surprised appreciation. "Better than we had hoped for."

"Can you get a fix on the landing party?"

"I can now isolate their comm-bracelets. It would appear they have entered the settlement." Deftly he ran his fingers over one area of his console, while concentrating on the read-out display at the opposite end. "There is a storm in the vicinity of the village," he added. "I am still unable to get accurate readings on the other life forms near them."

* * * * *

"Now remember", Wicasa whispered. "We're just here to get answers, then back out, okay?"

"And how are we planning to do that?" Sweeney asked.

Wicasa cautiously, glanced out from their hiding place in the alleyway. The next cobbled street, similar to the one they had just crossed, curved away from them in both directions; the village appeared to be built in concentric circles.

"There's no plan," he replied. "We play it by ear... Wattie," Wicasa whispered, indicating to a wider alleyway on the far side of the street. "Scout ahead."

Wattie edged into the shadow of the porch to his left, and then sprinted to the shadows on the far side of the empty street. Quickly he surveyed the alley then signalled to the others to follow. They both darted into the alley behind him, just as a door at the far end opened.

"Who's out there?" enquired an angry male voice.

"Under!" Wicasa hissed, as he threw himself to the ground, rolling into the gap below the floor of the house to their left. Wattie and Sweeney hit the ground simultaneously rolling under the floor space of the cabin opposite. All three lay silently, their breathing heavy, and restrained.

Wicasa was unable to see the villager descend

the steps from his house; he was on his back, facing in the wrong direction. He could see Sweeney and Cheung though, in the shadows across the alleyway. They were watching the booted feet of the stranger as he paced, apprehensively.

"Who's there?" the villager called warily, his voice thin…almost a hiss.

Sweeney and Cheung pushed further into the shadows to avoid detection. Wicasa watched their eyes as they followed the feet edging nearer.

A pool of light, from the lamp the villager was holding, entered Wicasa's field of vision. He must have been only a few feet from Wicasa's head. The Commander held his breath. The feet scuffed in the dust as the villager stepped closer. He halted momentarily, and then moved on to the far end of the alley.

The boots were now visible to Wicasa.

They were flat with no heels, made of rough hide. They had no modern fastening or laces; only strips of hide, bound in a criss-cross fashion, around the boot, and tied at the knee. What little he could see of the leggings, above the boots, also looked crude, a coarse sack-like material, which must have itched like the devil to wear. The clothing fitted with everything else they had seen since entering the village; old, not in years but centuries.

"What is it?" called a muffled female voice, from inside the cabin.

"I thought I heard prowlers," the male replied, as he turned, heading slowly almost sluggishly, for the warmth of the cabin again. "Must have scared them off," he said gruffly.

"Well come inside, it's getting cold," the female voice chided as the door slammed shut.

Then there was silence and darkness again. All three lay still for a few moments, to be certain the villager had gone.

Wicasa emerged first. "It's clear," he whispered, signalling for them to follow.

Sweeney and Cheung rolled into the alley together. They were on their feet, and following in a second. Dusting themselves off, they rounded the cabin and disappeared into the shadows of the next alleyway.

Moving quickly now, they hurried past the next few rows of cabins, halting as the last alley opened onto the village square; miss named since it was more of a village oval.

About twenty yards at its widest, more than a dozen cabins looked onto the cobbled 'square', their porches all lit by single oil lamps, casting a faint orange glow around the edges of the communal market place. In front of each cabin was a tethering post, only one of which was occupied at this late hour. Four horses were dozing on their feet, their heads bowed, reins securely tied to the post.

The setting moon reflected off the cobbles, and picked out the wide brim of a thatched awning in the centre of the square, which gave shelter to a public water pump and trough. Four wide roads lead onto the square from roughly the four points of the compass. The village was evidently a livestock market town and the square was the focal point of the region's cattle trade.

The cabin, outside which the horses were tethered, was on the far side of the 'square' from where the landing party were hiding, It was larger than the others they had passed and better lit. Through the opaque windows they could detect movement and there was music coming from inside. It looked warm and inviting.

"The local bar?" Sweeney whispered, jokingly rubbing his hands together enthusiastically.

"Let's stay focused," Wicasa replied.

"Just making an observation."

"Shh. Someone's coming." Cheung hissed.

They pressed deeper into the shadows as the tavern door swung wide. A hooded figure, its face hidden in the dark cowl of it's full-length black cloak, emerged. The short, stocky figure pulled its cloak tighter against the bighting, chill of the night. Weaving unsteadily, as it sluggishly descended the steps of the tavern, the figure paused for a long moment to gain its balance, then swung untidily, onto the saddle of the farthest horse, and rode north out of the village.

The square fell silent and empty again, none of the other cabins showed any sign of movement.

Cheung slid closer to Wicasa lowering his voice so that it would not carry. "I don't get any of this," he whispered. "The clothes, buildings even the look of the place, appears almost Middle Ages.

Yet there's a twentieth century battleship, rusting just outside of town."

"I'd say the only explanation we're going to get is in there," Wicasa replied, nodding towards the bar.

"These uniforms'll be a real give a way. We'll stand out like a Kraxian raiding party at a nudist wedding," Sweeney cautioned.

As though right on cue, the sky cracked and lightning again illuminated the alleyways around them. On the far side of the square, beyond the first row of houses, a washing line full of clothes flapped in the increasing breeze.

"Well, I suppose that answers the next question," Wicasa said encouragingly.

Avoiding the pools of light he set of at a crouch towards the washing line. Wattie arrived a few seconds later, followed by Matt.

"Isn't this steeling?" Wattie exclaimed.

"Only if we don't bring them back. We're only borrowing," Sweeney assured him. "Here," he said throwing a heavy, rough, cloak at him. It was similar to the one worn by the figure that had emerged from the tavern: long, black and hooded.

Quickly they pulled on anything that would adequately cover the upper part of their uniforms; the trousers they could possibly get away with, but the brightly coloured collar flashes and insignias of their shirts, would never pass for local.

Wicasa found a long, heavy woollen jacket-like garment. In the half-light it appeared a kind of dirty grey, and smelt vaguely of animal, but it was adequate, covering him from the shoulders to below the knee. He did up the four rough toggles at the front. As he did so, he noticed they were made of gnawed bone; two of which still had some dried meat on them. Either the jacket had just been made, or the owner was not very particular.

Matt grabbed a brown, rough, suede-like tunic that came down almost to his knees. He pulled it on, over his head, quickly tying the belt around his waist.

"Well we should pass for locals, as long as no one recognises their own clothes," Wicasa said encouragingly. "Let's take a look in the tavern."

Wattie crept to the corner of the cabin and searched the square. "Coast's clear."

Wicasa eased past him and led the way. "Wattie, maybe you'd better hang back, and keep watch out here."

"Okay," Cheung replied. Dropping back a little, he pulled the hood of his cloak over his head, as he slipped into the shadows adjacent to the tavern.

"Stay close," Wicasa whispered to Matt. "If we're questioned, we're just travellers heading north, looking for a place to rest for the night."

"We're not a touring rock band, then?"

Mounting the wooden steps to the tavern's porch, Wicasa did his best to stifle the involuntary smile that was threatening to break-out across his face. No matter the situating, Sweeney's irreverent sense of humour was never far away.

Although, to the casual observer, they appeared to be nothing more than tired, weary travellers intent on ale, their military instinct was embedded in them. As they approached the door their eyes swept back and forth, from the door, along the line of cabins, beyond, and back to the square which was to their right; constantly vigilant, always watching for movement.

Sweeney was visually scanning the shadows in the square when the tavern door suddenly opened and a figure emerged. Wicasa had no time to warn Matt. The figure crashed into him, and collapsed at their feet on the wooden porch.

Matt immediately reacted in character. "Sorry friend. Didn't see you there. Too busy thinking about a warm bed...." he said, with a good degree of levity, to defuse the situation.

"That's okay," replied the stranger. "No harm done." His voice, like the villager in the alleyway, sounded thin almost rasping as though he had trouble breathing.

"Here let me help you," said Sweeney offering his hand.

Firmly grasping the stranger's extended hand, Sweeney eyes went wide. The hand was green, covered with tough leathery scales. It had three long, thin fingers and a fourth, even longer, mounted further up the arm, which must have functioned as a thumb. On the ends of each finger were thick yellow, talon-like nails.

As the stranger rolled over to get to his feet,

his eyes locked on Sweeney. All three, Sweeney, Wicasa and the stranger froze. The figure at their feet was reptilian.

As the hood of his cloak fell back, the light from the oil lamp above their heads caught the creature full in the face, reflecting off its leathery, green scales which glistened gold, as though wet. In proportion and build, he was not dissimilar to humans. He had natures required essentials for evolutionary dominance: two arms, which were a little shorter than humans, and two long powerful legs. Its snout was wide and flat, above a wide, lipless mouth, which concealed jaws of razor sharp, dagger-like teeth. Licking at the air with a long, pink, forked tongue, the creature tasting the scent of the figures standing over him.

The whole incident happened so quickly there was little time to take everything in. But as far as Wicasa could tell, given his limited knowledge of palaeontology, the creature at their feet most closely resembled a velociraptor, with several million years of extended evolution. As the reptile's sharp, wide set, yellow eyes darted from Sweeney to Wicasa, their black vertical slits narrowed.

More than three hundred years ago, the human race had discovered warp technology: three hundred years of interstellar space travel in a shrinking galaxy. Discovering new life forms, had prepared Wicasa and Sweeney for life forms other than carbon based, mammals. Life, they had long discovered, could, and had evolved in a myriad of forms, as diverse and colourful as evolutions wide brush strokes could conceive. But they were shocked at what they saw lying at their feet. This was Earth and this creature did not belong here.

They were not nearly as shocked as the villager, though. The prostrate creature, was not just surprised, he was terrified, horrified. His yellow eyes went wide with shock. Kicking his heels at the boardwalk, he scraped and scratched, in an effort to escape these pail-skinned nightmares. Leaping to his feet he screamed.

"Devils!" "Devils!!!"

"Move!" Wicasa roared, grabbing at Sweeney's shoulder, hauling him away.

In unison they leapt from the boardwalk, hitting the cobblestones at a sprint, before the creature had the chance to scream a third time.

"Wattie!" Sweeney called as they sped passed the alleyway they had left him hiding in.

As they rounded the thatched awning in the centre of the square Wicasa slipped on the damp cobbles. His right foot skidded from under him and he hit the ground scrambling.

"Devils, devils!!!" The scream went up again behind them, splitting the still night air.

Bringing up the rear, Wattie grabbed at Wicasa. In one single movement without slowing, he hauled the Commander to his feet while at the same time vaulting over his stricken comrade, making good their escape. Finding his feet again Wicasa glanced back. The door of the tavern burst open and a crowd of villagers jostled in confusion, onto the porch to find out what the commotion was.

The terrified reptile, still shaken, pointed after the fleeing landing party. As he did his eyes rolled back into their sockets, tilting his head back, he opened his mouth wide. This time there was no frightened scream. He loosed a primal wail, a loud rattle, which pounded the air, like a hollow log being drummed in some far off glen. The sound pulsed through the chill air, shaking Wicasa to his bones. As he turned to follow Sweeney and Cheung into the alleyway, the sound was multiplied and amplified as the other villagers echoed the primeval warning-call.

The porch was soon crowded; more reptiles joined the commotion spilling out from the tavern and the surrounding cabins.

"Devils. Demons!" screamed a villager. "Demons are amongst us. They are returned!"

Another villager grabbed him by the shoulders, focusing his hysteria. "What do you mean demons? What did they look like?" he hissed, flickering his forked tongue.

"Pale," he stammered, still shaken. "Pale, like the face of the moon. Smooth, pink faces." He looked around the crowd. "Demons!" he screamed. "Like in the old prophecies," he screamed again. "Devils are returned."

As one, the rabble rejoined the primeval call, amplifying it till the cacophony was almost deafening. Adding to it, a high-pitched shrill, almost a whine coupled with the rattle, lifting it... giving it a new, more terrifying inflection. There was danger in the renewed call. This was a call to hunt.

Wicasa ploughed into the alleyway a few seconds behind Sweeney and Cheung. All three ripped off their borrowed garments, throwing them to the ground as they fled. They had been discovered, and would face their fate as Alliance Fleet officers, not as spies.

Lights came on in windows all around them. Doors banged opened. The commotion was reaching fever pitch. They had to move and move quickly.

"What's going on out there?" a voice called from the door they had just bolted past.

A large reptile, almost seven feet tall, stepped into the alley behind them. The towering lizard was broad, like an engine block across the chest with powerful crushing arms, and the two headed axe he was welding in his clawed hands added even more inches to his already impressive height.

"Move!" Wicasa urged, as he thumped his Comm-bracelet.

CHAPTER 8

"There would appear to be increased activity in the vicinity of the landing party, Captain," Jevak announced, his unhurried even tone betraying a slight sense of urgency.

"See if you can raise them," Lockhart replied. "They've been out of touch too long anyway."

Before Jevak could press the relevant pad on his console, the Comm system crackled to life.

"Wicasa …… eavour!." The First Officer's voice hissed and faded; distorted and fragmented.

"The storm over the settlement is disrupting communications," Jevak informed the Captain.

"Wicasa," Lockhart said stepping urgently to Jevak's science station. "What's going on down there?"

"………eleport….gent …." Wicasa's voice crackled through the bridge speakers. There was alarm and urgency in his voice.

Lockhart glanced at Jevak hoping for some good news. He had none to offer. "Teleports are still off line," he soberly informed her.

"Wicasa, teleports are still down," Lockhart shouted at the Comm. "What's happening?"

"....pinned down... rept..... urgent...."

A look of helpless confusion passed between Lockhart and her science officer.

"Wicasa!" Lockhart shouted again. "You're breaking-up. Please repeat!"

The Comm speakers crackled again. Wicasa's voice was virtually inaudible; lost in white noise. Then the transmission ended abruptly. Jevak hastily made adjustments to the comm system but was unable to re-establish contact. The Captain shook her head. There was nothing they could do to help the landing party; they were on their own down there for the time being.

Lockhart sighed helplessly. "Tell Cosique that...."

"Captain!" shouted Ensign Lawrence, staring anxiously at the main-screen.

Nicolle turned in time to see three Kraxian "battle beasts", de-cloaking at warp speed in attack formation, one hundred thousand kilometres to port.

Recently in the on going war against the Macaitians, Kraxa and the Alliance had all but cemented their uneasy accord, though they had been age-old enemies. This made the Kraxians virtually allies, but never quite friends. Lockhart, though, had come through the academy when Kraxa was still considered a simmering threat. No matter how close their two civilisations had become, the sudden appearance of three battle cruisers, de-cloaking in attack mode, still made her react defensively. She instinctively glanced back at Jevak although she already knew they had no shields, lasers or Warp-drive, but she glanced back anyway. He shook his head. Although they did have induction-drive and ion torpedoes they were no match for the firepower now facing them on their port bow.

"Lawrence!" Lockhart called, indicating towards Sweeney's vacant chair.

The young Ensign sprinted to the console, taking control of the helm. Nicolle strode briskly down to the main deck; fists planted firmly on her hips, her eyes narrowed, never leaving the screen.

"Report," she demanded.

"They are holding position at one hundred thousand, kilometres," Jevak replied. "We have been scanned, but as yet they have made no attempt to hail us, or to power-up weapons," he added, with a note of optimism.

It was galactic protocol, even between non-allies, to hail approaching vessels, signalling identity, co-ordinates, and intentions. This helped foster confidence in the security of space, and prevent accidental firefights due to miss-interpretation of purpose. The protocol was usually observed: it was being ignored at the moment. Which made Nicolle even more wary of their sometime ally. Lockhart paced to the rear of Lawrence's chair at helm control, deliberating over their options.

"Take us directly above the magnetic north-pole," she eventually ordered. "Maintain this altitude."

Without shields Endeavour was virtually defenceless. Placing the ship within Earth's magnetic field would confuse any attackers automatic targeting system, requiring them to target manually, and, with luck, possibly miss. Nicolle considered the move to be defensive, without being confrontational. She hoped the Kraxians would appreciate this.

Lawrence tapped her fingers lightly over the console. Endeavour responded immediately and smoothly, sliding gently, silently, north over the white ice caps one thousand kilometres below.

As she rotated Endeavour, bringing her round to face their assailants head-on deftly placing the Sun directly behind them, Lawrence noticed an anomalous reading on her console. Magnetic north had seemingly shifted, it was not where it should be. It was one point three degrees south east of its recorded position.

Magnetic north shifts slowly over long eons: hundreds of thousands of years. Endeavour had only been away a mere six years. A shift of that magnitude in that short time was inconceivable. Ensign Lawrence was about to inform the Captain when Jevak interrupted her.

"They are powering weapons, Captain!" He exclaimed.

"Hail them."

"Responding."

"On screen."

The screen shifted. Replacing the tranquil

scene of their slowly rotating blue home, was a wide view of the bridge of the Kraxian lead ship. Though Nicolle had never been aboard any Kraxian vessel, it appeared familiar; she had seen plenty via countless view-screens. It looked hostile and oppressive. Vapour leaked from exposed power conduits at various locations around the Spartan deck. Kraxians regarded comforts as a weakness. They were a proud warrior race and endured... no, relished their stark discomfort, as a mark of strength.

The commander was seated in his unpadded chair in the centre of the bridge. He was dressed in the customary Kraxian battledress; bright metal body armour perched high across his wide shoulders, covering black leather tunic and leggings. A chain-link vest-like garment hung loosely from his shoulders covering but not hiding his impressive muscular frame. Completing the intimidating appearance, his long black hair hung loose and un-kept falling about his shoulders. It was braided at the temples to accentuate his wide parting, not for any attempt at flamboyance but to proudly displaying both sets of horns... the horns of a warrior.

Kraxians are a formidable sight. If their dark green skin and red eyes were not intimidating enough their horns certainly got your attention. All Kraxians, even the females, though theirs are smaller, have one set of horns; short, thick, stubby and grey bony growths, high on their enlarged foreheads. Some of the males though have a second pair, lower on the forehead, just above their large and prominent eyebrows. Depending on how alpha the male is, and how testosterone fuelled his temper is, these second horns can be small grey mounds, or huge, almost as large as their primary horns. The Commander had secondary horns as large as his primary. He would have to be handled with kid gloves.

The Commander slid forward grasping tightly at the arms of his comfortless chair, his brow furrowed, almost knotting under his very enlarged lower horns, as he scrutinized Nicolle.

"I am Captain Nicolle Lockhart and this is the Alliance starship Endeavour," she pronounced assertively.

It was the only way to speak to Kraxians; they appreciated defiance over politeness. "Would you care to explain your unescorted presence in Alliance space?" She continued, making a show of swaggering boldly to the centre of the bridge her arms crossed defiantly. "The Kraxian imperial council has, as far as I know, yet to ratify any formal accord with the Alliance, and that therefore still requires you to be accompanied while in Alliance space."

For a brief moment the Kraxian Commander, looked puzzled. He shot a withering look to either side of his bridge, presumably at his subordinates, and then reacted.

"Krat yo tarr greakk storratan!" he growled, punching ferociously at the arm of his chair "Vatt-at-arr grougt!"

Lockhart backed slowly away from the screen. Glancing back towards Jevak, more in hope than expectation, she already knew the answer to her unasked question. The universal translator was way down the list of priorities for repair. Given that they had not anticipated requiring it, it was almost off the list altogether. With her back to the screen, she drew her fingers across her throat in a slicing fashion, indicating that Jevak should cut the audio on their transmission.

"How much Kraxian do you know?" she whispered, even though they could not be heard.

"Not enough to safely deflate a hostile situation, Captain," he replied earnestly, acknowledging the gravity of their situation.

"You and me both," Nicolle said looking hopefully at Lawrence, who shrugged and shook her head.

Pacing the bridge, Nicolle had to think quickly... "Cosique!" she almost shouted. "Get Cosique up here, now."

Jevak acknowledged with a nod, and hailed the engine room.

Nicolle paced a little more, mindful that she was probably irritating the Commander more than was advisable by putting him on 'hold'. She did not want to aggravate the situation more than she had to, but she had no alternative. Communication was out of the question.

"Any change in their status?"

"None," Jevak replied. "Still holding at twenty-five hundred kilometres."

Turning again to the screen Nicolle indicated

to resume audio.

"Ko chi, rakk," she growled, gutturally, from the back of her throat. Nicolle hoped she had pronounced it correctly. The inflections in the voice were paramount in Kraxian. The wrong emphases anywhere could change the meaning of any word. She hoped that what she had said was that they were on a peaceful mission, which was the best she could come up with.

The Kraxian Commander again looked confused, but this time there was anger bubbling near the surface of that confusion.

"Krat yo tarr greakk, storratan!" he snarled punching the air with both fists. He paused for almost a heartbeat then almost leapt at the screen snarling. "Krat yo tarr greakk, storratan!"

Nicolle held up both hands, palms forward in a vain attempt to calm the situation. She knew her actions were probably doing little more than annoying her opposite number, her body language could easily be construed as fear. But she could do little more, given their inability to communicate and the Kraxian's natural fondness for confrontation.

The lift door swished open behind her, Nicolle turned, to see Cosique step onto the bridge.

"Than goodness," she said, relieved that she could at least gain control of the situation again. "We seem to be having a little communication failure. Universal translators are off-line, and our Kraxian friends could be getting twitchy trigger fingers."

"Krat yo tarr, storratan. Vert yataraa!" the Commander growled again.

"He's demanding we identify ourselves," Cosique said anxiously. "Now, or he'll open fire."

Lockhart nodded. "You can let him know where we've been for the past six years, and how we managed to get back. Maybe that'll gain a little his limited sympathy." She turned her back to the screen, ensuring their conversation could not be observed. "But don't be too forth-coming on the damage we've sustained." She was cautiously guarded where Kraxians were concerned. "They've already scanned us, and they probably know that we're disabled, but let's play our cards close to our chest for now."

Cosique straightened; drawing a deep breath she locked eyes with the Kraxian Commander.

As the exchange began, Lockhart stepped to the side, giving her chief engineer room to play her hand. She watched silently as Cosique explained their situation.

The Commander at first listened intently, then rose to his feet, pacing his bridge as he bristle and growled at Cosique in what was obviously becoming a heated argument. The exchange, which had started out sounding aggressive and guttural, became more animated and intense.

It was difficult to tell when Kraxian were angry, since they always sounded that way. An idle thought passed un-bid through Nicolle's mind.

How strange Kraxian love songs must sound, she thought. It must be difficult to tell if a suitor wanted to steal you heart, or eat it.

Cosique seethed with fury. "He just called me a liar," she snarled. "He's accusing us of being Macaitian spies."

"What's he talking about, we're Alliance for God sake," Lockhart protested. "How can he possibly think that?"

"Captain. He says he says there is no Alliance."

The Captain caught her breath. In a heartbeat the slender, forlorn hope that there could still be some reasonable explanation for the lack of communication with Alliance Fleet was suddenly wrenched from her. Any hope, no matter how small, she had harboured was now dead. The Kraxian's confirmation that the Alliance had fallen hit her like a body blow.

"Ask him what happened," she urged. She was desperate for an answer to this confounding enigma that had plagued them since their return. "How was the Alliance defeated? What's happened to the fleet?"

Endeavour's chief engineer again locked horns with the Commander. This time the altercation started with snarling and shouting and intensified. Cosique pounded the rail, against which she was standing, in frustration; the discussion was not going well.

"We are an Alliance starship," Cosique screamed in English, through exasperation. "Why wont you listen, for God sake! What is this nonsense?" she growled hammering the rail with both fists.

"Cosique!" Lockhart interrupted.

She had to intervene; the dialogue was becoming a full-blown argument, and Cosique was losing control. Enraged Kraxians on either bridge, were the last thing any of them needed.

"Try to keep this under control," Lockhart urged, keeping her voice to a whisper.

"I'm trying to, Captain, but none of what he is saying makes any sense. He insists there is no Alliance." Cosique looked puzzled as she continued. "Not that the Alliance was destroyed, but that he's never heard of any Alliance. He claims that this is a barren region of space and that it is in dispute, and that unless we surrender immediately he will open fire."

An anxious call came from the science station, behind them. "They are closing on us, Captain."

"Cut transmission. Cosique get back down to engineering. We need warp drive and lasers... yesterday."

"Yes ma'am, we're almost there."

"Lawrence, on my mark drop us down to the edge of the atmosphere."

"Understood."

"Jevak, prepare ion torpedoes," Lockhart said, hastily making her way to her command chair. "I want three ready for immediate firing, and half a dozen available for manual deployment."

"Torpedoes ready," he replied.

Hurriedly seating herself in her command chair she pressed several buttons, readying her own tactical read-out on the arm of the chair. "Screen on," she directed.

The three Kraxian 'battle beasts' wheeled slowly in unison, above the gentle curve of the cloud covered, north Atlantic, banking to port as they did so.

"Steady Ensign," Lockhart encouraged the young inexperienced officer.

Even for Matt Sweeney, joining battle was always nerve wracking. His vast experience, and general bravado, just made it look effortless. But for Ensign Lawrence this was all completely new and she was scared, very scared. She had taken the helm many times before, but piloting the ship under fire was terrifying. The ship and all of her crewmates lives were in her hands; this was almost overwhelming.

For a brief second Lockhart tore her eyes from the screen, glancing at Lawrence. Like Wattie, the young ensign had joined Endeavour straight from The Academy. She had spent most of her six years aboard the starship in engineering, and was untested in front-line battle. But with so many of the crew engaged in repair teams, Nicolle had little option. She needed someone to fly the ship, and Elizabeth Lawrence, young and frightened as she was, was a more than capable helmsman; she would have to cut her teeth at some time.

"Just wait for my command, Ensign," Lockhart encouraged, calmly.

With out warning, the 'battle beast' to the left broke formation and accelerated, closing the distance to Endeavour in an istant.

"Now!" Lockhart shouted.

Lawrence stabbed at her console.

Instantly Endeavour responded. Her nose dropped and she plummeted, scraping the edge of Earth's upper atmosphere.

"Hard to starboard!" Lockhart roared.

The Kraxian spit a long burst of laser fire. Unable to target automatically because of the Earth's magnetic field, they attempted to 'walk' their lasers onto Endeavour.

Lockhart's gambit had paid-off. She had turned Endeavour just in time. The darts of burning green light shot high and wide, missing the port section by a mere twenty metres.

"Course 184 mark 3, ensign; scrape the edge of the atmosphere," Lockhart called urgently.

Remarkably manoeuvrable considering its immense bulk and lack of propulsion, Lawrence pivoted Endeavour nimbly through one hundred and eighty degrees, and dropped her south away from the Sun, into the planet's shadow. Acknowledging the Captain's orders the Ensign held Endeavour tight to the upper atmosphere, ploughing a shallow furrow. The ship's hull began to glow red as it scraped Earth's life giving, gas envelope, burning dangerously hot, trialling a glowing ionised tail in its wake.

Waiting a few seconds until the manoeuvre had commenced, Lockhart bellowed. "Now Jevak, drop four torpedoes in a linear configuration."

Dropping the weapons manually, rather than firing them, meant they would not be displayed on the Kraxian's threat indicators; the 'battle beasts' would be unaware of them until too late.

Four, red glowing orbs smoothly and swiftly exited Endeavour's battered hull, just above the for' ad deflector shield emitters, spreading out to form a straight line high above Southern Alaska.

Leaving the weapons drifting in her wake, Endeavour continued to descend over the far side of The Earth, keeping out of visual contact with the Kraxians. South-southwest, over Tibet, China, New Guinea, and Western Australia she came to rest just short of the South Pole, over the Antarctic coastline.

"Hold position."

As Lockhart had expected, the Kraxian lead vessel gave chase. It crested the North Pole, twisting as it dove south over Canada, heading southwest, following the obvious but all too inviting tail of glowing gas, straight into the path of the waiting torpedoes.

Too late their Commander saw the danger.

He stood screaming an oath of defiant rage, his veins bulging in his neck, as their starboard nacelle clipped one of the torpedoes. It exploded in a ball of blinding white light, debris ripping into the hull of his ship. The ship's twisting momentum sent what remained of the smashed vessel spinning into the atmosphere where it died burning.

The unseen explosion registered on the sensors of the two remaining vessels still beyond the curve of the planet. They split-up diverging port and starboard and circled around the Earth at its equator, in a now urgent attempt to locate their quarry. But Endeavour had made its self virtually invisible to their instruments, hidden within the magnetic field at the South Pole.

Both Kraxian vessels circled passed each other over the southern tip of India. From there they separated, one spiralling north and the other south, in a sweeping search pattern. As the vessel covering the northern hemisphere passed over debris and the remaining three torpedoes, deposited by Endeavour, it removed the hazard with a burst of laser fire.

"Our remaining torpedoes have just been neutralized, Captain," reported Jevak.

"It was a one shot plan, Jevak," Lockhart said with resigned satisfaction; the numbers were a little more manageable now. She perched forward in her chair, right up to the edge; she was working on adrenaline and nerves now. The crew were depending on her, and with no shields and minimal weapons she had no margin for error.

"Let's take this fight to them," she grinned. "Bring us round to course 117 mark 3."

"Laid in Captain," replied Lawrence tensely.

"Where are the other two?" Lockhart asked without turning to Jevak.

"They are both above us. One in a spiral search pattern, north. The other spiralling south, towards us."

"Let me know the second they both cross on to the night side," she instructed.

*   *   *   *   *

Wicasa threw himself at the wall. At the last moment he broke his fall by slamming his forearms on to it, just as an arrow sang past him, inches from the back of his head. It embedding its self, with a splintering thud, in to the doorframe of a house at the far end if the alleyway.

The baying mob had harried and hunted them through every street, alley and even one or two houses in the village; and they were hard on their heels again. They had been constantly running and dodging for more than fifteen minutes now, and were fast running out of options and breath. The three of them, fit as they were, where exhausted and had not been able to find an escape route out of the village. At almost every turn they found their way barred. The entire population of the village was on the streets, baying for blood, hunting them down. The reptiles had the scent of the kill and their quarry was cornered.

Though the dawn had already started to

lighten the sky overhead, it was not so bright that Sweeney could not make out the glow of burning torches from adjacent streets casting an orange hallow against the murky sky.

"This is hopeless," he heaved, breathlessly. "They'll have us surrounded soon. We've got to get out of here,"

The air sang as two flaming arrows, from either end of the alley, burned past Wattie a few inches in from his face. They exploded into the wall beside him. Cheung threw himself against the opposite building, seeking cover.

"I though you said soon?" he shouted at Sweeney, still managing to find sarcasm in a desperate situation.

Dropping to his knees, Wicasa, searched the under floor spaces of the houses on either side of them. He could see the streets beyond; they were crowded. Hundreds of booted feet jostled back and forth, searching for them, hounding them. The mob was screaming, becoming hysterical. The landing party were running out of time and places to hide and Wicasa knew it. He quickly weighed up their options. With nowhere else to run it was time to make a stand.

"Weapons set to stun," he ordered, with resigned acceptance, unclipping his hand-laser from his belt.

This simple recognisance mission was deteriorating into a conflict they really did not need, and Wicasa had hoped to avoid. Wattie looked at him questioningly. They all knew their orders had been to get in and out quickly and quietly. And that they were to strictly observe the Code of 'none interference'; using lasers on axe-wielding primitives was without doubt 'interference'.

"We've no Option," Wicasa roared in his defence. "This alley's as defendable as anywhere else we've found. Find some cover."

A battleaxe sliced the air above them, spinning end over end above their heads, it missed by mere inches, embedding in the side-door of the large building to their right.

Sweeney returned fire, but missed. The bright thread of concentrated blue light hit wide of its target, scorching the wooden wall of the building at the end of the alley.

The swarm of Reptiles, packed into the far end of the alley fell instantly silent, and then began backing away in mortal fear. This was some kind of witchcraft, evil. These creatures could lose lightning bolts from their hands.

"Surprise isn't going to keep them back forever," Cheung warned, as he took aim at the opposite end of the alley.

Wattie fired into the thick of the baying crowd. One reptile collapsed, hitting the dirt in a cloud of dust. His neighbour snarled with rage as he leapt to his aid. Kneeling beside his fallen comrade he screamed. "He's alive! He's alive! Their witchcraft has no power over us. Burn them. Burn them!"

"They're wise to us!" Wattie called to the

others.

A bright flame streaked the cold air, arching down the alley. Thud. The burning arrow hit Wattie square in the back, just above the heart. He dropped like a stone.

Wicasa hit the ground beside him. "Wattie. Wattie!" He hollered, dousing the flames with fistfuls of dirt.

Sweeney threw himself to the ground beside them, giving covering fire down both sides of the alley.

"He's still alive!" Wicasa shouted, over the noise of the baying hoards now pressing on them from both ends of the alleyway. Desperately looking about, he motioned towards a closed door a few feet away. "We need to get cover. Quickly get him inside."

As one, they grabbed an arm each, hauling their unconscious friend to his feet. Dragging him across the alley, they held off further attacks with covering laser fire in both directions, dropping a few of the snarling reptiles, to slow the mob down. Scrambling up the steps of the side entrance to the large building, they launched themselves at its heavily bolted door. It remained fast.

Two more arrows slammed into the doorframe to their left. Flames instantly caught hold, licked up the side of the dry wooden wall. Again they hurled themselves at the door, whilst continuing to drop reptiles with laser fire. The door gave a little. A third time and the door yielded, splitting the frame as they crashed to the floor inside.

Quickly Sweeney leapt to his feet. Stumbling backwards he found a long wooden bench, and jammed it against the splintered door, shutting it behind them. Wicasa meanwhile dragged Cheung further into the dark, away from the howling mob outside. Backing slowly away from the door Sweeney kept his hand laser levelled at it, waiting for the crash of splintering wood, as the villagers piled through the door and rushed them. He waited, and waited, but it never came.

It fell silent outside.

*   *   *   *   *

Ensign Lawrence had been holding her breath, her fingers poised above the consol touch pad for what had seemed an age. Her hands had begun to tremble with the stress. At last the Captain gave the word.

"Now Ensign!" Lockhart roared. "Full induction power, thrusters, everything we've got."

Endeavour screamed, at nearly three-quarters light speed, from her hiding place at the South Pole, arcing directly towards the Sun.

"Stay on this heading," Lockhart instructed Lawrence, while looking back towards Jevak, waiting anxiously for his next report.

A few moments passed, enough to put nearly five hundred thousand kilometres between them and the Kraxians, before the report came.

"We have been detected, Captain. They are in pursuit," Jevak confirmed

"All stop!" Bellowed Lockhart, as she leapt to her feet. "Come about."

Endeavour spun on a dime. Her bent and bruised hull groaned and protested as the G-forces she was pulling against almost twisted her beyond her limits. Jevak and Lawrence held tight to their consoles as the ship rotated violently and suddenly through one hundred and eighty degrees. Lockhart held tight to her chair gripping the arms to keep from being thrown across the bridge. Abruptly the G-forces subsided as Endeavour stabilised. Facing back in the direction they had come, the Sun now directly aft of them.

Though the Kraxian 'beasts' could detect Endeavour, as they burst from the far side of the Earth, pinpointing her was impossible. This close to any star their instruments were un-reliable. The solar wind coming directly at them: massive bursts of broad-spectrum radiation and electro-magnetic pulses, almost off the scale of their instruments, were blurring everything between them and their target.

Nicolle knew she had little more than a heart beat before they reacted, and split either above and below Endeavour, or to port and starboard, giving them a clear line of sight, with no Sun blinding their instruments. She took a chance that they would split left and right.

"Hard to port!" She bellowed. "Jevak, fire torpedoes to starboard, dispersal pattern Lockhart Delta!"

Whether it was her years of experience; the finest training in the Galaxy at Alliance Fleet Academy, or more likely just sheer luck, mercifully she had guessed correctly. The 'battle beasts' reacted just as Nicolle had hoped. Breaking from their hurried pursuit, they split to port and starboard. Shifting Endeavour's position had kept the Sun directly behind the ship in relation to the vessel currently tearing across their port bow, continuing to blind it. Leaving Nicolle to deal with the ship on their starboard side.

The vessel to starboard saw the torpedoes coming out of the Sun directly at them, but not quickly enough. It veered sharply to port and climbed, banking wildly, but the first of the torpedoes found its mark. The explosion tore through its main hull, destroying seven decks aft of engineering. It was wounded but it was still dangerous.

The other Kraxian ship saw the torpedoes launch, and targeted the launch co-ordinates.

Anticipating this Lockhart banked and dropped, rolling them beneath the port ship, as its laser fire sliced past Endeavour's upturned belly.

"Fire!" Lockhart roared.

The Commander of the second ship was a better warrior than she had thought, having fired he banked his ship to starboard, between Endeavour and his wounded comrade.

Endeavours second volley of torpedoes

missed completely.

Both Beasts, even the damaged one, were more manoeuvrable than Endeavour, but only because of her present condition. Rallying, they come round again, straight at Endeavour, searing the blackness with volley after volley of blinding green laser fire.

"Fire torpedoes, wide dispersal."

Both Kraxian vessels dropped, dodging the on-coming weapons.

"Ensign, take us back in, towards Earth!" Lockhart roared. "Swing port to starboard around the Moon. We'll hit them straight-on again."

Endeavour leapt toward the blue planet in the distance. The Kraxians reacted quickly; turning to give chase, losing lasers in Endeavour's wake.

"They are gaining on us, Captain. They will be on top of us in approximately one minute. We are one minute-twenty eight seconds from the Moon," Jevak said, keeping her tactically informed.

"Take evasive action," Lockhart instructed, hoping that Lawrence might manage to shake their pursuers long enough for them to reach cover.

"Captain," Jevak interrupted again. "Another ship is approaching, at extremely high warp."

"Can you identify it?"

"It is not Kraxian," he said shaking his head. "Other than that I am unable to determine its origins. I cannot be certain. It has some familiar characteristics, but…." he hesitated. "They are also powering weapons!"

The new arrival cut across Endeavours bow loosing a volley of lasers at the wounded Kraxian 'beast'. Completely destroying it with its first burst. The blast rocked Endeavour, throwing Nicolle back into her chair.

"Who ever they are, they seem to be friendly," she said, thankfully.

Swinging hard to port the unidentified ship turned to target the remaining Kraxian vessel, too late though. The 'battle beast' cloaked, bending starlight around it, as it disappeared.

Having luckily or miraculously outrun and outwitted three Kraxian 'battle beasts', Lockhart and her crew once again found themselves motionless, in orbit above their home, staring down the laser barrels of an unknown ally, or possibly another adversary.

"We are being hailed," Jevak announced. Then paused while he studied the received communication. Looking up from his console, his usually impassive face wore a look of utter confusion. "Captain," he said, his voice betraying his bewilderment. "They are claiming to be the Vaurillian security vessel 'Sorn'."

Lawrence looked to the Captain. Their faces both betraying the same questions Jevak was asking himself. What was a Vaurillian Security Vessel, why was it not Alliance? And why was it named after a long dead Vaurillian ship's Commander? Even if that Commander had instigated First Contact.

"They are communicating again, Captain,"

Jevak said.

"On screen."

As the view-screen shifted, Lockhart got to her feet, stepping closer. "Unidentified vessel," she said, a little cautiously this time, wary that they may have jumped out of the frying pan and into a fire. "You have our sincere gratitude."

The view screen shifted again to show the bridge of the new arrival.

Nicolle staggered, but she caught herself before falling. The shock and disbelief almost knocked her backwards into her command chair. Her eyes grew wide with astonishment. What the hell was going on here? She thought.

Ensign Lawrence gasped, loudly enough to be heard by Jevak at the rear of the bridge. Simultaneously, she and the Captain both shot a disbelieving look towards the science station, at an equally startled Jevak: although the Lieutenant being Vaurillian did his best to retain his composure.

Nicolle stepped closer to the screen. Looking back and forth between Jevak and the screen, her mind raced with confusion and uncertainty.

The Captain of the new arrival stepped up to his own screen. "I am Commander Jevak of the Vaurillian Security vessel, Sorn," he announced. "Please identify yourself."

Lockhart's disbelief was complete. Her mind raced with questions, a torrent of confusion, doubt, and answers that did not make sense, as she tried to make sense of this latest addition to the impossible conundrum they were living. This, on the screen, was Jevak, in every respect, in every detail, his voice, his face. It was Jevak, her own science officer, looking back at her from beyond their view screen, from another vessel.

*   *   *   *   *

Breathing heavily; a combination of fear and exertion, Sweeney backed further into the room, away from the barricaded door. He levelled his laser at chest height and waited, gulping in air. He'd expected at any second the already broken door to suddenly shatter, and hundreds of slashing, clawing reptilian villagers to surge through it and swarm over them. But that still had not happened. After almost a minute he realised that, for whatever reason they were not coming; they had chosen not to press their advantage and storm the door. As his breathing relaxed he could hear them milling back and forth outside, hissing and whispering. He could see their burning torches through a crack in the broken frame of the door; dozens of them. Gathering, waiting, but still they did not come.

Turning, he frantically searched the darkness. Squinting blindly into the dark corners, he staggered over the uneven wooden floor. A few yards behind him he eventually stumbled into Wicasa, kneeling over Wattie's motionless body.

The room they had inadvertently stumbled into was large. If Matt's echoing footsteps were a reliable indication, then the room was vast, and pretty much empty. It was old too, the heavy, still air was stale. It smelt musty, as though the room were used infrequently... if at all. The walls were lost somewhere in the imposing darkness. The only indication of how far away they were, were the three tall, narrow, slit windows down either side of the blackness which filtered shafts of dim orange light; the torch light from outside.

Matt switched on the flashlight, still strapped to his right forearm. He directed it around the room, checking for danger. The beam found the distant walls. The room was indeed vast. It was about forty, maybe fifty feet long, by thirty wide. On either side of them were two-dozen or so rows of simple wooden benches, arranged in parallel, each a few feet behind the other, in a classroom like fashion.

Looking beyond Wicasa Matt's attention was suddenly caught by something at the far end of the immense hall. Stepping past the Commander he focussed his torch beam above them, up into the darkness. There was no ceiling above them. The room extended up to the eaves of the high vaulted roof.

Matt caught his breath. His eyes went wide with confusion and shock.

High on the far wall was the carved wooden figure of a reptile, nailed to a wooden cross.

CHAPTER 9

Wicasa wished he had a medical palm-corder. He had no idea how badly injured Wattie was, though from what he could see, it was hard to imagine worse. The Ensign's shirt was already soaked with blood and a dark pool was spreading across the floor beneath him. It looked like he had lost about a pint already and was losing more, fast. From blood loss alone, he could tell Cheung would not last long.

The arrow, which had almost past right through him, was still protruding about three inches out of his back, just below his left shoulder blade, and about four inches out of his chest. From its position Wicasa could only guess how close it had come to his heart. It had punctured his left lung though, he was sure of that. Wattie's breathing was becoming erratic and shallow. Although unconscious he was in distress, struggling to catch a breath, blood frothing from his mouth. It wasn't hard to tell that his lungs were filling; he was drowning in his own blood.

Tapping his comm-bracelet, Wicasa again attempted to contact the ship. The bracelet chirped in response, but only to emit static. They were still on their own. They desperately needed to get Wattie back to the ship as quickly as possible. But for the time being, the best he could hope to do was to keep him from dying.

Quickly turning Wattie on to his side, Wicasa firmly grasped both ends of the arrow, as close to the Ensign's rib-cage as he could. Sharply yanking the tip downwards, he snapped the head off the arrow. Wattie stiffened in response, groaning and coughing pitifully, but remained unconscious. Wicasa then pulled the remainder of the three-foot arrow out of the ensign's back; his hands dripping with blood.

"Matt!" he called, looking up to find Sweeney staring up at the cross. "See what you can find to stem the bleeding!"

"What the hell is this?" Sweeney gasped, oblivious to Wicasa's concern for Wattie.

"Matt!" Wicasa shouted again, becoming impatient.

Matt remained rooted to the spot, his eyes wide, staring at this perverse symbol. Scrambling to his feet, Wicasa grabbed him by the shoulder, spinning him away from the carving.

"Pull yourself together Lieutenant!" he roared, pushing Sweeney back towards Wattie's fallen body. "Cheung's dying, now do your job and try to act like a Alliance Fleet officer!"

Sweeney reluctantly dragged his incredulous stare from the offensive carving, hanging over them. He crouched at Wattie's side; whether it was a conscious act or not, getting on his knees beneath that graven image was something he could not find within him. Quickly he assessed his friends' condition. Seeing the amount of blood he had already lost he grabbed at Wattie's tunic sleeve and with one single tug, ripped it off, bundling the material firmly against the wound in his chest.

"What the hell is this?" Matt asked, bewildered.

Wicasa knelt opposite him tearing his own sleeve off and placing it against the wound in Wattie's back. The Commander's Native American ancestry had no names for their Gods, or recognised physical representation of any deity. But that did not prevent him from sympathising with Matt's discomfort with the warped icon looking down on them.

"What the hell has happened to us?" Matt asked again, staring blankly at the dark puddle growing under Wattie.

Wicasa drew a deep breath, readying himself to voice what they all already knew, but had shied away from admitting, even to themselves.

"I don't know what's happened to us, or where we are, but this isn't home... At least it's not our home. It's Earth. But it's not the Earth we left, or the one we're trying to get back to.... Our species doesn't exist on this World, and by the looks of things possibly never has. Why this Earth has taken a different evolutionary path from our own I don't know, but it has. Humans don't exist here," he said relaxing the pressure a little on the exit wound.

"So ask yourself, why then would God send his son in any other form than that of the planets inhabitants. We're not here so why should the Son of God look like us. All this means is that whether we humans exist or not, God does... And there's the proof," he said nodding up at the carving.

Sweeney diverted his eyes to the floor. He was embarrassed. He had just made the same arrogant assumption that centuries of less enlightened zealots had also made; not that man was made in God's image, but that God looked like man, and a particular race of man at that.

As a result of that unenlightened arrogance, for nearly three thousand years Earth, had suffered from a cancer; religious intolerance and bigotry, to such an extent that through those dark centuries, more people had died of organised religion than had died of all of the plagues and viruses' humanity had ever come in contact with. It was only with the breakdown of old national boundaries after the World's economic collapse and the realisation that we, as a species had to find ways to work together, rather than find reasons to divide, that acceptance and an eventual embracing our differences, brought us together as a stronger, single inhabitant of our planet.

Sweeney had just displayed that same dangerous, religious intolerance his ancestors nurtured so dearly. Deeming his image of God, to be the one true image. The thought of another species usurping his physical representation of God, especially here, on Earth, even if it was not his Earth, was an unspeakable blasphemy.

What Matt, in his shock, had failed to come to terms with, was that if this were not his Earth why then, would there be anything other than a lizard hanging from the crucifix above them. Recognising this did not lessen the emotional shock to Sweeney's collective human ego: God exists, and it's not important to the Universe that we do.

Matt Sweeney had just had a rude awakening.

Glancing at Wattie's unconscious figure on the floor brought him back to his senses.

"This isn't working," he said squeezing the blood from the saturated piece of uniform he was pressing to Wattie's chest.

"Take a look around. See if you can find something to stem the bleeding," Wicasa replied, getting more concerned for Cheung's life.

Sweeney quickly scoured the vast room, while Wicasa placed the heels of his hands firmly against both sides of the wound in Wattie's chest in an effort to slow the blood loss.

As he knelt beside Wattie's prone figure, Wicasa's eyes were again drawn inexorably to the carved figure above him. Suddenly he felt very lost. On the opposite side of the Galaxy they had been closer to home than they were now.

* * * * *

"Explain your presence here!" Commander Jevak demanded. "This sector is disputed territory. You have no authorization to be here."

He had an imposing air about him, in the same fashion Lockhart adopted when confronting a potential opponent: just threatening enough without being confrontational. Striding resolutely to the centre of his bridge, he made it known, by his demeanour alone, that he meant business, and that there was a line he would not allow to be crossed. He folded his arms tightly across his chest, and lowered his gaze, his eyes glowering in a manner and bearing that Nicolle could never have imagined her Lieutenant adopting.

Commander Jevak looked in every respect identical to the Alliance Fleet officer behind her at the science station, the same height, build, grey skin colouring, and the same very pale blue eyes. They were identical, but only in the way that twins are. Where they differed was in their individual choices of appearance, and the knocks which life had dealt them. The commander was unkept, more ragged. His white hair was considerably longer, almost down to his shoulders and his jaw was accentuated with at least a four-day stubble. He sported several scars, the most prominent of which, just above his left eye, must have come close to depriving him of sight. The whole appearance gave him a more dangerous, almost cruel look. But in every other respect they were the same.

Seating himself in his command chair towards the rear of the bridge, the Commander perched forward, expectantly, urging Nicolle to reply.

As far as she could discern, given the tight angle the view screen was providing, the Commander's bridge was a pristine, uncomplicated, functional workspace: a gleaming, bright metal array of clean lines and no frills efficiency. There where two freestanding consoles either side of the command chair and half a dozen more along the rear bulkhead, all were manned by crewmembers busying themselves at their stations. Light flooded the bridge in a soft, calming, white glow. The whole scene appeared antiseptically clinical.

Nothing less than Nicolle would have expected in any Vaurillian ship, which was in stark contrast to the crews appearance. Their crew's uniforms looked especially out of place; a short, leather like, reddish-brown jacket, with matching trousers and boots. Nicolle had never known any Vaurillian, except those serving in Alliance Fleet, to wear anything other than their customary long, white robes.

The uniform though, was not unfamiliar to Lieutenant Jevak: he recognised it instantly as that worn by early Vaurillian space-farers, prior to first contact with humans. But Vaurillians had not worn that uniform in more than four hundred years.

Jevak attempted to remain analytical, assessing the situation for what it was, but he found the experience un-nerving; communicating with ones self in this manner was unnatural.

"Captain?" he said stepping down from the upper bridge.

Lockhart, without taking her eyes from the screen, raised her hand to halt her Lieutenant to silence him.

Since communications were down, Lockhart and her crew were completely unaware of what had been discovered by the away team, on the surface. Until this moment she was still under the misconception that they had made it home, that some catastrophe had befallen Earth, and that Alliance Fleet was somehow.... somehow, incapacitated. That mistaken assumption dissolved in that instant. Her heart sank as the truth was realised. Their mission had failed. They were not home.

"Commander, I am Captain Nicolle Lockhart of the Alliance starship Endeavour," she replied, composing herself. "We represent...." She paused, how was she going to explain this. "We represent the United Alliance of Planets."

Commander Jevak inclined his head. "I am unaware of such an organisation, Captain," he said, raising his left eyebrow as though questioning her authenticity. "I was under the impression that I knew of all species in this Sector. You must be far from home."

"Farther than you think," Lockhart replied, laughing ironically.

"Captain..." Lieutenant Jevak again pressed,

from the rail behind her command chair.

The slight movement to the rear of Captain Lockhart caught Commander Jevak's attention. His brow furrowed. As recognition dawned on the startled Vaurillian, his eyes grew wide. Until now he had not noticed any of Nicolle's crew. Lockhart saw the look.

"Commander," she said quickly, stepping up to the veiwscreen in an attempt to defuse the situation. "This is my science officer, Lieutenant..." She drew a deep breath; here goes, she thought. "...Lieutenant Jevak."

"What deception is this?" the Vaurillian Commander roared, getting to his feet.

"Commander...!" Lockhart urged. "In your position, I would doubt what I was seeing too. But believe me, this is no deception."

"Explain!"

"We are far from home... But this, is our home," she replied. "Or at least we thought it was."

"Riddles, Captain, will do no good. Explain!" he demanded again.

Turning towards Lieutenant Jevak she nodded confidently. "Return to your station," she urged him quietly.

This was going to be difficult to explain. If the tables were turned would she believe the tale she was about to tell? She doubted it. But Vaurillians were Vaurillians, she told herself, no matter in which parallel universe you find them. They had been humanities closest allies for more than three hundred years. 'Humans lap dogs', Kraxians had taken to calling them, so tight was their relationship. Could she foster that same trust here?

She had to remind herself to be cautious. Humanities relationship with Vaurillian had not always been so close, there had been stumbles along the way, not least the reconciliation with Tyreea. If this was to be first contact all over again, she hoped it would go smoother this time.

"We are human, Commander… homosapian. And this planet…. is called Earth, it is our home world," Lockhart said assertively.

"A lie, Captain. This planet's indigenous species has barely mastered basic metallurgy. Let alone warp technology.

"In this Universe, yes. But then, we are… not from this Universe," she said hoping for a positive response.

"An alternate Universe?" the commander ventured, almost sarcastically, both as a suggestion and a question. "How convenient, Captain. You expect me to believe that?"

It was obvious the only way to convince this, rightly sceptical Vaurillian was to be honest and open. It was what she would have expected, and respected, were she in his position.

She started at the beginning, carefully recounting the story of Endeavours original mission; the pursuit of the Johannesburg into the nebula to defend the freighter from a Macaitian attack. There they encountered the spatial anomaly, which had sucked the freighter through to a distant place in the galaxy. Endeavour had had to follow. Both ships were then trapped on the far side of the Galaxy, more than seventy thousand light-years from home, when the anomaly closed. She gave the coordinates of the nebula to permit the Vaurillians to at least confirm that part of her story. Commander Jevak confirmed that he knew of the region.

Picking her way through the major events of the past six years, Nicolle offered as much detail as she considered necessary to support her story. Bringing their story up to date, she described the ferocity of their near fatal passage through the wormhole. That brought an unexpected reaction from the Commander. He had listened dispassionately until this point, but visibly flinched as Nicolle described the terrifying destructive power of the barrier, and the vicious, brutal hammering they had barely survived on entering the wormhole.

There was no doubting that Endeavour had suffered a near fatal assault, and recently. The Vaurillian's sensors had detected the damage as they approached, and now they could see the full extend of the damage. Repair crews had shored-up the appalling external injuries in her hull. But there was still horrific scorching and visible blast damage along the rear section, and on all three nacelles.

"A fanciful tale," the Vaurillian Commander said dismissively, still not unconvinced.

Nicolle was about to jump to her own defence but she paused, almost imperceptibly. The

Commander's use of the word "fanciful" was...well a little fanciful for a Vaurillian, she thought. Their species were not known for overt use of language. In fact Vaurillians if anything, were deliberately concise; they had little use for hyperbole. Maybe there were greater disparities in this reality than just outward appearances.

"For what purpose would we go to the extent of such an elaborate rouse, Commander?" she insisted, becoming impatient. "You can see the damage we've suffered, as I've no doubt you've already scanned us."

"Indeed we have Captain. But the physical and systems damage, you have... apparently sustained, can be easily falsified. And as for..." His gaze went beyond her, to the science station. "Cosmetic surgery. What kind of fools do you take us for?" He paused briefly, deliberately, watching her intently for any flicker of a lie.

Dubious as her story sounded, the Commander was unable to ignore Nicolle's tale as a possibility. The ship was after all totally unlike any design he, or their data banks, had ever encountered. He could see no doubt or hesitation in her eyes.

"Please furnish us with the co-ordinates of this... wormhole," he finally demanded.

Lockhart nodded to Lieutenant Jevak.

"The anomaly is in the Massaran region," Jevak informed the Commander. "I am passing the co-ordinates to you now."

There was palpable discomfort in the short,

personal exchange between the two. Commander Jevak quickly looked away, fixing his eyes on Nicolle. She could sympathise with their uneasiness.

By definition, a parallel Universe is parallel because, in spite of the obvious duplication, in some respect, no matter how small or insignificant, it is different from our own Universe. Therefore, by extension, the you, from that alternate reality is also different and therefore not you, at least not exactly. Unable to abstract them selves from the situation, both Jevak's could only see the logic; that this individual had the same face, carried the same DNA, and was called Jevak. And that therefore they were looking at themselves. That made both uncomfortable.

Commander Jevak glanced to his left, to enquire if his subordinate had the received wormhole co-ordinates. As he did so, turning from the screen, he drew his hand across his throat, signalling to cut the audio on the inter-ship communication.

Lockhart did likewise.

"Engineering," she called to the comm-system.

"Cosique here."

"Lasers, Cosique?" Nicolle asked urgently.

"We're almost there, Captain. You'll have them in a few moments."

"Figuratively, or literally?"

"Literally."

"Excellent. Don't bring them online immediately, just dim the bridge lights to let me know they're available."

The Vaurillian ship would instantly detect weapons being brought line, and view that as an open act of aggression. Not wishing to alienate possible allies at such an early juncture, Nicolle decided on a more softly, softly approach. But she still wanted the weapons… just in case. She might not be able to convince these Vaurillians that they were friendly, and lasers could be her last bargaining chip.

"Understood."

Turning to face the screen again, she indicated to Jevak to resume audio transmission.

"Our long range sensors are scanning the region, Captain Lockhart," Commander Jevak said as the link resumed. "Let's hope your tail is not a fabrication." Still dismissive of Nicolle's account of their presence here, he added. "Even if a wormhole is detected in that region, it still proves nothing, it merely confirms a comprehensive and thoroughly researched alibi, nothing more."

"Commander, I can assure you, nothing of what I have told you has been concocted. As I have said, we represent the United Alliance of Planets. Endeavour is a ship of exploration. We're lost, and merely trying to find our way home."

The Commander's attention was caught by a voice to his left. He glanced to the side of the bridge, and then thought for a moment. "Captain Lockhart, I have a suggestion which may resolve this… impasse."

"I'm listening, Commander."

He raised a single eyebrow as he ventured the suggestion. "Would you be prepared to make your computer records available for scrutiny?"

Nicolle had a feeling that was what the Commander was going to suggest. She felt uneasy about it. She felt it was tantamount to surrendering her ship. But she had to admit it would resolve the standoff.

She nodded reluctantly. "Agreed."

The Commander obviously sympathised with her situation. Observing protocols he stood to attention and requested, "Permission to come aboard Captain?"

"Permission granted."

"My science officer and I shall teleport directly to your bridge."

The transmission ended.

Nicolle stepped away from the centre of the bridge. A few seconds later two columns of bright green, stars shimmered a few feet in front of her command chair. They took shape, resolving slowly into the two Vaurillian officers. Commander Jevak approached Nicolle and bowed slightly.

"Captain Lockhart, may I introduce my second in command and science officer......,"

The Captain froze, faltering momentarily, as she made to shake the Vaurillian female's hand. She could scarcely believe her eyes.... It was her! Without need of introductions Nicolle knew exactly who this female was… although the rest of her crew would know her merely by reputation. The face was older than she remembered, but then it had been more than twenty-nine years ago… yet it was her. She was still slim and attractive, given that she was now at least a hundred and twenty years old. Her white hair was still in that same bobbed style. Those high check-bones, and the mole at the left corner of her lower lip were unmistakable. Nicolle had seen this face only briefly, and although the nightmares had ceased, the memories of that harrowing encounter were as vivid and sickening as ever.

Nicolle had been young at the time, still a teenager, in her third year at the academy. It was the summer sabbatical and like the rest of her class she had been seconded to the fleet for a few weeks practical experience. The previous year she had spent a month on a freighter, this year though she had conspired to get herself on to one of the fleet's auxiliary vessels, the A.S. Atlanta; re-supplying personnel, stores and armaments along the still volatile Kraxian border.

One of the many ports of call the Atlanta had made during their brief tour that summer was to the Kraxan penal colony of Pentrea-Gasta. A convicted human prisoner was being released back into Alliance custody. Nicolle, to this day, could not remember who the prisoner was or what he had been convicted of; all she could recall was how utterly wretched and terrified he was when they reclaimed what was left of him from that hell-hole. The Alliance may not have approved of Kraxa's brutal penal system, but they did at least recognise that incarceration within it was infinitely preferable to the way Kraxians treated and executed their own.

Though the pitiful convict had spent only three years imprisoned in that desolate god-forsaken, medieval regime of brutality and fear, he was utterly broken, in spirit and body. Enduring forced labour, with death an ever-present threat on that barren, frozen rock at the wrong edge of civilisation he was a husk of a being when they retrieved him. Pentrea-Gasta was the Kraxian's flagship of penal reform; waking up each morning to find you had not mercifully died in your sleep was considered punishment in its self.

Nicolle though, did not have the same memory blind spot where this Vaurillian female, now standing on her bridge was concerned. Her name was T'Arran, and she could remember every detail about her and her infamous act of treachery. From the day the Vaurillian assassin had been convicted and exiled on that self same rock, it had been widely accepted, that there wasn't a hope in hell of her ever being released and that death might have been her own preference.

Seventy-five years before the young Nicolle's brief visit to the prison planet, T'Arran, the Vaurillian traitor had been a co-conspirator in the attempted assassination of the Kraxian Ambassador, on his way to Earth for peace talks. The assassination attempt had gone badly wrong and though thwarted, many of the ambassador's party had been killed in the attempt. The conspirators were dealt with harshly and swiftly; especially the Kraxian traitors; they and their families back home on Kraxa were brutally executed, (right of appeal on Kraxa is a notional concept). The three humans involved in the coup, had all been fatally wounded during the short sharp response from Alliance and Kraxian troops and so had been spared incarceration. The attempted assassination had not only failed, many to this day still ironically credit it with being the foundation, cementing the Alliance/Kraxa accord that the conspirators had so brazenly strove to derail.

Her trial on Kraxa had been without preamble. Sentencing to life, on Pentrea-Gasta for T'Arran, was immediate. The only surviving conspirator would die, broken and forgotten, on that bleak, pitiless rock.

To most she had been forgotten, until the morning that the A.S. Atlanta arrived to process the prisoner exchange. Nineteen-year-old Cadet Nicolle Lockhart had pleaded with the Captain to be included in the five-man landing party, to the high-security holding area. Reluctantly, after much badgering, he had relented. As the landing party materialised in the freezing rock cave, a hundred or so, feet below the hostile planet's frozen surface, Nicolle stepped cautiously away from the handover; the Captain had insisted that she take no part in the exchange. As a cadet she was merely there to observe.... No more.

The air in the dimly lit, semi-circular, cave was rank with the stench of death and putrid waist; it clawed at young Nicolle's throat, making her gag. She coughed up bile from her heaving stomach. The hot steam of her fetid breath dissipated in the still air, adding to the stagnant, rancid stench. Along the curved wall behind her and to her left were a dozen darkened cells cut into the living rock, each one of them no bigger than a doorway, four feet wide by six feet high and six feet deep. They each held at least one prisoner; some held two or three in stinking inhuman, cramped conditions, in which even Kraxians would not keep their dogs. Across each of the cell entrances, deterring any thought of escape, buzzed an invisible energy field.

Most of these prisoners were being kept separate from the rest of the colony because, either their sentences had been completed, and like their own charge were awaiting release, or because they were awaiting execution. This is where Nicolle met T'Arran; she had been confined in this security area for nearly fifty years, kept alone, freezing and filthy.... But in her case it was for the safety of the other prisoners.

Kraxian penal colonies are, to say the least, unremitting in there cruelty. They accept, even encourage several deaths per week among their 'work force'; they call it 'wastage'. It keeps the rest of the inmates fearful and subjugated. Here though with

T'Arran, the Kraxians had created a monster they could now never tame.

    T'Arran's mind was broken. Freezing, starving, battling the merciless conditions and fellow prisoners every day, just to survive, always expecting to die. They had tipped her into insanity. Vaurillians minds are their very core; their unyielding capacity for logic and clarity of thought is their essence, their extraordinary reason for being which sets them apart from all other species. At a comparatively young age they willingly and eagerly extinguish their capacity for emotions, unburdening their minds from the confusion of love, fear and joy and more, just to attain meticulousness mental precision. But in places such a as this, the darkness and fear bring their own demons, real and imagined. With no abstract, conceptual filter to her intellect T'Arran did not have the capacity to demonise her attackers and guards whose joyous sadism she found irrational. The mind of a Vaurillian that had never known emotion was now consumed and tortured by the most powerful of all. Her intellect stripped of its discipline and control, reduced to animalistic survival was a fearful beast and her strength as a Vaurillian made her formidable.

    T'Arran's crime had been against Kraxians she had merely mistrusted, but now hated. They could not control her, and even their brutal regime could not accept the horrendous and unabated slaughter of prisoners and guards, at her bare hands. So they locked her away, in the darkness, alone...... where she waited.

As the lights in the prisoner's processing area came on there was a low feral moan, almost a growl, in the darkened cell far to the landing party's left. The exchange prisoner who had been waiting, chained to a rusting post sunk in the rock in the centre of the processing area heard the low growl and shied away from it, looking pitifully to the landing party. He was quickly dragged, terrified, begging and howling by two Kraxian guards who unceremoniously dumped the filthy bundle of rags at the feat of the Atlanta's security detail. The prisoner, realising he was now accompanied by Alliance officers kicked-out in final defiance at his soon to be former captors. As he did he stumbled, knocking one of the Atlanta's security officers towards the ominous darkened cell where T'Arran was secured.

Security force fields are not solid, impenetrable walls; they are porous, and give under sufficient pressure. But they are designed to cause maximum, excruciating pain even to the merest of touches. If determined enough to attempt to push through one, they will all but shred every nerve ending in the body but still not kill; a powerful deterrent to those who might harbour thoughts of escape. T'Arran no longer feared pain. Her once brilliant mind no longer had the capacity to process the sensation; it was now merely a dark void consumed with loathing and blood lust.

It happened quickly, too quickly for either the Kraxian or Alliance guards to avert. As the helpless security guard stumbled forwards, too close to the mouth of the darkened cell, a stifled groan accompanied an arm thrust with ferociously speed through the force field. With flesh boiling and bubbling and nerves burning the twisted gnarled fingers grabbed the flailing guard by the face. The filthy, broken and twisted fingers plunged through his eyeballs skewering him, giving purchase to haul him, screaming, head first back through the barrier into the darkness.

By the time the force field had been deactivated and all the lights in the cave hastily turned on, T'Arran was gorging herself at the throat of the flailing guard. Four armed, Kraxian guards rushed the cell. Amidst the violence of the sustained assault there came the distinct loud snap as one of the guards was thrown headlong back into the processing area, his face partially torn away, his bloodied head hanging obliquely. The remaining guards finally subdued T'Arran. Snarling, clawing, kicking and screaming, they dragged her from her cell, blood and sinews still trailing from her gapping maw.

Then she had caught sight of young Nicolle, shaken to her soul, pinned to the far wall by her own fear and revulsion. As their eyes met, all Nicolle could see in those dark pools were loathing and feral rage. Nicolle knew that if the Vaurillian could be free, she would be at her throat in less than heart beat, tearing every part of her body from every other. There was nothing but hunger for death in those empty eyes.

"…. Sub-Commander T'Arran," Commander Jevak said, concluding the introduction of his Science Officer.

The Captain straightened, forcing a smile, flinching as she took T'Arran's hand. She fought to quell her repulsion at those memories, determined not to betray her mounting horror at the Vaurillian's presence on her bridge. She struggled to remind herself that this was a different universe and this was a different T'Arran….. But it was still the same face.

"Welcome aboard… both of you," she said maintaining a calm veneer.

T'Arran locked eyes with Nicolle; the Vaurillian's warm smile faded briefly. Had she noticed Nicolle's look of alarm? The Captain quickly looked away.

Suddenly the cordial atmosphere became frosty again as almost imperceptibly, the bridge lights dimmed briefly. It was apparent to everyone present that a standoff and mistrust had resumed. Smiling coldly, Commander Jevak eventually broke the silence.

"It would appear, Captain, you once again have lasers," he said, almost matter-of-factly.

CHAPTER 10

Sweeney hurriedly scoured the adjoining rooms, he made no attempt at subtlety; speed was of the essence. Throwing over pews, smashing through locked doors, he ransacked every room and cupboard quickly but thoroughly. He found nothing of use. The church was rustic, plain and unadorned. There were no drapes, cloth coverings on the walls, or on the pulpit, nothing at all that could be used as a bandage.

He found himself in what he assumed was the vestibule, about to return to the main hall with the bad news, when a scuffing noise to his left, over by the stone fireplace, caught him by surprise. Veering his torchlight in the direction of the movement he caught sight of a dark shape slinking, under a pew in a far corner. As the light caught it, it whined like a frightened animal. He leaped, clearing a desk and two pews in one bound. Charging down the scurrying figure whilst drawing his laser he kicked aside the bench the creature had take refuge under.

The reptile wore a long dark, heavy cloak; similar to the ones they had seen on many of the villagers at the tavern. Its hood was pulled back to reveal its terrified face, it's yellow eyes wide with fear, as it tried to scurry away on all fours.

"Obviously this seasons must have," said Sweeney sarcastically, as he grabbed the cloak near the creature's throat, hauling it sharply to its feet. It drew back from him, hissing and licking the air like a snake.

"Easy now," Sweeney rebuked firmly.

Cautiously holding the lizard at arms length he blinded it momentarily by directing his flashlight into its face. Beneath the cloak, Sweeney could see that the terrified reptile wore a cloth shirt of much finer, brighter material than anything else they had seen in the village so far. He guessed that, given their location, this must be their priest. Backing away slowly, the priest eventually found the wall. He pressed himself against it as tightly as possible, to get as far away from Sweeney as he could. Seeing the creature's fear Matt relented, taking the light from its eyes.

"I'm not going to harm you," he said holding up his hands in a calming gesture.

Putting his laser away, he let the priest see his hands were now empty, and that there was no danger. The creature, no matter what its species was after all still a priest, and Sweeney felt inclined to treat it with due reverence. As he reached out to grab the priest's cloak, and lead him through to the main hall, the creature dodged to the left.

"Oh no you don't," Sweeney grunted, hauling it around towards the door, drawing his laser and jabbing it into its ribs again. "This way!"

"Look what I found back there," Sweeney said as he re-entered the main hall, pushing the priest before him.

As they approached, Sweeney could see Cheung was deteriorating fast. Wicasa was kneeling over him trying to stem the blood from the seeping chest wound. He had torn another strip off Wattie's shirt and was holding it firmly against the wound.

"This isn't helping," Wicasa said despairingly. "His lungs are filling with blood... He's drowning."

Sweeney threw the priest onto the pew nearest Wattie's feet. "Stay there and don't move," he growled. Then added, by way of a thinly veiled threat. "And you won't get hurt."

Outside there was a mob, probably about a hundred strong, slavering for their blood; there was no reason to believe that this lizard, even if he was a priest, and given the chance, would not do the same.

"All I'm doing is soaking up the blood that's coming out of him," Wicasa said helplessly.

Behind Sweeney, the frightened priest shuffled away from them, farther along the pew. Sweeney spun, levelling his laser at the priest's yellow eyes.

"I said don't move," he barked.

As Wicasa eyed Matt's laser, an idea suddenly came to him. Quickly he drew his own. 'Maybe... Just maybe', he thought.

Adjusting the power setting to 'stun' and the also narrowing the beam to 'minimum', he rolled

Wattie onto his side, and placed the nose of his laser against the entry wound in the Ensign's back.

"What're you doing?" Matt exclaimed.

"I'm going to try to cauterise the wound," Wicasa replied.

"Maybe it'll kill him."

"He'll drown in his own blood in a matter of minutes, if we don't stop the internal bleeding. We've got to try something," he insisted. "Here, help me. Hold him."

Sweeney reluctantly had to agree. Wattie would not last long enough to get back to the ship, and without the Doctors help he would be dead in a few minutes.

Kneeling beside him, Matt secured Wattie by firmly pulling his unconscious body against his knees with his left hand, while his right was still otherwise occupied pointing a laser at their reluctant guest.

Wicasa loosed a single, prolonged volley of his laser's searing, orange beam, directly into the wound from point-blank range.

Wattie stiffened, groaning loudly, while Wicasa and Sweeney locked their arms and legs around his torso, stifling any attempt to shake them free.

Wicasa grimaced as he pressed down on the trigger. He knew the pain he must have been causing his friend, but this was necessary. He and Matt held tighter, preventing Wattie from shifting and causing him any further unnecessary injury.

Shifting the beam around in a circular motion, Wicasa eventually found the path the arrow had taken through Wattie's rib cage. The beam emerged through the Ensign's chest still bright and unbroken, just above his heart. It skirted across the room a few inches above the floor, striking the wall opposite them.

The Priest screamed hysterically. "Witch-craft!" "Witch-craft!"

He scrambled to get to his feet, clawing desperately to get over pews, which collapsed and fell around him. Struggling to get away, far away, his yellow eyes were wild with fear and uncomprehending shock. Matt loosed a volley of his own laser, deliberately missing the cleric by mere inches.

"I said don't move!" he roared.

It was a warning shot, but the hysterical priest got the message. He slid, whimpering fearfully to the floor, fighting to contain the madness, though still edging further away from them.

Rolling Wattie on to his back again, Wicasa examined the wound. It had been successful; the laser had sealed the damaged blood vessels. The bleeding had stopped, though Wattie's breathing was still shallow and laboured. Turning him over, he and Matt laid him out in the recovery position, allowing his airways to open-up, and hopefully, let blood drain from his lungs. Wattie spluttered and coughed, frothing red. They had done the best they could for him, they now had to find away of getting him back to the ship.

"He's stable for now, I think," Wicasa said, reassuring Matt.

Getting to his feet, the Commander tapped his Comm-bracelet; it chirped in response then hissed static.

"Wicasa to Endeavour," he said, frustrated. "Wicasa to Endeavour!"

"The storm's still blocking transmission," Matt said, looking up at where the gathering light was filling the windows.

The priest's eyes lifted to the light too.

The windows sills were a little more than fifteen feet above their heads. The windows themselves were tall and narrow, arched at the top, reaching almost to the eaves thirty feet above them. But the priest almost reached them with one thrust of his powerful legs.

"Devils!... Devils! Burn them. Burn them!!!" he screamed, clawing at the wooden sills, trying to warn the gathering crowd outside.

Sweeney rushed at him as he landed on the floor again. He grabbed him, wrapping his left arm around the lizards' muscular neck, while his right hand clasped tightly over its short snout, in an attempt to keep him quiet.

"Witches. Devils!" The priest continued, his muffled screams now barely audible.

As Sweeney hauled him to the floor their faces were mere inches apart. For a split second the priest stopped struggling. The look of terror in his eyes fell away and was suddenly replaced with one of loathing. The cleric's jaw tightened. Sweeney realised instantly the danger those powerful jaws held. His hand appeared miniature beside that wide, razor filled, maw. Matt felt the twitch; saw the look in the eyes of this evolved predator, as the priest's jaw made to snap. Wicasa sprang, pulling the priest back onto the pew. The moment was over. The danger had passed.

"Another stunt like that!" growled Sweeney. "And you'll make a fine pair of boots! You understand?" For emphasis he thrust his laser into the priest's throat, gouging it just enough to let him know he meant business.

"Matt!" Wicasa roared. "Back off. Can't you see he's frightened?"

Sweeney withdrew as Wicasa moved to the priest's side. "Take it easy," The Commander reassured him calmly. "We mean you no harm."

The priest shrank from him, still frightened. "I know you... I know your master... Satan," he hissed, pulling a wooden crucifix from inside his cloak. He brandished it at Wicasa, like a shield, holding him at bay. "I'll not be lured from the path of righteousness by soft words or false witness."

"Calm down," Sweeney said soothingly, having recomposed himself. He pulled his own silver crucifix from beneath his shirt. "See, we have the same God."

The priest howled hysterically. Burying his face in his cloak, he recoiled from them, chanting a prayer.

"See to Wattie," Wicasa said quietly, urging Matt away.

Sweeney nodded that he understood, then moved quietly to where Wattie lay. He knew Wicasa needed to talk to the priest, and he realised his presence was not helping. He backed away giving Wicasa space. The Commander righted one of the pews and took a seat beside the cowering reptile.

"We've no intension of harming you," he again reassured him. "You have my word."

"And what is the worth of a witch's promise?" the priest hissed from beneath his cloak.

"We're not witches or demons or anything like that. We just….we just look different from you, that's all." Thinking quickly he added. "We come from a far off land… across the ocean."

That sounded lame he thought. He felt himself cringe.

"No! Lies," the priest rebuffed. "Not from across the ocean, from his hellish lair."

Wicasa reached over and attempted to pull the cloak away from the priest's face. He wanted to look him in the eye. The lizard squealed, then hissed angrily, pulling the cloak in tighter but Wicasa managed to force it free.

"Look," he pressed, remaining calm. "If we were witches, or devils, would we bleed?" he said, indicating to Wattie's prone figure.

"Bleed?" the priest hissed, his yellow eyes

narrowing to slits, locking defiantly with Wicasa. "I know ye can bleed... Witches can even burn." Stretching out his log, scaly neck until he was almost face to face with Wicasa, he added, sneering. "And burn ye shall."

"The crowd are growing restless out there," Sweeney noted looking past the priest, up at the windows.

Even the gathering early dawn light could not veil the flicker of orange flame from countless torches in the alleyways. The mob outside had swelled. The clamour of angry voices, along with the clanking of weapons was becoming audible even through the thick wooden walls of the old church. The crowd had multiplied more than ten fold since they had entered the church and there were now nearly a hundred frightened, angry reptiles gathered outside: almost every male in the village. Their primitive blood lust was clouding their thoughts. Mob rule had taken over. They had the scent of the prey and a hundred tongues flickered furiously, tasting the air.

"Lets hope they've heard of sanctuary," Sweeney added.

"I think that's the only reason they haven't smashed through that door already," replied Wicasa.

"There'll be no sanctuary for ye... Satan's spawn," the priest spat, seeing the growing concern in Sweeney's eyes.

Both Wicasa and Sweeney checked their

lasers.

"You'll burn. Burn!" Springing to his feet he tried to leap at the windows again, screaming at the gathered mob outside. "Burn them! Burn them!"

This time Wicasa hauled him to the floor.

"If they burn us, they'll burn you too," Wicasa said through clenched teeth, holding the determined cleric down. "Your people wouldn't burn their own priest."

"They'll do what is needed," he hissed, struggling to be free. "They will rid the world of demons and witches again. This time for good."

"Again?.... For good?" Wicasa's mind raced. He stopped struggling as the implications of the priest's words became apparent.

The crew of the Eldridge.

He had almost forgotten them. This place. This Earth. It had not been their home either. My God, he thought. What had they done, those poor lost, 20th century fools. They had played with technology beyond their understanding, beyond their ability to control. In trying to simply 'cloak' a battle ship they had inadvertently torn a rift between universes. Opening a door to an alternate reality, which looked like home, had all the same stars in the night sky, had rivers, seas and continents exactly as they should be, but was populated by creatures borne of nightmares.

Wicasa's heart pounded. He suddenly felt afraid. Not for himself, but for those poor lost souls. Four hundred years ago they had taken a step into a dark void, few even in this century had taken. Alone in an alien universe, everything, everyone they had ever known, vanished, lost. All of their history, their species, completely erased.

He shuddered. "What happened to those who came before us?"

"Ye already know the answer to that. Demon!" Spat the priest.

"Would I be asking if I already knew?" Wicasa said, calmly, coldly… deliberately threatening.

The priest resisted, grunting as he struggled to pull free of the Commanders grip.

Straddling the prostrate reptile, Wicasa grasped him by the cloak, tightening it around his throat. "Now… what happened to them?" He growled through gritted teeth.

This was no way to treat a prisoner, but he wanted an answer, and quickly. Outside the crowd were pounding furiously on the walls. It may not be long before they grew determined enough to storm the door.

The priest looked confused, he could not understand the reason for this sudden barrage of questioning. Surely these demons would know the fate of their hellish kin, the spawn of Satan that had plagued their land four centuries ago. The eye that never sleeps; their all-knowing master should surely have revealed to them the outcome of his last foray into this world.

A window smashed above their heads, showering shards of razor sharp glass around them.

Sweeney shielded Wattie from the lacerating cascade, with his body.

"Were they killed?" Wicasa pressed. "Answer me!"

"N...no!" The priest stuttered in fear. "No...not all."

This was becoming a confrontation, and it was not going well. Wicasa needed to gain the creature's confidence, or at least reassure him that they meant no harm. He eased him back onto the pew, and backed off slowly, taking a seat opposite.

"We mean you no harm. I promise you," he reassured. "But I have to know what happened to the others."

The priest's nervous gaze leapt back and forth between Sweeney and Wicasa; if these two demons had been going to rent the earth, and beg hell devour him, they would surely have done so by now, he thought.

He calmed a little realising that they were more interested in their counterparts four hundred years ago than they were in slaughtering him.

"Not all were killed," he started reluctantly, uneasily. "Their legion was many, and their powers too strong. Our people fought bravely but we could do little to defend against their wizardry."

Wicasa nodded, he understood. A crew of frightened, but highly trained sailors, with twentieth century armaments, against these bewildered, barely iron-age, villagers. It would have been no contest.

"They came in the morning," the priest continued. "Not in darkness, when the spirits walk, but in daylight. A thick green fog crept over the lands to the east, from horizon to horizon, the colour of rot and decay; it shrouded their coming. Hiding them from our sight."

Wicasa understood. Earlier, on board the rusting hull, Jevak had gone into more detail on the 'Philadelphia Experiment'. As 'Project Rainbow' had gotten underway on that summer morning back in 1943, apparently the Eldridge had quickly been shrouded in a luminous green fog, as its massive generators powered-up, boiling the sea around it.

"Our forefathers were afraid," the Priest continued. "Many hid in fear at the unearthly fog, but the brave amongst them took-up sword and pike and marched for the river at Sunset, there torches burning through the thinning mist."

"As they neared the spot where the great metal chariot rests, they could hear voices calling for help, in their own tongue. We sought to help those in danger, never suspecting they were luring our villagers to their hell."

"As the villagers approached, the demons loosed their evil wizardry. First they blinded us with the rays of the Sun held prisoner in glass. Then they loosed their fire-sticks and thunderous death."

"Our people fled in fear as death cut them down like dry tinder before a fire." He spat these words at Wicasa. The priest may have been their captive, but he would not show fear in the face of the Devil's spawn.

"Our fore-fathers took flight," He hissed. "They hid in the hills, while the demons raised our village to the ground. They burned and looted. Then moved onto the next village."

He could not hide his distain as he recounted the tail handed down from holy man to holy man for the past four hundred years. His thin upper lip curled back angrily, displaying the deadly rows of razor-like teeth, as he spat each word in disgust at these new devils.

"Did your people do nothing to retaliate?"

"Eventually there were no more villages to raid. As they sent minions into the hills hunting food and water, we picked them off one by one. We still lost many to there few, but we drove them back," he said, sneering as he levelled his stare at Wicasa. "Back towards their iron chariot."

Wicasa shivered, not from the cold. He could see how much this holy man would love to be alone with him or Matt; he could see the loathing in those yellow eyes. 'Demons' had come amongst these simple creatures, bringing deadly magic and terror, and now it seemed with the landing party's arrival they had returned.

"This all happened a long time ago, how do you know?" he asked.

"It is written," the priest snapped, angrily.

He was a holy man, of letters and learning. He would not have his word doubted by this vile spawn of Satan.

"Were any ever taken alive?" Wicasa asked.

"Not for long," the priest sniggered.

"Did they tell how they came to be here?" asked Sweeney.

"Before they burned, they claimed they had been sent here 'as a test', to hide from the eyes of the one called 'ra-dar'."

Both Wicasa and Sweeney fell silent for a brief moment.

Four hundred years separated them from those poor misplaced seafarers. Their uniforms and their cause were different. The nation they had defended, and all concept of it, had long since dwindled to memories. But still, these were comrades. They served a cause; the defence of freedom, just as their Alliance, and had died in that service.... Greater love hath no man.

Wicasa broke the silence. "What happened to the rest?"

The priest shrugged. "Perchance Satan is using their bones to stoke hell's flames. We can but hope," he smiled, tilting his head mockingly.

"You don't know?"

"Nothing more is written of those who escaped the wrath of our elders," he replied slowly, letting the statement linger, watching their expressions for disappointment. But neither Matt nor Wicasa looked saddened, only perplexed.

"The raids ceased. They came amongst us no more," he eventually added. "Much was looted in the nights before they departed for ever; carts, horses, weapons, cattle, food. It was late autumn and our people were bled dry of everything. The winter that year was long and harsh. But the raids had ended. The devils were gone," he ended, smiling triumphantly. "And soon you shall be also...."

Smash!

A blazing torch crashed through a window above their heads, landing a few feet from where Wattie lay. As Sweeney launched himself at it another followed, landing on the far side of the room. Scooping them up, before they had time to ignite the timber floor, Sweeney hurled them back through the same window.

There was little time. Wicasa had to know. "Has anyone been to the iron chariot since?" he demanded.

"Only the village leaders and the priests can look upon the iron chariot. It is forbidden to all else, lest the demons return." He then added forlornly. "But they have returned anyway."

"Wicasa!" Sweeney shouted, startling his comrade.

He was pointing at the door they had barricaded. Smoke was filtering slowly under it, and through the gaps in its slatted panels.

"The fate of the demons is sealed," the priest sneered gleefully, backing away from them. "It would seam my flock are arranging a... warm welcome for you," he laughed.

Outside the villagers had piled branches, dry

timbers, anything that would burn, against the walls and under the floor gap, all were now burning furiously. The timbers of the building were very old, almost ancient. The flames took hold easily and quickly, devouring the church like a cornfield before a swarm of locusts.

Quickly the vast hall began to fill with smoke. It filtered in through cracks in the walls, floor, and down from the roof, pushing the precious air out of the room. Wicasa swatted the thickening smoke, attempting to clear it from his stinging eyes as it clawed and choked his throat and lungs.

Another blazing torch landed a few feet from Sweeney, then another, and another. He and Wicasa got to them quickly, returning them the way they had been delivered, but the floor was already smouldering filling the room with still more smoke.

It was getting hot, very hot, they were beginning to cook. Sweat poured from them, trickling down their faces mixing with the smoke, stinging their eyes. Sweeney wiped his face with his sleeve, smearing the blackening smoke across his face.

Their eyes began to fill with blinding tears. They were losing touch with their senses, becoming disorientated. They could hardly see the walls, mere feet from them, as smoke and flames began to fill the room. If they lost consciousness now they were doomed.

Wattie began coughing uncontrollably. Sweeney lifted him, away from the smoke filtering through the floorboards.

"Is there another way out of here?" Sweeney coughed.

The priest had no intention of answering. Instead he lifted his head to the roof, lost somewhere in the smoke above them. Closing his black and amber eyes, he opened his jaws wide, and vibrated his throat. The primeval sound he generated was a loud, pulsating clicking, which reverberated through the smoke, rising above the noise of the flames.

Through tightly squinted eyes, Wicasa could barely make out the priest's upturned, white throat. The smoke around it rippled, in ever expanding circles. Rolling outwards like the waves in a flat pond into which a stone had been dropt. The air around them pulsated, pounding with the primitive call to hunt. Outside the call wall answered. All around the church, hundreds of throats echoed the priest's ancient proclamation of the kill.

"For God's sake, you fool, they're going to kill us all. You as well!" Sweeney shouted, barely making himself heard above the building cacophony outside.

"Yes demon," the priest hissed. "For God's sake indeed." He made the sign of the cross, looking up to where the crucifix hung on the wall. "Sometimes the Lord's work demands sacrifices of us all."

Wicasa grabbed Wattie's left arm, shouldering it, taking some of the weight off Matt. "Is there another way out of here?" he demanded.

The priest, backed away, still refusing to answer.

Behind the priest, just bellow the middle of the three tall windows a plume of red, broached the wall, burning up and around the base of the windows. Within seconds the whole area beneath the high arches was ablaze. The wall warped and bent with the ferocity of the heat. Without warning two of the windows cracked and shattered, scattering shards across the smouldering floor.

The in-rush of fresh air fed the blistering heat. All around them columns of flames leapt towards the high angled roof.

Sweeney and Wicasa backed away from a blaze, which sprang from the base of the wall beside them, shielding Wattie with their bodies. Their uniforms began to smoulder, as the heat grew unbearable.

The whole building quickly became an inferno. Fingers of flames leapt across the roof, like grasping hands, tearing at the dry wood. Pews collapsed as they quickly turned to ash; they were little more than dry tinder.

At the far end of the room, the pulpit became a target. Flames, at first, licked tentatively at its base, working their way quickly around it, almost lovingly touching and stroking it. Wicasa looked away for a mere second, coughing and wiping the smoke from his burning eyes, by the time he looked back again the pulpit was a roaring inferno, flames leaping high to the rafters and across the roof.

"Help us for pities sake!" he yelled above the havoc of roaring flames and splitting timbers. "We mean you no harm...is there another way out of here?" Wicasa could barely form words in his burning throat, coughing and gasping desperately for breath, his lungs screaming for air.

The priest pulled his cloak tightly about him, wrapping it across his mouth, in a vain attempt to deflect the heat searing at his lungs. He screamed as another column of flame sprang to life a few feet from him. The reality of his own death was suddenly becoming very apparent to him.

Across the floor a carpet of flame rippled, like a gentle, but deadly wave easing on to a beach. As it reached the wall behind Sweeney it leapt vertically, roaring its malice as it spat and crackled, up towards the supporting horizontal beams above their heads.

Wicasa caught a look from the priest. His eyes twitched towards the anti-room behind the pulpit. There was another way out; that was where he was making for when Sweeney found him.

"Matt," Wicasa called, barely making himself heard above the noise of the cracking wood. He indicated towards the fleeing priest. "That way."

Above them a plume of flame lunged through the smoke at the roof's supporting beams, wrapping its self around them, snapping and cracking, as it consumed them.

High, to the priests left, the wall behind the pulpit cracked, splitting vertically, wrent by the heat. The crucifix teetered; swinging away from its anchor points as the flames greedily devoured its supports. Flames folded themselves around it, sending the icon plummeting to the floor, in an unrecognisable fireball. Its impact shattered the floor between the landing party and the priest, splintering it, throwing-up burning wreckage all around. The walls shook under the impact, twisting what remained of the support-beams above them, tearing a hole in the roof.

 The priest lunged at the door behind the blazing pulpit, throwing himself against the door-jam. As he threw the door wide, he prayed that there was still an escape route beyond it. Again the inrush of fresh air fed the inferno, and a column of flame roared past him, like a flamethrower, gorging its self on the new source of oxygen. He buried his head in his arms, pressing himself flat against the wall, as the door and its surround burst into flames. Beyond it the room was still clear. The way to safety was still accessible.

 Wicasa made to follow, dragging Wattie and Matt behind him. Suddenly a splintering crack from above sent burning debris showering to the floor around them. What sounded like an explosion followed instantly, as the roof began to collapse. Beams of seared wood smashed to the floor, throwing up flames all around, cutting off their escape. What was left of the building trembled and swayed.

 The priest hesitated at the door. Looking back into the flames, surrounding the demons, he caught his breath as more of the roof collapsed around them. They were doomed.

'Yes', he thought, '...Witches do burn'.

As the priest turned to flee, he could have sworn he glimpsed a corona of bright green stars descend around the forms of the demons. But he could never be certain. The remainder of the roof collapsed behind him, burying them. Their bodies were never found.

* * * * *

The few seconds it took for the Vaurillian's teleport to reassemble the billions of molecules in the human body seemed to stretch to hours. Lockhart stood to one side impatiently watching asced, taking shape, in the centre of her bridge. The huddled, forms of her landing party finally ceased sparkling, their blistering skin, hair and blackened uniforms still smouldering, as Sweeney collapsed to the floor.

"Doctor to the bridge. Immediately!" Lockhart called anxiously, at the ship's comm system, as she rushed to the aid of her stricken crew.

Wicasa attempted to stay on his feet, his scorched lungs screaming for air, Wattie's limp body still clasped tightly in his arms. Coughing and gasping he eased the Ensign to the floor then he too sprawled helplessly, dazed and half blind, on hands and knees beside him.

The air on the bridge was cool; Wicasa could

feel it blowing against his blistered face. He threw his head back, his chest heaving eagerly as he gulped in lungs full of it. It was good. His head began to clear, and his eyes began to focus.

The Captain was the first to them. She eased Wicasa gently to a sitting position. "The Doctor's on his way," she reassured him.

"Wattie …. See to Wattie," he coughed, wiping his scorched eyes with his still smouldering sleeve.

Ensign Lawrence; a split second behind the Captain, was at Matt's side in an instant, easing him gently on to his back, to let him breath, while urgently checking his injuries. Sweeney grabbed at the young Ensign's arm. Ignoring her urges to 'take it easy, and lie down', he hauled himself, unsteadily to his feet; Matt, as usual was too impatient to be a patient.

Seeing he was in no immediate danger, Lawrence quickly turned her attentions to Wattie.

Wicasa breathed deeply and gratefully as he focused on the crew gathering around them. The Captain, kneeling beside him, a sight he thought for a few moments, he might never see again, smiled warmly. Beside her was Jevak; he looked concerned, as Wicasa expected he would. Then, another figure came into his line of vision from behind him; it was also Jevak.

For a second he was not sure his vision had cleared. Then he realised that there were in fact, two Jevaks.

"I've got a bit of a tale to tell," Nicolle said a little flippantly, seeing the startled look on his face.

"You don't say," he replied sarcastically as he hauled in another lung full of oxygen.

"Has anyone noticed this?" Matt wheezed loudly, steadying himself against the helm console; he was staring incongruously at the view screen.

The arc of Earth's northern hemisphere turned lazily below them; a bright curve of blues and whites, against the black, star sprinkled Cosmos.

The Sun, behind them to starboard, was now high over central Europe, and the distinct line of the dawn was slowly creeping beyond North America's eastern seaboard. The margin, separating day from night cut south from the Arctic, through the great lakes, on south, clipping the southern extreme of Mexico as it headed for the Equator somewhere beyond the lower edge of the screen.

At first glance nothing appeared unusual. It was a sight they had all seen hundreds of times before.

One by one they all turned to look at the screen. One by one they all, except their visitors, realised exactly what Matt was staring at.

"The Gulf of Mexico," Wicasa rasped. "It's gone."

The great bowl of crystal clear, blue, Caribbean Sea was gone. A great landmass, more than a thousand miles across, had replaced the wide sweeping crescent of Mexico's beautiful, eastern coastline. From Cancun on Mexico's Yucatan peninsula, a wide, green expanse of prairie and mountains stretched north and east, joining the Texas coast line, a few hundred miles or so, to the west of Florida.

The Gulf of Mexico was gone.

There was no Gulf of Mexico. This Earth was different, and for a reason... a reason that was now all too clear.

CHAPTER 11

Nicolle half slumped against the recessed frame of the viewport in her Conference room. She sighed heavily, her breath misting the nine-foot high, curved diamond window, momentarily obscuring her view of the Earth below.

She was bathed in a cold harsh light, reflected off the Arctic's polar icecaps far below which emphasised the dark circles under her eyes. Nicolle was weary; she had not had a break from reviewing the masses of sensor data accumulated since the return of the landing party more than five hours ago. That, and the constant workload of trying to piece together her wounded ship, was draining her. Too much coffee and not enough sleep were winding her tighter than bowstring, and she needed to get away for a while to think, to digest everything that had happened to them since exiting the wormhole.

She stared vaguely at nothing in particular, her eyes barely focusing on the slowly dispersing patch of mist little more than a foot in front of her. She breathed again, misting the smooth hard surface a second time. Absently drawing her finger through the steam, she traced the line of the North American coastline. Her finger sketched south, from the pack-ice in the Arctic, which stretched farther south than she had ever know it to. The glistening white perma-frost extended all the way from the pole to Bangor, Maine swallowing the Great Lakes at the Canadian border as it did. On the Earth she knew, the ice had never come this far south, and it was still only autumn here. Sketching further she passed Florida then to the Gulf, but there was no Gulf of Mexico. She stopped. Nicolle had reached the crux of the conundrum she and her crew had found themselves in. Her eyes focused. She watched as the Earth turned slowly, fifteen hundred kilometres below her.... She caught herself, correcting her inner thoughts.... She had to remind herself again, this was not The Earth, but an Earth, an Earth so similar but so very different from her own.

It was now almost mid-day over North America's eastern seaboard; above which they were still orbiting. The Sun was directly behind the ship now and somewhere far below, Endeavour was casting a very feint shadow on an unfamiliar landscape that looked so much like home, but was so very alien.

In the short time she had been staring at this facsimile Earth, sixty-five million years of evolution had unfolded, and unravelled in Nicolle's turbulent mind: the entire history and evolution of sentient life on her world, and on the one below. Sixty-five million years since her warm-blooded ancestors, so very different from her, had replaced the dinosaurs as the dominant species on her world, but on this Earth that lineage had remained unbroken.

At this moment she felt very small and insignificant, bathed coldly in the light of another Earth. An Earth where evolution had seen fit to take a different path and her species, human kind, had been absent but never missed.

In Nicolle's Universe, sixty five million years ago a meteorite, more than six miles wide, swung out of deep space, hurtling through the solar system, and smashed into the Earth with such brutal force it wiped out almost all life, including nature's, until then, intended dominant species: the dinosaurs.

The impact was devastating. The entire planet trembled with the force of ten billion Hiroshima's. The earth convulsed wounded and broken. The sky darkened for years. The colossal impact caused tidal waves and tsunamis, earthquakes and volcanic eruptions, sudden shifts in the continental plates on an unimaginable horrific scale, reminiscent of the planet's birth. It threw debris and choking dust up into all levels of the atmosphere, where it rapidly encircled the planet from pole to pole, shutting out the Sun, and plunging the Earth into a freezing, dark winter, which lasted for decades. When the dust finally cleared, seventy-five percent of all life, including the dinosaurs were extinct.

The immense crater left by that impact is still visible today on that other Earth Nicolle called home: the Gulf of Mexico.

The Captain turned from the view port to sit on the edge of her conference table. Her gaze drifted north again, to the Earth's brilliant white arctic crown. As she stared, steeling the disappointment that this was not home, the reasons for this World's noticeably distinct climate became clearer to her. While on the surface the landing party had even noticed how abnormally cold it was for the time of year.

Not long after the landing party's return, Cosique's repair teams had managed at last to restore on-board sensors. Jevak's subsequent, urgent scans quickly ascertained several factors, all of which had contributed to their Earths dramatic climatic deviations, from the planet they were currently orbiting.

Magnetic north naturally shifts its position over millions of years driven by the tidal flow of Earths molten liquid core. The colossal meteor impact, sixty five million years ago had shocked Nicolle's Earth with untold ferocity, triggering horrendous tidal waves deep within that core. The liquid magma lurched and pitched on an immense planetary scale throwing the magnetic field into wild, erratic, chaotic patterns, rocking the planet for centuries.

The ebb and flow of the magma and with it Earth's magnetic field, did eventually calm though, settling into the slowly shifting pattern Nicolle was familiar with back on her own World. Its position on this duplicate, as Cheung and Wicasa, while on the Eldridge, had discovered earlier, was merely where it would have been had that fateful collision never occurred.

The massive collision, besides initiating colossal tides within the Earth's boiling liquid core, had also created a vicious oscillating of the planet its self, rocking it back and forth on its axis, like a balloon filled with water. The violent rocking effect had, over time, moved our Earth. Gradually shifting its orbit around the Sun, and altering its tilt, eventually spiralling it a little farther towards the Sun. Nicolle's Earth, as a result, was more than twenty thousand miles closer to the Sun than this Earth, raising her planet's temperature by four degrees. This Earth had not been shifted; it was farther from the Sun, and therefore naturally cooler.

That four degree jump in temperature had partially melted our ice caps, raising our ocean levels, and searing the tropics. Creating deserts, subtly altering the shape of continents and flooding coasts and rivers. The Delaware, as the landing party had discovered, was a meagre wide stream on this World, rather than the mile-wide tidal waterway they were familiar with back home.

The meteor's impact was not the only governing factor in her Earths altered climate. Here, lack of humans and their industrialisation and deforestation, over the past five hundred years, had also contributed to this Earth's lowered temperatures. Here there were increased oxygen levels due to extra vegetation around the more temperate equator. The accumulative consequence being akin to an inverse greenhouse effect; raised oxygen, lower carbon dioxide resulting in a further lowering of this planets temperature. Nicolle's world had been cruelly, and violently, robbed of this more balmy, Eden like climate.

Again Nicolle's eyes strayed to the Caribbean. On this Earth there was no Gulf. In this timeline that fateful meteorite had sailed harmlessly through the solar system, doing no damage, its passage unnoticed and unmarked. On this pristine, unblemished Earth, Mother Nature's first choice dominant species had endured, and evolved. There were no humans.

At this moment Nicolle felt very small and vulnerable. Her life, her existence, her very species it seemed was nothing more than the chance protégé of a worthless piece of space junk; and Mankind, she realised had been an evolutionary afterthought.

Quelle Curiosite. She thought, reverting, as always, to her mother's tongue in her head. Evolution was a curious and fickle phenomenon, she mused. It had no purpose or favour, for any particular or individual species, but It did, it seemed have an over-all plan. It had a design for life.

She realised that this fickle, curious phenomenon had a goal, an objective. And no matter what difficulties or obstacles are thrown in its path, such as Earth's meteorite, it will endeavour, at all times, to achieve that goal. Evolution, she pondered, seemed not to be the haphazard series of chance alterations in geographic, or climatic conditions that either promotes or suppress mutations. Evolution, whatever its original starting point, had a goal: to build towards a dominant species, and if that were true then its goal was pre-destined throughout Universe.

It seems it is irrelevant the number of species any world evolves, one will always emerge from the primitive disorder, and ascends to become the dominant species of that world. Evolution it seems demands it.

It is a curious paradox, that the dominant species of any world, exists at the top of that planet's food chain, but during the millennia of struggle for evolutionary supremacy, the top of the food chain almost never becomes the dominant species. To use Nicolle's Earth as an example; one would have expected the dominant species to have emerged from possibly, the big cat or the bear families, but curiously, it was eventually the humble ape who stood up-right to have dominion over her world.

Why? Because evolution favours dexterity over brute strength and killing prowess: Kraxians being the obvious exception. And for that reason, on all worlds where intelligent life has emerged, no matter what the species, the same basic body structure has always risen to dominance. This physical configuration; up-right biped, with two arms; hands for gripping and building; two eyes high on the front of the head, for depth perception, and two ears either side of the head, is evolutions pre-destined goal.

Each species has its individual distinctions, which are little more than cosmetic; Kraxian horns, Vaurillian's lack of external ears, and so on. But the similarities are incontrovertible; the dominant species on any planet, all share this same basic body shape no matter how many light-years separate them across the Galaxy. No matter the circumstances in which each species has evolved, to all intents and purposes, we are the same. Because this is what nature has intended. Because to become the dominant species, the principal life forms on any world, has to be this shape. This biped physical configuration has potential to achieve beyond the confines of more specialised species.

Humans, and the reptiles on the world below, are this shape because this is the optimum design to become the dominant species of this, or any world. This physical form is prevalent through-out the universe; Kraxian, Vaurillian, Rassilian and even on the far side of the Galaxy, Zerttral and Vadeusan; so many life forms, all so alike that they can even interbreed; Cosique, half Kraxian half Human being the immediate proof.

On Nicolle's Earth, it had always been evolutions intent, to evolve an upright biped, dominant species, and for that life form to reach out to the stars and find similar life forms. Unfortunately Mother Nature's carefully conceived plan was violently and devastatingly interrupted. In an instant, all of her painstaking endeavours were destroyed.

Two hundred million years of evolution, lost to a wandering meteorite. She'd had to start again. This time with mammals.

"Please repeat," Nicolle said, rousing herself from her dark brooding, as a voice over the comm-system dragged her back to the present.

"Commander Jevak is requesting permission to come aboard, Captain," Ensign Lawrence said again.

"Permission granted. Have him directed to the Conference Room, please. And remind the senior staff that there's a meeting in a few minutes."

"They're already on their way, ma'am."

Nicolle sighed again as she pondered the game of chance, the indiscriminate throw of a dice, by which an entire civilisation could rise or fall, and worlds die. We were an afterthought, a second choice in a game of chance.

As she gazed forlornly beyond the window, at the cloud covered blue orb, the lyrics to "Nowhere Man", tripped through her mind. She began to softly hum along, an ironic smile playing across her lips.

The synthesised chirp of the door chime brought her song to an abrupt end.

"Come!" she called, as the door swished open.

"Captain Lockhart," Commander Jevak said politely, announcing his entrance.

"I'm glad you could join us, Commander," Nicolle replied, fixing a smile, before turning to greet him. "We're just about to convene a staff meeting. My senior officers will be joining us shortly."

Directing him to the conference table she asked. "Would you care for a refreshment while we wait?" Nicolle poured herself her usual coffee.

Scenting the warm, pungent, Arabica beans, The Commander enquired. "What beverage is this?"

"Coffee," she replied, in a tone that almost questioned why he should be asking.

Then the significance of the situation suddenly became evident to her. This Jevak would certainly never have encountered coffee before, and that this was therefore first contact…. All over again. More than three hundred years after a pair of spiralling stars collided, Nicolle was about to retrace Captain David Robertson's famous steps. Repeating that pivotal moment in human history. It was time to go back to school. She was going to have to re-learn, how to be friends with Humanities oldest allies.

Eyeing the Commander, Nicolle felt somehow unsettled. A confusion of senses made her a little ill at ease, as though lost in familiar surroundings. His face, the voice, his mannerisms were all so familiar. This was the colleague and trusted friend she had known for so many years, even before she had been given Endeavour as a command. But this was not Jevak.

"It's made by filtering boiling water over the roasted beans of the coffee tree," she explained. "We then add milk and sweetener, to suit the individuals taste; it has quite an… alluring aroma," she said, inhaling the bouquet of her single, favourite indulgence. "We often drink it as an accompaniment to social interaction." After some thought she quickly added, reminding herself that being Vaurillian, Commander Jevak would baulk at the notion that coffee was also a mild chemical stimulant. "Would you care for some mineral water?"

"May I try it?" he asked, referring to the coffee.

The Captain was taken a-back, as he relieved her of her cup. She watched, fascinated, as he savoured first the aroma, and then sampled the drink, seeming to enjoy it.

She found it a little unnerving; a Vaurillian indulging in anything even remotely 'unwholesome'. Their whole society is built on strength of mind, and logic, anything, even mild caffeine is forbidden, since it weakens their intellectual control. She found his reaction to the coffee even more unnerving.

"Curious... very pleasant," he said, as a faint smile played at the corner of his mouth. "You appear surprised, Captain."

She was more surprised than he realised. Not only was this Vaurillian drinking coffee, but he was smiling as well.

"Just a little," she replied, dryly.

"Mmm, I think I would be too in your position, Captain." He said smiling again. "I've spent the last two hours studying your computer logs on Vaurillian culture in your Universe. There are, to say the least, considerable disparities between our two histories."

"That would seem to be stating the obvious." Realising she was not about to have her coffee returned, Nicolle poured herself another.

"Commander?" she asked, changing the subject. "Before the others join us, I wonder if I might ask you some thing?"

Sipping his coffee, he nodded politely. "Go ahead."

"We're eternally grateful for your intervention, back there. Your arrival was, to say the least.... fortuitous; just in the nick of time," She said, trying to gauge his response. She could see in his eyes though that her next question was already rhetorical. "It wasn't coincidence though, was it?"

"No Captain. We'd been monitoring your transmissions, and tracking you for several days. I suspect the Kraxians had been as well, that's why they were here to arrange the welcoming committee."

"I'd suspected as much."

"And I'd suspect that others have been too," he cautioned. "You have a remarkable ship, Captain Lockhart. Even from the little I've seen, you have systems beyond any technology I've encountered. Technology, which would be much prized." Then he added, a note of regret in his voice. "Your Alliance of Planets has achieved much."

"The accumulative expertise of more than one hundred worlds, Commander," she replied. "It's what happens when species come together, working for a common good. None of what we have, could have been achieved in such a short time individually.... We, our Alliance, as you can see, are greater than the sum of our parts."

The Captain turned away sipping thoughtfully at her coffee. She was pondering the dangerous ramifications of being the only Alliance ship in a hostile place.... Then she realised, their circumstances had not really changed that much in the past six years, only the natives. She was still pondering when the door chime sounded again.

"Come," the Captain directed, loudly.

Sweeney, Wicasa, Cosique, Lt Jevak, Salix along with Sub-Commander T'Arran, entered.

"Excellent timing. Please," she said, indicating that they take their seats.

She eyed T'Arran uneasily, trying to be discrete. It made her skin crawl being in such close proximity to her, although she endeavoured not to show it. After all, she kept reminding herself, this woman was not responsible for her counterparts' actions in another universe. How alike, she wondered though, was this Vaurillian to the one she had encountered in that dark frozen prison so long ago.

As yet Nicolle had not told any of her senior staff who the sub-commander was; they could all do without the gossip mongering. But she was certain T'Arran would not remain anonymous for long. Some in her crew were well versed in Alliance Fleet history. Her name would inevitably be recognised.

"I trust you're both ok?" Commander Jevak

enquired politely, as Sweeney and Wicasa seated themselves opposite him.

Wicasa instantly noted the Commander's use of abbreviated language; something no Vaurillian in their reality, would ever do.

"Minor burns and a little smoke inhalation; nothing the Doctor couldn't fix," Sweeney replied. "Wattie's being kept in for observation. As you can imagine, he's pleased at that."

"I believe we have you to thank for our timely extrication," Wicasa smiled.

The Commander acknowledged, nodding slightly. "I am grateful we could be of assistance," he replied, taking the liberty of pouring himself another mug of coffee.

"You don't think you could have cut it a little finer," Sweeney joked, expecting the usual Vaurillian disdain at his inappropriate use of humour.

"I'd no idea you might've such a... burning desire, to remain down there," the Commander reciprocated, astounding Sweeney with a sly grin and a playful wink. Turning to the others, as they took their seats, he smiled broadly.

It suddenly occurred to Nicolle how human he appeared. Of course, had she ever accused her own Jevak of such a thing, she would have been met with the appropriate Vaurillian response, that 'there was no need for insults'. But this Jevak had a warm, genuine smile. With his un-kept look, blasé manner and self-assured swagger, there was a roguish air about this Vaurillian that made him so un-Vaurillian.

The crew reacted in unison to the Commanders levity with stunned surprise. Every one around the table, except T'Arran and the Captain, shot questioning looks at each other; a Vaurillian who not only drank coffee but had a sense of humour. Just how different was this place, thought Sweeney. The Commander seemed not to notice the astonishment he had caused, and merely took another sip from his mug.

Lieutenant Jevak, seated opposite, shifted uncomfortably. His reaction would be understandable even if the Vaurillian in question were someone else, (Vaurillians feel a collective responsibility for maintaining their decorum and dignity in the eyes of other species) but that the offending Vaurillian shared his name and his face, compounded the 'shameful' display of emotion.

"The Commander has been reviewing our data-banks over the last few hours. He was just about to clarify some.... disparities, between Vaurillians here, and in our own timeline," Lockhart explained, as she took her seat at the head of the conference table. "Please continue Commander. I'm sure we'd all be interested in your findings," she said with genuine eagerness.

Commander Jevak passed slowly along the table, studying each of the faces of Endeavours senior staff in turn. He had known some of them for only a few short hours but already found much he liked in them, individually and as a species. They, in turn, returned his scrutiny with eager anticipation. Everyone at the table knew or could guess, that their absence as a species had impacted enormously in this Universe and that the Commander's knowledge could justify their existence in their own.

How 'George Bailey' is this, thought Matt Sweeney as the Commander locked eyes with him.

"I think we'd all be very interested in hearing how our two Universes differ," Wicasa urged.

"As I was just about to explain to your Captain," he said. "I've spent the past few hours correlating dates and events from your database, and ours. I've been trying to find our common history, and therefore, at which point in time, and for what reasons our cultures diverged." He paced around the table, talking to the assembled meeting, but looking mainly at Lt Jevak. "It would appear that until relatively recently, our histories trod a mutual path."

Like the Captain, Commander Jevak did his best thinking on the move.

"The crucial, pivotal moment in time, when our histories diverged was, as you have probably already deduced, March 19th 2158."

"First Contact," Lockhart volunteered, with no amount of surprise in her voice.

"Exactly Captain; First Contact. Our records show that there was indeed a Vaurillian survey vessel monitoring the converging star systems on that date, but it completed its mission without incident."

The Commander dallied for a moment as he passed behind the Captains chair at the head of the table. Approaching the view ports, he took a long look at the insignificant blue sphere beyond. It was an inconsequential, backward planet, which had suddenly taken on a new significance. A bright, dazzling beacon of missed opportunities and unattained potential, to his, and countless other worlds in the Galaxy. As he turned from the window to face his hosts again he felt a rage of pitiful loss wash over him. These humans... the impact these beings had had in their universe was immeasurable and it had been denied to his reality.

How different this world would have been, how different one hundred and fifty other worlds in the present, and how many countless more into the future would have been. A community of benevolence, strength and tolerance, had a wandering piece of space debris, drifted into this solar system on a different trajectory.

The full significance of the situations enormity was only vaguely apparent to those gathered at the table.

"The absence of humans, and I suppose, the non-existence of The Alliance, would explain a great many changes in your historical events," Wicasa said, glancing firstly at the Commander, then at Lt Jevak. "But there seams to be a cultural difference here as well." The last statement was also a question.

Commander Jevak sighed resignedly as he

took up his explanation.

"Yes Commander," he agreed. "To explain that, I'd have to tell you something of Vaurillian's history, in this time line." He began pacing again. "Approximately three hundred and fifty years ago, even before your 'first contact', small pockets, factions, within our society became disillusioned with the old ways. They rebelled against the restrictions, and constraints required to attain pure logic and mental clarity. These factions craved emotional release rather than clarity of mind; they embraced their passions. In a society, which required logic and inflexible mental discipline, their liberated expressionism alienated them. Eventually they were compelled to escape the constraints of Vaurilla, and abandoned our home world, to embrace a new, passionate existence, wandering the Galaxy as homeless nomads."

Lieutenant Jevak nodded his appreciation and understanding of the situation the Commander's home world had found its self in. A little uneasily he interrupted his doppelganger.

"In our timeline we also evolved small factions who rebelled," he stated. "But that was the limit of their expansion; small, random factions." The statement was also a question as to why the existence of these disenfranchised groups should have made any difference to the culture of Vaurilla.

"Different circumstances, Lieutenant." the Commander said, regretfully. Pacing again, he continued. "It is common to both of our timelines that about then, there was a long running territorial dispute with the Tyreeans. In this reality though, that dispute escalated unchecked. What had amounted to little more than skirmishes along our out-post borders, deteriorated to full-scale war." He turned to the Captain. "I understand that in your reality, that escalation was averted due to Earth and Tyreea intervening when Kraxa attacked my home world?"

"That's right," she nodded, a little taken aback by his wealth of knowledge so quickly accumulated from their databanks. "But the disputes weren't settled then; it took several more years to broker a lasting peace."

"Not for the first, or last time, human intervention saved the day." the Commander laughed emptily, as he glanced out at the empty promise that was this Earth. "Human endeavour, the salvation of your timeline, Captain. In our timeline the war with Tyreea continued for decades. Millions on both sides died. It took a massive toll on both worlds. Our populations and natural resources were almost decimated. Vaurilla was fast being stripped of everything."

"But then when things seemed at their blackest", he laughed ironically. "Kraxa, ever mindful of its neighbours fortunes, turned its expansionist eye towards Vaurillian, and Tyreea. With our armies depleted, we were both ripe for conquest. Soon we were fighting battles on two fronts."

He caught Cosique's eye as he began to recount Kraxia's eager and bloody entry to the galactic war, their eyes locked across the table, the accuser, and the accused. He felt rage and anger. Not towards Cosique personally, but having to share the same room, breath the same air, as a Kraxan, even a half Kraxan, was like a betrayal. His family, his friends his world had been brought almost to its knees at the hands of these war-mongering savages.

Cosique, who had spent much of the last couple of hours in main engineering, being assisted by T'Arran, as they tried to get the warp reactor back on line, therefore knew about the war, and how badly it had gone.

Endeavour's Chief Engineer shifted uneasily in that cold stare. She felt guilty for something she was not a part of. This war, which had raged for more than two centuries, was not of her doing, these were not her people, and this was not her reality, her Universe. She was not guilty. But she knew that her species was. She felt dishonoured, and culpable.

"In our Universe," she offered, in her species defence, "Kraxa isn't yet part of the Alliance, but we still hold out hope that one day it might. But it is no longer an enemy."

The Commander quelled his rage. Speaking softly, he said. "Once again Lieutenant, your Alliance, lead by humans has made the all important difference; the glue that holds everything together, nurturing galactic peace."

Turning away from her again he drew a deep breath as he retraced his steps around the conference table, back towards the view port.

"As the bitter wars raged," he continued, "It seemed that Vaurilla was doomed."

Again the Commander slowed as he caught sight of The Earth, he seemed continually drawn to that blue world now that he was aware of its full significance; that promise that had been denied. It was like a morbid fascination, or an itch that could not be scratched, how peaceful it looked, how tranquil. And how different, he thought, this Universe could have been, how many lives would have been saved, had that rock maintained its course.

Until a few hours ago Earth had been merely the third planet in a system, marking the vague boundary between the Vaurillian Protectorate and the Kraxian Empire. Now it represented an illusion, a tantalising notion, something out of reach on the edge of a dream. He gathered his thoughts again.

"We were faring worse than both of our adversaries," he said mournfully.

As he turned to confront the gathered faces around the table, his eyes slowly brightened. "But then our wandering, prodigal children returned," he continued, his voice gathering pace, his expression brightening. "They had left Vaurilla to drift the Galaxy, seeking pleasure and experience rather than enlightenment. But when Vaurilla needed all of her children, they answered the call," he smiled and said simply, "Our fortunes changed."

"You see," he explained, "In warfare, logic equals predictability, and that made our battle-fleets easy targets. The old ways were killing us. We were losing ships faster than we could build them, until our nomadic children returned."

"The few ships commanded by nomads, 'The Ghost Fleet' they became known as because, unlike the rest of the Vaurillian fleet they were like spectres amongst us; they were successful beyond anything the High Command could expect, or explain. Their emotions made them imaginative, resourceful, unorthodox and more importantly, ruthless. The enemy were at a loss to understand them, they thought that all Vaurillians were the same; systematic clones. They were wrong," he said coldly, again catching Cosique's eye.

"The 'Ghosts' routed an overwhelming Kraxian fleet as they attempted to annex Nimbus III."

"The Planet of Galactic Peace?" Wicasa asked, in disbelief. "Are there no Galactic accords, protecting Nimbus III, in this reality?"

Commander Jevak could not help himself. The humorous retort was too inviting to be denied. "Yeh, in a parallel Universe," he replied sarcastically.

The irony of the Commanders reply was not lost. An uneasy laughter echoed around the table. Everyone responded to the joke. Everyone, that is except Endeavour's Jevak, and unusually, Matt Sweeney.

Perhaps Matt just felt uneasy at being usurped as the joker in the pack. Perhaps, but he looked as though he had something else on his mind.

"The battle was over in a matter of hours," the Commander continued. "Forty ships lost to our seven. Soon the 'Ghosts' became legendary, especially amongst our impressionable young, those who had yet to undergo their first 'Purgat'. In droves, they abandoned the old ways, seeking to emulate 'The Ghosts'. Within a decade, there were no Vaurillian battleships crewed by the old order."

"The elders were powerless to halt the exodus from the ancient beliefs and disciplines." There was no regret in his voice as he recounted the death of his ancient culture. "Our monasteries soon fell into disrepair... The old ways were over. There are still a few who cling to the ancient culture, but they are numbered in hundreds, and becoming fewer... We are a different people."

The Commander looked directly at Lt Jevak as his voice became a little more solemn. "My father....Our father," he corrected himself, acknowledging for the first time their oneness, "did his best to dissuade me from joining the new order. He clung to his beliefs till the day he died."

Lieutenant Jevak visibly flinched; he looked as though he had been hit by a shuttlecraft. There should have been no reason for his reaction; after all it was not his Father the Commander was talking about.

"He is dead?"

"Twenty years now," the Commander replied, nodding solemnly. "He remained with his order, on our outpost on Gath'Vo, throughout the attack by Tyreean fighters."

"I am sorry for your loss," Lt Jevak replied flatly, but sincerely.

"Is....? Is our Father still alive in your timeline?" the Commander asked cautiously.

"He remains with his order. The monastery on Gath'Vo still flourishes."

"Is he still as... rash-eda?" the Commander asked, smiling.

Jevak was not sure he liked his father being referred to as obstinate. He inclined his head, raising one eyebrow. "He continues to be as... wise," he replied, correcting the Commander.

The Commander swallowed hard. "Stay close to him, Jevak," he said earnestly, quickly turning his back. "You never know when the last day will come."

He did not want these strangers to see the tears in his eyes, and especially not Lieutenant Jevak.

The old Vaurillian had tried to cling to their ancient values and culture, while all around the old ways were being discarded and torn down. He had tried to instil those values in Commander Jevak. 'Without our logic and culture, we are no better than the savages we fight', his father had said.

The Commander still found it hard to forgive himself. There had been no contact between them, since he had denied his fathers wishes, and rejected the 'Purgat'. He had tuned his back on that wise, gentle old man, forty years ago, vowing angrily, to live his life his own way. Even now he could not understand his own anger. He had been a head strong impetuous young Vaurillian. And he had spent the last twenty years regretting, every day, never having been able to tell his father how proud he was of him, how much he loved him, or being able to make his peace with him.

"Keep him close, Lieutenant," he repeated.

"Did the 'Ghosts' turn the war?" Lockhart asked, offering the Commander a dignified diversion.

"No...." he said, recomposing himself. "No, the war ground on, it descended into an interminable stalemate. The fighting became routine, sniping at border patrols, raiding outposts."

"This war has just kept going?" Captain Lockhart interrupted. Her tone betraying her disbelief at how the hostilities had been allowed to continue. "Was their never any attempt to step back; some sort of conciliation?"

"Step back, Captain?" he laughed, in disbelief, making no attempt to look anywhere but directly at Cosique. "Kraxa, or Tyreea, would've taken that as a sign of weakness; an invitation to send their entire fleet. No Captain there was no attempt to step back, but had we," he said regretfully, "it might have saved the Sector from the war we now find ourselves in."

He rounded the table, to the empty chair left vacant for him. Slowly he took his seat. He stared blankly at the table as he continued. "Macaitia was eager to enter the fray." He took a deep breath. "About fifty years ago their technology developed their first warp-eight engine, then the whole Sector came within their reach. They were so eager to flex their muscle, show the rest of us that there was a new challenger in the neighbourhood." He fell silent for a moment, remembering the onset of the Galactic war. Eventually he said, "Barva, their closest neighbour, was the first to fall."

"It was the same in our dimension," the Captain said grimly. "Barva fell under Macaitian rule for several decades."

"Same?..." He shook his head slowly. "No Captain. That is not how it happened here. They gave them no quarter. Barva was overwhelmed with firepower. Don't get me wrong," he added, "Barva fought back, but it was hopeless. It took almost a year all told, but the Macaitian fleet crushed them into submission."

He slowly looked around the table, at all the troubled faces of the Alliance officers. "And as every conquering empire has ever found, to its cost," he continued. "Policing territory already conquered, is labour intensive, and a wasteful drain on military resources, it is much more efficient to eliminate the problem, than to police it. Barva was sterilised, all life forms eradicated. In our reality Barva no longer exists."

Lockhart was shocked. "These Macaitians are more ruthless than they are in our Universe," she conceded.

"In this Universe there is no Alliance to contend with, Captain. And there in lies the difference. You see, your Alliance is not just a powerful military force; it is also an influence for good, throughout the Sector. It instilled a code of conduct in the Galaxy... even amongst its enemies. There is nothing like your Alliance in this timeline, and we are the worse for your absence."

Nicolle drew a deep breath, and ran a hand through her hair, turning her eyes to the ceiling. "For the want of a nail..." She muttered, quietly, sadly.

Commander Jevak looked at her, puzzled by her response. "Captain?" He asked.

"It is an old Earth saying." the Commander's Alliance doppelganger interjected. "English in origin. It refers to..."

Ignoring her Lieutenant the Captain re-commenced.

"For want of a nail a shoe was lost,"
"For want of a shoe a horse was lost,"
"For want of a horse a rider was lost,"
"For want of a rider the battle was lost,"
"For want of the battle the kingdom was lost,"
"And all for the want of a horseshoe nail," she finished, quietly, sadly.

Silence befell the room. It seemed smaller, darker. The Alliance officers around the table felt very alone.

"What does this refer to?" Commander Jevak

asked, puzzled by the Captain's unorthodox response.

"It's an old saying," Lockhart said, taking-up the explanation. "It refers to the cataclysmic, knock on, effects, a seemingly small, innocuous event can have. In this case the absence of a piece of space debris sixty-five million years ago, has caused countless wars and death on worlds, it never even came near... For want of a piece of space junk the Galaxy was lost."

"What happened after Barva fell?" Wicasa asked, quickly dragging everyone back from their collective melancholy.

"A slow, relentless onslaught through the Sector, which grew pace and eventually became a fast relentless onslaught."

"Seven years ago?" Wicasa asked, establishing a time connection.

"Yes, Commander. Seven years ago."

"The Alliance liberated Barva nine years ago, and it's been protecting it ever since," Cosique informed him, leaning in towards the commander she lowered her voice, almost conspiratorially. "There are some in the Alliance; the silent minority, who have long advocated an all-out attack on Macaitia. There are some in the Alliance, who recognised Macaitia's evil intent and the danger it poses to Galactic stability," she said, hinting at the growth of rebel forces within the Alliance.

"Lieutenant," the Captain reproached her. "This is no time for Alliance politics."

"There are countless billions in this reality Lieutenant, who wish that we had that option," the commander said despondently.

"How is the war progressing?" Lockhart asked, almost apologetically.

"Badly, Captain," he replied, gravely, his face darkening. "This is a war we cannot win." His voice became quieter, as though the fewer people could hear, the less chance of his prediction had of becoming reality. "We pull off small victories, here and there, but we're vastly out numbered and out gunned. There's no cohesion, no unifying force, or co-operation in the Sector. Your Alliance has stabilised your Galaxy, provided security, and protection. There's nothing like that in this reality. We have spent too many centuries fighting against each other, fearing our neighbours, to help each other now that the time has come. There has never been enough trust between any of us, to stand together against a common enemy. We've all stood alone. And now we fall alone, more than half the sector already has."

"Vaurillia has maybe another year, "T'Arran added, "maybe two at most, then the fate that befell Barva awaits us too. Kraxa may survive a little longer; their empire is spread wider, but their fate is also inescapable. For us though," she said shaking her head, looking to her Commander. "There's no hope. We will never surrender, but all we're doing is holding off the inevitable."

For a moment they both fell silent, letting the

gravity of their desperate situation sink-in. Eventually the Commander spoke again.

"This universe, Captain, is the worse for your absence." Looking up from the table, he scanned the faces around him; he saw sorrow and guilt in all of their eyes. Endeavour's crew felt somehow responsible, that they had some how failed to answer a desperate call for help.

Cosique, with her warrior nature responded first. "There must be something we can do to help," she said looking to her Captain.

The Commander was stunned by her demand for action. It was hard to imagine a Kraxan from this reality, offering assistance to any outside their own clan, let alone another species.

The Commander prevented the Captain from responding. "No."

"I thought you said you would never surrender," Cosique shot back impatiently.

"One ship will make no difference, to us, the Kraxians, Tyreeans, Tholtarians, none of us. Even fully repaired, this ship, with all of its lasers, torpedoes and new technology won't save any of us; won't change the course of this war one millimetre." He drew a deep breath, looking around the table, before continuing.

"Our ship yards are stretched beyond their limit, just maintaining our existing fleet; same with the Kraxians, Rassilians and everyone else. None of us have the capacity, or the resources to re-jig, to build from scratch a completely new design. It would take at least three years to complete a ship like this. Three years we don't have. During that time we would have to neglect our existing fleet, and that would only hasten our end."

"But surely there's something that we can do?" Wicasa added.

"You have come too late Commander. How is this war going in your Universe?" he enquired.

"We don't know," Wicasa replied, wondering what the Commander was getting at. "We left our alpha Sector six years ago, the war was only beginning to escalate. Macaitia had made a few raids along her borders by then, little more."

"Your war may be over by now, then. Do you think it was an easy victory?"

"If it is, it was probably won at a cost."

"And that, with an entire fleet; an alliance from one hundred and fifty worlds, fighting in co-operation, with uniform weaponry." He looked around the table again, for emphasis. "There is nothing like your Alliance in this reality," he said, slowly, deliberately, as though spelling it out. "Endeavour can not help us. If anything," he sighed. "It is more of a danger to us." He looked almost beseechingly at the Captain. "Were the enemy to somehow get hold of this vessel, it would hasten our destruction to mere months. They still have capacity to replicate. They could have an entire fleet of Endeavours, cutting a swath through the remainder of the sector in months."

"But that's not going to happen," Nicolle

firmly reassured him.

The Vaurillian Commander got to his feet, walked to the view port then turned to face the table. This was going to be difficult. He prepared himself for an adverse reaction.

Nicolle swivelled in her chair to face him.

"Captain...I've already received my orders from The High Command," he said earnestly. "I am ordered to take any means necessary... to ensure the enemy does not take control of this vessel."

A tense silence stifled the room.

"I thank you for you candour," she said tensely. She also got to her feet, fixing him squarely. "But as I've already said..., that will not happen."

"May I ask your intensions then, Captain?"

Another standoff was developing. The atmosphere became tense.

Nicolle did not answer immediately. She let the question hang for a while. She was about to discover if her assumption, that these Vaurillians could be as trusted allies as those in her own Universe, was accurate.

"This isn't our home. We've no right to be here. We've no wish to be here. As soon as we've restored warp power, I intend setting a course back to the wormhole, back to our own dimension."

Commander Jevak attempted to relax the situation with a smile. "Then, with your permission, Captain," he said. "We would be happy to provide you with an escort; to ensure your safe passage."

Nicolle knew that the offer was not just to ensure their safety. Should there be any possibility of their being intercepted enroot, the Commander's orders, no doubt, would be to destroy Endeavour to prevent her from being taken. Knowing the Commander was being as genuine as the situation allowed, Nicolle realised that were the circumstances reversed, she without doubt would have made the same offer.

"Okay," she said turning to her crew. "We still have our own 'Order of Business' to take care of."

The Commander nodded politely noting that the offer, though not accepted had also not been rejected and that neither he nor the Captain had had to lose face. He took his seat, appreciating her diplomacy.

The Captain also took her seat again, at the head of the table.

"As we're all now well aware, we have not made it home. So, firstly, people, the obvious question," she began. "How the hell did we get here? We've passed through wormholes before, none of them have ever opened into a parallel Universe, and there are no records of any wormholes ever doing so. So why are we here?"

Lieutenant Jevak responded to the question. "Captain if I may?"

"Please."

Getting to his feet the Lieutenant strode to the wall mounted display screens behind Matt, Salix and Wicasa. Lightly fingering the touch sensitive screen, he cancelled the standard ship status read-out, replacing it with a white-on-blue graphic, displaying Endeavours outline against co-incentric coloured bands radiating out from the ship.

"Observe," he said. "I have been reviewing our sensor logs during our passage through the wormhole. As you can see here, at this point, Endeavour crosses the phenomenon's threshold." He delayed while the graphic changed. "Closely pursued by two of the energy ribbons."

The graphic gradually shifted and altered, like time-lapse photographs.

"Here, the first impacted on our hull. The second, at this point impacted, then deflected towards the inner wall of the wormhole, impacting here."

The graphic suddenly disappeared, leaving the screen blank, apart from the outline of the ship.

Jevak turned to face his colleagues. "This is not a sensor malfunction. Nothing is being detected beyond the ship's hull, because there is nothing beyond the ship's hull to detect. For a brief moment, point zero zero zero seven two nano-seconds, to be precise, Endeavour existed in, for want of a better phrase, non-existence."

As the graphic resumed Endeavour was shown to exit the wormhole.

"As you will recall, prior to our entering the wormhole," he continued, "a probe was dispatched, to determine the location of the phenomenon's exit. Our records have established it exited into the Alpha Sector, of our own Universe. We on the other hand exited into the Alpha Sector of this Universe. Which would explain why, after we had stabilised onboard systems, we were unable to detect the whereabouts of the probe."

"Then the energy discharge must have opened a door between our two Universes," Salix offered.

"Precisely."

"To reopen that door then, we would have to re-create the same conditions?" Cosique asked rhetorically.

"How much energy was discharged in that impact?" asked the Captain.

"Incalculable, Captain. It was beyond sensors capabilities," Jevak replied, almost apologetically.

"Even a warp reactor overload can be calculated." Wicasa offered.

"There's nothing I can think of that we could use to re-create that amount of energy," Cosique said, "apart from maybe a collapsing star, and thankfully we always keep at least two of them down in Engineering," she added sarcastically, attempting to inject a little humour into a complex situation.

"Any ideas?" Lockhart asked, directing the question to every one at the table.

"Nothing as yet," Jevak replied, hinting that he was still hopeful of finding a solution.

The Captain sighed. "Keep me informed," she concluded, her voice betraying her deep concern.

Lt Jevak returned to his seat, deafened by the

silence of his crewmates.

"Well," Salix chirped, quickly changing the subject, "that explains how we got here, that just leaves the unexplained mystery of how that wrecked battleship down there, got here."

As the self appointed morale officer for the ship, as well as its chef, Salix felt compelled to ensure the meeting did not end on a depressing down beat. The little Talluriann was determined to divert them from their own dilemma; it was the best he could come up without having to resort to enquiring what they all wanted for lunch.

"I thought our historical data said that the… Eldridge, went into service and was eventually scrapped about forty years later. Even if it did disappear in some experiment, it came back. So how can it be here?" He asked.

Around the table the tension lifted slightly at the opportunity to mull over some one else's problem other than their own. Matt especially seemed to brighten at the mention of the World War Two wreck.

Jevak again was the only one to respond. "Having examined the data, and discounted the official line, that there was no such experiment," he said. "I have concluded that the U.S.S. Eldridge, which re-appeared in Philadelphia during 'Project Rainbow' in 1943, was not the same one which disappeared."

"How so?" Lockhart asked.

"Given that every U.S.S. Eldridge in all of the

infinite number of parallel Universes were being experimented upon at the same moment in time, it is quite possible that the energy build-up caused by the multiple quantum generators weakened the fabric of space in that geographical region. A doorway, as it were, was opened through which each then simultaneously disappeared, to re-appear in its neighbouring dimension, where another had moments before vanished." He raised his right eyebrow, indicating how logical and simple he believed the solution to be. "The Eldridge, which reappeared in our Universe, I believe, did not originate there. But, since the ship and crew appeared to be the same as the one which had disappeared, and since parallel Universes were a concept unheard of in that era, nothing untoward was suspected."

"But, since no Eldridge existed in this Universe..." Salix said, pausing as the thought became clear. "...So somewhere there's a parallel dimension, where a ship disappeared... and it never returned."

"I am afraid that would appear to be the case," Jevak agreed.

Again the room fell silent.

"Okay," Nicolle said springing to action. "Let's snap out of this. We have our own situation to worry about, and I don't want to spend any more time here than we have to. How are the repairs coming along?"

"Sub-Commander T'Arran has been invaluable in engineering," Cosique replied warmly. "The warp reactor's been repaired as much as we can, given the time factor, but we still have extensive repairs to carry out on both engine nacelles, so we wont be able to bring it on line for another hour... two at the very most. Shields will be a little longer. All weapons are operational though," she said brightly. "Teleports are back on line and censors are at maximum."

Nicolle was encouraged; at least the ship's status was improving. "Jevak?" she said, moving on.

"I have conducted an extensive scan of the region. To a distance of sixteen-light-years, there are no other ships in the area, apart from ourselves and the Commanders."

"Things are looking up," The Captain said encouragingly. "Alright, as soon as you can bring the warp reactor back on line. Shields can…"

"Err…. Captain. If I might suggest," Sweeney interrupted, apologetically.

Something was troubling Matt. Nicolle knew that there was something wrong. He had hardly contributed to the meeting at all, in-fact he had been almost silent; completely unlike him.

"What's on your mind?" she asked.

"I think… we may have an unforeseen, err… situation," Matt continued.

"What kind of situation?"

"I don't think we should consider breaking orbit yet. I think there may be humans on the surface."

"That's not possible," T'Arran replied for the Captain. "Your species doesn't exist in this timeline."

"There can't be any survivors from that ship," The Captain ventured. "It's been here four hundred years."

Matt did not reply, but remained resolute.

"Explain," Lockhart demanded, calmly.

"Well," he began. "While we were on the surface, searching the Eldridge, I took a look through some of the crew's cabins, while Wicasa and Wattie searched the Captain's. I found two cabins with what I can only assume were discarded...err." He hesitated, looking for the correct description. "...Feminine items."

"Such as?" asked Wicasa.

"Pink hair brush, panty hose, vanity mirrors, that kind of stuff."

"Why didn't you mention this before?" Lockhart enquired.

"At the time I thought the items were maybe just keep sakes, the crew hung on to, to remind themselves of their wives or sweethearts back home. But since we got back I've checked the database for more information." He looked intently at the Captain as he began recounting the battleship's apparent history.

"In August 1943 the Eldridge wasn't 'Navy' yet." he cast his eye around the table. "At the time 'Project Rainbow' was supposed to have taken place the War Department hadn't taken her into service. The ship would still have been civilian; under the control of Department of Defence scientists, not the navy. And there's no reason to suppose that some of those scientists, or technicians, weren't female. In fact you can bet that some of them were."

The weight of Matt's theory hit home.

"How many would you estimate?" Enquired Jevak.

"Impossible to say. But I found two cabins, with two bunks in each," he shrugged. "A minimum of four."

"Wait a minute," the Captain interrupted. "let's not get carried away with any kind of conjecture. This, if it did happen, happened over four hundred years ago. Are you suggesting that descendants of the survivors are still down there? That's pretty long odds, Matt."

"Possibly four women, to how many sailors?" asked Wicasa.

"Given that she wasn't in service and wouldn't have a full compliment yet, probably about fifty," Matt replied.

"That's the wrong ratio, Matt. A gene pool like that couldn't have supported anything more than a couple of generations." Wicasa argued. "If there were any offspring, congenital defects would've killed them off long ago."

"I can not agree, Commander." Lieutenant Jevak interrupted, apparently supporting Sweeney's theory. "Mr Sweeney may possibly, be correct. If there were any survivors, they would be alone in a hostile environment. They would quickly become aware that subsequent generations would be required for their own survival, especially into old age. Therefore, the gene pool would have to be deep and wide, enough to support future generations... Given a similar situation; were we to find ourselves stranded, do you not think this crew would take the necessary steps to ensure survival? A breeding programme, no matter how distasteful that may sound, would be implemented, the females having offspring with more than one male. Such a programme would ensure that an extensive and varied gene pool would be achieved?"

The Captain stepped away from the table. Her mind raced through the terrible possibilities. Were she and her crew to ever find themselves in such a situation, she was sure that they would take any steps necessary to ensure their, and future generations continued survival. Matt might just have a point.

She spun on her heels.

"All right," she conceded. "But it's been four hundred years, what makes you think their descendants have survived?" Nicolle was looking to Matt to convince her.

"Because their crew had the best possible blend of individuals they could've ever wished for, with skills and training which just wouldn't have let them perish. In fact they would have positively thrived." He explained enthusiastically. "A perfect mix of leader, warriors, thinkers, creators and builders; naval engineers who could build and maintain anything from a diesel engine to an ashtray with little more than papier-mâché. Scientists and technicians who designed and built the equipment that got them here in the first place. Sailors who had already fought in, what was until then the bloodiest conflict our planet had known. And a Captain, who……," he said, locking eyes with Nicolle, acknowledging her own leadership skills. "If my experience is anything to go by, would have seen them safely through a brick wall… Were I ever stranded in the same situation, I pray to God that I get stranded with people like that."

The Captain still remained dubious. This still was a long shot, but it was looking less unlikely.

"Ma'am," Matt pressed, using the Captain's official address; something he rarely did. "I'd like to think that somewhere back in our Alpha Sector, Alliance Fleet hasn't given up on us. That some how, some way they're still trying to find out where we are and find a way of getting us home. If there are humans down there, then we owe them that same consideration. They're lost. We can't abandon them. Alliance Fleet hasn't abandoned us."

Nicolle could not fault Matt's logic. He had convinced her…People like that could…would survive. "Okay, you've got two hours…"

"Captain Lockhart!" interrupted Commander Jevak. "If I might remind you…." he insisted.

"Commander," she said, stopping him in his tracks. "If there is any possibility that there are humans down there, I want to know. It is my sworn duty to protect the Alliance and all of it citizens;

they are human and therefore my responsibility, and under no circumstances will I desert them."

"But this is most likely a futile search. There are almost certainly no humans alive down there."

"Then we'll definitely be out of here in two hours. But until the warp reactor's ready to be brought on line, we have time to spare."

"Captain, I'd like to take one more Look at the Eldridge," Matt said. "I want to be sure of what the crew did before abandoning the ship. It'll maybe give us a clue to where they went."

The Captain thought for a moment. "Alright, but teleport directly to the wreck. I don't want anymore contact with the locals. The rest of you know what's required. Dismissed!"

Matt was first out of the conference room, heading directly for the teleport room.

As the others made their way back to their duty stations, Jevak found himself side by side with his counterpart. There was still an awkwardness between them, but mainly on the Lieutenant's part. The Commander was more intrigued by this Vaurillian who shared his name and his face, and who's ridged adherence to logic reminded him so much of his father. He resolved to get to know the lieutenant better.

"Commander, may I ask a question?" Lieutenant Jevak ventured uncomfortably, primarily to break the silence.

"Of course."

"I am puzzled. When the Kraxian battleship

confronted us after we arrived in orbit, their Captain's was reluctant to communicate directly with us. Yet the moment we made contact with you, although our universal translators were inoperative, you facilitated us with your own."

"In this reality, Kraxian 'battle-beasts' are not fitted with translators. They are a conquering race. They see no advantage in communicating with a ship they will, more than likely, shortly be destroying."

Jevak raised his eyebrows in that manner which acknowledged his understanding of a curious notion.

"I've also got a question for you," the Commander said quietly, not wanting to offend the humans. "How do you tolerate the smell?"

Vaurillians, in all Universes, apparently have a heightened, very finely tuned sense of smell and we humans are, to all intents and purposes, quite...... musky.

CHAPTER 12

By the time Matt arrived at the teleport-room, Wattie was already there, waiting.

"You're supposed to be in sick-bay," Matt said, reproachfully.

"I've had enough of the Doctor's bedside manner," Wattie replied, exasperated. "Even people who've never been ill have had enough of his bedside manner."

"Does the Captain know you're here?" Matt asked, stepping quickly on to the teleport pad.

"Of course."

Wattie was, 'by the book', never the type to do anything contrary to regulations; he believed him. Joining Matt on the teleport pad Wattie handed him a torch, hand laser and a palm-corder, then informed him that the co-ordinates had already been set."

Sweeney nodded, he could tell Wattie was as curious as he was. "Teleport," he said.

The teleport Chief engaged the controls, and began the process of dismantling their bodies, atom from atom. A few milliseconds later, on a sunlit, grassy slope, two columns of blue stars, condensed and resolved into their familiar shapes.

The instant they had ceased sparkling, Wattie stepped cautiously, away from the teleport co-ordinates, levelling his palm-corder to scan the area, while Matt took a look around.

The scene was different from what he had imagined, now that they could see it in daylight. The gentle grass covered slope they were standing on was the same one that they had descended the night before. About ten feet in front of them the gentle slope sharply then dropped away for about thirty feet, the grass there being replaced by loose shale and rock. It then levelled out again, to where the wreckage lay. The deck of the four hundred year old battle ship was almost level with them, listing towards them.

Beyond the wreck the long grass resumed, stretching for about five or six hundred yards in a gently declining plain towards the shallow, narrow Delaware, which snaked passed them from left to right. Even at this distance Matt could tell the river was emaciated; it looked barely twenty feet wide.

Beyond the thin ribbon of slow, meandering water, the land rose gently again for about half a mile, until it reached the edge of a dense pine forest. The carpet of evergreen blanketed the hills beyond, stretching as far as the eye could see. The eastern horizon, about ten miles away, was punctuated by the rise and fall of low, frost capped hills.

New Jersey looks even less inviting in this Universe, thought Wattie.

Matt tried to imagine the course of the mighty Delaware of his world, forging its path through this flat, cold landscape, but he could not. The glaciers, which had carved the contours of this land, had been driven by different forces; forces unique to this world.

Wattie squinted at the Sun, climbing towards its zenith. It did not seem any smaller, given that here it was an extra twenty thousand mile distant, but the unseasonably, cold autumn air confirmed the divide. He found himself having to remind himself again, that it was not this Earth that was different; it was theirs that had been altered. This was how nature had intended their planet to be.

A cold breeze caught them as it ruffled through the long grass at their feet. It swept across the gentle incline behind them, pushing the grass before it like a gentle wave skimming onto a beach.

Wattie shivered as he checked his palmcorder. "Coast's clear," he said.

Matt led the way down the crumbling slope, shuffling tentatively over the loose rock.

"Looks even older in daylight," Wattie observed as they stumbled to the level ground alongside the rusting keel.

Fifteen feet to their right were the scattering of spent cases, and the gouge they had entered by the previous night.

"If I'd known it was this badly corroded, I'd never have gone anywhere near it. We're not planning on going inside again, are we?" Cheung asked, hoping the answer was no.

"Don't worry, not the way we went. This way," Matt said, indicating towards the stern to their left.

Crouching, out of instinct, rather than necessity, they passed through the narrow gap between the keel and the rocky out-crop, where the Eldridge had lodged, defying gravity.

The pitted metal above their heads was crumbling. The original impact, as the ship had toppled, had holed the keel, splitting it from its mid-section up to the deck. Over the years, as corrosion had continued to devour the structure, bending and warping the welded plates, the ship had gradually tilted further, as the metal continued to weaken. The whole structure would probably collapse completely in about another fifty years, if there were anything left to collapse.

Passing below the precarious overhang, Matt continued aft, closely followed by Wattie. Rounding the massive bowl of the stern, they continued scanning with their palm-corders as they went. The readings were about what they expected; sixty two percent iron oxide, on average.

Matt knew why he had returned to the wreck, and therefore what he was looking for. Wattie on the other hand, had no idea. He diligently continued scanning and recording the available data for scientific posterity anyway. Wattie's understanding of what they were examining was minimal, he probably would not recognise anything of significance even if he knew what the object was. And so he followed closely behind his colleague, relying on Matt's judgment.

Sweeney's knowledge of twentieth and early twenty-first century technology and culture was borne of a fascination; he loved everything about that era; their cars, aeroplanes, movies, any kind of gadget. Wattie was pretty sure, that being an Alliance Fleet pilot, Matt would have fitted into that era seamlessly. He could see him as a Grand Prix driver or an action hero in the movies...No, he corrected himself... probably just a driver.

At the rear of the wreck, they found that the keel here was embedded deeper in the hard earth than anywhere else along its length. The ship was not just tilted port to starboard, but also, it seemed, stern to bow.

What was visible of the huge, twin brass propellers came to about shoulder height on Matt and Wattie. About a third was buried beneath the rock and gravel at their feet. As the ship had materialised here, the props' had still been turning, grinding their huge blades into the earth, smashing and pulverising the rock below the surface. Much of the debris was still scattered around their feet, huge rocks, gouged and hacked from the solid stone. The rudder had long since disintegrated. All that was left of it were the hinges by which it had hung.

They continued on, round to the port side.

***********   **********   **************

The door to the conference room slid open with its customary swish.

Besides this being the ship's meeting room, it was also Nicolle's private office, where she could work when she was not required at her post.

Commander Jevak had spent a little time on the bridge, getting to know Lieutenant Jevak, whilst waiting for a communication from the High Command. He now wanted to speak to the Captain.

Nicolle again had her back to the door as the Commander entered. Again she was deep in thought, perched on the edge of the long sofa, which ran half the length of the bulkhead, below the view ports. She was lost in some daydream as she gazed out at the Earth below.

As she turned to greet her guest, Commander Jevak again caught that fleeting, forlorn look, before she fixed a smile for his benefit. It was the same look she had banished as she greeted him earlier.

"Commander," she said with practiced cheer. "Please." Indicating that he join her.

"I've been in communication with Vaurilla, Captain," he began. "I have explained your situation, but the High Command are still anxious to have Endeavour underway as soon as possible."

"We're attempting to do that Commander," she replied firmly, but politely.

"I have explained that too."

What the Commander had omitted to say was that a fleet of Macaitian battle cruisers had been detected twenty light-years on the far side of the Orion sector; easily within intercept distance.

The Commander took a seat beside the Captain, glancing uneasily out at the distant stars as he did.

"Relax, Commander," she assured him. "I am as anxious to leave this Universe behind, as you and the High Command. But until we've restored warp power there's little point in getting underway. And we plan to have warp capability in less than two hours."

Endeavour still had induction engines, but as she and the Commander both knew, two hours on induction-power would barely take them beyond Pluto. Which was little better than remaining where they were. And the nacelles could be more effectively repaired whilst they were stationary. So Endeavour was staying put.

Changing the subject, in an attempt to ease the atmosphere, Nicolle adopted her flippant, quizzical look, and said. "Commander. Something has been puzzling me."

"Ask away."

"When we were first in communication with you, there was a short period when we both cut audio."

"Mmm?" He said, unsure of what she was getting at.

Nicolle paused briefly, surprised again by this Jevak's casual use of language. No Vaurillian she had ever met employed abbreviated words, let alone substituting grunts in their place; their diction was always impeccable.

"During the transmission break," she continued, setting the observation aside. "Engineering contacted me, to let me know that lasers would be available soon. I told Cosique not to bring them on line immediately, just to dim the bridge lights as a signal to let me know they were available."

Again to Nicolle's amusement, Jevak grunted his understanding.

"Then, when you'd come aboard, when the lights did dim, you knew exactly what the signal meant. How could you know?"

Commander Jevak smiled, stifling a laugh. "Is that all?" he asked. "I thought it was something serious."

For all the highly advanced technology the Alliance obviously possessed, Commander Jevak found it strange that something so rudimentary could be a mystery to them.

"It's really quite simple. It's not even high-tech, in fact it's very, very low-tech," he replied. "To be honest I was surprised that your Alliance doesn't employ something similar in your own vessel."

"Our sensors are programmed with a subroutine," he explained. "During our initial conversation, our sensors scanned your outer hull, recording and analysing the minute vibrations caused by sounds from within the ship; conversations, movement, that kind of thing. Even in the vacuum of space, a ship's hull still vibrates due to internal sounds."

Nicolle nodded, furrowing her brow a little with surprise, as Jevak's explanation unfolded. She had expected something more, some new technical innovation beyond the Alliances ability. She could not believe the explanation was so simple.

"Our computer singled-out the vibrations caused by your particular voice pattern. Then, when transmissions are broken, we simply continue scanning your hull, for that particular vibration, translating it back into speech patterns." He shrugged dismissively. "It really is that simple. You see, in a Galaxy constantly at war for centuries, we've found that information gathering is a premium."

Nicolle was speechless. How unbelievably simple, she thought. She was about to quiz The Commander further when she was interrupted by her own Jevak's voice.

"Bridge to Captain Lockhart." His disembodied voice said, via the ship's comm.

"Go ahead Jevak."

"Sensors have detected a large group of villagers making their way towards the wreck of the Eldridge."

"Let Matt and Wattie know, and keep me Informed."

"Understood."

**************   **************   **************

The flames consuming their tranquil, little, church had finally been quenched. And though they had searched meticulously, no trace of charred bodies, or bones, could be found anywhere amongst the smouldering ashes.

The priest needed no more proof that their tiny, pious, hamlet had once again been visited by demons. Demons, who had called on their Dark Lord, to spirit them away from the jaws of fiery death.

He had immediately gathered the males of the village together, rousing them with a 'hell's fire and brimstone' rant, demanding their faith, action, and if necessary their blood. He urged them to rid their God fearing land of this hellish blight, which would undoubtedly return if they had not the courage to take-up arms and destroy the Devils chariot, which still remained to the east. This was the second time that evil had visited them; he vowed there would not be a third.

The defences their forefather had constructed; the sucking bog, and brier filled mote, had merely deterred their own, inquisitive young from approaching the metal chariot. The protection of their village would demand direct action against the demons to prevent any future returns. This night would see an end to the demons grip on their land. By nightfall the chariot would be lain waste once and for all. The demons would have no more dominion over this world.

Taking-up axes, pitchforks, swords, knives, burning oil, torches, anything they could use as a weapon, they set out to destroy the chariot.

********** ************** **************

"Thanks Jevak," Wattie said. "Shouldn't be a problem though, I don't think we'll be here that long. Landing party out."

As they rounded to the port side, about twenty yards from the stern, Matt found what he had been looking for: an almost rectangular hole, deliberately cut into the hull, giving access directly to the engine room. The hole was about ten feet long by seven feet high; four complete hull plates had been removed to fashion it. Its edges had been neat, precise incisions at one time, but four hundred years of rust had eaten into the metal, leaving them ragged.

Wattie switched on his torch, playing it around the inside, while Matt scanned the edges of the serrated, crumbling hole with his palm-corder.

"How did you know this would be here?" Wattie asked.

"I didn't, but I figured they'd need certain things. With no cranes to hoist, they'd have to find another way of getting them out." He said, concentrating on the readings on his instrument.

"What's the matter?" Wattie asked.

"Just trying to work-out how they cut this hole. The plates are almost an inch thick."

Wattie shrugged, unable to help, his lack of knowledge of twentieth century engineering, evident. "Wouldn't they have some sort of cutting gear?"

Matt did not answer.

"Do we go inside?" Wattie asked, anxious to get going, now that he knew the villagers were on their way.

"Gi'me a minute." Matt replied, crouching as he examined the keel, the ship's backbone, exposed on this side due to the vessel's tilt.

A few yards further along, near the mid-point of the keel, he stopped, sighing desolately. His shoulders dropped visibly as he realised the full extent of the disasters, which had befallen the ill-fated Eldridge and her crew.

"What've you found?"

Matt got to his feet, looking at the geography of the land around them. "On our Earth, standing here, we'd be under water just now. Wouldn't we?"

Wattie came over to join him, trying to imagine the land around their wide Delaware transposed onto this landscape. He looked back and forth, from the far side of the river, to the rise on the opposite side of the wreck.

"Yeh, if the stream were the mid-point of our Delaware," he confirmed. "Probably by about twenty-five, maybe thirty feet."

Matt crouched by the keel again. Wattie could see now what he had found. The keel, at their feet, was buckled and holed. A mangled, gash, almost a foot wide had been ripped in the ship's backbone.

"I'd been wondering why they hadn't just disconnected the propeller shafts, restarted the engines, powered-up those generators on deck, and gotten themselves home again," Matt explained. "That's why. They materialised here, where there was no river, about twenty-five feet above solid ground. Can you imagine the impact: several thousand tones of battleship smashing down onto solid rock?"

He put his hand inside the gash, shaking his head incredulously. "Directly below the fuel tanks. They must have lost every drop of diesel, thousands of gallons, in minutes. They'd have no chance of plugging the hole. Probably didn't even know it was holed, with all the confusion, until it was too late."

"Playing with technology they didn't understand," Wattie sympathised.

"Come on," Matt said, switching on his torch. "Lets see why they cut that hole."

The first thing that struck him, as he cautiously entered the dark belly of the engine room, was the feint smell of oil and diesel. The industrial fumes, though heavily masked now by musty, dampness and metallic decay, had diminished over the four hundred years the ship had lain dormant, succumbing to the elements and oxidisation, but the smell was still present.

Wattie, following closely behind, peeled to the right, as he entered. The deck-plates under foot were again slick with slime, so he had to watch his footing. But that still did not prevent him from accidentally kicking some unseen object, ricocheting it around several pipes and the machinery. The sound echoed dully off the desiccated walls of the cathedral like engine room

"Careful," cautioned Matt, from Wattie's left. "What was that?"

Stooping to retrieve the object, Wattie replied, "Another of those shell casings. There's even more in here than we found outside."

Matt crouched, running his torch around their feet, where he found more. Picking one up to inspect it, musing, "None of these have been fired either. I wonder why they needed so much of the propellant?"

Second-guessing events, after almost half a millennium was fruitless. Time they did not have was being wasted, and so he pressed-on. Getting to his feet Matt directed his torch across the high, bleak, wasted, walls.

The engine room was spacious. It occupied about a quarter of the lower decks, but its high roof and the convex walls, the internal curve of the hull, gave the impression that its dimensions were greater. The walls were brown with rust, but darker in some areas, where water had penetrated through the upper decks and accumulated, seeping inevitably down.

Wattie directed his flashlight low into the corner to their left, where a series of various diameter pipes descended from the deck plates above. Following the pipes up, he caught his breath. A dismembered pelvis, rib cage and skull fused between the array of aged pipes and the deck above, hung upside down above them. One of the pipes dissected the skull through the frontal lob and the face.

"It's hardly surprising, they didn't have time to notice their fuel disappearing, with this horror going on around them," Matt said.

Wattie instantly pulled his torch beam away. "What do you need me to do?" he asked, recomposing himself.

"Scan the room for lead," Sweeney replied, still stung by the sight of the human bones materialised within the mass of the ship. It again reminded him of his own fear, the first time he was teleported, and his relief as the painless process, re-materialised him safely.

"Their electric batteries were mainly lead-plates and acid." He added, turning away from the horror.

*************** ***************

Nicolle's eyes momentarily strayed to the view port beside them. The Commander caught the fleeting glance again.

She was troubled; it did not take a "telepath"

to see that. Commander Jevak was sure though that it was not for herself, crew, or her ship. But she was troubled, and that perturbed him. It could be disastrous beyond imagination if Endeavour were to be delayed for any reason…especially for some ill-conceived notion of belonging.

Her periodic glancing indicated some pre-occupation. This, he thought, would have been understandable, if she felt some emotional tie to this world they were orbiting. But she was a strong woman. She could detach herself from the disappointment she must have felt at discovering they had not made it home. This, he felt, should merely be just another world to her, a mirage, which she now planned to leave behind.

Jevak's species had until recently, sought clarity of mind. A mere three hundred years of emotional gratification in this alternate reality, had not robbed Vaurillians of centuries of genetic coding though. While not completely telepathic, they had an insight into the minds of others.

He could sense it; something down there on the planet's surface troubled her. He could see it in her eyes. Or was it, he wondered, something that was not down there, something absent, that was bothering her.

The momentary silence stung her to her senses.

"Sorry, what were you were saying?" Lockhart asked, awkwardly.

"I didn't say anything."

"I'm sorry. I'm just a little distracted."

"Are you concerned about the possible survivors down there?" Commander Jevak asked, casting a mental line into the still, deep running, waters of Captain Nicolle Lockhart.

"No, I...."

He did not let her finish. "Or are you concerned about the humans who never existed?"

"What makes you say that?"

"Three times now, I have seen that uneasy way you look at this 'mirror' world of yours. You seem..." He faltered, searching to put into words, what he sensed from her. "You seem almost.... afraid of what you see, and yet there is only one dissimilarity."

He turned to look at the planet, trying to connect to her feelings.

"You...you are disturbed by the ease at which another species has taken your place, as the dominant species of this world?" It was both a question and a statement. "That you were so easily replaced." He smiled ironically. "Captain, it is not you who were replaced, it was them." He motioned out of the view port.

"I know that. It's just so disturbing to see how well our own world could get on in your absence, that our species wasn't really necessary, we were merely a replacement, but not the first choice."

"Not necessary?" Jevak said a little exasperated. Lockhart was feeling sorry for herself. "Captain, as you so rightly said, 'For want of a nail', countless billions across the Galaxy, would not have perished. This Galaxy has been devastated because you do not exist here."

"I know, I'm sorry but…"

"No Captain, no buts. I know how you feel, because I have to live with this reality. I live on the other side of your 'mirror'." He got to his feet, turned to the window and lent against it with both hands outstretched.

"Can you imagine what it is like", He continued. "To be shown another road, another path? Had you turned left instead of right, said yes instead of no? To have all of your past alternatives laid before you, and know that you chose wrong instead of right. To see a world, a life on the other side of the looking glass. To glimpse salvation, and know that it is forever denied to you, but was given to others. To glimpse heaven from the black bowels of hell. To know that the grass is indeed greener in someone else's garden. Do you know what torment that is?

He drew a deep breath as he turned to face her, adding. "Until two hours ago I…, none of us in this reality knew that there was another side of the looking glass, where others were given what we'd been denied."

"You think that you were natures second choice; the reserve pulled off the bench to replace the injured first team player? I doubt that Captain, I doubt that very much. I think they were the mistake. They've had a sixty-five million years head start on you, and haven't evolved nearly as far as you have in a shorter time. Your species has done more than just fill a gap. Nature, if you like, realised its mistake, and put it right."

"And do you know the irony...?" He went on. "And I don't know why I get this feeling, but I think the mistake was put right, in all of the other parallel universes apart from this one. This one is the lab rat. This one is the control that proves the success. So please Captain, stop feeling sorry for yourself. In some things it is best not to be the first... just as in love it is preferable to be the last."

Nicolle turned her gaze to the floor, she felt ashamed. Beside the dangers and constant threat of annihilation, these beings faced on a daily basis, her personal emotions paled to insignificant.

"I'm sorry," she apologised. "My insecurities are trivial beside the troubles you face." Turning her back on the view port, she added. "I really wish there were something we could do to help."

"You don't belong here, this isn't your war. The best you can do Captain is to help yourselves," the Commander urged. "Get your ship back to your own reality. Our fate here is already sealed."

Lieutenant Jevak, via the ship's comm-system, broke the awkward silence that followed. "Bridge to Captain Lockhart," he said with unhurried, even, measured tones.

"Go ahead."

"The landing party have completed their survey of the vessel. They are teleporting up as we speak."

"Did they encounter any of the locals?" Nicolle enquired.

"Negative. The villagers are still approximately one kilometre from the wreck."

"Good," she said, relieved that the landing party had avoided further contamination. "Have them report to the conferance room, yourself and Wicasa as well, Jevak."

"Understood."

Nicolle's mind was not entirely on the landing party's findings. Whatever Matt and Wattie had found down there was not immediately crucial to her ship and crew. At the moment, Commander Jevak's warning, that they should find away back to their own Universem as quickly as possible, disturbed her. That, she thought, maybe more easily said than done.

Until now she had shied away from considering the difficulties they might face in making that possible. But the moment of truth was becoming imminent.

A unique set of circumstances had accidentally opened the door between these two parallel realities; a unique situation, which existed only at the far end of the wormhole, and possibly only in their own dimension. How was she going to re-create those unique circumstances, which brought them here?

The two-note door chime sounded, rousing her from her dilemma.

"Come," Nicolle called.

Wicasa entered, closely followed by Matt, Wattie and Lt Jevak.

"Well?" she said looking directly at Matt. "What did you find?"

"Exactly what I'd expected Captain," he replied eagerly. "One of its four engines has been dismantled and removed, along with all four electric generators and all of the ship's batteries."

"I barely understand the technology, Matt, and I'm sure the Commander has no idea at all. You'll have to spell it out for us."

"Each of the ship's engines, apart from turning the propellers to drive the vessel, produces electricity too, by driving a generator." He looked around him at the expectant faces. "The survivors took everything they needed, to make and store electricity."

"So where does that put us?" asked Wicasa.

"They intended, not only to survive here, but to thrive," Matt replied triumphantly. "With the means to produce electricity, they could maintain their 20th century lives in a iron-age world. They could maintain their technology, culture, lifestyle, all of their home comforts, and develop more. With this unique World they found here they've possibly even developed things we didn't."

Lockhart looked quizzically at her helmsman. "Okay, lets not get ahead of ourselves," Nicolle urged him. "You've had time to consider this. You think you know where they might have gone?"

"Yes Captain."

The obvious next question would be, 'where', but Nicolle asked, 'why'. She wanted deduction, before destination, that way she could draw her own conclusions.

"Their 20th century culture and society was wholly dependant on their technology, which was in turn dependant on energy production; electricity," Matt explained. "To maintain their society they would have to preserve that technology. They'd have moved to where the oil is, that's what powered their diesel engines; generated electricity." He stepped up to the view port, and looked out at the 'mirror' Earth. "Texas."

"If I remember my history," Wicasa offered. "Prior to industrialisation, before we started drilling for oil, in the nineteenth century it was found lying in pools on the surface. Back then it was pretty easily come by. I'd imagine it was the same here."

Matt nodded eagerly.

Nicolle and the others joined him at the view port. "Texas was a pretty big state," she said.

"There are two ships in orbit, Captain," Lt Jevak said eyeing his counter part. "And therefore two sensor arrays."

"Again, if I can be of service," Commander Jevak offered, a little reluctantly. He was becoming more concerned that further delays could be fatal. But he had to put himself in the Captains shoes; if the situation were reversed, he would be equally as concerned if fellow Vaurillians were in need of his aid. And besides…he was becoming just a little curious as well.

CHAPTER 13

It had taken Lieutenant Jevak and his opposite number, the tactical officer on the Vaurillian ship, almost thirty minutes to scan the target area. Jevak had scanned north to south, while the Vaurillian ship had carried-out a similar procedure south to north. After correlating data, both had arrived at the same conclusion. There were no signs of human life on the surface. But they had discovered signs of an abandoned settlement, which were beyond the capabilities of what they understood to be reptilian technology.

As far a he could tell, sixteen, possibly seventeen stone built, habitable constructions had been abandoned for some considerable time; how long exactly he could not estimate.

The village was situated in a shallow bowl on the west fork of the, much depleted, river San Jacinto, about sixty miles north of where the vast gleaming, vibrant, metropolis of Houston would have occupied on a more familiar Earth, but where now vast prairies and unspoiled forests stretched as far as the eye could see.

Jevak had been drawn to these co-ordinates

by an unexpectedly high trace of complex hydrocarbons; a by-product of petrochemical production, in the surrounding vegetation and soil.

Overlaying the sensor readings with the known co-ordinates of their own Earth, he realised he already knew this area, as would most of the rest of the crew. It was a region they were all familiar with, though not in this guise.

He'd had cause to visit this location on several occasions many years ago. The lake, on who's tranquil shores he had lodged though, was now conspicuous by its absence; it having being man made, and there being a distinct lack of men on this planet to construct anything.

On their own Earth, in the early twentieth century, a considerable oil strike in this locality, south of the small town of Conroe, had prompted an acceleration of population and wealth to this rural backwater lumbar trail.

Fifty years, and many millions of barrels of crude later the San Jacinto River Authority elected to dam the river north of the town of Conroe, creating the lake Jevak was so familiar with: Lake Conroe.

Primarily the dam had been created to provide a secondary water source for the near by city of Houston, but it also attracted the usual water and recreational activities to its idyllic shores. Completing the regions millionaires' playground image, yachting marinas, golf courses, plentiful recreational fishing and summer homes blossomed around the lakes idyllic shores.

Subsequent to the global financial crash of the late 21st centuary, after the first warp ship The Odyssey returned to Earth bringing news of diamonds as far as the eye could see, the community around Lake Conroe diminished, as a man's labour became currency rather than coins.

Following 'First Contact' though, man's recognition of his small place in the galaxy, and his realisation of his responsibility to his species and his planet brought a clearer awareness of the way ahead. National boundaries became redundant. A new global government recognised only citizenship of Earth; nationalities were a thing of humanities divisive past. When the exchange of paper and metal disks was no longer recognised as currency, a man's time, sweat, and labour were given freely, as was his neighbours, and the fruits of that combined labour belonged to all men.

With society's rebuilding, lake Conroe again flourished.

As Alliance Fleet's ranks of multi-species recruits swelled, Earths new symbol of unity, created a cadet summer camp on Lake Conroe's shores. A place where young recruits, far from home and in a strange culture, could get to know each other and grow together, helping each other, in a none disciplined environment. This was the reason for Jevak's first visit to the area.

Barely thirty years old, scarcely a teenager in Vaurillian terms, Jevak spent three summers on the lake's placid, tranquil shores, learning about these irrational humans. Its serene, peaceful waters had provided ideal ambience for meditation.

Though it was his second visit, almost twenty years later, which held the most memories for him, and not pleasant ones.

On his first tour as a young bridge officer, Jevak had the misfortune to serve aboard the A.S. Orion on her fateful inaugural mission. Along with thirty-two others, although having suffered severe injuries during a Macaitian attack on a Barvan outpost, he had survived. The young ensign Jevak was sent to Alliance Fleet's Lake Conroe Rehabilitation Facility, to recover from massive neural injuries.

As he looked over the schematics of the area, Jevak's Alliance Fleet career came flooding back to him: memories with no emotional attachments. He then realised the survivors of the U.S.S. Eldridge must have recalled the oil strike from a few years before their own fateful inaugural voyage.

Captain Lockhart barely hid her disappointment on hearing the sensor report. Like Matt, she was beginning to harbour a forlorn hope that this mission had not been a complete failure, that they might at least be able to do some good by rescuing survivors.

Unrelenting, Matt would not be dissuaded, until he had absolute proof. He wanted... no, needed to see the settlement with his own eyes, to be certain of the crew's fate. There might still, he thought, be some clue as to what had befallen them.

Lockhart had to agree; she could not deny

him. Until she had received the sensor report, Nicolle had begun to harbour hopes that Matt's theory of the Eldridge's crew's survival might be correct. His conviction, that the crew could have survived, had been so unshakeable. Besides her own curiosity had now gotten the better of her and she also wanted to see the settlement for herself.

"Okay," she said, looking round the bridge at the disappointed faces. "We've still got about an hour before Cosique can bring the warp reactor back on line. Matt, Jevak and myself will teleport down to the settlement to see if there's anything that'll give us a clue as to what might've happened to the survivors."

Turning to Commander Jevak she asked. "Would you care to join us? This may not be our World, but it's not that far removed. It'll maybe give you some idea of where we come from."

"Thank you Captain, I'd appreciate that," he replied courteously.

As the four members of the landing party made for the lift, Lockhart added, "You have the comm, Wicasa. Tell the Doctor to meet us in the teleport room; he'll be joining us. We'll report in every fifteen minutes. If the warp reactor's ready before Cosique's estimate, let us know."

Wicasa was about to remind her of Alliance Fleet's regulations governing Captains leading landing parties, and their disapproval of such cavalier behaviour, when Wattie cut him short.

"Err, Captain…" Cheung said, pleadingly.

Matt and both Jevak's had already entered the lift, and were waiting. Lockhart halted just short of the automatic doors. "Okay, Wattie," she nodded sympathetically to the anxious ensign. "You too."

Wattie deserved to know what had happened down there as well.

As the lift doors closed, Wicasa reflected that he had already savoured this 'Earth', and that Nicolle also deserved her chance to see 'home' again.

The six columns of blue, dazzled in the bright mid-day sun, the shifting particles gradually giving way to the figures condensing within. The instant they had ceased shimmering, Lockhart stepped away from the teleport co-ordinates. As she did, she turned a three hundred and sixty degree ark, levelling her laser, surveying their perimeter. To her left Commander Jevak did the same. Lieutenant Jevak and the Doctor had their palm-corders powered up, and scanning by the time the two commanding officers had assured themselves the area within visual range was clear of reptiles.

"Anything?" Lockhart asked, referring to hostiles.

"Negative, Captain. Nothing within sixty kilometres," Lieutenant Jevak confirmed.

"Okay fan-out, let's have a look around. Remember, be quick.... but thorough," she said, reminding them that time was against them.

They had materialised in the centre of what, at the time, must have been a village green. All of the sixteen buildings bordered onto a central, grassy square, about forty feet along each of its sides.

All that remained of the crumbling single storey, cottage like buildings, were the dark red, stonewalls. The windows, roofs and floors, had long since fallen victim to time and gravity. The empty shells, with their gaping eaves, looked like a nest of hungry, squawking chicks, craning skyward, demanding to be fed.

In the centre of the square there was what appeared to be the remains of another construction; considerably smaller than the perimeter buildings, it could never have been a dwelling, but was not instantly identifiable.

Beyond the square, a little further up the rise to the east, separated from the others, was a much larger building. Broad and sturdy, it was about five times as large as the others, with an immense stone chimney, which more than doubled the height of the imposing construction.

Jevak made directly for the central building, scanning as he paced slowly around it. Matt and Wattie separated, fanning out to two adjacent buildings on the east of the square, running their palm-corders over them as they approached. The Doctor did like wise, heading beyond the perimeter of the ruins to the south.

"Is this as you remember it?" The Commander asked, taking in the green rolling hills, which stretched from the edge of the village to the horizon.

Nicolle closed her eyes and took a deep, satisfying breath. The air was sweet; there was a faint scent of honeysuckle on the mild breeze. She had longed for this for six long years. It felt like home.

Exhaling slowly, she sighed. 'All that glitters...' She thought. No matter how much it looked like the real thing, this was only a facsimile.

"The climate's a little cooler," she replied tersely, steeling her emotions against her confused senses. Pointing south, to the thick blanket of trees, she added, "As far as the eye can see, that should all be dry, flat prairie."

The settlement, they had teleported to, nestled high on the slopping side of a deep semi-circular hollow. The hollow its self was indented into the south facing, slope of a sparsely forested hill, bordered a little more than a mile to the south and east by dense pine forest, and by grass plains, stretching to the distant hills to its north and west.

The hollow was immense, about a thousand yards in diameter, enclosed to the north and west by the wide arc of a sheer cliff face; the dark red rock face plunging fifty feet, from ground level above them, to its base. From high above, the hollow must have resembled a massive, semi circular heel print, imbedded in the soft hillside.

At the foot of the cliff a small lake had accumulated, fed by an emaciated San Jacinto. The river, shrunken in this reality, tumbled through a narrow gorge, about twenty feet wide, in the north face of the cliff. Hundreds of thousands of years of fast flowing water, thundering over the sheer face, roaring to the rocks below, had laboriously dissolved the porous, fragile rock, eating into the precipice.

Within the damp gorge, bushes clung precariously to the sheer face, fed by the constant spray of the waterfalls crashing torrent.

From the edge of the lake the land rose gently, south and east to re-converge with the original elevation of the hill. The settlement rested on the gently rising slope, about thirty yards from the edge of the crystal clear, cool water.

Like much of Texas, there were oil fields subterraneously peppering the land mere hundreds of feet bellow the surface. It was just such a pocket of oil which had created this hollow; the self, same oilfield which had instigated the economic boom around Lake Conroe on Lockhart's own Earth.

Approximately three million years ago the vapour pocket sitting on top of this particular oil seem had vented, under increasing pressure from the constricting weight of the rock above it. The massive outburst of explosive gases, venting through the Earths crust had split the porous rock, which offered little more resistance than meringue on top of a pie, leaving a vacuum, into which the hillside had collapsed.

The mechanics of the collapse had shaped the hollow to this particular fashion. The hillside had imploded like a flap, hinged on its south and east sides. The failing rock had plunged fifty feet to expose the cliff face, to the hollow's north and west sides,

On Nicolle's mirror Earth, this same oil field had been forcefully vented sixty five million years earlier by the impact of the meteor strike less than a thousand miles to the south; hence there was no corresponding hollow on her own World.

The scene was idyllic; four hundred years ago the Eldridge survivors must have found everything they needed within this beautiful, natural hollow.

But to Lockhart the geography and flora were all wrong. Had she had to place this scene anywhere it certainly would not have been Texas. Probably Quebec or Newfoundland, she thought, certainly somewhere much further north.

This was their World, but with different scars.

Nicolle and the Commander strode to the nearest ruin. Letting the Commander enter the ruin by himself she dallied a moment outside. Touching her comm-braclet she said quietly. "Lockhart to engineering."

"Yes Captain."

"Cosique, what's left of the three the shuttle crafts?"

"We've cannibalised all three of them, Captain, to get the ship operational. There's very little left that's still serviceable."

"Is there enough to make one serviceable warp reactor, within a basic, manoeuvrable, empty hull?"

The transmission went dead for a brief moment, while Cosique evaluated the situation. When the transmission resumed she sounded a little puzzled.

"Yes Captain. And I can give you more than an empty hull."

"Basic, manoeuvrable hull, will be sufficient."

"I'll get a team on to it right away."

Cosique was about to ask what the shuttle was needed for when the Captain cut her short.

"How's… our visitor, Sub-Commander T'Arran coming along?" Nicolle asked, endeavouring to make the question seem as casual, and innocent as possible.

She was still troubled by T'Arran, though the Vaurillian had not given her any reason to doubt her, and she seemed perfectly at home with Endeavour's crew. Nicolle was still concerned that leopards do not change their spots, and that a Vaurillian with good reason to hate Kraxian's, in this reality as well as her own, might be compelled to act with vengeance.

"She's been invaluable, Captain, she and her repair crews," The chief engineer replied enthusiastically, then dropping her tone to a conspiratorial whisper she asked. "Captain I was wondering…Is she…I mean, T'Arran isn't a common name amongst Vaurillians… Is…?"

Cosique was astute enough to note the Captain's attempt to single out the Sub-Commander for special mention whilst trying not to be obvious about it, and so had put two and two together. As a child back on Kraxa, the monster, T'Arran had been the subject of ghost stories and tales to frighten naughty children. Cosique did not need the obvious to be pointed out to her. She realised her initial instinct concerning the Vaurillian Sub-Commander had been correct.

"First Officer T'Arran is a visiting ally, and as such I expect her to be treated with respect and consideration. Keep what you think you know to yourself Lieutenant ...I don't want damaging gossip sweeping the ship."

"Aye Captai..." Cosique almost replied before being interrupted again.

"Cosique.... Keep an eye on her anyway....Lockhart out."

Turning towards the dilapidated ruin again, Nicolle entered by the low, crumbling doorway. She had to dodge around an assortment of boulders, dislodged from the dried, crumbling walls, as she stepped down into the weed-filled foundations. The wooden floors and joists had apparently disintegrated long ago leaving empty, damp husks.

Inside, a narrow alley, which had been a hallway, lead directly the rear of the cottage; exiting to the back door.

The hallway had three other openings, one leading right, to the large living room with a yawning fireplace against its far wall, and two others leading to the left.

The first door, closest to the front of the

building, lead to another hallway, which ran the length of the building and from which five adequately sized rooms could be accessed; probably bedrooms, Nicolle thought. The second opening in the main hallway, further to the rear of the building, looked as though plumbing could have been fitted through circular openings at the base of the outside wall; undoubtedly a bathroom or kitchen. What it had been used for, she had to remind herself, did not really matter, where the occupants had gone, did.

It was in the rear most room where she found the Commander. He was by the exterior wall, examining the structure.

The thick, stone walls were constructed in the old way; almost a metre thick, so thick, dampness could not penetrate. A clay and mortar-like adhesive, plastered between the red boulders held them in place. Thick green moss had taken hold in places, between the stones, growing into the weathered crevasses, eaten away by time and rain and wind.

"It'd certainly appear that the indigenous reptiles couldn't have built these," the Commander commented as she approached.

"More importantly, it hasn't been lived in for a long, long time," she replied pushing her thumb into the dry, crumbling mortar between two of the stone blocks. The mortar crumbled, scattering around their feet. "There's been no attempt to maintain it since they were built." Looking around she added. "But at least it confirms the survivors made it this far."

To the south of the hamlet the Doctor halted, stopping short of a thick forest of Maple, Hickory and Black Ash trees, which nestled in the small valley between hills. The forest was vast and dark under its canopy, continuing unbroken south, towards Galveston Bay about fifty miles away. He had stopped to scan an area about the same size as the village, just beyond the dip of the hill's southward slop.

He was still revelling in the new found sensations of fresh air and green grass when his palmcorder picked-up a reading not far below the surface of the hill, which though disturbing, was not entirely unexpected.

Nicolle moved quietly between the dilapidated rooms of the old building, followed closely by the Commander. She could find nothing, nothing to indicate that the building had ever been used as a home. There were no artefacts. No remnants of daily living; broken plates, kitchenware, ornaments, discarded clothes, nothing that would place humans in these surroundings, which surprised her. Even if the fledgling community of misplaced humans had failed, there should still be some record of there having being here, besides the ruins.

At the vacant window in one of the rear facing rooms, Matt suddenly appeared.

"This is strange Captain," he said.

"I know," she replied, appreciating his suspicions.

"These houses haven't been abandoned, they've been deliberately dismantled."

Wattie appeared behind the Captain at the doorway.

"You mean sacked by reptiles?" asked Commander Jevak.

"No," Matt explained. "If reptiles had attacked and killed everyone, or even if they had come upon the place after the humans had died, because the community was unviable, there would still be signs of destruction; even after this time. This place has been, as they used to say on old cop shows, 'hoovered'. It's completely clean."

"He's right Captain," added Wattie. "Even the wooden joists and beams which held the floors and roofs in place have been carefully removed, not burned or destroyed." He stepped into the remains of the room, kicking through the over grown weeds in the foundation. "The large building at the rear appears to have been a workplace, where they made everything they needed. There're heat scorch marks in the foundations that would suggest there'd been a furnace of sorts there at some time. But it's completely clean otherwise. No broken tools or even remnants of charcoal, which you would've expected."

"These people didn't abandon this place, they weren't killed and removed forcibly, and they didn't just die-out. They packed-up and left," Matt concluded.

"Could they have found a way back to there

own dimension?" The Commander asked.

"Why tidy-up. It's not as if the lizards were going to come after them and complain about the unsightly mess they'd left," Matt joked.

"Then the only other possibility would seem to be..." Lockhart paused. She was about to disappoint Matt, and that would be hard to take, especially since she had started to believe herself that they might find survivors. "...that there were no females on the ship. The only survivors were male, and they all died here."

"No... No Captain I can't accept that," Matt said still unswerving, Shaking his head, he cast a quick glance around at the ruin. "This is what you do when you have a future, when there's a reason to establish a community. This is domesticity. This is somewhere to come home to after a hard day in the field. This is somewhere to call home. This is not what men do when they have no hope, when they're waiting to die. These people were building for the future. If there had been no hope, these people wouldn't have trekked all this distance from Philadelphia to set up a permanent community. They wouldn't even have stayed together. They'd have split up, taken their chances in the wilderness. Die living, grasping the remainder of your life by the throat." He shot the Captain a sidelong, playful smile. "It's a guy thing," he shrugged.

Nicolle knew exactly what he meant, though he was wrong about it being a 'guy thing'. When Endeavour had arrived in the Gamma Sector, six years ago, she had been determined to get home. She had not accepted defeat, and waited to die in some far, alien, corner of the Galaxy. If there had been no hope for them, she would never have set out on this journey. They had gotten this far because she, they, always believed there was hope.

She looked around again at what those twentieth century survivors had build; these people had hope. They came here to build, and grow. They must have left some kind of clue as to where they went, and why.

Still looking for something that might support this she sighed, asking. "Okay then, what about the things they removed from the ship, any sign of them?"

"Indeed Captain," Lieutenant Jevak said, appearing behind them at the doorway. "If you would come this way."

They followed Jevak back through the doorway, out into the square again, where he indicated towards the central building.

"I believe, Captain," he said. "That this was where the inhabitants housed their communal, electrical generator. I have discovered minute traces of hydrocarbons in the soil within the buildings foundations, and within the remains of the walls." He stepped around the building checking his palm-corder for any anomalous readings. "It would appear, Mister Sweeney, that this was where they located the internal combustion engine, which was removed from the ship wreck." He stepped into the centre of the ruins. "There is also evidence of disturbed soil, approximately a metre below the surface, radiating out in straight lines, towards each of the other constructions."

"Power Lines?" Matt asked.

"That would be a worthy assumption. Along each of these lines, there remain indications of polarisation, as a result of intense, electromagnetic fields."

"Each of the buildings also had pretty remarkable plumbing, given that they had to start from scratch. That's all been removed, too," Matt added, supporting Jevak's discovery. "There's the remains of an extinct pumping station below the surface of the lake."

Jevak was about to add something else when....

"Doctor to Captain Lockhart." The Doctors voice interrupted him.

Nicolle lightly touched her comm-braclet, in response. "Lockhart here. Where are you Doctor?"

"About three quarters of a mile south, beyond the lip of the hollow."

"What have you found?"

"The village cemetery. One hundred and seventy three graves."

"Stay where you are Doctor." She said, cutting him off, then immediately re-tapped her braclet. "Lockhart to Endeavour."

"Yes Captain," Wicasa responded.

"I need a site to site teleport. Lock on to the

Doctor and have him teleported here immediately."

"Aye Captain."

The single column of blue sparkled a few yards from the waiting landing party.

The Doctor materialised, facing away from the waiting group. He glanced around him, then turned, feigning surprise at seeing his assembled colleagues.

"Ah, there you are." He said, attempting humour.

Wattie stifled a snigger. He found the android Doctor's attempts to humanise his mannerisms, absurdly amusing.

The Captain ignored his jocularity. "You were saying," she pressed.

"I was saying," he coughed. "I have found one hundred and seventy three graves at the base of the hill. They would appear to contain the remains of both male..." He turned his attention to Matt. "and females. In fact", He added triumphantly, "almost a seventy-thirty split. The last of which was buried approximately two hundred and eighty years ago."

"That time scale would tie-in with all this," Nicolle said looking around at the ruins. "They've been deserted just about as long."

"Looks like you were right," she said, smiling with satisfaction at Matt. "How many of a crew, did you estimate the Eldridge would have?"

Matt thought for a moment. "For a ship that size..., no more than about fifty."

"They lost some of their number in the initial

experiment, we know that." She said, wondering away from the group. "Some more, defending the ship against the reptiles." She turned, still pacing. "It's probably safe to assume that they would've lost some more on the journey here." Stopping, she looked around again, taking in the scale of the survivors' achievements. "Maybe about two thirds of the crew, plus the females made it this far."

"Then what's buried in the cemetery," the Doctor butted-in "is probably the result of two generations of very successful controlled breeding, or three, of moderately successful."

"Either way, their initial success seems to have been cut short," Wattie said. "Where are they now?"

"Could they have fallen victim to congenital defects, due to inbreeding?" the Captain asked.

"No." Replied the Doctor, fervently. "Even if only one female had survived along with the crew, it would have taken more than one or two generations before defects became evident, and then only minor ones, certainly not lethal to the entire community... Besides, having scanned the graves, I am pleased to say that at least five females were in the initial survivors group." He smiled smugly. "A genetic pool, deep and wide enough to support many, many healthy generations."

"Then we're still no further forward," The Captain said, still mystified.

"Captain. As I was about to say," Lieutenant Jevak interrupted.

"Sorry, Jevak, continue."

"One of the electrical power lines lead directly to the cliff face", He indicated towards the waterfall. "From there, up to a sizeable cave, behind the waterfall. According to my scans, it would appear the cave is man made."

Nicolle paused for a moment, evaluating the situation. She checked the chronometer on her palm-corder. There were still forty minutes until the deadline set by Cosique for bringing the warp reactor back on line. It was time to make a decision.

"Okay," she said decisively. "We check out the cave, but if there's nothing to indicate where these people went, or what happened to them, then it's time to return to the ship, I want to start preparing to break orbit."

Matt was about to object, but she cut him short.

"I'm sorry Matt, but we've got to consider the possibility that these people may not have wanted to be found. You said yourself that the place has been 'cleaned'. They did that for a reason."

"Okay Jevak, lead the way," she commanded.

Skirting the lake, they set out at a brisk pace, picking their way through the knee-high grass, the two hundred yards or so to the base of the cliff. Jevak took point, closely followed by the Captain and Commander Jevak, then the Doctor, and bringing up the rear Wattie and Matt.

The air was still and warm, the hollow being sheltered from the westerly breeze by the cliff to their left. As they walked Nicolle felt another pang of regret; this could so easily have been home, she mused. To the rear of the column she heard Wattie chattering to Matt about something, she decided to listen-in on the conversation, to distract her from her disappointment.

"So how come, with a sixty five million year head start on us, they're still not as evolved as we are?" he asked, quizzing Matt about their reptile captors.

"Beats me."

"How about you Jevak?" Wattie shouted to the front of the column.

Jevak dropped back a little. "The answer is quite simple," he replied, in his inevitable, dispassionate fashion.

"Chillingly simple, in fact," joked his counterpart.

Jevak carried on unperturbed by the Commanders flippancy. "Reptiles are cold blooded," he said, finishing his answer.

"Care to expand on that," Matt asked?

Turning, once again, to his counterpart, Lieutenant Jevak politely enquired, "Would you care to continue the explanation?"

"No. Please, carry on."

"Hey Doc," Wattie said a little more loudly than was required, ensuring everyone could hear what he was saying. "Isn't that the first sign of madness, when you start talking to yourself?"

The joke raised a laugh from everyone, except, once again, Lieutenant Jevak, who merely raised an eyebrow to demonstrate his indifference.

"Ignore them Jevak," Nicolle urged. "Let's hear your theory."

The Commander had known these humans for only a few short hours, but already found himself growing to like them. They seemed a sociable, trustworthy, amiable species. It was easy to see why these companionable people had been the cornerstone of their Alliance, in their own dimension. He smiled as he thought, how much fun they would be in a bar.

"It is not a theory Captain," Lieutenant Jevak continued. "It is a universally recognised fact that all reptilian life forms, evolve at a more retarded pace than their mammalian equivalent, simply by virtue of the fact that they are cold blooded."

"Each generation," Jevak announced to everyone in general, "No matter what the species, throws up mutations in their genetic code. These mutated genes, if the environmental conditions in which the species finds its self are conducive to the mutation, can benefit its survival, even enhancing its development, there-by evolving the species. For instance the ability to sweat only becomes part of a species genetic code if the species inhabits a warm climate, since the mutation is beneficial. If the ability to sweat mutates into a species which inhabits a cold climate then the mutated gene is not beneficial and is therefore through time, discarded."

Nicolle walked on a few paces in front of the

others, trudging through the long grass she listened absently to the 'lecture' Jevak was giving. The talk of reptilian evolution was taking her to a far off distant place, 65 million years ago. The roll of a dice, she thought. How callous.

These creatures she pondered, were never equipped to evolve quickly enough for the Galaxy's needs. Humans were not the saviours of the Galaxy, it was arrogant to think so, but they were the necessary catalyst, which brought the Galaxy together at a time when it was needed. These reptiles would have taken another thousand years or more, to reach the Moon, let alone venture out into the Galaxy. And then what would they have found when they got there, after the Macaitian empire had crushed the life out of the Alpha Sector.

"Mammals," Jevak continued, "because of their warm blood, have the innate ability to exist in wider and more varied, harsh, almost intolerable climatic conditions, from a planets frozen poles, to its burning deserts. Therefore there are greater opportunities for beneficial mutations to emerge within the species, and aid its survival. The more varied the environment, the greater the probability of an essential mutation emerging. A more diverse species therefore adopts a greater number of mutated genes, thereby fast-tracking the species evolution."

"Reptiles on the other hand, by the restrictive nature of their cold blood, are confined to warm, unchallenging climatic condition, thereby reducing the probability that any mutated gene is of benefit. Therefore their evolution is retarded."

Wattie stepped to the front of the group and scanned the mouth of the gorge. It was overgrown at its base, with thick briars. Pulling some of the branches aside he revealed neatly fashioned steps, cut into the cliff face, leading up the side of the gorge, to the rear of the waterfall.

Lockhart did not look too surprised. "Let's take a look," she said, indicating that she would lead the way up.

At the rear of the group Matt watched as the Captain began to ascend. Just then a movement at the edge of his peripheral vision, caught his eye. He could not be sure if the movement was close-by or distant, only that it was certainly not one of his colleagues, since they were all in front of him. Spinning on his heals; he caught his breath. A young woman stood almost a meter or two behind him.

"Hi," she smiled, quite calmly.

CHAPTER 14

On the far side of the Orion sector, fifteen Macaitian ships suddenly, and inexplicably, broke-off a sustained attack on bedraggled Rassilian fleet.

The battle had raged for over two days, across a distance of more than ten light-years, and already cost the helpless, out-gunned and out-manned, Rassilians dozens of their best attack ships. The desperate, retreating Rassilians, facing a crushing defeat, had been decimated, reduced to three attack ships and seven badly damaged cruisers. The battle was all but over. None of their Commanders expected to survive the next few hours.

Then suddenly and without warning the attack had abruptly ended. The Macaitians ceased fire, assumed a pursuit formation, and vectored across the Orion nebula, burning-out plasma injectors and frying warp coils, to push their ships beyond their maximum velocity.

*************** ********** **************

Her name was Samantha; or Sam as she preferred. She must have been about twenty, maybe twenty-one years old at the most, thought Matt Sweeney, and almost un-naturally beautiful.

She was tall and slender. Her long, almost black hair fell about her shoulders emphasising the extraordinary paleness of her skin; pale like milk, as though she had spent too much time in some very dark place. She had the most piercing ice blue eyes Sweeney had ever seen, framed by arched brows and high, prominent cheekbones, which gave her that very attractive feline look; the kind of look that men prefer to think of as 'predator'.

She stood a few feet behind them looking quite unfazed by the sudden appearance of strangers.

Dressed in soft hide trousers and brightly embroidered blouse, she eased past Sweeney and the others, and approached the Captain. Nicolle was about to introduce herself but Sam cut her short.

"Please," She said calmly. "Won't you join us?" She looked at the Sun's position in the sky. "We will be eating soon, and there's more than enough to go around." Starting up the steps, Sam indicated that they should follow.

Again the Captain tried to introduce herself, but Sam, already a dozen or so steps ahead of them took no notice.

Her response, or lack of it, was unexpected to say the least. A little shock, surprise, or even mild hysteria, might have been expected. After all they had been stranded here for four hundred years; they had just been found, and were about to be rescued. But her response almost bordered on indifference.

Shooting surprised glances at each other, The Captain signalled that the landing party remain silent.

"Us?" Lockhart asked. "How many of you are there?"

"Please," she said again. "Come. You'll see."

They followed, warily to begin-with, mounting the stairs in single file, behind her; Captain Lockhart followed by Commander Jevak then Wattie, the Doctor, and Jevak, Sweeney as usual brought-up the rear.

The narrow stairs curved steeply, along the inner wall of the gorge, hidden from the ground below by the thick greenery clinging to the walls of the narrow cut. As they ascended, Jevak, Wattie and the Doctor diligently continued scanning, recording everything they could.

A few yards from the waterfall, the stairs levelled out onto a wide, flat platform, which veered to the right under a wide overhang behind the tumbling torrent.

Passing behind the cascading curtain of water they came to a narrow perfectly angled, vertical slit in the cliff face; the opening was obviously not the work of nature. Though it had been cut into the solid stone by tools, there were no obvious marks on the rock to indicate this; so precise was the workmanship. The cut was deliberately wider outside, at its mouth becoming narrower as it progressed inside. This gave anyone inside a full view, and aim, at any hostiles approaching from any angle, whilst from outside there was next to nothing to aim at.

A perfect, defensive design, thought Lockhart as she examined the cut.

Sam stepped to the far side of the door. "Please," she said, loudly enough to be heard over the sound of the thundering torrent.

"No, after you," Lockhart declined.

Sam smiled, partly to show she understood the Captains caution, and partly to reassure her that there really was no danger here. She ducked under the low overhang above the door and slipped inside. After a moment's hesitation Lockhart followed.

Beyond the narrow mouth the cave opened up to a wide semi-circular room about twenty feet radius and seven or eight feet high. It was clean, dry and comfortably warm.

Nicolle was not sure what she had expected to find as she stepped inside. Certainly not primitive damp, slime covered walls and animal skins; Sam's contemporary attire assured her of that, but the almost sterile appearance of the room was way beyond her expectations. She was agreeably surprised. The smooth, pearl like white wall curved around them, away from the entrance. It angled towards a broad staircase at the far side of the cave, which was framed in a carved arched doorway. The stairs leading upwards though, not down, as Nicolle might have expected.

Looking around her, Nicolle noticed that the floor was also smooth like the walls, almost polished like marble and that it sloped up and away from the doorway towards the stairs. Another defence design, she thought. Under an attack this floor would easily and quickly become slick with blood, the slope would make it almost impossible for the few who might gain entry through the narrow slit to gain a footing and advance. What she had not noticed but which Jevak had, as soon as he entered, was that the room was flooded with much more light than the two burning torches, either side of the staircase, could possibly produce. Also there was no smoke staining on the walls behind, or above, the flames.

The rest of the landing party followed one by one, since the opening was only wide enough for one person to enter at a time.

Three a-breast they mounted the stairs, the Captain and Commander Jevak either side of Samantha, behind them Wattie, Jevak and the Doctor, Sweeney, again as always, brought-up the rear.

The assent was not a long one, a mere twelve steps, elevating them to just above the height of the entrance room behind them.

Looking back Nicolle caught sight of a faint chink of light at the angle of the sloped floor and the far wall, directly under the cave mouth; a drainage hole, through which to flush spilt blood. She could now see that the whole room was a deliberately created bottleneck, a killing ground. A dozen or so well armed defenders could comfortably repel an army, coming through that doorway one by one. It was unlikely that any attacker would make it beyond these steps. These people had spent four hundred years alone, on an unfriendly world; defence would have been paramount.

The top step was in fact a broad landing, so large it was almost a room in its self. It stretched about thirty feet towards another arched opening at its far end. Four burning torches, two at either end of the landing, again lit the smooth, milky white walls. Beyond the far opening the stairs descended again. This time the descent was steep and long, plunging them deep into heart of the hillside.

Sam took the lead again.

Commander Jevak dropped back alongside Sweeney. The battle-hardened soldier, who had spent most of his life in the defence of his World, had seen too much death to be complacent. He was wary of unseen danger in such a confined space.

Their footsteps began to echo as they descended further. Lockhart lost count of the steps they had already covered, but she was fairly certain that they were now well below the level of the lake; millions of tons of rock above them. The air continued to grow a little warmer the deeper they went, and unusually sweeter. This far below ground she expected it to be heavy and stale.

"This must have taken years to excavate," she

said attempting some sort of meaningful communication.

Sam made no reply, but continued her swift descent.

As they approached the bottom of the steps, the final twenty or so became gradually wider and shallower, slowing their eventual descent. The walls and ceiling fell away, opening into a vast subterranean cavern. It felt almost like emerging from the noisy end of a clarinet onto the set of one of Matt's favourite old twentieth century, black and white musicals.

The sight that greeted them was completely unexpected, and breathtaking.

The cavern was immense, larger than any of Endeavours spacious cargo holds. What immediately caught Nicolle's attention though, was a little disconcerting. The cavern was about a thousand square yards, and about fifteen feet high, but there were no visible means of support for its vast, single span ceiling. Considering the colossal weight, the mountain of rock above it, Nicolle was somewhat perturbed.

In fact, she was a little taken a back by the entire room; its look and feel exuded fine living. These people had not just survived on a hostile, alien world they had apparently prospered.

The floor of the cavern, which was completely covered with some unfamiliar thick, luxurious, animal pelt, appeared to be deliberately uneven. It was laid in an informal step design. Some areas of the floor were raised higher than others, while others were sunken, creating natural, communal, gathering areas for the occupants to lounge within.

There was no identifiable furniture anywhere in the vast expanse, but there was an abundance of abnormally huge, comfortable looking cushions, scattered across the sumptuous floor, some of them even filling the floors deep indentations.

The cavern's irregular shape was accentuated further by the dozen or so smooth but massive rocks and boulders protruding into it. The walls had been cut meticulously even and straight, but had been deliberately fashioned around the contours of some of the larger rocks within the mountain. Leaving them exposed with in the living space. Some of the larger boulders even had cushions strewn across them, making them part of the furniture. The rocks did not so much intrude into the living space, but that the living space had incorporated the stone into it, giving the cavern a harmonious, natural form.

Reinforcing this natural harmony were the half dozen or so rock pools scattered about the vast space, which had formed at the base of several of the larger outcrops. Crystal clear water that had filtered down from the surface far above gently trickled over the smooth surface of the rocks and collected, forming shallow, languid ponds, which had then been stocked with brightly coloured fish. The pools were lit from beneath. The light from them scattered, rippling and dancing across the walls and ceiling, where they tangled in an eternally shifting kaleidoscope of dancing rings, lighting the whole cavern in a soft warm glow.

The centrepiece of the cavern was an enormous open log fire, which was raised on a wide circular stone plinth. The flames from which, licked and leapt at the air, almost to the height of the ceiling. The blaze though gave off no smoke or fumes and much less heat than would have been expected. Given Jevak's other findings he suspected that the fire was not so much for warmth as decoration since apart from the pool lights, there was no other illumination anywhere in the cavern.

The massive underground vault looked and felt… homely, Nicolle thought, but it seemed at odds with its self: it was a contradiction. Despite its overwhelming ungainly size and the fact that it was hewn from cold stone, it had a cosy welcoming ambience. There was a peaceful, tranquil quality to its design; a harmonious fusion of nature and architecture.

This, Sam informed them was the Great Hall.

Groups of young people; apparently Samantha's fellow descendants of the original Eldridge crew, lazed, chatting in the hall's various nooks, crannies and opulent alcoves. There were about fifty in total, all of them in their early twenties and all of them like Sam unusually pale and unusually beautiful. Every one of them appeared serene in their comfortable, enviable surroundings. No matter how harsh and fraught their ancestor's survival on this World had been, four hundred years on their descendants certainly appeared to want for nothing.

As the landing party followed Sam, descending the last few steps to the floor of the Hall, the faintly echoing noise of chatter and human interaction subsided to silence.

The silence was suddenly heavy. Wattie could hear his own breathing. Fifty pairs of eyes followed them, scrutinising them, watching them. But other than that there was no reaction to their being here. No display of surprise, joy, or excitement. Nothing. These people had been lost for four hundred years. Here now were their rescuers, the first humans, out-with their own community, any of them had ever encountered, and yet they appeared, either not to care, or they were too shocked, or overwhelmed to be emotional.

Lockhart somehow suspected it was not the former; they were all too calm.

"Where's Michael," Sam asked one of her companions, as she led the away team to their right, towards another dimly lit corridor one of several that led off the Hall.

"He's with Joe and Mark, they went down to the second level," the striking, young blonde replied.

"Can you let him know we have visitors, Sarah?"

The blonde got to her feet and hurried off in

the direction of another corridor, at the far end of the Great Hall.

"Is Michael your leader?" ventured Nicolle.

"We... have no leader," Sam replied, then paused before continuing. She had to consider how she was going to phrase this. This was the first time any one in their community had ever had to explain anything about their hierarchy, or rather lack of it, to any one. No outsiders had ever attempted to communicate with them. All they had ever known of the reptiles they shared this world with, since the day they were born, was hatred and violence. This was a little strange to Sam.

"Michael is the eldest," she shrugged, seizing at the simplest explanation she could.

"I see."

Following Sam down the wide corridor, they passed several curtained doorways, spaced about twenty to thirty feet apart, on both their left and right. Arriving at the third opening on their left Sam pulled aside the heavy, buckskin, which screened the room from the corridor. As she stepped inside the light level automatically brightened from dark to a little more than subdued without her touching anything, or directing any command.

"These are my quarters. Please make yourselves comfortable," she said, indicating that they should take a seat.

The room was modern, which surprised Nicolle, it could almost have been contemporary twenty-fourth century in style, a room she would not have felt out of place in herself. She still expected to find something in this subterranean world to be basic, almost rustic, with at best a few attempts at mimicking a technological existence, but the room was warm, inviting and stylish.

The accommodation was constructed on two levels; the sleeping quarters on a raised mezzanine floor above the living quarters. The smaller, upper level was accessed by an ornately carved spiral staircase, and safely enclosed by a waist high wooden, slatted railing. The whole room, upper and lower, was carpeted with the same animal pelt as the Great Hall, with more of the obligatory cushions scattered around. Most of the light in the room came from three massive, glass, fish tanks, embedded in the wall opposite the doorway. These housed more than a dozen brightly coloured tropical fish; most of which the crew did not recognise. The light from the tanks caught reflections from the ripples on the water's surface, playing ever changing designs across the floor and walls.

Captain Lockhart took a seat on the larger of the two over-stuffed dark-brown leather couches, almost sinking into it as she did. Although stylish, thought Nicolle, Sam's accommodation lacked the trinkets and ornaments to give it a more personal touch. But what was really lacking, and made the room a little claustrophobic, were windows, but considering they were several hundred feet below a mountain, that was a little impractical.

"Your colleague said that Michael was on the

second level," the Doctor said, stepping a little closer to Sam.

He was not really that interested in the question he was about to ask her, but he needed to refine the information being gathered by his palm-corder, which he was holding casually at his side, and therefore required to be in closer proximity to the subject.

"How many levels are there?" he asked, then added, for further diversion, "This is a considerable feet of engineering."

Sam flinched at his approach. The reaction was almost imperceptible, barely noticeable, but it was there. She was uncomfortable by the Doctor's proximity. Backing away to maintain her distance, she directed her reply to the Captain.

"There're three levels. This is the accommodation level. Below this are the mess hall, galley, and some of our recreation facilities. The level below that, houses the swimming pool, saunas, gymnasiums and suchlike." She turned towards the door. "If you will excuse me a moment, I'll go and find Michael," she said politely. "In the meantime, please make yourselves comfortable. Our home is yours."

When she had left Matt waited for a few seconds, and then pulled the curtain back, checking the corridor.

"It's clear," he said, ducking back into the room, but remained near the door, listening for footsteps.

"Well, I wouldn't imagine you'll be getting a Christmas card from her," Wattie said sarcastically, referring to Sam's reaction to the Doctor.

"I wouldn't imagine any of these people have ever seen an android before," the Doctor replied indignantly. "Her reaction was hardly surprising."

"And how would she know you were an android?" Lockhart asked then looked searchingly at the others. "And how come we couldn't pick-up any human life signs."

"Our sensors could barely penetrate the atmosphere until about half an hour ago, Captain," Wattie replied. "If they were below ground..." He did not get to finish.

"That was in orbit Wattie ...we're on the surface now. Out there, when she appeared behind us," Matt argued. "We had three palm-corders burning the air around us and still not one of us detected her."

"Doctor?" Lockhart said looking for an explanation.

"I don't understand this Captain, her life signs haven't registered at all." He continued scrolling through the data on his palm-corder. "Neither have any of the others in the Hall. My palm-corder is registering three Humans, two Vaurillians and an android. There's no one else in these caves. According to this we are apparently the only beings in the entire complex."

"Captain," Lieutenant Jevak interrupted. "The caves occupants are not the only apparent anomaly. The entire cave system is in its self, ambiguous," he said, continuing to scan the clouded, glass like walls. "...This cave has not been excavated by any method I can comprehend. It has not been dug, blasted, or cut by laser. I can detect nothing that would indicate by which means it was created. It is simply here. It exists. As for life support," he continued, "There is no indication of any power sources anywhere within the cave system, no means of creating heat or light, and yet there are both. These torches are also an anomaly, they are emitting less light than there is in the room."

"That's not possible," Nicolle replied in disbelief.

"But it is the case, Captain. I can detect no other light sources, but there is more illumination within the room than these torches are producing. Also," he said, stretching up to put his hand to the naked flame, "There is virtually no heat being emitted by the flame."

"Is any of this real?" Lockhart enquired. "Are we standing in a barren, empty cave, but being made to think that it's all been transformed into habitable living quarters? Do these beings possess some kind of telepathic ability, and they're creating all of this for our benefit; an illusion that we're being made to believe?"

"It's not an impossible a scenario," Sweeney offered.

"Could these beings be alien life forms, intent on making us see what they want; making us believe we've found human survivors, because that's what we wanted to find?" Lockhart ventured.

"Or possibly they might be some species, native to Earth in this reality," Wattie offered. "We really don't know what differences there are in this Universe."

"Either way," Sweeney asked, "why would they want us to believe we had found the descendants of the Eldridge survivors? Why would they want us to believe an illusion?"

"Is there any way of knowing who, or what they are?" Lockhart asked.

"It's impossible to tell, since I can't detect any life signs, but that in its self might imply that they're not human. On the other hand..." the Doctor shrugged. His eyes slowly widened as a thought came to him. "That's possibly why she shied away from me. If she has telepathic abilities, being an android she couldn't read my thoughts."

"How can we trust anything they tell us, then," Said Sweeney, anxiously. "If they are aliens and can read our minds and manipulate them too, then they can make us believe anything they want."

"Captain, if I may?" Commander Jevak interrupted. "Speaking as an observer," he said as he walked to the nearest chair and took a seat. "I don't think there's any manipulation going on here," he looked to his duplicate for support. "At least, I can't sense any untoward telepathic connections being made."

"I agree, Captain," said Lieutenant Jevak. "Our

empathic abilities make us receptive to telepathy; I also can detect no manipulation."

"So," the Commander continued, "looking at this objectively: you and your people arrived at this location on this continent, by your crews own expertise and deductive reasoning," he said acknowledging Matt's input. "You weren't drawn to it... These beings haven't coerced you into finding them; if anything I'd say they've done their best to avoid detection. Only when we were about to stumble right into their home did they make themselves known to us. I don't think we've been enticed here. But I'm pretty certain that something's going on. Our friend Sam's holding something back."

"You don't have to be an empath to see that Commander," agreed the Captain. "The reaction to us, or lack of it, from her and her friends out in the Hall seams proof of that."

Matt sprang away from the door. "Someone's coming," he whispered, as he swiftly moved across the room to the foot of the spiral staircase, assuming a casual air as he quickly planted himself on the bottom step.

The curtain swung back and Samantha entered, followed by a young man.

"Hi," he said casually looking around the room. "I'm Michael."

He was tall with a thick mop of long, dark brown hair, which fell casually across his broad shoulders. His features were chiselled with cheekbones that stood proud above a strong, square jaw line and like Sam he had piercing blue eyes. The loose fitting shirt he wore did little to disguise the thick muscular arms and chest below. He was an almost perfect specimen of a man, but like all of the others they had seen in the Great Hall, his skin was unusually pale.

They were all surprised by his appearance. When Sam had said that Michael was the eldest, they had assumed he would at least be middle-aged. If he was older than Sam at all, it could only be by months or possibly even weeks.

Michael's appearance, and that of the others they had seen while passing through the Great Hall were adding to Nicolle's suspicions. Apart from their pale colouring, they all seemed perfect, too perfect. She considered that if an alien race were to attempt to replicate the appearance of humans for the landing party's benefit, they might make the mistake of replicating a too perfect image; a flawless image. Possibly, she thought there appearance could be an amalgam of images held in the landing parties subconscious minds, of how perfect the human form could be, but then, why their unnaturally pale colouring? That was a feature that could never have been gleaned from any of their minds. There must be a reason for that.

"I'm Captain Nicolle Lockhart, of the Alliance starship, Endeavour," she said, getting to her feet, extending her hand in greeting.

Without hesitation, or any sign of confusion at the gesture, Michael took it, shaking hands firmly, in what appeared to be a genuine display of welcome.

His hand felt warm, normal. She was surprised. Nicolle did not know what she had expected, but normal was not it. She had hoped for something... something that would betray him as fake.

"A starship?" Michael said sounding surprised. "Humanity made it to the stars?" he laughed. "We'd thought that someone would eventually just replicate the experiment. Open-up another 'doorway', after they'd ironed out the problems. I'd never have thought it possible or necessary to come after us in a starship."

There was an uneasy silence. For a brief moment Michael looked confused at the lack of reaction. Then the reality of the situation dawned on him.

"You...you haven't come to find us. You were coming home.... Or thought you were....." He said, looking around the room at the grim faces of the landing party. "You didn't even know we were here," He laughed ironically.

Stepping away from the Captain, Michael walked to the centre of the room and turned to face them all, He laughed again, adding. "You're as lost as we are. Some rescue party."

Gauging the authenticity of Michael's reaction was difficult. This was, in a way, pretty much how she might have expected him to react; if they had been lost here all these years. But if he was not what he seemed then this could all be part of the deception. Nicolle decided it was best to maintain the illusion and continue the pretence, that they believed them to be the actual descendants of the Eldridge survivors until they could prove otherwise.

"What did they think had happened to the Eldridge? Has no one been looking for it?" Michael asked.

Lockhart took her seat again opposite Michael. She looked at him earnestly. "Do you understand the term, 'parallel universe'?" She asked.

"Of course I do Captain, I was born in one."

"I don't mean to sound patronising," Lockhart reassured him. "But I'm not sure how much you understand, about your circumstances, and therefore how much you don't know, and how much I need to explain."

"Our ancestors realised pretty early on, what had gone wrong with the experiment, and where they were. They were highly intelligent scientists, Captain. After all they created a device back in the 1940's that could open a doorway between dimensions."

"But that wasn't their intention." The Captain said. "This, by all accounts, was a compete accident, they were meddling with technology far beyond their understanding."

"What made them realise where they were?" asked Wattie, introducing himself.

"Those that weren't scientists were seafarers," he replied, glibly. "A simple sextant can accurately plot your position anywhere on Earth, using the stars. And since the constellations were still the same, they knew they hadn't moved. They were still on the Delaware, off Philadelphia."

"It must have been quite a leap of imagination," Nicolle again put in. "Parallel Universes weren't exactly an everyday topic of conversation back then, it wouldn't have been their first conclusion."

"No. But it didn't take them long to come to terms with the reality. They knew exactly what was involved in what they were trying to do. Invisibility requires the bending of light, which in turn requires the manipulation of time, and therefore a dalliance with other dimensions. They understood what they were 'meddling' with, Captain, and the risks involved. What they couldn't understand is why no one bothered to come looking for them."

That touched a nerve. Nicolle suddenly felt a deep sympathy. If these were the descendants of the Eldridge crew, they'd been stranded in a terrifying nightmare for four hundred years. Endeavour was also vanished, beyond the reach of home. Nicolle and her crew were just as lost and abandoned. Whether or not Michael was what he appeared to be, the Captain felt obliged to explain. A deep sense of camaraderie with those ill fated, doomed seafarers, lost in a nightmare all those years ago, compelled her to set the record straight. Someone should know why they had been forsaken. Besides, she reminded herself, further discussion of the events of 1943 might betray Michael for what ever he really was.

"No one came looking for them," Lockhart started sympathetically. "Because no one knew they were missing."

Both Michael and Sam looked surprised by this. But then wouldn't they do that to maintain the illusion?

"How could they not know?" Michael asked incredulously.

"In our parallel reality the Eldridge reappeared," she assured him. "It never went missing. And since then, governments and authorities have consistently denied that any experiments ever took place. The whole story of the experiment, in our Universe, has been rumours and second hand conjecture," she shrugged almost apologetically. "The rumours about the experiment were dismissed as conspiracy theories. The Eldridge didn't go missing…so why should anyone come looking."

"But, how can that be!" Sam asked, stunned.

Nicolle explained their theory; that each Eldridge, in each parallel reality, had moved one reality over, replacing its counterpart in the neighbouring Universe. Since in each Universe a USS Eldridge reappeared, even accepting the horrendous damage and loss of life, the ship did reappear. There was no reason to suspect that it was not the same ship, and so no reason to mount a search.

"But if that's true, then somewhere there's a

parallel universe where, since our ancestors didn't re-materialise, then they are missing an Eldridge," Michael concluded.

"True, and I've no doubt that in that Universe, they've done everything possible over the last four hundred years, and possibly still are doing everything, to discover the whereabouts of their missing ship. But given an infinite number of parallel realities, what are the chances that they might re-open a 'doorway' to this specific reality?"

Nicolle watched Michael closely, there seemed to be genuine emotion in his reaction to the news that there never was any rescue attempt mounted.

"Then, is it also possible that you are not from the same Universe as us?" Sam asked.

"That's quite possible," Lockhart said. "In fact, given the odds, more than likely."

The Doctor, still loitering over by the ornate fish tanks, suddenly took a keener interest in the conversation; his interest peaked by Sam's observation. Calmly adjusting his palm-corder behind his back, he continued to scan their hosts, surreptitiously.

Michael looked shaken. His shoulders slumped. "There was no need for them to die," he mumbled to himself.

Lockhart shifted in her seat, leaning forward towards him. "No need for who to die?" she asked softly.

"The crew," he replied. "The survivors of the

Eldridge. If they'd known that they weren't going to be rescued, more of them might have lived." His gaze shifted to the far wall, as he stared into the middle-distance. "After about a month or so, it came time for he survivors to decide what they were going to do; if they were going to remain with the wreck in the hope that they might be rescued, or move-on and find somewhere to settle permanently. About a quarter of them wanted to remain with the wreck. There was a mutiny. Seven of the crew were killed in the fighting; the Captain was one of the casualties." He began pacing as he recounted the story. "You see the wreck was their last physical contact with the world they'd left behind. The ones, who wanted to stay, were sure that a rescue attempt would still be mounted, and that it'd be sent to the same place. They thought if they moved they'd never be found. After the mutiny was quashed, though they were still reluctant to cut the only tie to the old World, they all headed south. If they'd known..." His voice tailed off.

"What triggered the mutiny? Why didn't the group who wanted to remain with the wreck just let the others leave?" Lockhart asked.

"There were only four females on the ship, and they were all in favour of moving-on. In fact it was the women who'd instigated it. For there to be any chance of survival into subsequent generations all of the females had to remain together. The men who wanted to stay with the ship took some of the women hostage; a man needs a reason to survive,

Captain," he said, explaining their actions, though not attempting to justify them.

"An ugly situation." Lockhart observed.

"A man'll do ugly things when he has nothing to lose. These men weren't just fighting for their lives; they were fighting for a reason to live. The women were eventually freed. But the lose of life was tragic, men had killed their comrades and friends."

Lockhart had been studying Michael as he recounted the tragic events. The tale, and his reactions, seemed genuine, she thought. But then a little embellished fiction, mixed with facts that, if he were telepathic, he could have acquired from any of their minds, might make this illusion considerably more plausible.

Matt had moved away from the staircase, and had slowly paced across the room to the rear of the Captains chair, while the conversation progressed. The mention of fighting had given him an idea. He now lent against the back of the Captain's chair.

"The fighting must have been unnecessarily brutal," Matt said. "There were an awful lot of shells fired. You don't need several hundred rounds of 4.5 inch shells to kill a half dozen men; bullets'll usually suffice."

Matt was searching. The Captain and the rest of the landing party knew it. They all knew that the shells had not been fired, but deliberately emptied, though none of them understood why, not even Matt. A little inspired bluff might force Michael's hand.

Michael looked a little unsure. Was he searching their minds for a plausible reason, which, since none of them knew the answer, none of them could offer? He searched their eyes.

"The shells were not fired...." he eventually replied, ending the statement with a questioning look.

"Lieutenant Sweeney," Matt said, answering the unasked question.

"And I think, Mr Sweeney, you know as well as I do that they were not fired."

"Can you explain why?" Matt pressed.

As Michael again studied the faces around him his brow furrowed. He looked troubled. If he were telepathically searching their minds for an answer they would believe, there was none that could be offered. No one on Endeavour knew why the empty shells had been dismantled, not even Matt. If Michael was using their minds against them, he was now on his own, and Sweeney would be able to deduce if his answers were a fabrication. Michael's reasoning would depend on an intimate knowledge of 20th century warfare. Which if he were not genuine, Nicolle doubted.

"The Eldridge was a brand new ship," Michael eventually replied. "She'd not yet gone into service, hadn't even undergone sea trials, but they'd earmarked her for the 'Project Rainbow' experiment."

Matt nodded he understood, whilst Captain Lockhart shifted in her chair to enable her to observe the interaction between them.

"She hadn't been fully fitted either," Michael continued. "But for the purposes of the experiment, everything had to be as close to the conditions they would encounter in battle."

Again Matt nodded, but remained silent, allowing Michael enough rope.

"Everything that the ship'd require at sea was on board, but not in the quantities she would have in service. It was an experiment there wasn't any need to fully fit her; she carried only enough personnel, ammunition and stores to evaluate the effect of the electro-magnetic field. There wasn't a full compliment of crew, but enough for the purposes of the experiment. They needed to know how the human body would react to the field. Unfortunately they discovered that the human body, or the deck plating it was standing on didn't remain solid."

"We saw that," Wattie said.

Michael acknowledged Wattie's remark; his eyes adopting a sadness, as he reflected. "There wasn't a full compliment of engineering supplies, again, just enough to evaluate the experiment. That also meant that there wasn't enough acetylene to cut through the hull, when it came time for the survivors to remove one of the engines. What little welding gases they had, they used to cut a groove on the port side. Then they removed the propellant from the ammunition, packed it into the groove and ignited it. It took a long time, and all the propellant they had, but they eventually cut through a section of the hull."

"Wouldn't gunpowder spill out of a groove?" Wattie asked.

"Modern ammunition uses cordite, it isn't a powder, it's like solid sticks of spaghetti. You need to be careful with it, but if you heat it up, it can be moulded to fit any shape."

"We didn't see any sign of the hull plate that had been removed," Matt said.

"They used it to haul the engine down to the river, loaded it on to a barge they'd built, and floated it down the coast."

"That must have been heavy," Matt replied.

"Not really. The spent shell cases came in handy as rollers to drag the hull plate over."

Lockhart shot a questioning look at Matt, to which he nodded slightly; affirmatively. It seemed Michaels story was not just plausible: it was feasible.

Nicolle was all but satisfied they had indeed found the descendants of the Eldridge survivors. Everything seemed to fit, even if their initial reaction to her crew's sudden appearance had been strange. There was just one more question she needed answered. Leaping to her feet she slapped her comm-bracelet, which chirped in response.

"Wicasa here, Captain."

"Commander, access the historic data base. See what information we can get on the original crew manifest of the USS Eldridge."

"Yes ma'am," Wicasa's disembodied voice replied.

Turning to Michael she asked, abruptly. "What's your surname, Michael?"

Michael hesitated a moment, he looked stunned. The question had come out of the blue. Looking around the room at the expectant faces, his brow furrowed.

"Van Allen." He eventually replied.

There was a short pause while Lockhart waited for Wicasa to comeback to her. She adopted her usual pacing the room, fist planted firmly on her hips. The room adopted an expectant silence while they waited.

"We have it Captain," Wicasa eventually said. There was a shorter pause while the Commander assessed the list. It did not take long to find the name he was looking for; it was second top. "Lieutenant William K. Van Allen; he was the Eldridge's first officer, Captain."

"Lockhart out."

"Well Captain, do I pass?" Michael asked, flippantly.

Lockhart smiled warmly. She was convinced.

Michael knew from the beginning that he was being tested. He was neither disappointed nor offended that he had not been accepted for who he claimed to be, given the circumstances, he realised he would probably been equally sceptical. His hesitancy in giving his surname had not been because he did not know the answer, but simply because in his entire life, no one had ever asked him that question before; no one had ever needed to. Living all of his life with people he was related to, he had never had to be any more than simply Michael.

'Do I pass?' reverberated and echoed deep in Commander Jevak's brain; the part of his brain where the Vaurillian empathy originates, the part of his brain that was sensitive to extrasensory energy. A telepathic link had been suddenly and deliberately connected. A door, which had until now been tightly closed and guarded, had suddenly and intentionally been thrown open and Michael was now loudly announcing his mental prowess to the Commander.

The Commander shot a startled look towards Lieutenant Jevak. His Alliance Fleet double seemed unaware of Michael's telepathic declaration. Maybe Vaurillians in his Universe were not as receptive to telepathy as in this, the Commander speculated. What kind of game was Michael playing, if it was a game?

For the moment the Commander kept his own counsel, saying nothing of their host's telepathic ability.

CHAPTER 15

The discussion had cleared the air somewhat, though not entirely. There were still some things that were not sitting right with Nicolle that she wanted answers to, but there was certainly less tension now that suspicions of their host's authenticity had been dispelled. Only Commander Jevak still remained dubious. That brief telepathic contact with Michael disturbed him. For what purpose would Michael camouflage his telepathic abilities only to later display them so brazenly, but only to him? Could it be that there was still some malicious intent? The Commander said nothing; he kept his distance, watching closely.

Michael, in the mean time, was playing the perfect host. He had offered the landing party some refreshments in their mess, which Nicolle had graciously accepted.

Passing through the Great Hall again, Michael led them to the main corridor at the far end of the hall. It took them down to the next level of the cave complex via a wide stone spiral stairway.

The stairway opened directly into the mess hall. It was lively to say the least. About forty of their hosts where gathered in groups, chatting eating and generally socialising, much like any mess, on any starship.

The room was about twice the size of their own mess back on Endeavour and, as with the rest of the rooms and quarters they had seen in the cave complex, it was designed with ecology in mind. Massive, rocks and boulders, again punctuated its smooth, milky white, walls, protruding into the room's uneven spaces, creating shaded alcoves and secluded corners, which lent a measure of privacy to its patrons who might require intimacy.

In the centre of the mess, a wide, circular, granite galley, stood proud and sure-footed. Its wide black, polished surface laced with veins of white and cream, gave the room an air of grandiose and distinction. Above it hung an array from which an endless assortment of brightly polished metal utensils, ladles, knives, pots, pans and so on, swayed.

Although the mess was large and reasonably empty, their attractive, fair-skinned hosts were crowded mainly in and around the galley. Some sat on high stools around it, but the majority stood, constantly moving, reaching and passing morsels amongst the throng, as they mingled chattered and laughed, while preparing their food. No one seemed to be in charge of the preparation. No one seemed to be taking care of any particular part of the preparation; every one was doing everything. It appeared that cooking was considered to be a game rather than a chore.

"Salix'd love this place," Wattie commented.

"Yeh, like a kid in a toyshop," Matt agreed.

"We'll tell him about it later," added Nicolle.

"Would you like some coffee?" Michael asked all of them.

Nicolle's eyes brightened at the offer. "Oh yes," she replied enthusiastically.

She was a devotee and quite the connoisseur of coffee, and it had been four long years since she had last tasted the real thing, having had to survive on replicated instant for their entire exile in the Gamma sector.

"If you enjoyed the stuff we serve on the ship," she commented, turning to Commander Jevak, "Wait till you try this. This is how coffee was meant to taste." To Michael she added, out of genuine interest rather than simply making conversation, "Where do you grow the beans, the climate around here is surely too cold for coffee?"

"Twice a year, several teams of us head south with pack-wagons, to the Yucatan Mountains in Mexico. Our ancestors planted hundreds of acres of coffee on the lower slopes. We've been tending them ever since," Michael replied.

Rather poetic, thought Nicolle; humans, on a world where they should not exist, utilising a mountain range for sustenance, which does not exist on their own world.

Michael left them for the moment, mingling and surfing through the throng at the galley, while he arranged their refreshments. Nicolle found the scene mildly amusing, even heart warming. It was almost like a mini carnival. These people had had to endure extreme hardship and isolation and danger, but still appeared not to have a care in the world.

The landing party remained apart from the organised chaos going on around them, admiring the simplicity, yet complex dexterity involved in merely boiling an egg. This complex dance could never have been considered a production line; but it was amusing.

The Doctor took the opportunity, now that Michael had moved away to approach Nicolle.

"Captain," he said in a loud whisper, not wishing to draw too much attention to himself. "Something Samantha said back in her quarters, made me reassess the lack of readings we've been obtaining from our hosts, here."

Turning his back to the throng in the centre of the mess, he flipped open his palm-corder, shielding its display from prying eyes.

"We have been unable to detect them because we have been scanning in singe band widths. These people are only detectable through multiple band widths," he said incredulously.

"I don't understand," Wattie said, stepping closer to listen.

The rest of the landing party also stepped a little closer to listen in to the Doctor's explanation.

"At a sub-atomic level," the Doctor began again. "All matter resonates at a particular frequency. This resonance is constant, and cannot be altered in anyway. The resonance defines the particular reality from which we, and all other matter, originate. It allows identical matter, from all of the infinite number of parallel Universes to co-exist, occupying exactly the same space, without interaction or interference. We resonate at a different frequency from Commander Jevak and all other things in this Universe, because we do not belong here." He hesitated, looking around the room at their hosts. Certain that their conversation remained private he continued. "These people resonate at several frequencies. That is why we have not been able to detect them with any of our instruments. Their multiple resonances appear to keep them in a physical state of flux; neither fully existing in this universe nor in the one from which there ancestors originated, or in any other, for that matter."

Matt attempted to interrupt, but the Doctor cut him short.

"Yes Mister Sweeney, I'm quite certain that if their resonances were audible, I'd imagine they would sound like the Beach Boys," he said, grinning smugly; secure in the knowledge that he had beaten Sweeney to a punch line.

"How did he know I was going to say that?" Matt squawked at Wattie, feigning irritation.

"Ooh, that's gotta hurt... out smart-assed by an android. You're becoming predictable, fly-boy," Wattie grinned.

"I've been accessing the crews personality profiles," the Doctors said; shooting a sidelong, sly, glance at the Captain. "Mister Sweeney's infantile humour can be quite amusing at times," he said, grinning like a Cheshire cat.

"Yes, quite." Lockhart responded, dryly. "What's caused this?" she asked, earnestly. "You said that resonance was constant, and can't be altered?"

"It can't," he replied. "But these people were born in a place where they don't belong, where they shouldn't exist. They and their ancestors, for four hundred years, have been breathing oxygen, eating food, drinking water, all of which resonates at a different frequency from them. In the womb they were formed and nourished by elements that resonate at a frequency alien to their atoms; it cannot be altered. But they," he said looking back at the cheerful gathering behind them, "have been created this way."

"Does it affect them in any other way, besides existing in a state of flux?" Lockhart asked.

"I can't be certain yet, it may take a little time. I'll have to reconfigure my palm-corder to scan across multiple band widths."

"Might I suggest we all reconfigure our palm-corders?" Lt Jevak added.

Nicolle nodded her agreement. She was quietly relieved that another reason not to doubt these people had been discovered. "Keep me informed," she instructed the Doctor, Jevak and Wattie.

Michael returned with a tray laden with coffee cups. As he did, Matt noticed Sam making her way up the stairway, out of the mess.

"Captain. Would you mind if I took a raincheck?" he asked. "I'd like to have an other look around topside."

"Okay, but keep in touch with the ship. We don't have long, and I don't want to lose anyone."

Wattie gave him a knowing wink as Matt brushed past him heading for the steps. "You should take her some flowers," he joked.

Matt wavered a beat as he made to come back with one of his renowned witty retorts. He had a well-earned reputation aboard the ship as a bit of a Romeo and he had a natural urge to remind Cheung just how well earned that reputation was. But his mind wasn't quite in the game; he was more intent on his new prey than exchanging witticisms.

"We'll see" he smirked, hurrying after Sam.

Michael laid the tray of coffee on the table, passing cups to each of the away team. Lieutenant Jevak naturally declined, explaining that Vaurillians did not indulge in chemical stimulus, not even caffeine. Michael was therefore surprised when Commander Jevak accepted his cup. The Vaurillian Commander savoured the fine aroma, commenting to the Captain that it was much better than the brew she had served on the ship.

Michael was about to hand a cup to the Doctor when he paused, unsure.

Turning to Lockhart he said, looking a little

bewildered. "There is so much I need to ask you Captain."

Lockhart's mind raced with four hundred years of unimagined questions. This was a situation no human could ever have contemplated; it was completely unprecedented. Alliance Fleet had a wealth of experience when it came to first contact with alien species, but never in her long distinguished career had Nicolle ever imagined first contact with her own kind.

"Like wise. Why don't we take a seat?" she suggested calmly, hiding her eagerness.

She slid on to one of the six, high wooden stools around the table beside them. Michael left the Doctor's un-offered cup on the table and joined her.

The Doctor, unfazed, continued scrutinising his palm-corder readings.

Lifting her eyes slowly, from her coffee cup Nicolle asked. "I've noticed how you, and Samantha, reacted to our Doctor. Neither of you have spoken to him, nor made any attempt to interact with him. You seem to know there's something different about him. How can that be?"

Michael did not answer immediately. His delay was not hesitancy; he was trying to formulate the words to explain something he himself did not fully understand. He found it hard to explain because his ancestors had not had a word for the condition that he and the others had been born with.

"We....we are different, Captain. Living in

this reality has somehow changed us. We see the World.... with more than just our eyes," he explained.

"Telepathy?"

"No. It's more than that. It's.... It's difficult to say, it's like a one-ness; a connection to all living things. You'd maybe call it a sixth sense, but it's much, much more." He glanced over at the Doctor. "We can feel... empathise with other creatures. But I can't feel anything from him, it's like he isn't there," he said frowning in disbelief. "He's a little un-nerving."

"The Doctor is an artificial life form," Nicolle said, then she began explaining robotics.

She tried to keep the explanation simple, but Michael was hungry for knowledge, he was desperate to know everything that had happened in the centuries since their ancestors had left their own Universe.

The explanation became long and laboured. She had to continue reminding herself that, intelligent as he seemed, Michael's technological understanding was based on four hundred year old, internal combustion and copper wire, engineering. In the end his grasp of her explanation seemed pretty complete. She had to wonder though if he had eventually, resorted to delving her mind for the explanation, rather than battle with incomprehensible concepts.

Nicolle was equally hungry for information. There were no records of the failed experiments that had stranded the crew of the USS Eldridge here. Everything relating to those fateful events had been covered-up and denied for centuries. She needed to know what had really happened in Philadelphia in 1943.

She was about to enquire about the experiments when Michael got another question in first. "How did you find us Captain?" he asked. "If you weren't looking for us, what brought you here?"

That was a long story, she thought. Where to begin?

Six years ago; the chase through the nebula of unstable dust and debris, where sensors were, at best unreliable, in defence of an Alliance freighter, had thrown them to the far side of the Galaxy. Their subsequent quest for shortcuts home, had brought them to the wormhole, which, in turn, had led them here.

"Like your ancestors," Nicolle began. "We find ourselves here as a result of a series of unfortunate, unforeseen events."

She quickly outlined the Macaitian Empires warmongering, and the Alliances response. She hoped her explanation of wormholes was a little more comprehensible than that of androids.

********** ********** **********
****

The early, afternoon sun, shone directly through the crashing, curtain of water, as Matt emerged from the cave mouth. A cool breeze caught the gently, drifting spray which hung in the air, like a shimmering mist of bright diamonds, wafting it across his face, cooling him after the stiff climb, from the Mess Hall, below.

Turning left, he ducked from behind the waterfall, emerging at the top of the staircase. Sam was nowhere to be seen. She had not been that far ahead of him, but Matt could not see her anywhere as he began to descend the steps towards the hollow.

At the foot of the stairs, where Sam had first approached them, Matt shielded his eyes from the sun, searching the hollow for any sign of movement. From the ruined village up the slope to his left, to the lake, which filled the base of the vast depression, he could see no sign of her. The lakeside, though, with its scattering of shore side bushes and trees offered the best hiding places, so he made for the lake.

A narrow, well-worn dirt path skirted the lakeshore. It meandered beneath several shading Maple and Willow trees and was punctuated by thickets and bushes, which huddled close to the waters edge.

Although Sam was still nowhere in sight Matt declined to call for her. He had planned on their bumping into each other being 'an accident', and he was not about to give the game away.

Looking back and forth along the length of the pathway, he could see from one end of the lakeshore to the other. There were not that many places for someone to hide; yet he could still not find her. Matt was puzzled; where else could she have gone. The hillside, up towards the ruins was completely exposed and offered no hiding places at all. She could never have run so fast as to get over the brow of the hollow before he had gotten to the bottom of the steps. Endeavour's quick-witted pilot was completely baffled.

Passing under the shade of one of the giant Maples, he heard an exaggerated cough from somewhere behind him. Spinning on his heals he was stunned to find Sam casually lounging back against the broad trunk of the tree. She was almost beside him, almost close enough to touch and yet he had not seen her. She had not have been there when he passed the tree, and there was nowhere she could have been hiding either; he could not have failed to see her but some how did.

"You wouldn't be following me, would you, Mr Sweeney?" she asked teasingly.

"How d'you do that?" he asked, completely failing to hide his astonishment. "That's the second time you've sneaked up on me."

"Just a trick," she smiled, shrugging dismissively. "It's just something I do. Come, sit. Since you seem so intent in finding me."

"I just …needed some fresh air," he responded quickly, playfully countering her allegation.

"Of course you did. Sit," she said, patting the ground beside her.

It was a friendly, yet reserved invitation, it seemed to Matt. Sam's manner was not exactly cold, but she was standoffish. He was going to have to use every ounce of his roguish charm to break down these defences. But then, he thought, there was no real hurry; he would have all the time he needed when they were all back aboard Endeavour.

"You're not afraid out here, all alone?" Matt asked, deciding to take the heroic, protector approach, as he sat down on the grass beside her.

"Why. Should I be?"

Reclining back, against the tree, he suggested. "Well, there must be reptile settlements near-by. You never know, they might be lurking anywhere," he suggested, eyeing the top of the cliff. "Ready to attack. Those bushes over there, for instance." He indicated towards a thick undergrowth at the far end of the lake, just below the southern cliff face.

"I think I'm pretty safe, Mr Sweeney."

"Please, call me Matt," he insisted, smiling his most disarming smile.

She returned the smile, a little more coolly than Matt might have hoped. "There isn't a reptile settlement for more than a hundred miles in any direction. They're terrified of this whole region," she assured him. "There's absolutely no possibility of us being attacked."

"Terrified?" he asked, letting the flirtations drop for a moment.

Sam nodded. "Wouldn't you be? The evil spirits of, 'The Devil's minions' haunt these hills, didn't you know?" she joked. "Or so the stories go. The reptile's old stories of us are enough to deter any unwanted visitors. They stay well away from here, believe me."

"Wasn't there ever any attempt to make peace with the locals?"

"You've met them. What do you think the chances are of living in harmony with them are?"

Matt shrugged.

"These creatures are on a par with us, as we were back in the middle-ages," she went on. "And back then we burned witches, made human sacrifices and tortured, mutilated and killed other human beings just for the colour of their skin, or their religious beliefs. These creatures aren't any different. The simple fact that we exist at all, or that stories of us persist, makes them live in fear of the night, the wind, of anything they can't explain. No Mister Sweeney, they don't want to live with us. They want to wipe us from the face of their Earth. We're the reason their crops fail, the rains come too late or too early, why diseases kill them, or even that a horse throws a shoe. We're witches," she shrugged, matter-of-factly.

"That's why," she continued after a while, "after the caves were made, we dismantled the old village. If they thought we'd gone, maybe they'd stop hunting us. But stories of the 'smooth faces' still persisted. We couldn't avoid them completely. Every now and then one of our hunting parties bumps into some unsuspecting lizard, and the horror stories they tell around the fires at night, kick off again. But they do leave the hollow alone, so we're both safe," she said winking cheekily.

The heroic approach was going to be a non-starter, Matt thought. Best just make small talk; take it from there.

Looking back, up towards the waterfall, were the cave entrance was, he asked. "The caves must've taken decades to excavate?"

"No. Not really. The original cave was just a damp hole in the cliff face, but we expanded it pretty quickly."

"You mean your ancestors did?" He corrected her.

"No Mr Sweeney...we did."

Matt looked surprised. "That's a lot of work for one generation."

He picked up a flat stone, and playfully threw it across the calm, surface of the lake. It skimmed once, twice.... five times, before sinking beneath the surface.

"It must've taken a long while," he added for emphasis. "Our Mr. Jevak couldn't work out how the excavation had been done. There's no sign of digging, or blasting, or anything like that." He looked seriously at her, determined to get an answer. "So how was it excavated?"

"The caves are the way they are because that is how we will them to be," she replied simply, also picking up a stone.

"And how do you do that?" he persisted.

Sam did not throw her stone; she merely flicked it with a slight movement of her wrist. It skimmed five, ten…seventeen times, to the far-side of the lake, then turned, skimmed a further dozen or so times, in a figure of eight, before eventually sinking.

"We just do," she giggled playfully.

Looking at her, Matt was suddenly swamped by the realisation of how beautiful she really was. He could not help but notice how completely exquisite she looked. Her auburn hair shimmered a myriad of warm colours in the autumn sunlight. She was statuesque like, elegant and…

His surprise and amusement at her little performance quickly turned to astonishment as the truth suddenly struck him. They're perfect specimens of humanity, he thought, because they can be…. because they can be anything they want.

***********   *************   **************

Nicolle finished her coffee and slid her cup to the middle of the table.
"Finding the Eldridge was a complete surprise to us," she said.

Michael had sat silently, mesmerized as she recounted their unbelievable tale. Space travel was something that had only been imagined by the Eldridge's generation, and had become no more of a reality to Michael's. It was still the stuff of fantasy. Visiting other worlds had already been done in the cinemas of the 1930's and 40's before the experiment, so the illusion was at least tangible. But meeting someone who had actually crossed the distance between stars was fascinating.

"We have absolutely no records of 'Project Rainbow' ever having taken place," Nicolle continued. "When we checked our historical database the only mention of it, or the 'Philadelphia Experiment', was with reference to cranks and conspiracy theorists. As far as official records go the Experiment never happened. We have no idea what or who were involved."

"Well Captain we're living proof that the experiments did take place. But you're absolutely right; they were dealing with forces far beyond their control or understanding. But they believed in what they were doing."

"Do you know who put the theory together?" Lockhart asked.

"From what I understand, the greatest scientific minds of the time were supposed to be in control of the project. I only know what's been passed down to me. Einstein and Oppenhiemer." Michael shrugged, unable to offer more. "Do the names mean anything to you?"

"I've... come across them," she smiled coolly, keeping her answer brief. She was too engrossed in his tail to offer distracting snippets of her own information.

"Well who ever they were," he smiled. "I suppose we owe them a debt of gratitude,"

Nicolle found this a strange thing to say. If it

were not for these scientists, Michael and the others would not be stranded on a world where they did not belong. That was nothing to be grateful for.

"Without them none of us here would exist. All of us are alive," he indicated, glancing around the mess at his companions. "Because of an exceptional set of circumstances; circumstances which wouldn't exist in yours, or any other parallel. Circumstances, which brought the crew and technicians permanently together, and when they realised there was no way home resulted in an un-natural, but essential breeding programme, to ensure the continued long-term survival of the community. Those circumstances don't exist anywhere but here in this Universe. We exist purely because of that. Unlike you," he said, nodding for emphasis towards the Vaurillian Commander and Lieutenant Jevak. "In all of the infinite number of Universes which exist in parallel to this, we have no counter parts. We are singular entities. We are completely and utterly unique. We exist here, and only here.

He paused, gathering his thoughts, before drawing a deep, well considered breath. "Have you ever wondered, Captain Lockhart, why so many different cultures across the globe, some separated by thousands of miles of ocean, hold a common belief that at the moment of death your whole life passes before you?"

It was a strange question, thought Nicolle. It caught her a little off guard.

Before she could answer though, Commander

Jevak cut-in with an observation. "That's a common belief on many planets across the Galaxy, not just on your world."

Michael acknowledged the observation then continued. "There is a reason why," he explained. "…..It's true." He let the statement hang in the air for a moment then added. "But to a greater extent than you could ever imagine."

The conversation was taking an unexpected turn. Nicolle was surprised, intrigued and just a little unsettled.

"At the exact moment of death, your lives, plural…" he emphasised, "not life, pass through your diminishing consciousness." Locking eyes with the Captain he went on. "Every life lived by every Nicolle Lockhart in every one of the infinite parallels, comes rushing at you. In that final moment you suddenly become aware of all alternate paths your life could have taken. All the opportunities you never took, but some other alternate you did. Every door that was closed to you, but stood ajar for another. Every time you said 'no' instead of 'yes'. When you turned left another Captain Lockhart turned right. All of the different outcomes your life could have culminated in, and the possibilities unimagined; they all come rushing to you."

Releasing her from his gaze he added, thoughtfully, "I suppose that could be what we call Heaven or Hell. In that final moment, that last glimpse of life when it's all too late, to become painfully aware of how much more you could have been; the innumerable chances and opportunities you had squandered. Or the certain, and reassuring knowledge that you made the most of what life offered. What greater joy or deeper despair."

"How do you know this?" Nicolle asked.

"Because as I've said, we have no counterparts in other dimensions. We, unlike your selves, are not an infinitesimal segment of a single, shattered being, scattered across infinite parallels. We are singular. Whole. Complete. Therefore our awareness is not diminished by fragmentation. Our consciousness expands beyond this World, beyond this reality."

Nicolle drew a deep breath and sat back in her chair, as her mind raced. This was hard to accept. Less than an hour ago they had found, against all odds, the descendants of survivors from an ancient experimental accident. Now she was having to come to terms with.... What? Super-beings?

"No Captain. I know what you're thinking." Michael said calmly, reassuringly.

His awareness of what was going through her mind, was not as a result of any unusual abilities, but because her misgivings were written all over her face.

"We're not super-human I can assure you. We're mortal; we bleed. To be honest, if I had to analyse what has happened to us here, I'd say our circumstances have merely forced our natural growth, we have been advanced, propelled as it were, by the extraneous environment we live with, to some next stage in human evolution."

"How far do your... powers go?"

Michael said nothing he merely finished the remains of his coffee.

Laughter from the galley caught Nicolle's attention. Wattie was causing a stir with his jovial antics. He was either teaching two of the females how to make an omelette, or showing them how to juggle eggs. And since Nicolle knew he could do neither, she rightly assumed he was just simply showing off.

Michael slid his chair away from the table and got to his feet. Leaning close to Nicolle he whispered. "Don't be concerned. What's happened to us is fate. We were conceived and born into a Universe that was alien to us, nothing more."

Stepping away from the table, "I'd like another coffee," Michael announced casually. "Anyone else?"

As Michael gathered-up their cups, Wattie tore himself away from the throng around the galley, to rejoin his colleagues. At the same time the Doctor seeing his opportunity to talk freely to the Captain again also moved swiftly to join the group at the table.

"Captain," the Doctor whispered, urgently. "My scans have revealed some remarkable inconsistencies."

Knowing what she now knew about their hosts, Nicolle had not expected anything less but was still eager to find out what more the Doctor had discovered.

"Captain. These people have evolved beyond us," he said, confirming Michael's earlier self-assessment. "So much so," he continued. "They are almost a new species. They are almost as different from you, as you are from the apes."

Nicolle was shocked that such a dramatic change could have been possible in a few short generations. "In what way?" she asked.

The Doctor eyed the room, making certain he would not be overheard. "I don't mean that since their ancestors arrived here that subsequent generations have gradually evolved. I mean that they, themselves as individuals have, and as we speak, right now, are continuing to evolve. They are continually, physically altering."

"Explain."

The others around the table gathered a little closer.

"Well, to begin with their cranial cavity's are considerably enlarged. Their brains are approximately thirteen to fourteen percent larger than normal, and structured in a completely unfamiliar arrangement, parts of which I have no idea of their function. But, and here is where it gets really interesting, although thirteen percent could be construed as a relatively minor increase, the electrical output of their brains has been multiplied exponentially. The computing power of just one of their brains could easily run several starships."

Wattie sucked in air.

"But it isn't just their brains which have been transformed. Physically they have lost some of the superfluous organs which still burden the rest of the human race," the Doctor continued. "Mainly, they have no tonsils or appendix, since these organs have been largely redundant for centuries, they have been evolved out of their DNA. But," he said, hesitating, to emphasise what was to follow. "More importantly though, these people, all of them are not only impotent, they have no sexual organs at all, nothing.... They are all asexual. It's as though nature, having denied them reproduction, were rewarding them with long life and continued evolution, but at a much more accelerated pace. In about another hundred years or so, your DNA wont even be compatible with theirs."

Wattie smiled wryly to himself, and took a mental note to take Matt aside, for a little 'locker room' style gossip. He had some very disappointing news for him.

"They've altered that much in...what, twenty years?" asked Commander Jevak.

"No not twenty years Commander... More than three hundred," the Doctor corrected him, barely concealing his own astonishment. "This is not the fifteenth, or sixteenth generation who have survived here. These are the third. Their grandparents were the original survivors; the Eldridge crew. These individuals are over three hundred years old.

*********** ************* *************
******

The afternoon sun sleepily arced towards the south-western rim of the cliff, casting a deep shadow over most of the southern end of the lake. A mist had begun to form there, hanging in the cooling air a few feet above the surface fed by the evaporating, still warm waters below.

Dragonflies, dozens of them, buzzed the heavy air. Their delicate, gossamer wings catching the orange glow of the waning sun, illuminating them like fireflies in daylight, as they danced and flitted in the warm early Autumn. Further along the bank, to their left, the towering willow's languid, limp branches pawed lethargically at the still waters, tracing lazy ripples on the lakes otherwise glass like surface.

It was a perfect day.

Matt breathed deeply, slowly. His eyes closed as he drank in the familiar sounds and smells that should have reassured him that he was home. Sighing, he opened them again. They would have to leave here soon. This place was beginning to frustrate him. Looking so much like home, yet it was not. It was an illusion, a bad joke that was now wearing thin. As his eyes refocused, a crimson, three pointed maple leaf, falling from a branch not far above their heads caught Matt's attention, as it drifted, swaying to and fro to the grass at their feet. Hardly an unusual sight, considering it was fall, except that on the branch from where it had fallen there were already buds and young leaves, in place, ready to continue the trees growth.

Sam caught the look on Matt's face and followed the line of his gaze. She smiled at his bewilderment. He was still coming to terms with the differences on this Earth. She was about to explain when, as though he had read her thoughts, he interrupted her.

"This Earth is tilted at a lesser angle than ours," he said, almost as a statement. "The seasons aren't as distinct here, are they?"

"We've only ever known this World," Sam explained. "But from the stories handed down to us, it would seem that this Earth's a lot more temperate that yours. The climate and changes in the duration of daylight, aren't as severe here."

Looking at him, Sam could see his disappointment and frustration growing. She did not require her extra senses to tell that he was becoming impatient. This World was becoming a painful reminder that he and the rest of Endeavours crew had failed. This road had proved to be a blind alley.

"Did you ever try to recreate the experiment, to try to get home again?" Matt asked, painfully aware of his own need to get to his own World.

She nodded, turning her gaze towards the lake.

"It was almost ten years before this place was fully secured," she replied, remembering the stories handed down to her. "Ten years of struggle... Every day was just about survival, in a hostile place. Ten years of scratching a living off the land; hunting for meagre food whilst being constantly hunted themselves," she said referring to the Eldridge crew.

"Seven more crew members were lost during that time. Three to reptile hunting parties, and the other four to disease. Thankfully, for the community, none of the women died," she added, gently tossing some pebbles into the shallows. "But eventually after a time they were able to devote their time to more that just survival... The crew built three more generators, to go along with the one they brought from the wreck."

"They linked them to a single metal chamber, big enough for one person, around which they wound copper coils. The electro-magnetic field they produced was beyond anything they had expected."

"For the first trial, they used a dog. As far as any of us know, it went well. The dog de-materialised...didn't reappear. So they thought it would be okay to try with a human. That went the same way, crewman Rusedski disappeared without any hitches. The next two attempts went horribly wrong, though. For some reason both crewmen spontaneously combusted." Sam looked shaken as she recounted the story, as it had been told to her. "After a couple of years of taking the equipment apart and starting from scratch, they tried again with another dog. Same again, it spontaneously combusted as well. There were no more attempts, it was unpredictable and too dangerous."

"They accepted their fate?" Matt asked. "They gave up?"

"What else could they do? They weren't prepared to sacrifice any more in some vain attempt at the impossible."

Matt shivered at the thought.

To be denied hope. It was beyond his comprehension. Hopelessness was something Endeavours crew had never known.

In the six years they had been lost on the far side of the Galaxy, none of them had ever abandoned the belief that they could get home, would get home. Even when the distance had seemed impossible they had always had hope. Captain Lockhart's belief in them, her crew, and her ship, had carried them on. But these lost souls, in the end, they had been denied even the possibility of hope. It must have been a cold feeling; the desolate finality of having to accept their fate, embracing defeat. Abandoning all possibility of ever getting home again. To know that this gilded cage, so much like their own Earth, was forever their prison.

It was something Matt could not come to terms with. He felt a cold, empty gnawing in the pit of his stomach. He knew some how that Endeavour would get home. He could never give up hope.

He was about to sympathize with the helplessness that lost crew must have felt, when suddenly Sam sat bolt upright.

"You must go... Now!" she gasped.

********** ************* ************* *******

"You must go... Now Captain!" Michael suddenly gasped.

"What's wrong?" Lockhart asked.

"Now Captain! You must go!" Michael barked, kicking his chair away, getting to his feet.

Before she had time to ask again, Nicolle's comm-braclette came to life. Wicasa's voice cut the air.

"Bridge to Captain Lockhart," he said, his voice betraying urgency.

"Lockhart here."

"Captain. Long range sensors have just picked up a fleet of fifteen Macaitian battleships on an intercept course with the wormhole."

Commander Jevak's communicator chirped furiously. On answering it, he was given the same information.

Nicolle face dropped.

"Now Captain, please!" Michael pressed.

Turning to Commander Jevak, Nicolle asked. "How many can your teleports cope with at one time?"

"No Nicolle," Michael interrupted. "We are not going with you."

"We can get you out of here, Michael," she

urged. "We can get you...."

"Where Captain? Home? No. Where ever we originated from, it wasn't your Universe, and we now, no more belong in your reality than we do now in our own."

"Maybe not, but you definitely don't belong here."

"On the contrary, we are what this reality's made us, this is our home, it's where we belong, and I'm sorry, but we have no intention of leaving."

"This is insane. You can't stay here. You're the only humans in a Universe that's alien to you," Lockhart insisted.

"We'd be even more alien in you Universe. And in a hundred years or so, how much more alien would we be? Yes Captain we can stay here, we belong here. I believe there's a reason why we are here, we have a purpose, and I believe that purpose will be made clear today."

"Captain Lockhart..." interrupted Commander Jevak. "We must go."

"A moment Commander," she replied firmly.

"Captain..." The Commander persisted. "Every second we delay puts them closer to the wormhole. There's no time for this."

"Michael......."

"No Nicolle. But you must go. Your presence here isn't just endangering yourselves, you're also putting whole worlds in danger."

She stepped away from the group, deliberating possibilities. The deliberating did not take long.

She, as always, was sharp and decisive. This argument was over and she could not, she knew, change Michael's mind. She had to take action, and her ship and crew were now her only priority.

"Wicasa," she said tapping her comm-braclette. "Prepare for site-to-site teleport. Get us directly to the bridge"

"Is there anything we can do for you before we leave?" she asked Michael.

Jevak, Wattie and the Doctor joined her, ready to teleport. Commander Jevak took-up his teleport position at the opposite side of the mess hall.

"No Captain, but thank you," Michael replied with gratitude. "Unfortunately the circumstances we find ourselves in haven't allowed us to get to know each other better. I'd have liked to have learned more about the last four hundred years on your World."

"Like wise," she said, her voice tinged with regret.

"Safe home Nicolle," he smiled regretfully, stepping away as four pillars of blue and one of bright green stars shimmered to either side of him.

CHAPTER 16

Sweeney was already at his station when the four pillars of light ceased shimmering in the centre of the bridge.

Almost before the figures had coalesced, Lockhart, Jevak and Wattie were moving, diverging to their stations. The Doctor, still wishing to see out the mission, remained on the bridge, getting out of the harms way though, he took-up position at the rail behind the Captain's chair.

"Status?" Lockhart demanded.

"Cosique's in the process of bringing the warp reactor on-line. We have weapons, sensors and navigation, but still no shields." Wicasa replied.

Since coming through the wormhole, Cosique's engineering teams had performed miracles, working flat out to repair all of Endeavours near fatally damaged systems. But even after eight days, and with more staff having been seconded to her from other areas of the ship, there just had not been enough time or manpower to get everything back on-line.

"Engineering."

"Cosique here Captain," came the response,

via the comm-system.

"Cosique, I need warp power right away."

"You'll have it in exactly two minutes, Captain."

"Good work."

Tuning to Wicasa she said, "We'll be travelling alone."

"They couldn't be persuaded, then?"

"They had their reasons," she replied dolefully then added, "I don't know why but Michael was adamant that they were staying; he feels they have a purpose and that it's here."

Nicolle did not feel right about, as she saw it, abandoning humans in need. She could not have known that Michael's decision was not of his choosing, because even he was unaware that the choice had never been his to make.

"I just couldn't persuade him," she concluded.

"The Sorn is hailing us, Captain," announced Jevak.

"On screen."

"Captain Lockhart, we'll deploy our tractor beam to tow you..."

"No need, Commander." Replied Nicolle, enthusiastically. "Our chief engineer is about to bring our warp reactor back on-line."

The news was not greeted with an equal show of enthusiasm. "Is that wise?" He asked, his voice revealing his concern.

"We've had a tried and tested procedure for cold starting a warp reactor for the best part of a hundred years now," she assured him. "It's never a preferred option, but nobody's died of it yet. Don't worry, we'll be ready when you are."

He was not quite convinced of the Captain's faith in her technology, but if Endeavour were to destroy herself, by her own misfortune, here and now, it would save the High Command any further concern that the ship might yet fall in to Macaitian hands.

"As you wish, Captain. Sorn out," he said, ending the communication.

The screen shifted, retuning to the high orbit view of Earth's, now sun lit, northern hemisphere.

"Warp power coming back on-line now," Sweeney announced triumphantly.

As he did the lights on the bridge brightened noticeably.

"Well done Cosique," Lockhart praised. "Let's get underway. Set a course directly back to the wormhole... Warp eight."

"Laid-in already, Captain," Sweeney replied.

"Engage."

The image of Earth, on the view screen, slid away to one side then vanished as Endeavour dipped and turned.

"Switch to aft viewer," Nicolle instructed.

The view screen instantly altered to present the shrinking blue planet, flanked by stretched points of starlight, fast disappearing in their wake.

"Full magnification."

Again the screen shifted.

The azure blue sphere, flecked by wisps of white, once more filled the screen. Gradually though, the corners of the huge display gave way to the blackness of deep space, as the Earth continued to recede.

The bridge fell silent.

A heavy, solemnity descended. The crew as one stared silently at the screen. Each lost in their own private mournful regret as the sight they had longed to see again, slipped away from them. Each one of them submerged in their own personal loss.

Lockhart sighed quietly to herself. She could not let her crew know the crushing disappointment she felt, although she knew that they all felt the same. As always she had to be strong for them.

"We made it once people," she announced robustly, turning to look at each of them. "We will do it again...Screen off." As the display again became blank she added determinedly, confidently. "Let's go home."

************ ********** ********** *******

Across the expanse of the alpha Sector six more Macaitian ships joined the original fifteen as they tore at warp reactor searing velocity, across the divide.

Angling to starboard, all twenty-one hugged perilously close to a nearby star, grinding through its crushing gravity to slingshot around it, in an effort to increase their speed beyond the limits of their warp engines. As they did, shearing the thin atmosphere of the star, twisting violently through its corona, a solar flare leapt into the void, engulfing two of the rear most ships. Both exploded in the searing plume, sending debris smashing and tearing through another. It in turn vaporised as it tumbled helplessly into the scorching maelstrom.

The remaining eighteen continued on without slowing, seemingly oblivious to their comrade's demise. Bending light in their wake, pushing at the warp envelope, desperate to close the gap to the wormhole.

*********** *********** ************ **********

"Time to the wormhole?" Nicolle demanded.

"Thirty four minutes, twenty six seconds, Captain," Jevak replied instantly.

The distance it had taken them eight days to cover, powered by the ship's induction engines, was now disappearing rapidly behind them in a fraction of the time. Their current warp eight was devouring the light years.

Nicolle rested on the rail behind her chair. She felt whole again. Her ship was functioning almost as normal, and she was in control of both hers, and her crews destiny again. Behind her the sound of lift doors swishing open roused her. She spun on her heels.

"Ahh, Sub-commander T'Arran," she said almost warmly, greeting the Vaurillian as she stepped onto the bridge. "I believe we have you to thank for the swift repairs to our warp drive. I can't tell you how grateful we are."

"You have a good crew, Captain Lockhart, and Cosique is an exceptional engineer," she replied. "She did more than I, I was merely an enthusiastic assistant."

"None the less, your help was invaluable, we're indebted to you."

Side by side the Captain and T'Arran stepped down to the lower bridge. As they did the Vaurillian cast an approving eye around Endeavour's bruised and battered bridge. Nicolle eyed her intently, wondering again about that day twenty-five years ago. It still felt wrong to have the Vaurillian traitor on her bridge, much less feeling indebted to her for her help.

"Well Captain, have you reached a conclusion?"

Unsure of what T'Arran was referring to, Nicolle did not answer immediately, but metered her response with a questioning look.

"Nature or nurture, Captain? Isn't that what you were wondering?"

Nicolle looked startled, as though she had just been caught with her hand in the cookie-jar. "Ahh... You know," she replied, with note of resignation.

"It's a curious prospect to have the opportunity, as one of your human poets apparently put it,

'To see ourselves as other see us'. When you made your computer records available, I couldn't resist the urge to discover the fate of my counterpart in your Universe...So... what do you think, nature or nurture?"

"Does it worry you, that you might have the capacity to be that other T'Arran?"

"Until a few hours ago, I wouldn't have considered her existence as a possibility, but there must be a part of her in me, we're essentially the same person."

Nicolle smiled. "I'm not so sure, Sub-Commander," she said. "Twins are genetically the same person, carbon copies of each other. They are raised in identical environments, but they still invariably grow to become separate, unique personalities; they can be told apart."

She had not had much time to get to know this T'Arran; much less time or inclination to get to know the other, but she felt sure that this Vaurillian could never take the road the traitor still languishing in a cell on Pentrea-Gasta, had chosen. That T'Arran had feared changes; sought to hinder the new order. This T'Arran would, like all beings in this reality, embrace that 'Undiscovered Country' her counter-part had so mistrusted.

"Different circumstances have brought you to where you are now. Her life took her somewhere dark, somewhere I don't think you would even know how to find," the Captain assured her.

The Sub-Commander smiled as she again cast

an appraising eye around Endeavour's cannibalised bridge. Nicolle could not help but notice it was an approving look, tinged with a degree of envy. Even in her current state Endeavour was still faster and more deadly than anything in the High Command's arsenal. A puzzled look dawned on T'Arran's still grease smeared face.

"Captain?" she said, quickly changing the subject; she was evidently as uncomfortable with the thought of her counterpart as Nicolle was. The Sub-commander had learned that in The Captain's reality, the former Lieutenant T'Arran's name, on many worlds since her incarceration, had become the stuff of legend, vilified as a euphemism for 'Bogeyman', to frighten errant children. "Why are there so many miss-matched technologies aboard your ship?" she hastily asked.

"Well...," began The Captain. "We've been far from home for six years. No space-docks or engineering stations, and most of our repairs have been done while on the run for our lives. We've begged, borrowed and, I'm not proud to say, stole systems that were so incompatible we've had to shoehorn them in..."

She did not get a chance to finish her explanation.

"Captain! Long-range sensors are picking-up multiple warp trails on an intercept heading!" Wattie interrupted urgently.

"Go to red alert...! Distance?"

"Thirteen point four light years, and closing

fast."

Before she could respond, Jevak announced: "We are being hailed by the Sorn."

"On screen."

Seated in his command chair, Commander Jevak looked grave.

"We know, Commander. Our sensors have just detected them as well." Lockhart confirmed.

"Commander, Endeavour still has no shields," T'Arran said stepping closer to the screen to speak directly to her own commanding officer.

"We can extend ours to encompass both ships," the Commander offered. "If you can keep a parallel course, within eight hundred metres?"

"Can do," Sweeney interrupted.

"Captain, I must return to the Sorn," T'Arran said, quickly stepping to an empty spot in the centre of the bridge. "Thank you for this brief glimpse through the looking glass, Nicolle, it fills me with hope knowing that the beings of the Alpha Sector, in some other reality, know how to live together. Safe home Captain." She snatched a final, regretful look around Endeavour's bridge as her outline dissolved in a pillar of green stars, and was gone.

"Time to wormhole?" Lockhart demanded, turning to Jevak.

"Six minutes, seventeen seconds."

"Time to intercept?"

"Five minutes, twenty," replied Wattie.

They were going to need the Sorn's shields.

************* *************** **************

The first wave of four ships, cut across their bow, strafing shafts of lasers along the length of Endeavours starboard nacelle. The envelope of protective shields, surrounding the two ships glowed brightly as it safely dissipated the energy beams.

"They're attempting to disable us, Captain," Wattie informed her.

"Sorn's shields are holding," Jevak announced, calmly.

"Return fire. Target their warp reactors."

As the four vessels twisted, pivoting around their target, they continued to loose their lasers on Endeavours nacelles.

Simultaneously Alliance and Vaurillian vessels opened fire, targeting the rear Macaitian ship. Both Captains had the same plan. Their combined firepower cut through the Macaitian's shields, instantly renting its hull through to the power source at its heart. The ship exploded in a shocking, silent, blinding flash, which tore through the blackness, pummelling Endeavour and her Vaurillian escort.

"Three more coming at us from the rear," Cheung called, keeping the Captain continually appraised of the threat.

"On screen," she said, reacting instantly.

Endeavour's port viewers tracked the three ships, as they swept past, unleashing another continuous volley of lasers at their port nacelle.

"Ready ion torpedoes," Lockhart instructed, as she studied the path of the vessels. "Wait," she commanded. "Wait….. Wait…Fire!"

Sweeping port to starboard, in close formation, at warp eight, none of the three had time to react, as four bright orange globes streaked from beneath Endeavour's for'a'd section, directly into their path.

The first two ships were destroyed instantly as the torpedoes ripped through them. The third sustained horrendous crippling damage as the two close proximity explosions, and millions of tonnes of shredding debris tore through its shields, then its hull. As the fatally damaged ship attempted to turn out of Endeavours path, the G-forces rend its weakened hull, tearing it apart; it too inevitably died in a numbing flash that shocked the empty void.

These Macaitian had never had the misfortune to come up against Alliance tactics before. That gave Lockhart a slight advantage over them, for the time being at least, but they would soon learn.

The remaining ships split port and starboard, burning at Sorn's shields with continuous laser fire.

Incapable of withstanding such a sustained, ferocious assault, Commander Jevak ordered evasive action. The Sorn dipped twice then plummeted into a steep dive. The manoeuvre caught the Macaitians off guard; it would also have taken Matt Sweeney a little by surprise, had he not caught the exaggerated dips.

An open comm-link between the two ships, enabling them to co-ordinate their defence would have been preferred, but that was suicidal. The enemy might as well have had someone on both bridges broadcasting every intended move.

There was no alternative Sweeney would have to be on top of his game, alert to any movement of the Sorn, ready to match her or Endeavour would be left vulnerable, naked and dead, without cover of the Vaurillian's shields.

Sweeney pushed at his controls. Endeavour dipped, plummeting after the Sorn.

"Stay with them!" Lockhart urged, by way of encouragement, knowing that that's exactly what Sweeney would do anyway.

If any helmsman in the fleet could fly blind in a battle, it was Matt Sweeney; he had a natural instinct for this. She knew they were in the safest hands.

At the bottom of the dive Sorn banked sharp to port and for a brief moment Endeavour slipped out of the Vaurillian's protective shields. Sweeney reacted instantly, adjusting their course, bringing them back with in the envelope. But not before a volley of lasers cut across their port side, ripping through decks four and five, as though the nanocrystalline hull were no more than damp tissue paper. Endeavour trembled at the savage pounding.

The laser fire continued, hammering relentlessly at the Vaurillian's weakening shields.

"Three, no, five ships in pursuit," Wattie

called, loudly.

All five of the pursuing ships scorched their laser banks, diverting every joule of available energy to their weapons. Still the Sorn's shields held, glowing, like burning liquid gold as the energy they were absorbing dissipated across them.

"Sorn's shields are down to eighty four percent!" Jevak announced, as another barrage of weapons fire slammed Endeavour's battered hull, burning out conduits behind his science station, showering the Vaurillian with scorching debris.

Immediately a second wave of four ships cut across their starboard bow strafing both ships with a continuous volley. The Macaitians were coming at them with a ferocity bourn of desperation; Endeavour had to be stopped. They had to have the superior Alliance technology she contained.

Again the Sorn twisted, angling sharply to starboard, cutting across the wake of the receding second wave. Matt reacted and followed. As they did the Vaurillian ship unleashed a volley of lasers at the second wave's aft sections. Endeavour did likewise, burning a shaft of searing laser energy at the four ships in the next wave, pursuing to their rear. Both ships were giving as good as they got for the moment, but they were vastly out numbered and out gunned, and when the Vaurillian ship's shields were gone they would both be dead.

Nicolle was straining at an imagined leash, she felt shackled. Tied to the Vaurillian ship was curtailing her ability to muster any kind of convincing defence strategy. They were doing little more than swat at a circling swarm, of buzzing hornets.

"How far to the wormhole?" she called, steadying herself.

"Two minutes and seventeen seconds," Jevak replied, almost apologetically. He knew as well as the Captain that, under this onslaught, Sorn's shields would give out long before that.

Nicolle had to do something.

"Matt, take us out of their shields," she said forming a plan. "But keep the Sorn between us and the Macaitians." She demonstrated with her hands what she wanted him to do. "Weave back and forward, up and down. Give them a target, then duck out of the way behind the Sorn. If we can draw their fire for long enough, it'll save Sorn's shields and maybe burnout a few Macaitian laser banks in the process."

It was a simple plan, Nicolle knew it, probably a little too simple, but sometimes they worked as well. She could not just sit on her hands and hope. She had to act, and maybe it might just buy them some time, because right now that was exactly what they needed.

Matt deftly played his hands across his console. Endeavour dipped, slipping down below the Sorn, out of her protection, inviting an assault.

Three attackers instantly reacted, swinging to port, angling down. As they did Endeavour slid farther to port and climbed, keeping The Vaurillian ship between them, dodging lasers as they went.

Commander Jevak immediately grasped what Nicolle was attempting. Doing his best to assist, he swung the Sorn viciously into the path of the pursuers, forcing them to dodge to avoid a collision, loosing lasers as he did.

During the interchange two of the pursuers were hit, though not fatally.

Sweeney managed to pull off the faint twice more, narrowly avoiding lasers, before the Macaitian's Commander decided it was time to eliminate this obstacle once and for all.

Every Macaitian ship targeted its lasers on the Sorn, intent on ridding it and Endeavour of shields.

Both ships dodged and weaved, diving and climbing to avoid the onslaught.

"Shields at forty percent!" Jevak announced, as the Sorn's faltering shields glowed ever brightly under the bombardment.

There were still about a minute and a half until the wormhole came within visual range, and at least another minute before Endeavour was inside.

Another, continuous volley of laser fire pummelled both ships. Power conduits exploded all over Endeavour's bridge. Above the Captain's and First Officer's chairs the bulkheads cracked raining searing debris down on Wicasa. A second explosion threw him crashing to the deck, his uniform and face singed down his left side, smashing his arm as he landed. Rushing to his aid, the Doctor too was thrown aside like a toy, his power matrix faltering momentarily as the bombardment pitched Endeavour, buckling the bridge deck plates.

Sweeney fought to hold their course; it was becoming almost impossible to stay with the Sorn as the pounding tore at the ship.

Holding desperately to his console, Jevak called, "Shields are almost gone!"

It was over. They could dodge and weave for as long as it took for one of the attackers to get an accurate weapons lock on their nacelles, but this race was run.

Suddenly the lead Macaitian vessel dropped out of warp, falling behind them in an instant.

The barrage continued, when just as suddenly another two inexplicably dropped out of warp, disappearing in their wake.

Lockhart looked incredulously at the screen, then rounded on Jevak.

"What just happened?" she demanded.

************   ****************   ****************

"What just happened?" Commander Jevak demanded turning to T'Arran.

"I can't explain," she responded. "There are no detectable spatial anomalies in the immediate area, nothing that could destabilise a warp field."

"Yet three enemy ships have just bizarrely lost warp capability," the Commander stated, looking to his science officer for a rational explanation.

Four more Macaitians rounded on them, spraying the vacuum with laser-fire, targeting Sorn's warp reactor and Endeavours weapons and nacelles, when three of the four suddenly and again inexplicably fell behind them dropping out of warp.

Dropping instantly from warp eight, all six of the stricken vessels were suddenly billions of kilometres in the wake of the battle. Unfortunately for Endeavour, it took only a few seconds for them all to re-establish their warp fields, and once again they were in deadly pursuit.

The single remaining Macaitian, still intent on the two fleeing ships, was still targeting Sorn's reactor. It loosed a sustained volley of lasers. Endeavour instantly responded in kind hitting the lone ship broadside. It lurched viciously as its hull shredded then vaporised, a shock of blinding light and mangled wreckage erupted from it as it died in the freezing silent vacuum. Endeavour and Sorn simultaneously angled for the exploding hull, diving through the confusion of debris and flame, using it as cover to mask their escape. The remaining eight ships, who had not fallen victim to the bizarre assault on their warp fields, twisted and spun around the explosion, still focusing on their quarry.

"Sorn's shields are down," Jevak confirmed, as both fleeing vessels crashed through the maelstrom of burning wreckage.

One single Macaitian ship pulled away from the pursuing pack ferociously snaking after the now vulnerable prey.

"They're targeting Sorn's warp drive!" Cheung bellowed.

Before either ship could respond the lone Macaitian inexplicably again dropped out of warp.

Commander Jevak straightened. His eyes grew wide as a sudden realisation dawned on him. Somewhere deep in the part of his brain where the Vaurillian empathic power resided, the lobe sensitive to telepathic energy, there was a deep and powerful echo. An echo of the same sensation he had felt back on Earth in the mess hall with Michael. His mind raced at the possibility.

"Michael," he whispered in astonishment as a smile spread across his sweat and smoke stained face.

It had to be. Something in the deep, ancient core of his Vaurillian brain told him it must be. Michael, or the commune, was reaching out with their minds, destabilising the Macaitian's warp fields.

A dazzling burst of Laser slashing across their screen, exploding on a Macaitian's shields, brought him quickly back to his senses. Endeavour was keeping two more ships at bay.

"Six vessels rejoining the attack, Captain," Lieutenant Jevak confirmed to Captain Lockhart.

That they had survived for so long, defending against such a sustained and savage attack was, in no small way, due to the combined skill of both Commanding officers. But the main reason for their continued existence had been the fact that the Macaitians desired to possess Endeavour, rather than destroy her. This restraint had, of course, shackled their battle plan. Aware that the attackers were afraid of inadvertently destroying their prize with a stray laser aimed at the interfering Sorn, Lockhart and Commander Jevak conspired to give them even less of a target; corkscrewing furiously about each other, while maintaining warp eight. The fleeing vessels were a confusing spinning maelstrom, offering little more than brief, fleeting glimpses of any target. Never the less, the pursuing fleet still maintained their barrage, sniping at the twisting blur.

Sorn pitched as she took a glancing blow to her starboard side. The laser strike impacted adjacent to main engineering, searing through three decks, venting them to the vacuum, killing ten crew and destroying four of her ten warp induction coils in the process. She faltered, forcibly decelerating to warp six point two.

"Stay with the Sorn," Lockhart hollered.

They had protected Endeavour this far; Nicolle could not desert them now. Besides, they were still too far from the wormhole to consider a single-handed sprint for home.

"Eight ships breaking away from the main body, Captain," reported Wattie.

"Wormhole now within visual range," Jevak added.

The eight ships accelerated past Endeavour, making directly for the phenomenon, intent on cutting off any escape.

"Ion-torpedoes;" Lockhart ordered. "Delta dispersal."

Five dazzling, deadly orange globes streaked from beneath Endeavours for'a'd section, screaming after the departing Macaitians.

Luck proved it could be with both sides. All but one torpedo missed their targets, harmlessly overshooting their prey, as the Macaitians snaked and dived to evade the closing weapons. One though, found its target. As the rear ship swerved to dodge one torpedo it slid into the path of another, brutally reducing their number again. Then as the remaining seven accelerated away, again one, though only one, stuttered, faltered, then fell out of warp tumbling helplessly into the path of two of its comrades. All three were destroyed.

It appeared that the enormous distance was taking its toll on Michael's ability to help. As the Earth grew distant, Commander Jevak could sense the extraordinary human's influence wane. The Commander prayed for just a little more time. In about thirty seconds Endeavour would enter the wormhole. That was all he needed just a few more seconds.

The Sorn convulsed as she took another blast of laser. Behind the Commanders chair bulkheads exploded, throwing him and his navigator across the bridge. Flames and burning debris spewed from the mangled, twisted hole, flooding the bridge with choking smoke.

As their velocity decreased they were becoming an easier target.

Another bulkhead exploded.

Once more, one of the ships buzzing the Sorn faltered and fell back, though only a few thousand metres. Just managing to maintain its warp field, accelerating to rejoin the attack, it continued to target the wounded Vaurillian.

Sorn took another blow to engineering, reducing their velocity still further. One more and her warp containment field would fail, then it would be over. Endeavour reluctantly slowed to stay close, like a leviathan remaining with its wounded mate.

The wormhole was so close, yet seemed to be getting further away.

Endeavour took a direct hit on her starboard nacelle. Fighting to hold her steady, Sweeney adjusted, correcting for the imbalanced propulsion. The lack of forward momentum was beginning to make it difficult to remain in such a tight twisting helix with the Sorn.

Endeavour and Sorn simultaneously returned fire, spraying the still shielded Macaitians with everything they had, doing little but hold their undaunted attackers at a distance.

"Port nacelle being targeted, Captain. Multiple sources," warned Jevak.

She had no more options, nowhere to run. But Nicolle Lockhart was stronger than that. She refused to accept the inevitable. This situation was not hopeless; she would not accept that. She would not let this battle end this way. She would not be beaten.

"Evasive action!" Nicolle raged.

Sweeney attempted to dive, but the helm was heavy, Endeavour was sluggish and unresponsive. The damage they had already sustained was taking its toll.

Commander Jevak, struggling to his feet, saw the threat. As the Macaitians opened fire, Sorn swung, viciously to port, screaming between the attackers and Endeavour, shielding the Alliance ship, knowing that one more hit would destroy the Vaurillian. More than ten billion joules of laser energy burned at both floundering ships.

None found their target.

A dozen lances of searing energy harmlessly dissipated across some invisible barrier interceding between the helpless prey and the glowering pack. As the Macaitians ceased-fire, beneath the invisible barrier, background stars flickered and wavered disappearing as a concealed ship took shape, blocking-out their light.

"Kraxian Battle-Beast de-cloaking," a shocked Wattie announced loudly. "They're arming lasers!"

This was all they needed. Lockhart was about to order a pre-emptive strike, when Jevak interceded.

"We are not the target, Captain"

The Kraxian lanced lasers beyond Endeavour and Sorn, destroying a Macaitian, which was attempting to cut across their bows.

This was the third Battle Beast; the same one that had retreated from the Sorn's attack in Earths orbit a few short hours ago. It had been tailing and eavesdropping on them ever since.

"Wormhole. Go!" Nicolle roared at Matt.

Endeavour dipped as she accelerated, angling directly at the yawning phenomenon. With one nacelle already damaged her top speed was a hobbling warp five. Never a match for the pursuing fleet she was still going to have to battle her way to freedom.

Sorn attempted to keep-up but gradually faded aft, explosions peppering her burning, crippled hull. But Commander Jevak still refused to abandon Endeavour to be picked off by the pursuing pack. Swinging port and starboard, Sorn denied them a clean shot at the fleeing Alliance ship's rear. Targeting everything that moved to threaten, she bravely held two of their pursuers at bay, as they banked port and starboard, cutting to within a thousand metres of Endeavour. But a single, well placed, laser shot ended the Vaurillian's valiant defence.

Lockhart, and the newly arrived Kraxians, both saw the attack coming. Endeavour had targeted the chasing Macaitian with ion torpedoes, while the Kraxian ship scattered the vacuum with lasers, but to no avail. Dodging sharply to port and climbing, the Macaitians had narrowly evaded the closing weapons, loosing, as they did, a single volley of lasers across the annoying Vaurillians bows.

Sorn's main engineering exploded instantly. A numbing shock of blinding light heralded its breaching warp reactor. The rest of the ship followed in stages shredding like pounding heartbeats as explosions ripped through it deck by deck

Commander Jevak, in his final few seconds, as his bridge disintegrated burning and exploding around him, struggled to voice his final hyperspace transmissions message to the High Command. His ship, crew, and he along with them, were dying and yet all he could focus on was the message. It was a message he desperately needed to get through. His body, smashed, bleeding and broken, he ordered 'send', just as Sorn vaporised taking with it all hands. He died never knowing if the communication had made it. For the sake of the Galaxy he hoped, with his last thought, it had.

As Commander Jevak's waning mind descended into that final oblivion, memories that were not of his life came rushing at him. Memories of others who had also borne the name Jevak filled his dwindling consciousness. Faster and faster the images came at him passing in a blur as time became short, yet clear, defined and meticulous in detail they seamed to him. And amongst those beautiful, joyful, and bittersweet recollections were Lieutenant Jevak's memories of their father. The life memories the Commander had never known, wrapped themselves lovingly, warmly around his failing mind, easing him gently to his end.

Michael had been right.

Seven of the Macaitian ships, had taken-up a linear formation, barring the mouth of the wormhole as Endeavour and the Kraxian bore down on it. The Kraxian accelerated in front, shielding Endeavour, while Lockhart targeted the pursuing ships. They closed on the phenomenon, at warp six, with all lasers blazing. The Macaitians reciprocated. The Kraxian's shields began to fail immediately; the continuous bombardment was stripping them bare.

"Time to wormhole?"

"Fifteen seconds," replied Jevak.

The Kraxians shields would not hold that long, but there was nothing Nicolle could do, they were out of options. Staying tight to the Battle-Beast, for protection, she doubled the Kraxians efforts, both ships targeting the centre ship at the mouth of the wormhole. They had to clear a way into the phenomenon.

"Ten seconds," Jevak called.

"Torpedoes! Fire," Lockhart ordered.

Four sets of lasers and five ion torpedoes succeeded in clearing a small opening in the barricade. The centre ship disintegrated in a fury of flames and debris. Instantly, though, the remaining six closed ranks, barring their way again. Again they targeted one single Macaitian ship.

"The Battle Beast's shields are almost gone," Jevak reluctantly announced.

"Torpedoes, aft!" Lockhart barked.

Four bright globes issued directly into the paths of the pursuing pack. At warp six; a closing velocity of warp ten, it was almost impossible to evade them. Two of the Macaitian ships instantly shredded as the torpedoes found their marks. Endeavour balked as the explosion bounced her dangerously close to the underside of her Kraxian shield.

"Six seconds... Shields have gone!"

The Battle Beast swung side on to the waiting Macaitians, offering her broadside, giving Endeavour as much cover as possible. The Kraxian ship instantly took a full volley of lasers, opening up a wide gash in her starboard side. She was dead and her commander knew it but he held her course, continuing to give Endeavour cover.

It was all too apparent to Nicolle, that the damage the Kraxian vessel had sustained was fatal. With time fast running out she ordered an open communication channel to the Battle Beast. The Captain could not let the bravery and scarifies of these Kraxians go unacknowledged. She did not know their Commander; a short while ago they had been adversaries, and yet he had been willing to give his and the lives of his crew for theirs.

Endeavour's view-screen shifted to reveal the oppressive Kraxian Bridge, burning like a furnace, choking fumes and flames leapt high across the stark consoles and roof, explosions ripped through bulkheads as though they were little more than paper.

"Ramming speed!" The Kraxian Commander roared at what was left of his crew.

This mirror Universe had already thrown-up an excess of surprises to Nicolle, but she found herself once again catching her breath as she confronted another twist in this skewed reality. This Kraxian Commander was known to her, or at least she recognised his face.

"You have no place here!!" He growled her. "This is not your war!! Your presence brings death to us all... Go, now!"

"Thank you.... Groth," Nicolle replied choking on her words, her eyes wide in disbelief and regret.

Cosique was the only female Kraxian in the Alliance Fleet, but she was not the only Kraxian. Over the years, some, but not many on Kraxa had seen the necessity and wisdom of standing with the Alliance against the Macaitian invasion; Lieutenant Groth Motan, son of Kang Motan had been one such. He and Nicolle had served together and been close friends on the A.S. Dauntless when Nicolle had been a mere Ensign, and as far as Nicolle knew Groth was now serving aboard the A.S. Valiant, protecting the Rassilain border regions.

"You have much honour, where ever we find you," she added, her voice cracking with wretchedness.

The Commander echoed Nicolle's hesitance for a brief second, at the sudden comprehension, that this being from a species he had never known of, or encountered till this day, knew his name. She knew him. He flinched visibly, stiffening against his command chair, as the significance of that recognition hit him like a sledge-hammer to the chest. A wave of rage crashed through him. Somewhere in another plain of reality, another Kraxian who bore his face and his name was known to this alien creature.

Smashing his gloved fist into the armrests of his command chair, buckling the bare metal in his fury, he leapt to his feet. The veins in his dark green neck bulged with rage and hatred at that other Groth.

In that instant Commander Groth, of the Kraxian Imperial Guard, shared in the weight of Nicolle's crushing regret, knocking the wind from him. Another Groth, in another time and another place who shared his name, had been gifted a life far different from his own. That Groth was known to these beings, this female. And that other Groth..... had been called friend. A life that had been denied to him had been bestowed on another in a Universe of unity and benevolence; another Groth would endure in peace, where as he and his kin would, he knew, soon meet a brutal, violent end.

"You have no place here!" he growled at Nicolle from the viewscreen. "These dogs would use you against us. Go. Go now!"

For a brief second there was silence between them, as he studied this strange being. Drawing closer to the screen he locked eyes with her.

"This Universe is a sorry place for your absence, human," he said, a little more softly than a

Kraxian was accustomed. Then quickly recomposing himself he snarled, "Now go!"

Turning from the screen, to his crew, he roared, "Prepare to ram!"

The transmission ended.

The Battle Beast banked sharply to port, directly down the throat of the lead Macaitian ship, then accelerated. She was disintegrating, shedding hull plating, which careered aft, ricocheting off the unprotected Endeavour. But bearing down on the barricade, there was still enough of her tattered hull intact to smash a hole through their barrier.

Endeavour swung directly at the tear in the defensive wall exposed by the exploding Battle-Beast. Diving through the erupting debris and flames, loosing lasers port and starboard, as she did. The nearest Macaitian attempted to bar her way, but for a brief moment its warp field faltered.

And Endeavour was gone.

"Slow to Warp Two," Lockhart instructed.

"Captain?" Sweeney questioned, knowing the Macaitians would be right behind them in a few seconds.

"Warp two," she repeated, confidently. "Now."

As Matt slowed the ship Nicolle almost hauled him from his chair, taking his place at the helm.

"Okay, now I need you to man the Auxiliary Engineering Station, it's been rigged so the shuttle can be piloted remotely from there," she said.

Uncertain of the Captain's reasoning he did as ordered, scrambling to the opposite side of the bridge, adjacent to Jevak's Science Station. Passing his hand over the flat black panel recessed into the wall, he brought the Engineering Station to life.

"On line," Sweeney confirmed.

Nicolle raised her voice to the Comm-system. "Shuttle bay!"

"Cosique here Captain. The shuttle is ready, but it has a coolant leak which we were unable to seal."

"It doesn't matter. Launch it."

"Shuttle away," Jevak informed her.

"Matt," She said urgently. "It has to exit the other end of the wormhole before we get there."

Lockhart's logic suddenly became clear, not only to Matt but to the others on the bridge as well. The far end of this wormhole opened into the Gamma Sector, in the wrong Universe. The accident, which brought them here in the first place, had to be recreated. Another energy ribbon would have to ignite against the wormhole to weaken the barrier between Universes, enabling them to exit into the Gamma Sector of their own reality.

"On its way, Captain," Sweeney confirmed, a note of grim determination in his voice. "Warp eight point two. That's all she's got!"

"Make it count," Nicolle urged as she, steadied Endeavour into the slipstream of their fleeing shuttle.

A wormhole, far from being a uniform

straight pipe with an opening at either end, is more like an enclosed rollercoaster ride; twists, turns, dips and terrifying hairpin bends. And although it had been considerably more than a few years since Nicolle had last been at the helm of any starship, just like riding a bike, it was something she never forgot. She settled into the chair and took control, deftly manoeuvring the ship along the constantly snaking tunnel.

"Count us down to the exit, Jevak," she instructed.

"Thirty two seconds, Captain."

Behind them the blast had barely subsided, the crushing debris of two massive hulls, barely scattered, when three of the Macaitians swung through a wide ark, punching straight down the throat of the wormhole.

"Twenty nine seconds..."

"Three ships in pursuit!" Wattie called.

"Matt?"

"Shuttle's approaching the exit, Captain," he replied, focussing totally on the unfamiliar console.

The cannibalised, scorched remains of the tiny shuttle burst into the Gamma Sector. Were it not for the tail of leaking plasma trailing in its wake it would have been almost lost, like a microbe in a football stadium, in the vast swirling dome at the heart of this duplicate nebula.

Without slowing, Matt banked the ailing craft, angling it towards the heart of the energy charged void, which straddled the twin orbiting stars. He had to remain vigilant though; the shuttle had no shields and one lash from even a minor burst of energy and it would be instantly vaporised, and all would be lost.

"Twenty four seconds."

The energy field bristled, sparking its fury. Deadly tendrils teased at the approaching shuttle; lashing-out, flickering at it, like a cobra tentatively tasting its quarry before striking.

Sweeney delayed, holding the craft in orbit, edging it closer, tempting a fatal strike. Surely that was enough, he thought, as he turned her through a long, lazy ark. He had let her linger for as long as he could, tempting the energy field to strike. Running his hands across the console he quickly set a course back towards the wormhole.

"Twenty seconds."

"Re-entering wormhole," Sweeney announced, still concentrating.

"No reaction from the energy field," Jevak added.

"Bring her about!" Lockhart demanded. "Again, quickly. Take the shuttle through the energy field again, closer."

Again, without slowing from warp eight, Sweeney swung the shuttle through a tight one hundred and eighty degrees. She came about, full circle, never coming close to touching the sides of the wormhole's vast throat. Back, he took her, into the alien Gamma Sector.

"Seventeen seconds."

Matt pressed deeper into the gas dome this time. Closer. The shuttle was almost directly between the orbiting twins. Tendrils as thick as a planet cracked and whipped around the tiny craft but still, even at this close proximity the shuttle was having no effect.

"Thirteen seconds... The Macaitian ships are closing," warned Jevak

"Time to intercept?"

Jevak looked grave. "Ten seconds."

They would be on them before Endeavour could reach the exit. Reluctantly Nicolle increased their own speed to warp three point five.

"Fourteen seconds to intercept," Jevak said, revising his estimate.

"Captain, the shuttle's too small," Wattie exclaimed. "It's like the probe we sent in earlier, the energy field's oblivious to it."

It took her less than a second to evaluate their options and come to a decision.

"Vent its plasma. All of it," she roared, hurriedly turning to Matt.

They all knew what that meant; without plasma flow the shuttles warp reactor would breach. But if this attempt to restore their own Universe failed then that and every thing else would not really matter.

Nicolle did not know if the idea would work. But it was entirely possible it might, and that was reason enough to try. Warp plasma is ionised, electrically charged, theoretically it should therefore attract the energy ribbons. But again, it might just as easily repel them. This as they all knew was grasping at straws, but there was only one straw left to grasp at.

"Venting plasma," Matt confirmed.

"Eight seconds to exit," Jevak reported, continuing to countdown.

The cloud of plasma fanned-out aft of the shuttle as it hurtled through the charged field between the twin stars. Almost immediately it had an effect. The cobalt blue ribbons of energy crackled and stabbed furiously at the passing shuttle, like grasping fingers, as Matt turned it back to the wormhole.

"Six seconds."

As it neared the mouth of the phenomenon two ribbons launched at the shuttle punching after it like barbed fists. Matt swung it to port hugging the rim as it re-entered the anomaly. The ribbons followed, striking like snakes.

"Three seconds....Exit within visual range."

Nicolle looked up at the screen just in time to see the second ribbon strike at the shuttle...but miss. It exploded instead against the inner wall of the wormhole.

It happened. Imperceptibly, but it happened.

For a brief millisecond, the ephemeral beat between thoughts, Endeavour, and the chasing Macaitians, were frozen in nothingness. Caught in an empty, timeless, abyss. They were trespassers in a place where they could not belong; beyond existence... the space between universes.

Then they were back.

Endeavour exploded from the wormhole, into the vast dome of cloud. Nicolle hauled her up and to starboard, turning her away from the waiting energy field. Her hull groaned and protested as she twisted, pulling G-forces she was never designed to withstand, up and away from the lashing ribbons.

"Captain...." Jevak grunted, anxiously grasping at his console, as the bridge seemed to slide away from under him. "We are... again receiving... telemetry from our probe... It is directly aft."

The probe was once again behind them, at the other end of the wormhole, in the Alpha Sector of their own Universe. They were home, or at least, back in their own reality.

Behind them in the wormhole the three Macaitians swung at maximum warp, around the final bend in the snaking tube. Bearing down on their quarry they were no more than two seconds behind. They would have them soon. Suddenly it was on them. They had no time to alter course or take avoiding action. The lead ship bore down on the abandoned shuttlecraft heading directly at them also at maximum warp. In almost the same instant as the collision the shuttle's fragile warp reactor breached. The explosion was terrible in such a confined space. A blinding, brilliant, white flash issued from the anomaly like an enormous searchlight, as bright as a million suns. The combined eruption tore through the following Macaitian ship as well, melting through its shields and hull, vaporising it instantly. Only the rear ship managed to avoid the crushing detonation. Throwing all of its engines into reverse and redirecting all of its shields for' ad had saved it from the blast. But nothing could save it from a collapsing wormhole.

The force of three warp reactors breaching, had compromised the phenomenon's stability. Silently, suddenly, the curved walls around the tiny Macaitian ship closed in, tightening as though being throttled. Both ends of the anomaly, separated in real space by more than seventy thousand light years, tumbled inextricably towards each other. Closing in the blink of an eye. Imploding the wormhole.

Scientists and physicists have long debated, even before they were ever proven to actually exist, the fate of matter caught in a collapsing wormhole. None have as yet come to any definitive conclusion; since logically any hypothesis can never be proven. But one hundred and fifty seven Macaitians now knew, and from this moment until the end of time, would continue to know the fate of matter caught in a collapsing wormhole; trapped forever beyond time

A single energy ribbon leaped, reaching for the fleeing Alliance vessel, but dissipated harmlessly against the inner curve of the clouded dome as Endeavour climbed safely into the nebula. Nicolle kept her on a straight course, and within a few moments Endeavour emerged into the star encrusted void they had come to know only too well; the Gamma Sector.

"Matt," she said, relinquishing her post at the helm.

As Sweeney took up the vacated seat he asked, "What course?"

"Back to Gar-Jevva," she replied, exhausted. "Maybe their offer of assistance is still open. We've an awful lot of repairs they could help with."

She knelt by the Doctor who was still administering to Wicasa.

"Home the long way?" The First Officer asked easing himself up from the deck.

"It would appear so........ The long and winding road. Lets get you to sick-bay," she smiled wearily, as she and the Doctor eased him to his feet.

EPILOGUE

Through a dark mirror, on the far side of another galaxy in another Universe, so similar but so totally different, the Sorn's final hyperspace transmissions message had been despatched un-encrypted.

For the security of the fleet encryption was obviously of the utmost importance but in the heat of battle, just getting the message out had been little short of a miracle; there just had not been time to ensure that standing orders were adhered to. Besides Commander Jevak had hoped the message would be intercepted, and understood by as many other worlds as possible.

The message was received on Vaurilla less than twenty minutes after the Sorn had been valiantly cut down; Kraxa, Rassila and Macaitia had all intercepted it within a further thirty minutes.

There had been little preamble; the High Command reacted instantly. Six ships were despatched immediately from Vaurillian Space Dock. Four of them had just completed a total re-fit, the other two were still under going extensive repairs. But needs must, so teams of engineers were seconded to the fleet to complete the repairs en-route; every available ship was now urgently needed, they had a duty to fulfil.

Urgent hyperspace transmissions messages were sent to the remainder of the fleet. Every Vaurillian ship in the Alpha Sector reacted immediately, re-vectoring to rendezvous at the given coordinates.

Kraxa reacted similarly despatching every available ship, as did Rassila, Tyreea and their close neighbours the Sauril, every serviceable ship in the sector desperately sought-out the same destination. The destiny of the Galaxy was now, more than ever, in the balance.

The Kraxians being in closer proximity to the objective had a significant head start, but Vaurillian ships are smaller and faster, it would be close but the Vaurillian fleet should reach the destination first, they hoped.

En-route five more Vaurillian battle cruisers joined the six, then a further two. Thirty-four hours later, by the time they were within sensor range of the target, eighteen ships in all had joined the attack formation. As they passed through the Sirius System, just ten light-years from the target, sensors detected twenty-three Kraxian Battle-Beasts ready and waiting in orbit, and a further seven within ten light-years. The spearhead of the Rassilian fleet were approaching on a parallel course a few hours behind. Within the next few hours this sector would be a tense, bristling, battleground.

Red alerts and battle stations were sounded across the diminishing void, between the closing fleets. The Commander of the lead Vaurillian ship ordered his fleet out of warp, slowing to half induction as they approached the waiting Kraxians, head on. Instantly, shields were raised on both sides.

The Kraxians had adopted an inverted 'V' formation, the apex pointing away from the approaching Vaurillians, with one single ship at the centre of the two converging lines. Slowly, cautiously the Vaurillians approached, manoeuvring their lines to mirror the Kraxians. The formation nullified either sides attempt to mount a surprise offensive.

Forty-one fully armed battleships, held their positions, gauging each other. Waiting for the order.

Across the void the total firepower of two worlds, two ancient, hateful, mistrusting enemies waited anxiously, motionless. Centuries of war and bloodletting had conferred on these old adversaries, a common history; a deep-rooted hatred of each other.

They dallied along time, hanging suspended in the endless dark cold, each waiting for the first move to be made. The vacuum between them, buzzed with frantic sensor activity, each side eager for something, anything. The waiting became intolerable. Gunner's fingers twitched over laser banks.

Still they waited.

Curiously, neither side had, as yet, charged weapons.

Then there was movement. Tentative. Hesitant. It came from the Vaurillian ranks. The lead ship manoeuvred slowly, warily on docking thrusters alone. Climbing slowly, until it came to rest three hundred metres directly above its own lines.

On the Kraxian ships, Commanders restrained their snarling crews, baying like packs of rabid dogs, howling for blood, hungry to loose their firepower at the insipid grey skinned empaths.

But still their lines held firm.

Still neither side charged weapons.

The lead Vaurillian vessel pivoted slowly, turning horizontally until it presented its stern to the Kraxians. Then slowly, deliberately it moved, reversing across the void towards the Kraxan lines.

Halting almost directly above the lead Kraxan vessel, the Vaurillian flagship began its slow descent until it sat alongside its opposite number.

Gradually, one by one the entire Vaurillian fleet turned slowly and repeated the manoeuvre backing towards the Kraxians and slotted into their lines. Forty-three ships combined to build one single defensive line. Ancient enemies laid down centuries of mistrust and hatred to combine their firepower, and within the next few hours their numbers would swell further to nearly ninety ships; not much, but all that the free worlds could muster.

In a high orbit, just beyond the planet's single Moon, Vaurillians, Kraxians, Rassilans, Tyreeans and Sauril were ready to set aside ancient mistrust and conflicts to stand together and defend a world none of them had, until a few days ago, deemed worthy of spilling blood over, but now they were more than willing to die defending, against the might of the entire Macaitian fleet now massing along the border.

Two hundred thousand kilometres above a small, blue, insignificant, backward planet on the outer spiral arm of the Galaxy, a sixty-five million year old mistake was being put right. An Alliance was being born, catalysed by a displaced commune of humanity.

Below in the Great Hall, Michael gathered them all together.

It was time.

The reason for their whole existence was now.........

The End

Author's picture by: Mark Runnacles.

An award winning, national newspaper photographer, in has native Scotland, who has captured Royals, Presidents and wars; this is John Gunion's first novel.

He is happily retired now, still living in Scotland and in Spain with his partner Sue and their cat.

john.gunion@yahoo.co.uk

Printed in Great Britain
by Amazon